The Tie that Binds

Kelly Leigh Halsch

This is a fictional story based on fictional characters. Any resemblance to real persons or real circumstances is purely coincidental.

Unless otherwise indicated, Bible quotations are taken from the New International Version of the Bible. Copyright © 2005 by Tyndale House Publishers.
All rights reserved.

ISBN: 0615917216
ISBN 13: 9780615917214
Library of Congress Control Number: 2014900514
Legacy of Beauty Books, Carlsbad, CA

To the Lifehope Community in Halesowen, UK who supported all that was going on in my life during the writing of this book, especially to my teammates Anna, Lilamaria, and Crystal, and a very special thanks to Allie and Karen.
The difficult moments of life are made so much sweeter when there are those that walk alongside you.

Chapter One

As a little girl, Amy Monahan could remember her mother talking about the day when her firstborn daughter would get married. She talked of it often, as if the day would be just as special for her as it would be for Amy. Her mother talked of white dresses and flowers, of walking down the aisle on her father's arm. She talked about true love and happiness, making it sound like it would be the happiest day of Amy's life. Of course, she always told her daughter that a wedding was one day, and a marriage was a lifetime. But the number one thing that Amy's mother instilled in her young daughter's heart was that she already had a built-in maid of honor: her younger sister.

Amy could remember sitting on the floral printed chaise lounge in her parents' large bedroom as she watched her mom help Amy's aunt get ready for her wedding day. Mom helped with Aunt Mary's makeup, touching her up before a photographer came in to take a few pictures before the bride walked down the aisle. Amy wished that she could wear makeup. Mom told her that five years old was too young to wear makeup, but she put a little lipstick on Amy's lips just the same. Amy liked the color it added to her small mouth. It made her feel more grown up. She even got to wear a pretty dress for the day. She got to wear a white dress with a dark brown sash around it. She had practiced the night before at the church, walking down the aisle holding the small basket in her hands. She was the flower girl at her aunt's wedding, and she was very excited for the role she got to play.

She knew the day was all about the bride, but Amy couldn't help but watch her mother instead. Elizabeth Monahan looked purely radiant in the chocolate brown dress she wore, like the other bridesmaids. But it truly accentuated her features, matching her dark hair and endless blue eyes. She was the picture of elegance to her daughter, and Amy wanted to be just like her when she grew up, although she looked nothing like her mother. Amy had inherited her father's light complexion with blonde hair and light brown eyes with a sprinkling of freckles across her cheeks. But she didn't have to look like her mother to be just like her.

"I hope you feel like a princess on your wedding day," Aunt Mary said to Amy with a smile, reaching down to playfully touch her nose with a rose petal she had been toying with in her hand, like the many that Amy would soon adorn the aisle with. Amy breathed in the warm, sweet scent as she laughed and pushed her hand away.

"How can I be a princess without a prince?" Amy asked innocently, thinking of some of her favorite fairy tale stories that her mom had read to her countless times before she went to sleep, or on lazy rainy days when they would curl up together on the plush couch in the living room. Amy would stare outside the large floor-to-ceiling windows at the rain and imagine the world the words created. She loved reading about princesses.

Aunt Mary laughed at her, as did all the others in the room, making Amy blush. What was so funny? The whole bridal party was getting ready in her parents' bedroom, and Amy felt privileged to be counted among them. Technically, her sister was supposed to be another flower girl, but she had been so fussy at the rehearsal dinner that Mom had to send her home with a neighbor. She had been stubborn and refused to walk down the aisle on cue. Amy was happy that now the title of flower girl was hers alone.

"Someday your prince will come," Aunt Mary assured her. "Mine certainly did." She smiled wistfully.

"Will I get to wear a pretty dress on my wedding day?"

"Of course," Mom and Aunt Mary replied at the same time.

"You'll get to hold a beautiful bouquet of flowers as well," Mom added. "Maybe we can even put together something from my own garden," she hummed. And of course, that is exactly what Amy wanted as soon as her mom suggested it. Her mother's garden was like Amy's own personal fairyland.

"I want to wear a dress just like yours," Amy stated. She wasn't referring to Aunt Mary's dress, although it was gorgeous. Instead, she turned and glanced at the wedding picture that rested on the side of her mother's vanity, where Amy watched her mother get ready almost everyday.

"You might change your mind when you get older," her mom said with a laugh, but Amy knew she wouldn't. She decided right then that she would wear the exact dress that her mother wore when her special day came. Mom had once shown it to her. It was in a special white bag hanging in the back of her parents' large closet. Amy had once gone looking for it. Mom had found her and had chastised her for snooping through her things, but had shown her the dress just the same.

"Will I have a whole bunch of friends to walk down the aisle with me?" Amy asked, glancing at the others in the room chatting excitedly. They had all walked down the aisle successively at the rehearsal dinner the night before. Amy was learning a lot about weddings simply by participating in Aunt Mary's. It was all so exhilarating.

"Of course, you can have as many bridesmaids as you want," Aunt Mary said.

"But you also get to choose a maid of honor," her mom stated.

Amy knew that was her mother's role in Aunt Mary's wedding, although she didn't know what it meant. But it made her sound more special than the other bridesmaids to be called the maid of honor. Amy already knew that her mom was special.

"I get to choose anyone I want?" Amy asked.

"You already have the perfect maid of honor," Mom told her.

Amy's eyebrows furrowed together. "Who?"

Mom smiled warmly. "Your sister."

"Beth has to be my maid of honor?" Amy asked, referring to her three-year-old sister who was named for their mother.

Mom didn't give her a yes or no answer. She simply told Amy that there was a tie that bound the hearts of Amy and Beth together, no matter what happened. It was a tie that not anyone or anything would be able to break. They were sisters, and would always be a part of each other's lives.

Amy never fought her mother on the subject, even as she repeated the same statement to her multiple times as Amy got older. She always stressed the fact that Amy and Beth had a special role in each other's lives. Therefore Amy never imagined anyone but Beth to be her maid of honor.

"Oh Beth," Amy sighed into the early morning air. The one thing her mom had never told her was what to do if Amy and Beth were so completely the opposites of one another that they couldn't see eye-to-eye on anything. She never told Amy what to do if she and Beth couldn't stand in the same room without arguing. And she certainly didn't tell Amy what to do if Beth ran away from home, forsaking her family simply so that she could live her own life and do what she wanted—leaving Amy behind to pick up her pieces. No, Amy had never been prepared for any of that. As a little girl she had wanted to please her mother. She had nodded her head in agreement anytime that her mom suggested that she and Beth would be each other's maid of honor.

"I'm sorry to disappoint you, Mom," Amy said to the cool air, "but it's not going to happen."

Amy could see her breath in front of her, and rubbed her arms in response, hoping to create some heat with the friction. All she had to do was go inside to her warm bedroom, but she liked being outside in the crisp darkness of the predawn hours. She was too wound up to sleep just yet. She had just had the perfect night, and she wasn't ready to give it up for the peace of sleep. She wanted to keep dreaming about it as she stood awake. She could only hope that she would dream about it in her sleep when she finally forced herself inside.

Tonight, David Carpenter, the prince she had dreamt about all her life, had gotten down on his knee and asked her to marry him. She could barely wait for him to finish asking her before she responded with an excited yes. She couldn't wait to be David's wife. She had dreamt about it for so long. She had been dreaming about her wedding day for as long as she could remember. Amy would finally get to plan that special day that her mom had always talked about. However it wouldn't be complete. Her mother wouldn't be there to share it with her.

Not a day went by that Amy didn't long for her mom. It was almost nine years to the day since her mother had perished in a car accident. It had happened so quickly. One day she was simply gone. It had been extremely hard, and still was sometimes. But life goes on. Her wedding day would never be what she used to dream about as a child without her mother. And now she wouldn't have her sister either. But if truth be told, Beth's absence was more of a relief than anything else. Life was less complicated without Beth around, even if it meant that Amy had to pick up all the responsibilities she had left behind. But sometimes Amy liked it that way. If Beth were here, Amy was sure she would find a way to ruin this special time for her.

When the cold got to be too much, Amy headed back into her bedroom, ready to get cozy underneath the down covers on her bed. Her eyelids were starting to get heavy, no matter how hard she to tried to fight it—after all, it was really late.

David had been her dream for so long. She wanted nothing more than to spend forever with him, to have a wonderful loving relationship just like her parents had had, till death parted them. Her father never stopped loving her mother, and she knew that he wouldn't. He still wore his wedding ring, even after nine years. A lot of people remarried after losing spouses, but something inside Amy just knew that her father never would. His heart would continue to beat for his beloved Elizabeth Monahan until they were reunited again in Heaven.

Amy admired it, really. But she wanted her dad to be happy, even if that meant that he met someone new. However, Julian Monahan would never look at someone the way that he looked at his wife—part of Amy was glad. As much as she had said she would be okay with it over the years if it happened, she had a feeling she would have a difficult time with anyone trying to encroach on the place her mom had held. No one ever could though, not really. But she knew she didn't have to worry. Her father was far too busy, anyway, running the family business that was fast becoming Amy's responsibility.

Amy had spent her whole life in Colorado, growing up at the base of Mount of the Holy Cross—the northernmost 14,000 foot peak in the Sawatch Range, known for its steep gullies resembling a giant cross when filled with snow. She loved being situated at the foot of the Rockies. It was her favorite place in the whole world. And it was where her father ran the business that was started by his own father. Amy's great-grandfather had owned the vast land that her grandfather made into a large ski resort. Now it was the only family operated ski resort of its size left in all of Colorado, and a very sought after place for corporations to try to buy them out. Her father and grandfather had been presented with many offers on the ski resort, offers that would make them more money than they could ever possibly imagine having. But her grandfather had turned them down, and so had Amy's father. The business had never been about the money, anyway. And soon it would be placed in the hands of Amy when her father retired for good. She would continue to carry on the family legacy. She loved it too much to ever sell it away. It was home, where she had taken her first steps and learned her first words. It was the home that her mother knew as well. And Amy would never let that go. This was home, the home that she shared with her father. And it was soon to be her home with David.

Chapter Two

When Amy awoke the next morning, she awoke with a smile on her face. Dreams of David certainly had come to her in the night. They didn't make sense, but they were all sweet. She dreamt of their wedding, which had started in the backyard in her mom's garden and had ended at a tropical beach. She dreamt of him proposing, which was nothing like the reality, but still wonderful. And when she was awake, he was the first person that she wanted to see.

Amy walked to the French doors that opened up to a balcony off her large bedroom, which overlooked the town of Holy Cross. Her grandfather had built the very house she lived in with his own hands—Monahan Ranch. It wasn't really a ranch, however. They didn't keep any animals or even work the land at all, except for the horses, but they were kept at a stable a few miles away. But he had chosen the name, and built the large mountain house that she lived in. It had been modernized and added onto since he had originally built it, and had only become grander since then. Rather than resemble a log cabin, it was more like a log manor house due to its size. It fit perfectly hidden in the woods from the main road, with the long gated drive. And Amy absolutely loved it.

Amy let out a sigh of contentment as she breathed in the crisp autumn air. The sky was completely clear, no sign of snow. But Amy was sure that more snow would come. After all, it was only mid November—although it seemed like it had gotten cold early this year. Winter was just getting ready to stop teasing them with little squalls and stay for a while. Ski season would be in full throttle in no time and continue on as long as there was snow. It could last even into June depending on the weather.

Although she loved winter, if truth be told, summer in Colorado was Amy's favorite. Winter was busy season, and it meant that she didn't see her father for days at a time, depending on the amount of work to be done. Everyone was busy, but they were doing something they loved. Although there was still plenty to do in the mountains in the summer, it meant more down time with her father and the rest of her family. And while Amy stood on her balcony in the frigid November air, she imagined the perfect summer wedding in the garden of her home. She had been dreaming about her wedding for as long as she could remember. And ever since she was a little girl, she knew she would get married in her mother's garden that her mother had always tended so carefully.

Her cell phone ringing on her nightstand snapped Amy out of dreamland, forcing her back into reality. There was work to do and people to see. Never mind that she had a wedding to plan. Ski season was just beginning. And if she planned to take over the business one day, she had to be ready for anything.

"Hello?" Amy said into the phone, switching into business mode, letting the chilly air still pour into her room through the open French doors. She was used to the cold, and she welcomed it.

"Hi, I would like to speak to my fiancée, please," David jokingly said into the phone.

"She's not here," Amy said, teasing him right back, pleased that it was not a business call.

"Oh, well that's too bad. If you see her, tell her that there's a beautiful brunch awaiting her in the dining room."

"A brunch?" Amy said, dropping the joke with the mention of food. She had to admit it, she was really hungry. She didn't actually eat dinner last night. She had been too surprised and excited about David's proposal that the fact that they hadn't eaten didn't even seem to cross either of their minds. They were too busy celebrating and calling everyone that they knew.

"Yes, and a fair amount of people who would like to offer their congratulations," he added.

"I'll be right down," Amy stated. "I just have to get dressed." She actually longed to stand under a hot shower, but she couldn't keep people waiting. She would just have to wash her face, put on a little makeup, and hurry down.

"Excellent," David said. "And if you see my fiancée, tell her to come, too."

Amy laughed. "I'll make sure to pass on the memo."

Amy hung up the phone and headed to the large bathroom connected to her room. Although she knew she had to be down as quickly as she could, she couldn't help but scrutinize her face, as she did every morning. There was a sparkle in her light brown eyes this morning as she glanced at her grinning face, which only made her smile wider. She usually hated her eyes—she thought them dull. Her curly blonde hair, which was typically styled in a cute little bob, was mussed from sleeping. She did her best to tame the natural ringlets with a little water. Her short hair was new to her, and she was still trying to figure out the best way to style it. She had taken a picture of a well-known movie star from the 1930's to her hairdresser and asked for her hair to be styled the same way. She loved the old-fashioned look. Although she certainly didn't look old-fashioned and elegant when she descended the stairs twenty minutes later. She had simply powdered her face and put on a little eyeliner—not her usual routine. The only way to get her hair out of her face was to pin it back with bobby pins. And she was wearing jeans and a sweater, which was typical winter apparel. But it didn't matter. David was waiting for her at the bottom of the stairs, and he looked at her with such love in his eyes when she came down that she could care less what she looked like. He loved her no matter what.

"Oh, I see you got the message about brunch?" David said with a teasing grin.

"Yea some girl told me about it," Amy replied back.

"Well I'm glad you could make it."

"I'm glad *you* could make it," Amy said wholeheartedly.

David smiled at her and pulled her close, giving her a lingering kiss before putting his arm around her waist and leading her toward the large dining room where people were waiting to greet them with congratulations—bringing back memories of grand brunches from her childhood that her mom always catered. Amy could hear the happy chatter of the people she loved most in the world before she even rounded the corner and walked in.

"Amy! David!"

"Congratulations!"

"The happy couple!"

There were greetings coming from all over the place, but the first person to come and greet her with a hug was her father. His caramel-colored eyes looked just as joyful as her own as he held his firstborn in his arms.

"I'm so happy for you," her dad said to her, and then releasing her from his warm hug he glanced at David. "I'm happy for the both of you. Welcome to the family, son," he said, holding out his hand for David to shake. As soon as David took it, Julian pulled him into a hug. Amy loved seeing David welcomed into the family, but she knew he had been considered a part of it for a while now. Falling for David had taken Amy by surprise, but it was a happy surprise. She had been so busy working that as much as she had dreamt about her wedding over the years, she didn't have time to let the reality of it cross her mind. But then David came, and he changed everything. She loved him.

With winter quickly approaching, there was a ton of work to do for the family that owned a large and prosperous ski resort. But Amy spent the day surrounded by her family, who were always there whenever she needed them. They were as excited for her as she was for herself.

"Have you guys talked at all about wedding plans?" Aunt Mary asked Amy. Of all of Amy's aunts and uncles, she was closest to Aunt Mary, probably somewhat because Mary was Amy's mother's only sister. Amy's dad came from a large family, and they all lived in the area and worked in the family business, but Aunt Mary held an extra special place in Amy's heart.

"Not at all," Amy said truthfully, but Aunt Mary knew quite well that Amy had been dreaming of her wedding since the day she sat in her parents' bedroom watching Aunt Mary get ready for her own.

"Summer in the backyard?" she asked, amused.

"You know me so well!"

"Well I'm here for you, whatever you need to help plan the wedding. Your mother would be so proud of you."

Amy smiled. "I wish she were here for all of this."

"We all do, sweetheart. We all do." Aunt Mary pulled Amy close in a hug, a knowing hug. Aunt Mary felt the same sad sorrow that rested in Amy's heart, felt the same gaping hole that only Elizabeth Monahan could fill. She couldn't have her mother, and that broke her heart. But she had the second best thing instead.

"I've got you," Amy said softly in her aunt's ear, and Mary only pulled her closer.

Mary pulled away and grasped Amy's hands. "And I'm going to help you plan the best wedding you could ever imagine!" she declared. Amy had no doubt that she would.

Brunch turned into a daylong affair, as many of their family's parties did. Her father ordered takeout food from town, as if they hadn't had enough food in the morning, bringing enough Italian takeout home to feed double the amount of people that were at the house—they would have leftovers for days, which served Amy well since she wasn't the best of cooks. Amy felt surrounded by love, the love of her family and friends, and the love of David. But as she glanced at her father as the last of their guests left that evening, she knew that he was thinking that there was one person missing, one person needed to make this picture complete. Beth.

Chapter Three

Rolling over in bed, Beth squeezed her eyelids as tightly shut as she could, trying not to let in any unnecessary light. She wanted to sleep for hours longer, but the sun seemed extra bright as it snuck in through the slits of the plastic blinds. She could tell from the position of the sun shooting through the dirty apartment window that it was late afternoon.

Just when Beth started to get comfortable on her side, the annoying chimes of her cell phone alarm clock went off. She groaned as she reached for it, mechanically turning it off without even looking at it. It was silent again, but she threw it under her pillow for good measure. Even with it silent, she could still hear the echo of the chimes in her ears.

Beth groaned as she got out of bed, feeling the aches in her back from a not-so-satisfying night sleep on the pullout sofa, stepping over clothes that had been strewn on the floor. Someday, she promised herself, she would sleep in a wonderful pillow-top bed again, with a fluffy down comforter to keep her warm. But she knew that day wouldn't come for a long while, although she refused to believe that it would never happen. Someday her life would be on track again. Someday.

Beth put her hand over her eyes as she reached to turn on the bathroom light. Slowly, she let her eyes adjust, but the light still stung nonetheless. Once her eyes were opened, she got a decent look at herself in the mirror, groaning at what she saw. Her eyes were slightly puffy and bloodshot, with dark circles underneath, evidence that she had cried herself to sleep once again when she had returned home in the early morning. The curls that had flowed down her back in a perfect wave the night before were now jumbled into a giant knot.

"Manny will not be pleased," Beth said cynically, referring to her boss.

She turned the shower on, letting the bathroom fill up with steam before she even got in. A hot shower would do her good. So would some aspirin and a large coffee, which she knew she couldn't have. No caffeine. But none of those things would make her feel better about herself. While she should have been washing her hair and letting the previous night fade away, she sat on the floor of the bathtub hugging her knees, sobbing while the hot water left her skin red. She didn't want to do this anymore. She didn't want to live her life this way, but what choice did she have? She was in so much debt that she needed to work, work that made her a lot of money. She had a place to live. She had a job. But she just felt so empty. And now she needed a plan more than ever. Beth couldn't just worry about herself anymore. She was already too much of a responsibility for herself, and now she had to care for the little life growing inside her—or at least figure out what to do about it. She couldn't go on denying its existence forever. It wasn't easy deciding for two.

"Babe, I'm home!" Tyler's voice boomed through the bathroom door, snapping Beth out of her fit of tears. Tyler couldn't hear her cry. She wouldn't allow it. She wouldn't let him see that she was vulnerable. She had to be strong. She had always been strong. She blamed her tendency to cry on increased hormones from being pregnant. But really she knew that her life was in a hopeless pit right now. However, she needed Tyler to see her as strong and as confident as ever. She wouldn't let him have more of a hold on her than he already did.

"I'm just getting ready," she called back, her voice sounding much more in control than she felt on the inside. She forced herself to stand up, and went through the routine of showering. While towel drying her hair, she studied herself in the mirror again, looking past the obvious signs of a fitful sleep into her clear blue eyes. Beth was beautiful, and she knew it. In fact, she often used it to her advantage. She looked just like her mother, with the same distinct blue eyes and dark hair, which she had been growing out since high school ended. It was extremely long now, always falling in perfect waves down her back. It almost scared her how much she resembled her mother. But there was a difference. Beth's blue eyes didn't hold the same warmth as those of the mother she was named after.

"I'm a shame to your name," she said out loud, as if her mother was listening. Her mother would never approve of the life that Beth was living right now. Beth didn't even approve of it. But right now, she didn't have any choice, not until she could dig herself up out of this hole she had put herself in. And she had to do something, quick. She was four months into her pregnancy. Pretty soon she would start showing and wouldn't be able to hide the secret any longer—she could already feel a tightness over her abdomen, like something was going to pop out any day. She had done her best to eat extremely healthy since she had found out she was pregnant—although she wasn't completely sure why she cared so much. It's not like she wanted a baby. And just as she always had, she still went running everyday, keeping her slender figure in shape. But a baby couldn't be hidden forever, as much as she would try. Beth was good at being deceptive.

Beth had to open the bathroom door a crack to let the steam escape as she brushed her hair out. She didn't even have to worry about styling it. Her hair always dried into the same perfect waves that always looked like those of celebrities who had been professionally styled on the cover of magazines. It had been the envy of many of her friends. Sometimes she straightened it, just for a change. But mostly she just let it do its own thing.

The last thing she did was powder her face to get rid of the shine, and added a touch of mascara. She was the kind of girl that looked beautiful even after just waking up in the morning, even after crying herself to sleep the night before. Makeup had never been a necessity to her, but she put it on just the same, to make her feel better about herself. Most of the girls at work wore tons of makeup, anyway. Manny had suggested that she go all out with the eyeliner and lipstick like the others, but she had refused. She may have enjoyed completely dolling herself up in high school, but she had come a long way since then. She would play the part she was required to play for now, but she wouldn't compromise on everything. She was a natural beauty, and she wasn't going to paint herself up to sell herself even more. The extent she would go to would be wearing false eyelashes, but today she wasn't in the mood to even deal with putting them on.

"You're going to be late if you don't hurry," Tyler said when she came out wrapped in a towel. He didn't even bother to look at her. He was too focused on the game on the small TV and the pizza he was consuming that he had brought in with him—he frequented the pizza place down the street. But when Beth went to the small closet and pulled out her undergarments, as well as her work uniform, she could feel his eyes on her as she changed, and she hated it. And she was half afraid that he would notice the slight roundness in her stomach that she wasn't actually sure was there, or if it was her imagination. Although she was sure that by now the roundness was becoming more pronounced everyday. She had started wearing loose-fitting shirts to try to hide it.

To everyone she talked to, Beth described Tyler as her boyfriend, but she felt nothing toward him whatsoever, except maybe pure loathing. Of course, when she had first met him, she had thought he was everything. He was incredibly gorgeous, attracting attention everywhere he went for his looks. They looked like a model couple together—he even had been a model for a while. But all the people that admired them as a beautiful couple didn't know what Tyler was like once you got to know him. He wasn't a nice guy at all. He was greedy, selfish, and uncaring. They lived together, but they weren't really a couple—they never really had been. There was no emotion to this relationship. Purely lust, and more on Tyler's side than her own. For Beth, it was about survival. If she had her choice, she wouldn't be here with him. But until she had more money and a distinct plan, she had nowhere else to go. Plus being with Tyler was a heck of a lot better than where she was before he came along. She had agreed to play in this charade for her own purposes, not for any feelings she held toward him.

Beth gave herself one last glance in the mirror to make sure she looked all right before she reached for her jacket. She could tell by Tyler's appraising eyes that she met his approval. A year back she would have given anything to have someone look at her the way Tyler was now, but she didn't care anymore. She didn't care about attracting anyone. He wasn't looking at her with love in his eyes. He just saw the object of his desire. He liked having a hold on her, because he loved seeing the same look he was giving her in the eyes of other guys—it gave him satisfaction. They all wanted her, but he was the only one who got to have her. He liked feeling like he owned her.

Beth grabbed her long pea coat, which covered her outfit completely, leaving only her heeled boots showing at the bottom. She felt safe in her jacket, covered up. She even clutched the neck closer together, which was completely buttoned up already, as if she could conceal herself even more. But she was headed to work, another horrible night doing something she hated.

"I'll see you later," she said, reaching for her purse.

"You're coming here right after work, right?" he asked from the couch, no longer interested in watching her now that she was covered up with her jacket.

"Where else would I go?" she asked, the bitterness evident in her voice. She wished so desperately that she had somewhere else to go. He turned to look at her now, his eyes narrowed on her face in disdain.

"I'm staying in tonight, so don't be late." It was a warning. She didn't care though. Tyler thought that he was the one in control in this situation, that he called all the shots. But she knew that she had a power over him. In the end, she would be the one calling all the shots. One day she would break free from him, and there would be absolutely nothing he could do about it. And she would laugh in his face.

Instead of answering him, she merely rolled her eyes and slammed the door behind her. He would be asleep when she came in anyway, she was sure. When he told her he was staying in, she knew it meant that he wanted her. On the nights when he wasn't there when she returned from work, she knew he was with some other girl. And he thought she was foolish enough to believe that he loved her. Thankfully she ceased to care what Tyler did with his life months ago, if she ever had at all. Their arrangement was purely out of necessity.

Beth walked down the steps that led up to their third-floor studio apartment that was over a Laundromat, out onto the chilly autumn San Francisco streets. It wasn't the kind of cold she was used to, growing up in the mountains of Colorado. It wasn't even winter yet, although she knew by now that summer could really be the coldest time of year in San Francisco. But the wind blowing off the cold Pacific waters of the bay weren't friendly as they slapped her in the face on her way to work.

Work was her personal hell. She could handle Tyler and the bad situation she had gotten herself into with him, but the second the sign of the gentlemen's club appeared a few blocks from the apartment, she grimaced. She hated her work, but had to accept the job six months back. It paid really well in tips, and helped her to dig herself out of the even deeper pit than the one she was in now. Everyone that had known Beth growing up would never have pictured her to hit so low as to literally have no home and nowhere to go. She had lost all her money, and quite a lot of her dignity. She spent a month hopping from friend's houses, crashing on their couches and eating their food. But even that couldn't last—she wore out her welcome with people she thought had cared. Just when Beth was going to be thrown out onto the streets for good, she had met Manny. He offered her a job at his club without specifying just what kind of club that it was. But she was desperate. She would have said yes to anything, which was not a fun position to be in.

"You're late," Tony said as she walked up to the door. He took his job as a bouncer almost too seriously—he was like a guard, making sure only the right people got in, and making sure not to let Manny's girls out. At least, that is how she felt. It was her own personal prison. But she walked away with so much money every night made simply in tips that it blew her mind. It was a job she hated, but in some ways it was helping her get back on her feet. At least she could pay back some of her debt. But right now she felt like she was in the bottom of a huge, deep pit and she had no idea how to get herself out. She walked in every night with the intention of quitting, but lost her resolve on the way out with a wad of cash in her hand.

"Well, I'm here," she replied with a roll of her eyes, walking under his arm as he held the door open for her. She walked into the back room, stashing her jacket and purse in a safe location. And then she went about her routine.

When Beth first took the job, Manny informed her that he would only have use for her as a showgirl. He wanted her to prance around in next to nothing, and be there merely for the pleasure of the gentlemen who came into his club. He told her that she would have to do whatever it took to satisfy her customers, assuming that since she was the type to express interest in this kind of job, that she would agree to anything. But she refused flat out. Even being merely a waitress, Beth knew that she was selling herself. She didn't need to be a prostitute to know that she was selling her body—it was something she had done even before Manny had offered her a job, in her own way—Beth knew how to get what she wanted. But she told Manny that she would only work for him as a waitress. The only reason he agreed was because he saw the way the men reacted to her when she was in a crowd. Beth was just another little gem to him, and he wanted to have her no matter what it took—like she was part of his own personal treasure collection.

So Beth was a waitress. She carried drinks on a little tray to all the guys that came into the club. She turned on her seductive, flirty smile, knowing it was the best way to get tips, all the while tuning her heart and her emotions out.

She was disgusted by what she was doing, but felt glad that at least she wasn't prancing around onstage being so close to naked that she might as well take her clothes off—even being here for six months hadn't made her comfortable with the fact that she saw way more of her coworkers bodies than she ever wanted to. She had to wear a short and sexy dress, kind of like many guys' fantasy of a little French maid's outfit. It definitely wasn't tasteful, but it wasn't the bare minimum.

Beth strutted across the club all night, entertaining men and letting them think they had one ounce of a chance with her until her shift ended. She was used to customers buying her drinks, and Manny told her that it was good of her to accept. He told her sobriety made her uptight. But in all reality, Beth hated to drink—even in college, when she had partied her nights away, she had hated it. She hated the taste of alcohol. But she often came away from her shifts feeling awfully tipsy, that is, until she found out she was pregnant—although she wasn't sure why she had cared enough, but somehow the presence of this baby was forcing her to change her habits. She simply started refusing any offer of a drink, and Manny had lashed out at her for it. But the gentlemen found it even more entertaining.

Everyone who was a regular at the club knew that little Beth was hard to get, so they tried even harder—the mere chase of her was so exhilarating to so many of the men that she got even more attention than before—sometimes more than the naked strippers strutting across the stage. But at least she got away with not having anything to drink. She didn't want to do any of this anymore. But when a bundle of cash was placed in her hand when her shift ended at four in the morning, she knew that she would be back there the next night. She would be back until she absolutely couldn't anymore. Her uniform was like a corset. It wouldn't hold her in for long—it was getting tighter everyday, and she had already secretly exchanged hers for the next size up a couple weeks ago. There was no larger size now, not one that would allow her to keep her job. But she was already planning her escape, anyway.

"Do you want to go for some food?" one of her coworkers asked who was also getting off. Most of the girls went out to the twenty-four hour diner down the street after their shifts ended, at least those girls who weren't going home with various gentlemen, but Beth had yet to accept. They never stopped asking, however.

"No thanks, I'm just heading home," Beth replied, following the group out of the main entrance of the club.

"Suit yourself."

Beth sighed and wrapped her jacket around her tighter. She felt chilled to the bone, but not just from the autumn winds. She just felt cold inside. She was utterly ashamed of herself, and even more annoyed because she had thought that she had stopped caring months ago. But she knew what she was, and deep down she wasn't okay with it, as much as she told herself she was.

Before heading in the direction of home, Beth glanced across the street in a moment of desperate hope, already expecting to be disappointed. But she was wrong. Sitting on the sidewalk with elbows rested on his knees was Johnny Harris. She had met him months ago in a flower shop, and then carried on a conversation with him for a while, strangely enough, about the proper care of orchids, until he was called to the back of the shop for a meeting with the owner. It was the first conversation she had had in a long while when someone wasn't trying to work her, to get her to do something for them—she could tell from the innocent look in his eyes. It was just a simple conversation in a flower shop, one she frequented from time to time to spend precious money on flowers. She loved their bright burst of color, but they always died, kind of like how she felt like she was dying inside. The day she had met Johnny was the last time she had walked into a flower shop.

She had seen him again that very night after leaving work, and she could tell that she caught him completely by surprise, coming out of a gentlemen's club, although she did wonder what he was doing meandering around the streets at 4 a.m. The next three nights after that he waited outside on the curb for her, simply offering to walk her home or take her to eat. She didn't know him at all, and had no idea what his interest in her was—even though she knew it had nothing to do with what every other guy seemed to want from her, but she had declined all his invitations. And then he disappeared, and she was glad to finally be rid of him, but then two weeks later, there he was, trying all over again. She felt bad, knowing that he sat out there in the cold for her for some reason, and agreed to grab a bite to eat with him—a decision that had taken her by surprise as soon as she had made it. She had nothing in common with him, and they only talked about superficial things. But he came back the next four nights. And then he disappeared again. The same thing had been going on for the past three months. He would be there multiple nights in a row, and then he would be gone for a week or two. This had been the longest time he had been gone, nearly four weeks.

She didn't know why she hung out with him at times, and their conversations often left her angry—not at him, but at herself. She wasn't sure if she even liked him. But somehow, seeing him had always been a sigh of relief once she got out of work. She glanced hopefully to the curb every night when she got out of work to where he always sat waiting, telling herself that she didn't actually want him to be there, and she was starting to think that he wasn't going to come back.

Johnny glanced at her with a smile, like he was genuinely happy to see her despite the fact that she had just come out of a gentlemen's club. She knew enough about his personality by now to know that he was the kind of guy that normally wouldn't be caught within miles of a place like this. He was one of those rare, truly genuine, good men. A kind of guy that Beth definitely could never deserve, that she had never even crossed paths with before and didn't even know existed. She had no idea why he seemed to pursue her. All she knew was that he wasn't like the other guys. He didn't look at her with condemnation like so many others that knew what she did—even some of the regulars at the club would give her a look of disgust if they saw her out in public, only to chase after her later that night when the rest of the world wasn't watching. But for some mystifying reason, Johnny cared—about her.

"Hey there," he called across the street.

"Hey," she replied back, half-surprised, half-annoyed, frozen on her side of the road.

"Want to grab a bite to eat, or walk for a bit?" he asked hopefully.

She simply gazed at him for a moment, fighting a battle inside herself. Did she really want to go with him, or did she just not want to go home to Tyler? Why did the difference matter to her?

"I should probably head home." She didn't want to encourage him. Why did he keep seeking her out? She had nothing to offer. She had nothing to offer herself.

Johnny stood up and started walking in her direction. For a split second she thought about running for it, but something held her to the spot. She knew she would regret it more if she did.

"You look like you need some warming up. Come have some coffee with me."

She rolled her eyes and crossed her arms. "It's four in the morning. Shouldn't you be sleeping?"

"I like early mornings."

"Well I like to sleep," Beth argued. Although when she got home, Beth knew that Tyler wouldn't have sleeping on his mind, at least, once he did wake up and realize she was there—the thought made her feel sick. She usually went running right when she got home from work. It helped to clear her mind of anything before she crashed until work again. Running helped to relieve her frustrations—even if the euphoria only lasted until she walked back into the door of Tyler's apartment. She refused to think of it as her own as well. It was a temporary situation.

"Come on—what's more fun, sleeping or hot chocolate?"

"What, are you four?" she asked sarcastically. She actually thoroughly enjoyed hot chocolate and wasn't sure why she was giving him such a hard time about it. She just wanted him to leave her alone. But then again, if he walked away from her right now, she felt like she would cry.

"You ordered hot chocolate last time we went out to eat."

Beth's eyebrows creased together. "Oh, right."

"So will you come with me?"

Beth sighed, not caring enough to hide the sarcasm. "Only if you can find me hot chocolate with the little marshmallows."

"Oh, I think I can handle that," he said with a laugh, although she hadn't meant it to be funny.

So Beth left with Johnny, not sure where they would end up. But he was the lesser of two evils. She would deal with Tyler later.

Chapter Four

"So, how are you?" Johnny asked from the other side of the booth. They had found another twenty-four hour diner to go to, walking in silence all the way. It was the same chain of restaurants where all the girls went, but far away from the gentlemen's club, something that Beth appreciated, and something that Johnny seemed to instinctively know. They always went far away from the club.

"I'm fine, how are you?" she asked hollowly, reaching to the middle of the table and grabbing a French fry against her better judgment, not enjoying the pretense of pleasant conversation. They were both sipping hot chocolate and sharing a plate of fries. It wasn't the most conventional meal, but it was hitting the spot. She felt a little guilty to be eating fries, knowing that she really needed to watch her figure. But at the moment she just didn't care. Sometimes salty French fries were just necessary—especially doused in vinegar, just like she liked them. Plus, she was starving. She knew that she probably wasn't eating the amount she should be to be supporting another person inside of her.

"I'm doing well. Just in town on business."

That's what he always said. He didn't tell her what he did, and Beth never asked. She kept a wall up between her and Johnny. She wasn't even sure if they were friends. But somehow his presence had become the image of hope to her over the past few months, and in many ways that was unsettling. She had run out of hope a long time ago and was merely trying to keep her head above the water. She was afraid to hope. Every time she did, she sunk deeper than before.

Pretty soon she wouldn't be able to pick herself back up again. Not unless she thought of something quick.

Johnny wasn't like any of the guys that Beth had grown up knowing. She had always had an extremely bubbly personality, and had been more of a flirt than anything else. Her boyfriend in high school was the most popular guy in school, as well as the most attractive. Beth had always been in the popular crowd. But she could tell that Johnny wouldn't have fit into the same sort of high school group. He was cute enough, but she would never look at him and think he was gorgeous—not like Tyler, even if the thought of Tyler made her cringe.

Johnny had straight golden blonde hair, which she wished she could help him style, and hazel eyes that had just a touch of gold to them. When he smiled, one side of his mouth always went up a little further than the other, giving him a boyish grin, but she knew he had a couple years on her. Beth could tell that he was the kind of guy who as a kid had been the chubby boy, but puberty had done him well and he had thinned out a lot—she could tell he had a lot of strong muscles on his body, even if he was really thin. He was the type of guy who would turn heads at his ten-year high school reunion because no one would have expected him to turn out looking as handsome as he was. He wasn't the type of guy that she would have been friends with in the past, but that was before she had become the Beth that she is today. That was before she left home ready to conquer the world and had ruined her life instead.

"How's work?" he asked. The question was sincere, but she thought she caught a bit of a mocking glimmer in his eyes. Either way, she narrowed her eyes on him. They did not discuss her work. It was supposed to be off limits.

"Horrible as always. Why do you ask?" she wanted to know, crossing her arms.

"If it's so horrible, why do you do it?" Johnny wondered.

Beth's eyes narrowed, and she almost didn't answer at all, but instead she reached into her purse and pulled out the wad of cash she had received in tips. She held it up in front of him to see his reaction, but she could tell he wasn't impressed. Honestly, she wasn't that impressed herself, however much the money would help her.

"You know, there's lots of ways to make money."

She sighed. He wouldn't understand. She could tell that he had been brought up in a loving, caring family, and he hadn't thrown that all away like she had. He didn't know what it meant to be drowning in the midst of your own chaos.

"Not when you're desperate."

"Why are you desperate?" he asked. She didn't mean to give such an honest answer. It was pushing the conversation past the borders she always set up when they were together.

"I just am," she replied, crossing her arms and looking out the window of the diner to the dark streets. But the endless burst of tears started to stream down her face, and there was nothing she could do to stop them. She hated that he was so interested, that he kept pushing. Why couldn't he just leave her alone? He made it sound like a way out was easy. He didn't understand at all.

Johnny handed her a napkin to wipe her eyes.

"Thanks," she said, almost meanly, wiping her eyes and trying to control herself. Her outbursts were surprising her. She hadn't cried in months, and now all of a sudden everything was hitting her—the nothingness of her life. She had learned how to turn her emotions off, but apparently the dam had broken. Lately all of her emotions were flooding out of her, and she didn't know how to make them stop.

"Why don't you get out?" Johnny asked. She could tell by his voice that he would personally help her get out if she would just ask, although one look at him and she knew that he would be no match for the crowd that she ran with. There was no way for him to help her.

"I can't just walk away. It's not that simple."

"Why not?"

Beth looked into his hazel eyes, and saw only compassion written all over his entire face. For some reason, he actually cared about her. They didn't even know each other, but he actually cared for her well-being. And he was probably the only person who did. She couldn't understand it, and that made her nervous. She had been with plenty of people she had thought cared about her, and they had only ripped her to pieces. She could tell he was different though, and the unknown was terrifying. She couldn't understand him.

"You don't know anything," she said, not in a mean way. In an honest way. "I'm not doing this because I want to. I'm doing this because right now there is no other option."

"I can help you," he said. And for a moment, Beth really did want to take him up on his offer. But he couldn't help her. He didn't even know her. He thought she was simply talking about her job, but her whole life was in shambles. And she had to fix it somehow. For the sake of the child she was carrying within her, she would.

"You can't help me," she stated.

"Why not?"

"You don't even know me."

He leaned back into his seat, like he was getting comfortable, as if he planned to stay awhile. "So tell me about yourself."

Beth glanced at him warily for a second, and then relaxed. For some reason, she actually wanted to tell him about herself. Or at least tell him about what brought her to this point. It was such a burden to carry all on her own. But she was ashamed of herself, and she knew anything she said to Johnny right now would send him running. And she was mad at herself for caring enough, knowing that she didn't want to not ever see Johnny again. She didn't want to send him running because she was afraid of the emptiness she would feel without him. It made her almost want to laugh, in a completely non-humorous way. This guy that she didn't even know had somehow become integral to her existence.

"You don't want to know," she answered.

"I wouldn't have asked if I didn't want to know."

"Johnny," Beth began, "I'm not a good person. I've made some huge mistakes."

"Who hasn't?"

She shook her head. "I have so many regrets."

"That means you're human."

"I've messed my life up in so many ways."

"Not beyond repair. Never beyond repair."

Beth stared at Johnny, almost as if she were sizing him up. She couldn't tell him about herself, because then he would be out of her life. He was her one beacon of light right now, and she couldn't mess that up.

"Let me help you," he said, leaning forward and placing his hands on the table, almost as if he were reaching for hers. She could feel the increased pounding of her heart from the simple gesture. Her instincts were equating Johnny with safety. It terrified her.

"You can't help me. No one can help me."

"That's not true."

"Johnny, you know nothing about me!" she declared angrily.

"Then tell me."

"Fine! You really want to know who I am? You really want to know the horrible person I've become? Fine!"

So out of her anger and desperation, Beth started to tell him. She took him back to the very beginning, about two years ago when she made the first big move. The memory haunted her now. She had done the unthinkable to her family, but at the time she thought she was right. At the time she thought it would make her free. It disgusted her now.

Growing up, Beth always had to battle with her older sister, Amy. She knew that Amy resented Beth simply for being born, which Beth could never understand. They never had much of a warm relationship growing up, but not for Beth's lack of trying. And then when their mom died, everything got worse for a while. Beth was only thirteen when her mom died, but she missed her everyday. It had been a really hard time, but then life continued on. Beth started high school, and started working for the family's ski resort.

All throughout high school, Beth taught ski instruction for four-to-seven-year-old kids. She helped the older instructors, and she loved it. Amy was more interested in the business of actually running the ski resort, something that Beth could care less about. She hated growing up with this expectation that she would simply join the family business. She wanted to do her own thing and become her own person. She wanted her own identity apart from her family's enterprise. Her father knew that she had no interest in running the ski resort, so he worked with Amy, preparing her to one day take over the business. And Beth hated her for it. Just because Beth didn't want to do what was expected of her didn't mean she wanted to be cast out of the family legacy entirely.

"It isn't fair!" Beth declared one morning in her father's office. She was twenty, and had just returned home from her second year of college in Boulder. She didn't care if her sister had just graduated college with a business degree and was looking to take on more responsibility. It wasn't fair.

"What isn't fair?" her father asked, sitting at his large mahogany desk and looking up at her as she paced back and forth across the room.

"Amy gets everything handed to her on a silver platter, and I'm just left in the dark!"

"What do you mean Amy gets everything handed to her on a silver platter?"

Beth stopped pacing and glared at her father.

"You're handing Amy your legacy, and I get nothing. She gets the whole business, everything, and I get nothing." Beth started pacing again. She was sure that her sister didn't even want it. She took it just to spite Beth, to be on their dad's good side.

"Beth, you've made it clear that you want nothing to do with the resort."

"So what if I don't want to work here? You're still going to hand everything to Amy as if I don't exist? Her whole future is provided for, and I get nothing. It's all or nothing, Dad."

He was being very patient with her, but she was too fueled up to care or notice.

"It's not all or nothing," he replied quietly.

"Yes it is!" Beth yelled. "I either have to join the family business or I'm out cold in the streets."

"You would never be left out cold in the streets. You know that isn't true."

"Yes it is! And I don't want to be a part of the ski resort! Sometimes I don't even want to be part of this family!"

Her father didn't answer her for a few minutes. He just watched her as she continued pacing back and forth across the room. She knew her words hurt him, but she was too angry to care. After a few moments he leaned forward on his desk.

"Then what is it you do want, Beth?"

"I want to do what I want and not be chastised for it. I want to be provided for just like Amy. I want to be my own person and get out of this place!"

She continued pacing in rage, not paying attention to her father as he opened the top drawer of his desk and pulled out his checkbook. She didn't notice him as he raised his pen, or when he tore the check away from the rest.

"You've always favored Amy! You give her anything, and I'm just expected to do everything on my own or be just like her. I don't want to be Amy."

Her father just looked at her, pain reflected in his eyes as he watched his baby girl red with fury.

"You want a chance to find your own way—here," he stated, holding the check up to her, no malice in his voice, just sorrow.

Beth stopped pacing and glanced at him, wary for a moment before she approached the desk and took the check. Her eyes got wide when she read the amount.

"What is this for?" she demanded.

"You said you didn't think it was fair that Amy received the business and you got nothing. So take it, it's yours."

Beth glanced at the check again, astounded that she had procured part of the inheritance she always assumed she would get. Now she had the money to do whatever she wanted, to get as far away from Holy Cross as she dreamed. And she did. She took the check and ran upstairs to her room and packed her bags. Without so much as a thank you or goodbye, Beth stormed out of the house in the car she had gotten for her sixteenth birthday. She drove far away from her childhood home. She drove all the way to San Francisco where her best friend from high school was living and going to school. Together the two of them flew to Europe to have the time of their lives. After two months, her friend had to fly back to the states to go back to school, but Beth stayed in Europe. She didn't care about going back to school. She was too busy having the time of her life.

For ten months, Beth traveled all around Europe. She had always been an extremely bubbly person, and made friends wherever she went. She was having so much fun being on her own and being independent. And she didn't just tour around Europe, she did it in style as well. She only stayed in the best hotels. And she spent tons of money on a brand new wardrobe of only the most expensive designers. She was free to do as she pleased, and she loved it.

Three months before she returned to the states, she met Marcello. She fell madly in love with him, or so she thought at the time. She never wanted to leave his side. They spent a month together in the south of France, where she met him, before returning to his native Italy. They were planning on moving in together, into a beautiful refurbished flat in a small Tuscan town. She wanted to spend the rest of her life with him. At the time she didn't realize that he would be one of the biggest mistakes of her life.

Beth wasn't familiar with Italy at all. She couldn't speak Italian. So when it came to the purchase of their flat, she placed the burden in Marcello's hands. He said that he would handle it all. So she did everything he said. She transferred her funds into a joint account in Italy so that he could access the funds and take care of buying their home. On the day they were expected to close, Beth waited for him outside of the realtor's office, and he never showed. It was then she learned that the whole purchase had been a lie. She went to speak to the realtor that Marcello had been talking about to find out that there was no realtor by that name in the office that he told her to meet him at. When she checked the bank account, all of her money had been withdrawn. Marcello had taken everything. He had been playing her all along.

Beth went to the authorities and told them everything that happened. She could tell merely from interacting with them that they were doubtful she would ever see her money again. Marcello had disappeared. And Beth was left with nothing.

Beth was devastated, not only because Marcello had stolen all her money, but because she had thought that she loved him. Thankfully, she had enough in savings to get her back to the states, but she knew she couldn't return home. She wouldn't go back now. She wouldn't show her father and her sister how she had failed and lost all her money. She had to make it on her own, and Beth was determined. She would continue on her pride alone.

Beth bought a plane ticket to San Francisco, where she had a few friends from high school, and from college as well. She tried to find a job, and was becoming desperate. She sold the car she had driven to San Francisco when she had left home, but even the money from that ran out all too quickly. She wore out her welcome with all of her friends, and was about to be homeless. Then one day, when Beth was just walking the streets of San Francisco in hopelessness, which she did often, she ran into Manny on Pier 39. She was merely leaning on the pier, glancing at all the sea lions on the dock, listening to the multitude of people around her yet hearing nothing, when Manny came and stood next to her. He struck up a normal conversation with her, as if he was just an interested stranger. When he mentioned that he owned a club, Beth asked if he was hiring—more like pleaded with him for a job. That's how she got started in her new line of work. She went to work for him on a trial run that very night, and received enough money in tips that she was able to rent a cheap motel for the night so she wouldn't be on the streets.

Beth worked at the gentlemen's club for a month, waiting on all the guys who came in and putting on her seductive charm before she went home with Tyler one night. He had been there every night she worked, and she thought he was one of the most handsome guys she had ever seen, even more attractive than Marcello. She went home with Tyler every night for three weeks and was convinced that she was actually starting to like him until he found out that she lived in a motel. That's when they struck up a deal. Beth moved in with Tyler because it got her out of her sad situation at the motel. It meant that she could live in relative comfort, even if only in a shabby studio apartment with a pullout couch rather than a bed. At least there was a kitchenette, where she could cook actual meals. And it felt homier than the motel.

He knew that she hardly had any money when he asked her to move in. Their original bargain was that she would be the payment. But after a few weeks of that, Beth wanted out. Unfortunately she had nowhere else to go. Tyler was furious when she presented him cash for half the rent. It went against the deal they had made. It was that night that he first started going out seeking excitement elsewhere—he had taken the cash anyway. But in the end, she got to stay. She couldn't afford a place on her own, so it was the best she could to do. She and Tyler continued to pretend to be a couple, even though there was absolutely no emotion in their relationship.

A week after Beth had presented the rent money to Tyler, she found out she was pregnant. She was devastated. She couldn't take care of herself, and there was no way that she was prepared to take care of a baby. But it forced her to think of other options. She didn't want to live with Tyler anymore. She didn't want to work at the gentlemen's club. Her baby became a lifeline in some ways. Because of the baby growing inside of her, she couldn't do nothing. She had to think of a way out. She was forced to act. She needed to make something of herself. She wouldn't bring a child into the world she was living in—whether or not she kept it.

Beth sat there telling Johnny everything about her life since she had left home. It felt so good to tell somebody. It was still her burden to bear, but at least someone else knew. Her terribleness wasn't her secret anymore. Now Johnny knew the real her. He knew everything but about the baby she carried.

She couldn't risk telling anyone about her baby. If word got back to Tyler somehow, she was afraid of what the consequences would be. He could not know about their child. She knew she could trust Johnny with the information. Something inside of her instinctively trusted him, and she had no idea why as she had learned long ago to trust no one but herself. Johnny would never run in the same circles as Tyler, but she was unable to make the words come out.

"You're still here," Beth stated when she had finished telling her tale. Her hot chocolate sat cold on the table, the French fries only half eaten.

"You're surprised?"

"To be honest, yes."

"Why?" Johnny asked. He had sat in silence throughout her whole tale, watching her face, watching her regret. And he didn't leave.

Beth didn't answer him. She didn't know what to say.

"I can help you," Johnny said again.

She couldn't ask Johnny for help. She just couldn't. But when she left him on the corner near her building after he had walked her home—the first time she had let him do so—she left regretting that she didn't take him up on his offer.

Chapter Five

A week and a half later, the day came when Beth knew she had to leave. It started when she woke up at noon despite the fact that she had gone to bed at seven that morning after being up all night out of habit. She never woke up early in the day if she could help it. She usually slept until late afternoon until she had to do it all over again. But for some reason, she woke up at noon when Tyler left for work, and she was unable to go back to sleep. So she got up and made herself breakfast before heading to the shower and getting ready much earlier than she had to.

It was as she was standing by the closet in her towel, about to throw on comfy clothes until she had to get dressed in her uniform, that she caught a good look at herself in the mirror. She took her towel off and stared at her bare stomach. It was then that she noticed it. It was tiny, but there was a light bulge over her lower abdomen. It was slight, and since no one knew she was pregnant she guessed that no one would really notice—but it was definitely not her imagination this time. When she went to try on her uniform, she was unable to get the hooks on the front of the corset to close over her stomach. The fabric wouldn't stretch enough. She had been off the past three days, and it had been enough to make her uniform too small. It had felt far too tight the last time she had worn it, and she had even left a hook or two undone. There were no larger sizes available.

"Shoot," Beth said to herself, turning around to catch glimpses of her body at different angles.

There was nothing she could do. She couldn't return to work because she couldn't get in her uniform, and explaining that she simply couldn't fit anymore would not do. She had to be in tip-top shape to continue in her line of work. That meant she had to leave, lest Tyler find out that she was carrying his baby. She couldn't ever let that happen. She had almost told him on multiple occasions, but a voice in her head warned her every time she tried to form the words that it would completely endanger her and the baby she carried.

Beth threw on a sweater and a skirt, one that was short enough that when she put her usual jacket on over it, it would appear that she was wearing her uniform under it. She packed her suitcases full of her clothes, unable to fit all her possessions. But she brought all she could in her two large bags that had come home with her from Europe, willing to leave whatever else there was left behind.

Beth called for a cab to pick her up. While she was waiting, she put on her heeled boots and brought her bags down to the curb. Her shift started at eight, and Tyler would return home around nine. She had just enough time to disappear and he wouldn't know right away.

When the cab came, the driver loaded her bags in the trunk. She gave him the address of the gentlemen's club, and he looked at her in the rearview mirror with a raised eyebrow. She wouldn't have gone back at all if there wasn't a paycheck there waiting for her. She would walk in the front like always, as if she was coming for her shift, and then sneak into the office and grab her check. Then she would go out the back and meet the cab driver. She didn't know where she'd go after that, but she knew it would be far away from Tyler.

She told the cab driver to pull over a block from the gentlemen's club and then walked the rest of the way.

"Hey, Beth," Tony said, opening the door for her.

"Hey, Tony," she replied. She walked inside and greeted the bartender as she slipped into the office. Manny wouldn't come into the club for another hour or so, plus she wouldn't look suspicious at all just grabbing her paycheck. It was payday, anyway. Everyone would be coming for their money. She would just be taking her check before her shift, not after.

Once she grabbed her check, Beth came out of the office and headed into the back storeroom. That's where the door was that led out into the back alley.

She closed the door behind her and breathed a sigh of relief. That is, until she heard the door open behind her as she was about to slip down the alley.

"Where is it you're going?" a voice called behind her, and Beth cringed.

She turned around. "What are you doing here?" she asked, trying to subdue the sense of panic that immediately came over her.

Tyler smiled at her maliciously.

"I got out of work early. When I got home I saw that all your bags were packed and caught you climbing into a cab. But I knew you wouldn't leave without your paycheck. You're all about money, aren't you Beth?" he asked, walking closer to her.

"Oh, I'm the selfish one, huh?" she taunted back.

Tyler just shook his head at her.

"Where do you think you're going to go all on your own? Who's going to take care of you?"

"I don't need anyone to take care of me."

"Oh, don't you?" he asked, reaching his hand around to the small of her back and pulling her up against him. "You don't know how to be on your own."

"I'll learn."

"You'll fail."

A dangerous sense of confidence came over her. "I'll risk it."

Tyler yanked her harder against himself.

"You're not going anywhere," he said nastily, his face inches from hers.

"Well I'm certainly not staying with you," she declared.

Tyler smacked her so hard across her face that she staggered backward. Beth covered the sting of his slap with her hand

"Really, Tyler?" she called, her own anger prompting her further. "You're really going to hit me?"

"You can't just leave me."

"Watch me," Beth said. She turned around and quickly headed down the alley to the street, trying not to show her fear, but Tyler caught up with her before she could make a run for it. She knew that if she could just get out on the street she would be safer—Tyler wouldn't chase her down in public.

"You're not just walking out on me."

Tyler hit her again, this time splitting her lip. She could feel blood as it dripped down her chin.

"Why waste your time, Tyler? You tell me everyday that I'm not worth it," she stated, knowing that she shouldn't provoke him more. But she couldn't help herself. She hated him. She truly hated him. And there was no way she was going to show him how breakable she was.

"Go to hell," he told her

"You'll be going right along with me," she said back.

Tyler knocked her down onto the ground. She smashed the side of her head against the cement. He then proceeded to hit her a few more times. When she was too winded to fight her way back up, he reached for her purse and took her stash of cash and put it in his jacket pocket.

"Let's see how far you get without any of that," he stated.

Beth glared at him, but was in too much pain to move. He walked over and stood over her again, and she prepared herself for the impact of another blow, looking back toward the club wishing she were inside—which was a first. But he tried a different tactic.

"You're not going anywhere until I'm through with you. You owe me for taking you in like I did," he stated. He pulled his shirt out of his pants and was about to unbutton them when someone pulled him back and thrust him up against the wall.

"You better not lay another hand on her," Johnny warned.

"What's it to you?" Tyler spat in his face.

Johnny slammed him against the wall again. At any other moment she would have been impressed to see Johnny intimidate a guy like Tyler, but she knew he was no match.

"I mean it," Johnny stated. "You hurt her again and I'll have to hurt you."

Beth slowly pushed herself up. When she was completely on her feet, she swayed from the nausea in her stomach and the fogginess in her head from being hit too many times. She fell back toward the ground, trying to brace herself with her hands. She blacked out before she could feel the pain of smacking her head against concrete one more time.

———

When Beth opened her eyes and tried to sit up, she fell right back against the pillow. She could hear her pulse in between her ears as she put a hand to her head to try to quell the dizziness, shutting her eyes against the spinning room. But her hand pressed against a bandage that was covering the left side of her forehead. It put pressure on the wound it was covering, forcing her to let out a little yelp of surprise.

Beth took a few deep breaths and then opened her eyes again, completely confused by her surroundings and how she had gotten there. The room she was in was small but cozy. She was lying on a plush queen-sized bed, covered in a down comforter. It was the bed of her dreams. But she would have been able to enjoy it more if she wasn't in so much pain and if she actually knew where she was. She was completely disoriented, and it was making her nervous.

The room was cute. It was painted blue, with bursts of yellow accent colors in the curtains and the paintings on the walls. There were also fresh flowers on the nightstand near her, as well as a glass of water and a bottle of aspirin.

Beth was trying to decide whether or not it would be to her benefit to call out to someone when there was a soft knock on the door. Before waiting for a response, someone opened it.

"Oh good, you're awake," said a middle-aged woman. She had straight blonde hair, and wore a cheery smile on her face. She came right up close to Beth and sat down on the side of the bed. "How're you feeling, honey?" she asked, placing an ice pack over the bandage covering Beth's forehead. Beth shied away from her touch, not liking the feel of anything against her head, even the cold relief.

"Um...I...where am I?" Beth asked, looking up into this woman's face. She had hazel eyes. Familiar hazel eyes. They had gold in them.

"Johnny brought you here," the woman responded. "I'm his mom. You can call me Ellie."

"What happened? What am I doing here?"

"Johnny brought you here, and I'm so glad he did," Ellie replied with motherly concern. "You had a concussion, and had to get a few stitches right above your eyebrow and on your lip. You also fractured your wrist."

Beth didn't answer for a moment, letting that sink in. She glanced down at her wrist and noticed that it was in a temporary cast.

"How long have I been here?" Beth wanted to know. She was baffled by everything. The last thing she remembered was Tyler yelling out to her when she snuck out the back of the gentlemen's club. She faintly remembered hearing

Johnny's voice. Looking back on it now, it was like she had dreamed it all—except she could feel all over her body that it hadn't been a dream.

"Since early this morning. Johnny took you to the hospital last night before bringing you here. You've been out since you've gotten here," Ellie told her, reaching for her hand and giving it a squeeze as she held the ice pack up for Beth.

Beth's mind was going a mile a minute, trying to remember what had happened in the last twenty-four hours, and surprise over ending up in Johnny's house, with his mom tending to her.

"I went to the hospital?" Beth asked.

"Yea, he took you in the city."

Beth pulled the covers back and reached down to pat her stomach, feeling the small bulge.

"My baby," she stuttered, feeling a sense of panic. "I'm pregnant!" she yelled as some details started to come back to her. She remembered Tyler throwing her to the ground. Why hadn't she thought to protect her stomach?

"The doctor at the hospital did a full examination. Everything is fine with your baby," Ellie smiled at her.

Beth let out a sigh of relief. "Oh thank God."

"How far along are you?" Ellie asked.

"About four and half months."

"Wow, and you're still so small!" Ellie said with a laugh.

Beth rubbed her stomach again, feeling the small bulge over the abdomen, suddenly comforted by it, and suddenly feeling a need to protect it that she hadn't felt before.

"I'm starting to show," she replied.

Just then there was another knock on the door.

"How's the patient?" Johnny asked, stepping into the room. Beth's eyes widened. Johnny's nose was black and blue, and it looked like there was a small bandage over it. But he smiled widely on seeing her awake. It made her uncomfortable. She could tell it was genuine.

"I'll leave you two alone. Dinner's almost ready," Ellie said, glancing at Beth. "I'll bring a plate up for you. You should keep resting in bed."

Beth nodded. "Thanks," she said, still out of it.

Ellie smiled sweetly. "You're more than welcome."

After she quietly closed the door behind her, Beth turned to look at Johnny. "Are you okay?" she asked.

"I'm fine," he said, as if nothing at all had happened to him.

"What'd he do to you?"

"It's just a little bruise," Johnny said, trying to pretend it was no big deal.

"It's a big bruise. Did he break your nose?"

Johnny didn't answer. She took his silence as a confirmation.

"What happened?" Beth asked.

"I got to you just in time," he said. "Who was that guy?"

"Tyler," Beth said, folding her arms across her chest, turning to look out the window, but the blinds were closed.

"Is he the father?" Johnny asked.

Beth glanced at him again. "You know?"

"When we got to the hospital, you kept saying 'my baby, my baby' over and over again. You left that part out when you told me your life story last week."

Beth was surprised. She didn't remember the hospital at all. And she was also surprised at this motherly concern that had apparently come over her, even if she couldn't recall it whatsoever.

"How'd you find me?" she wondered.

"I was coming to your apartment," he stated, pausing long enough to catch the surprise on her face. True, she had finally succumbed to his desire to walk her home for a change. He flat out refused to let her go home alone, so he knew where she lived. He had probably watched her from the corner where she left him until she got inside. She didn't want Tyler to see him and have what happened, happen. That's why she had always refused to let him walk her home in the first place.

"Okay," she stated, waiting for him to go on.

"I saw you leaving with all your stuff, so I got in my car and followed you. I wanted to make sure you had somewhere to go. I saw you walk in the club, and then you didn't come out. I heard yelling from the alley so I came to check it out."

Beth started crying. She couldn't help it. She felt bad that Johnny had gotten hurt, and she was just feeling emotional right now. Why couldn't she ever stop crying?

"Thank you," she said. "You really saved me."

Johnny gave her a half-smile.

"Are you okay?" he asked.

She sighed heavily. "I will be." She had to be. She was determined to be. It didn't happen at all how she intended, but she did get away, and there was a big relief in that, even if she had no idea what came next. Now she had the rest of her life to figure out. She was determined to make something of herself. There was no going back.

She studied his face, feeling a growing sense of nausea in her stomach. He really risked himself to save her, and she didn't know what to do about it. A tiny part of her was angry at him for it, because now she owed him. Now she had to repay him for saving her, and she was afraid of what he'd want. She knew it would never be what Tyler had asked of her—Johnny was too good of a person for that. But that fact alone scared her. This was unknown territory for her.

"So, what do you want from me?" she asked, hearing the coldness plain in her voice.

Johnny's brow furrowed. "What do you mean?"

"Why'd you bring me here?"

He looked surprised by her words, especially how she went from crying out her thanks to this.

"I wanted to make sure you were safe."

She sighed, feeling the tears come to the surface again. What was with this guy? What did making sure she was safe mean?

"For what price?" she asked, her voice dead.

He pressed his lips together and nodded in understanding. She was shocked that he looked like the one who was going to cry now. Johnny sat down on the edge of her bed, near her feet, a look in his eyes that brought her up short, completely silencing her. She had no idea what to think of this guy. She couldn't put him in a box.

"You've forgotten what freedom tastes like, haven't you?"

Beth opened her mouth to speak but no words came. Instead, all she could feel was this longing in her chest at the word he had just said, freedom.

Johnny looked like he was about to reach for her hands but then thought better of it.

"Beth, not everything comes with a cost."

She bit her lip and looked away, pressing down so hard she nearly drew blood through her stitches. It hurt though—she had forgotten how the impact of one of Tyler's blows had caused her lip to bleed.

She didn't believe Johnny. Everything had a cost, he was just too naïve to notice. She had learned the hard way.

"You're going to be okay," he said when she didn't respond.

Beth looked back into his face and shook her head.

"You will be," he reassured her.

"I don't even know what that means anymore," she nearly whispered. It was the most honest thing she had said to anyone in a long time. "I don't even know what I'm looking for."

He gave her a half-smile. "You'll find out."

She laughed at him, at the utter absurdness of the situation.

"And just how exactly am I supposed to do that?"

" 'Ask and it will be given to you; seek and you will find; knock and the door will be opened to you. For everyone who asks receives; he who seeks finds; and to him who knocks, the door will be opened.' " he quoted.

Beth rolled her eyes, thinking he was crazy, and then studied his face, truly studied it. His blonde hair was ruffled, like he hadn't stopped moving in quite some time—and he probably hadn't. His hazel eyes were warm as he looked upon her with empathy. She could see it in his eyes, in his honest expression. He truly didn't want anything from her. He didn't expect anything from her. He just cared. She didn't know why, but he did. It made her uncomfortable. She was afraid of what caring in return would do to her. She wasn't even sure she was capable of caring anymore. The past two years had sucked the life out of her, but she could feel it. The small flame of hope was still there. It had always been there.

She nodded at his expression and attempted to offer him a smile. It was the only thing she could give him.

"What happened after you got me away from Tyler?" she asked. She couldn't remember much of anything.

"I grabbed your bags from the cab and helped you to my car then took you to the hospital. They said you'd be fine. You had a minor concussion and they said to just take it easy the next couple of days and you'll be fine, although

I had to wake you every couple hours at first, which I'm guessing you don't remember. They also stitched you up and fixed your arm."

Beth nodded. "Thanks for taking care of me," she said again. She really did mean it, and she hoped he could hear it in her voice.

Johnny smiled more fully this time. "You're going to be fine."

Beth smirked.

"Trust me, you will be. You'll be fine—in all ways."

She smiled at him, a smile of gratitude. No matter what happened next, she knew she was safe for right now. She could feel it. "You brought me to your home?"

"My parents' home," he corrected. "I live in a little apartment about three blocks away, so not far," he said with a little laugh.

"Are we still in San Francisco?" she asked.

Johnny stood up and walked the few steps to the window, pulling up the blinds. Beth let her eyes focus on the large mountains, covered with snow on top. Her heart swelled with a kind of longing that she hadn't felt in a very long time. For a moment she thought she was back in Colorado, back in her childhood home. But she knew her mountain like the back of her hand, and this wasn't it.

"Where am I?" Beth wondered.

"Lake Tahoe."

Chapter Six

Ellie brought dinner up to Beth that night, but Beth was feeling so stressed and out of it that she could barely get herself to eat. Although for the sake of the child within her, she forced the food down her throat. It had been over twenty-four hours since the last time she had eaten, if her calculations were correct. She knew that couldn't be good.

After dinner, Beth walked across the hall to the bathroom to take a hot shower and wash away the mess. She felt extremely groggy from the past day. But she knew she could only wash the outside clean. She was still marred inside. She was still ashamed of herself, even if for the time being she was free from the horrible life she had been living. But she still felt disgusted with herself. She couldn't believe that she had fallen so low. She once had everything, and she threw it all away. She knew she only had herself to blame.

Beth stayed in the shower until she scrubbed herself clean and the hot water gave out—giving no thought to the cast on her arm, which she should have taken off before getting in the shower, ignoring the throbbing pain in her wrist. And she had no idea if it was bad for her stitches to get wet. When she got out of the shower, her skin was red from all the scrubbing and hot water that had burned as it rained down on her. She scurried across the hall in her towel, making sure to peer out the door to make sure no one was around. She put on the pajamas Ellie had left on the bed after bringing her dinner, and brushed her hair, but was still disgusted by herself as she glanced at her reflection in the mirror on the back of the door.

She was sick of herself. She was sick of being beautiful. Being beautiful had gotten her nowhere. It had gotten her caught up in whirlwind romance with Marcello, which turned out to be a lie. It had a gotten her a job that made her a decent amount of money, but caused her to sell her body in return, and sucked the life out of her in the process. It got her a place to live. But what did that really mean? Where did that really get her? Nowhere. Pregnant and alone, with no plans and a baby she was still partially in denial about. Beauty meant nothing. It had gotten her nowhere she wanted to be. Getting attention for her looks was no longer something she enjoyed. She wished no one would ever look at her again.

Beth walked across the hall to the bathroom again, rummaging through the drawers until she came across a pair of haircutting scissors.

"Perfect," she said to herself.

She gathered her long hair together, the hair that had drawn a lot of attention as it fell down her bare back every night at work—the pure silkiness of it being enticing enough. She held the scissors up, and started chopping at random. Long strands fell to the floor, leaving her hair short and choppy—very disheveled.

"That's not going to work," she heard Johnny's voice call out. Beth glanced at him in the mirror, startled. He was leaning against the doorpost.

"What's not going to work?" she said.

"You're still going to be beautiful no matter what you do to your hair—or yourself."

Beth sighed, placing the scissors on the counter. She looked at the mess she had made of her hair. It was short, cut in various lengths around her shoulders. It looked horrible, but he was right. She was still herself. She still looked the same. He had said it, she was still beautiful—even with uneven hair and red splotches on her face. By the time her hair dried in curls, the unevenness wouldn't even be that noticeable.

"Maybe I should shave it," she stated, half-jokingly. In a strange way the idea appealed to her, yet at the same time the thought of losing all her hair made her cringe. It had been something she actually used to like about herself, before she started hating everything about herself. Maybe she should go for something slightly less drastic than losing it completely. Dyeing it?

Johnny scrunched up his nose in distaste, and then winced in pain.

"You okay?" Beth asked.

"I'm fine. You okay?"

"No," Beth answered honestly, exasperated. Johnny was the one guy she could be completely honest with. He knew everything about her, nearly, and he had still come back. After that one night she hadn't seen him again, that is, until he came to her rescue. He not only took her to the hospital, but he brought her to his home. And he called her beautiful, but not in a way that made her cringe. She wasn't sure what to think of that.

"You will be."

"So you keep saying," she replied sarcastically. She was getting really sick of hearing it.

"Well I believe it."

Beth turned around and glanced at him. She noticed all the hair on the floor and sighed. Seeing all her hair on the floor made her a little sad—she immediately regretted what she had just done. But she leaned down and started gathering it up and threw it in the wastebasket, inwardly thankful that her hair grew almost annoyingly fast—it would be longer again in no time. When she was finished, she walked past Johnny back to her room and sat on the bed. He followed right behind her.

"Thanks for taking care of me," she said again. She didn't know what to do to make it up to him. Thanking him incessantly was the only thing that came to mind, but it sure didn't feel like enough.

"You can stop thanking me."

He looked down at her arm in the cast, which she was cradling in her free hand. He reached for it.

"It's soaking wet."

She shrugged in response, and then glanced at her things.

"I guess I have to start making some plans," she stated, pulling her arm free from his. She didn't want anyone touching her ever again, even someone as seemingly nice as Johnny.

"Well, I can help you with that."

"How?" Beth asked skeptically. "I have to get a job and figure out my life."

"You're more than welcome to stay here," Johnny offered.

Beth narrowed her eyes on him.

"I can't stay here. This is your parents' house."

"They said it was okay."

"I can't stay here," she said again, more forcefully.

"Well if you won't stay here, a few years back we renovated the garage and turned it into an apartment for some extra income. Their previous tenant recently left, so it's up for grabs."

Beth wasn't sure what to say to that. It was a really nice offer, but what was she supposed to do in Lake Tahoe? What was she supposed to do with herself? And how on earth was she ever going to repay Johnny and his family for what they have done for her already? She had been with them one night, but that was one night free from Tyler. She was free from him. She had no idea how to repay Johnny for that, let alone everything else he had done for her.

"I can't accept that," Beth said.

"Why not?" Johnny asked. "What else are you going to do?"

Beth decided not to be offended by his comment. He didn't mean it to be mean, but it stung. Maybe because the truth hurt even worse when she heard it aloud. She had nothing else to do.

"I need to find a job," she said.

"You can work with my parents. Help out the family business."

Beth glanced at him warily.

"What?"

"The family business?" she questioned, darkly amused. "I have a bad track record with family businesses if you remember correctly. We don't really get along."

"Well this has nothing to do with owning a huge multi-million dollar ski resort."

Beth rolled her eyes. "What's the family business?" she wanted to know.

"My parents own a flower shop," he stated. Beth glanced at him in surprise. She loved flowers. She used to spend hours with her mother in her garden, and continued to tend to it after she died. She loved arranging flowers in beautiful displays. She just loved them. They were so naturally beautiful, and just always added brightness to everything. She also loved to paint them.

"I met you in a flower shop," Beth stated.

"Yea," Johnny smiled, as if it were a good memory. "We do a lot of flower arrangements and ship them all over the country. But I go back and forth to San Francisco sometimes doing marketing and stuff. I don't really have anything to do with flowers personally, I'm just into the advertising and keeping up with the website, where the majority of our orders come from."

Beth was astonished. It was a family business, but completely different than her own. And she loved it—at least the idea of it. Flowers made her smile.

"Your whole family works there?"

"My mom works in the shop, and my younger sister, Crystal, works there a few days a week after school. You'll meet her tomorrow. She's at a friend's house working on a project for her science class."

Beth nodded. "What does your dad do?"

"He's an accountant. He works for an actual accounting firm, but does all the accounting and financial management stuff at the shop. Same with me—I do advertising for a few other places on top of the shop. All local businesses."

"Wow," Beth said. "That sounds cool." She couldn't deny it. As much as the thought of family businesses made her feel shaky, working in a flower shop was a dream.

"My mom's a little shorthanded, so if you want a job, she's already said that she'd love to have you."

Beth's eyebrows rose in surprise. "Your mom doesn't even know me."

"She can get to know you."

Beth smirked. "And what about you?"

"What about me?"

"I hardly know anything about you," Beth said.

"What do you want to know?"

She thought for a moment, but couldn't come up with many good questions. Her head was pounding a bit, and now that her hair was drying, she could tell how much lighter it felt since she chopped it off. On top of that, her cast felt extremely uncomfortable on her arm since it had gotten extremely wet in the shower. She wasn't sure how long it would take to dry out. A fleeting thought made her worry it would smell as it dried.

"Uh…how old are you?"

"Twenty-five. You?"

"Twenty-two," she replied. "Where did you go to school?"

"San Francisco," he replied. "You?"

"I'm a college drop-out, remember?"

"You still went for two years, where'd you go?"

"I went to school in Boulder. I was an art major."

"Art?" Johnny seemed surprised.

"Yea, it was part of my whole desire to be independent thing. But I've always loved painting."

"That's really cool," Johnny said. "What do you like to paint?"

Beth gave a sheepish grin, almost like she was embarrassed, which was hard these days.

"What?" Johnny laughed, seeing her expression.

"Flowers."

"Flowers?"

"I love to paint flowers," she shrugged.

Johnny smiled, a gleam in his eyes. "Perfect."

Chapter Seven

Beth woke up early the next morning. It was odd for her to actually sleep through the night. Usually her schedule was flopped, and she would sleep throughout the day. But now she had a new life ahead of her, and could do things differently. She would do things differently.

Beth tiptoed around, feeling fairly refreshed despite her injuries. She got completely ready for the day before realizing that it was barely six in the morning—her suitcases had been brought up to her room, and a toothbrush left in the bathroom with a note saying it was for her. The house was still quiet. Beth assumed that everyone else was still in bed. She didn't know what to do with herself until everyone woke up. In all honesty, she didn't know what to do with herself even when everybody woke up. Maybe the quiet stillness was better than what awaited her.

Since no one was around, Beth decided to take the opportunity to wander around the house. After stepping out of her bedroom, she looked down the hallway, really paying attention for the first time. There was a closed door at the end of the hallway, which she assumed was the master bedroom. There was another closed door diagonally across the hall from Beth's room, and she guessed from the long dangly necklace hanging from the door that it was Johnny's sister's room. The only other open door, beside the bathroom, was a small home office.

Beth walked down the stairs to explore some more. The whole main floor had a wide-open layout. The house wasn't large, but it felt homey and comfortable. The family room had plush, oversized chairs. The kitchen opened right up to the dining and family room. There was also a formal living room, which seemed to be doing double duty at the moment housing a treadmill and weight machine.

There were sliding glass doors in the kitchen that led out to a deck and a little backyard. Beth could tell that her bedroom looked over the back of the house, because she got the same view of the mountains. She couldn't believe that she was in Lake Tahoe. She had skied here as a kid with her parents and sister on a family vacation. They had skied all over the place. It was ironic to her that Johnny's safe haven for her was a ski town.

Beth turned around and glanced around the updated kitchen. She debated whether or not to search for some food. She felt bad rummaging through the cabinets of a stranger's home, but she was starving. She never finished her dinner the night before, and she really needed some food.

After debating for a few minutes, Beth decided not to worry about appearing rude. Why did she care? She went all out and searched the kitchen, grabbing fresh vegetables and eggs. She found a pan and started to make an omelet, not letting her wrist impede her cooking skills. Just as she was about to flip it, she heard the front door open. Her heart rate started accelerating. She felt like she was about to be caught doing something terribly wrong and be reprimanded for it.

"Hey there," Johnny said, rounding the corner into the kitchen. He seemed surprised to see her there, like he thought he was greeting someone else at first. "I see you're making yourself right at home."

She smiled guiltily. "I'm sorry."

He laughed. "Don't apologize. It's a good thing."

"I was just starving and I've been awake for hours."

"You don't need to explain," he said. He stepped over to the stove to see what she was making. "That looks good."

She smiled. "Want one? Omelets are my specialty." Food would be a good place to start in terms of saying thank you. Thank you would never be enough. That fact worried Beth.

"Oh really? I think you'll be a hit with my family then."

Beth nodded, not quite sure what he meant, and if that was a good thing. She wasn't sure she wanted his family to like her. She didn't know if she was capable of being liked anymore. And she didn't want to owe them anything more than she already did.

"Well I can make you one," she said again. "If you want."

"Sure, that'd be great," he answered.

He told her what he wanted in his omelet, and she went to work making it, taking bites of her own as his was cooking, pouring herself a glass of milk to wash it all down. She tried to keep Johnny talking, wanting to learn a little more about this guy who had saved her from nearly being raped and beaten even more, who had continually offered her a way out of her personal hell and didn't rest until he did.

"So do you ski?" she asked. The two of them sat down at the dining table to eat their omelets together, even though Beth was nearly done.

"No," Johnny said, pursing his lips.

"Not ever?" she asked, surprised.

He shook his head.

"How do you grow up in Lake Tahoe and not even try?" she wondered. "Do you not snowboard either?"

He shook his head again.

"Wow," she stated, taking a sip of her milk. "You've never even wanted to learn?"

"I just…" he began, trying to find an explanation. "I mean…the idea of sliding down a mountain on small little sticks just never really appealed to me."

Beth smiled, amused. "You were too afraid?"

"Those are some steep mountains!" he yelled, embarrassed.

Beth laughed good-naturedly.

"It's really not that scary," she stated, knowing that wouldn't help.

He looked at her like he didn't believe her. "How long have you been skiing?"

Beth thought for a moment. "I think since I learned how to stand," she answered. "I got my first pair of skis for my first birthday."

"Wow," Johnny said. Now he seemed impressed by her. "Can you snowboard as well?"

Beth nodded. "Although I prefer skiing. Or I'm better at it—not really sure."

"That's really cool," he stated.

"I guess."

Just then Beth heard footsteps above her, and a moment later someone else appeared in the kitchen.

"Morning," Johnny said. The girl grimaced in response. She didn't seem to want to be awake. She didn't even acknowledge her brother as she plopped down on the couch.

The girl was dressed in long pajama pants and a sweatshirt. Her blonde hair was piled on top of her head in a messy bun. She looked a lot like Johnny. They had the same nose and hair.

"This is Beth, by the way," Johnny said.

The girl turned her head to the side, clearly surprised to see someone else in the kitchen. She sat up, brushing her stray hair out of her face, trying to make herself appear more composed. Beth noticed that she also had the same color eyes as her brother.

"I'm Crystal," she said with a bright smile, her sleepiness vanished.

"She's my little sister," Johnny explained.

"I gathered that," Beth replied. "It's nice to meet you."

"Nice to meet you, too," she replied warmly. Crystal got up and sat down at the table with them, firing off questions at Beth, not at all shy. Beth felt weird having someone she had just met be so interested in her life. She asked her about growing up in Colorado and what Beth liked to do in her spare time. Beth tried to answer her questions to the best of her ability, skimming over many things that she never wanted to mention to anybody. It startled her to see someone so interested in her life, especially someone who didn't even know her. Beth surmised that Johnny had yet to tell his sister exactly what he had rescued her from.

"Have you thought of any names for your baby?" she asked excitedly after quizzing Beth on her favorite kind of flowers to paint. Beth hadn't been able to give a good answer. She wasn't sure she had a favorite.

"Crystal!" Johnny said, trying to deflect the question from Beth.

"What?"

"Just chill out a bit."

"I was only wondering."

Beth forced a smile, feeling a pit in the bottom of her stomach. "To be honest, I haven't decided if I'm going to keep it yet."

Crystal seemed surprised by her answer, almost upset. "You're not going to keep it?"

"Crystal, leave her alone!" Johnny yelled, looking agitated.

"Are you going to get an abortion?" Crystal asked.

"Crystal!" Johnny shouted again, standing up in his anger.

Beth appreciated Johnny trying to help. She didn't know what to say, especially to someone as young as Crystal who had the whole world in front of her. They weren't that far apart in age, not really, but Beth felt like she had lived a million years after what she had been through since leaving home. She didn't want to destroy Crystal's bright-eyed innocence.

"No, I'm not going to get an abortion," Beth stated quietly. She glanced down at her glass of milk for a second, hoping that Johnny and Crystal wouldn't notice the heat that crept into her face. No, she wasn't going to get an abortion, but she almost did. That was the reason she had stopped spending her precious money on flowers after meeting Johnny—to afford it. She got all the way to the table at the clinic for her appointment, the doctor giving her an exam before the procedure, when she started to have a panic attack. She couldn't do it. She had no idea what propelled her from the clinic that day, but she couldn't go through with it. No—she would carry the baby until term. From there, she wasn't sure if she would give her baby up for adoption or keep it. The reality of carrying a life inside of her was still sinking in. Beth didn't even know how to handle herself. What was she going to do with a baby?

Crystal seemed relieved by her answer, although Beth wasn't really sure why. It really was no one else's business what she decided to do with her baby, and there were times in the beginning when she wished she could find the strength to just get rid of it. She still doubted her decision sometimes. But that day in the office, Beth's own selfishness had caught up with her. For her, choosing whether or not to end her pregnancy was the difference between life or death. Between sinking further in despair and doing whatever she wanted without concern for anyone else, and turning her life around. Beth wouldn't extend her own selfishness onto the life of this baby, no matter what she decided to do with it.

Crystal just kept chattering away, as if there hadn't been any awkward moments at the breakfast table. Beth made her an omelet while Crystal talked about school. Beth discovered that Crystal had recently turned seventeen. She was halfway through her junior year of high school, and hating every minute of it. She told Beth that junior year wasn't fun at all. It was just piles and piles of schoolwork. Beth tried to be sympathetic. She didn't really miss school, although she hated being considered a college dropout. She was a failure in so many other areas that she wasn't sure why she cared.

Ellie and her husband, Mark, came down the stairs just as Beth was finishing cooking Crystal's omelet. Beth thanked them for their hospitality and apologized for rummaging through the kitchen uninvited. They didn't care at all, especially when Beth placed steaming omelets in front of them. She felt extremely awkward sitting down with the whole family. They all seemed to truly love and care for one another, even if there was a lot of good-natured joking. Beth hadn't witnessed a healthy family in a long time—not even her own. Sure, she had a good life growing up, but things only went downhill after her mother died. And she and her sister certainly never had a healthy relationship. Still, her family had been great, she just never took the time to realize that.

Because of their time sitting around the table and chatting, Crystal hadn't gotten ready for school. When Mark left for work, she was already missing part of her first class, which Beth noticed Crystal digested with a triumphant smile.

With Mark and Crystal gone, Beth cleared the dishes from the table, but Ellie told her not to worry about cleaning them. Instead, she left the dishes in the sink and Ellie and Johnny took her to check out the garage apartment.

"Wow, this is really nice," Beth exclaimed when Ellie opened the door. The whole apartment was decorated with different blues and bright accent colors, much like the guest room that Beth was currently in, which she found out used to be Johnny's room until he moved out.

The garage was connected to the house through a large room off the kitchen that appeared to do double duty as a mudroom and laundry room. There were benches and hooks for the family to hang jackets, as well as racks to lay out wet boots in the winter. There was a washer and dryer, which Ellie said was for the family to use, as well as any tenant. Aside from the entry to the kitchen, there was a door that opened up to the backyard, and then the door leading into the actual apartment.

The apartment was basically one big room that had been sectioned off into smaller spaces—much like a studio apartment, but much better done than the other studio apartment coming to her mind. There was a small sitting room, with a nice looking couch and coffee table. There was also a small table pushed up against the wall. The extra chair was in the corner, trying to save space. There was a small kitchenette, with enough there for Beth to be able to make herself omelets in the morning if she wished to, as well as a door that opened up to the side of the house so the apartment even had its own entry. The bedroom was partitioned off creating an actual room. There was a queen bed with a down comforter on top—Beth's dream. There was a tiny closet, as well as a fairly large dresser. There was also a full bathroom just off the bedroom.

It was more than Beth could ever hope for, and definitely more than she could afford. Something as nice as this little apartment had to cost a lot. It was hard to tell that it was even a garage—although from the outside of the house Beth was sure it appeared to open like any garage door, but from the inside a wall had been created in front of it so that you would never know. It was a spectacular use of space.

"What do you think?" Ellie asked, leaning against the counter in the small kitchenette.

"It's wonderful," Beth replied honestly, her gaze drifting to the window that looked over the backyard to the mountains she had seen from the bedroom upstairs. Truly, it was a dream. "But how much is rent?"

Ellie smiled at her. "Don't worry about it, honey. You just recuperate a bit. Put your money to good use." Beth noted Ellie's quick glance to her stomach.

Beth stared at Ellie in startled surprise. "I can't take this place rent free."

Ellie shook her head. "Really, the apartment's just sitting here. I'm just glad there is someone to use it."

"You have to let me pay you for it."

"Just deal with paying for your own groceries and such," Ellie explained.

Beth looked from her to Johnny, who had taken a seat on the couch, completely at home, while Ellie took the time to show Beth throughout the whole apartment. He was just sitting there with a contented smile on his face. Beth wanted to weep. For some reason, being with Johnny's family scared her more than her life with Tyler did, more than contemplating how she was going to escape him. These people were unlike any she had ever known, and she didn't know what to do with that. They were offering her a home, a place unlike anything she could have imagined finding for herself. They were offering her a piece of her life back. It scared her to death.

"You can have your own space out here and just get back on your feet again," Ellie explained. "Of course, we would love to have you join us in the main part of the house whenever you want, if you want. Please feel free to be in the house as often as you wish. Consider it your home, too. You are more than welcome to join us for meals any day. But I totally understand if you need some time to yourself as well."

Beth stared at her, almost unable to comprehend the situation. Johnny and his family weren't just helping her until she figured out her next move. They weren't just offering to let her use their garage apartment. They were telling her that they wanted her to consider herself part of the family though they barely knew her—no strings attached.

Chapter Eight

A week later, Beth was still trying to get used to her new life. With the help of Johnny carrying her bags from the guestroom to the garage, Beth moved into the little apartment. She unpacked all her clothes into the sizeable dresser and the closet, realizing that she had left a lot behind when she ran away from Tyler, a lot of the beautiful designer clothes that she had purchased in Europe—but she didn't care. Her whole life felt like excess baggage. She only had the pair of high-heeled boots she had worn when she went to pick up her paycheck one last time, which certainly weren't suitable any longer. She wanted to burn them and have them gone from her life forever.

Ellie let her borrow a simple pair of tennis shoes until Beth went shopping, which was great except that they were too big. She had to wear two pairs of socks so that her heel didn't slip out the back, and even still, the constant rubbing was giving her blisters. She had tried to go running in them, and learned quickly that it was a bad idea.

Whoever had lived in the garage apartment before her had left some things behind. There was a t-shirt that had been scrunched up in the back of one of the dresser drawers, which had a logo for a baseball team in Los Angeles. There was also a hooded university sweatshirt that had been hanging in the closet. On top of the small table next to the bed, there was also an old worn-out leather book. When Beth went over to check it out, she was surprised to see that it was a Bible. It wasn't necessarily the fact that it was there that surprised her, but the fact that it was obviously well read and studied over. She flipped through the pages, seeing verses, sometimes entire passages, underlined on nearly every page. There were also tons of notes in many of the margins. She put it back down on the nightstand, realizing that the name "Jonathan Harris" was embossed on the cover. She hadn't noticed it when she picked it up—the book had been lying upside down. So it was Johnny's Bible.

She wondered what it was doing in the apartment. He didn't even live with his parents anymore. She made a mental note to bring it into the main house with her sometime so she could return it to him.

Somehow it was fitting to her of the image she was putting together of Johnny for him to pour over the Bible. It wasn't something that Beth could understand, but she remembered another person who spent hours devouring the Word of God—her mother. She soaked it up, like it was life to her.

Beth's parents had both been strong Christians. Her dad used to read the Bible aloud to Amy and Beth every night after dinner—or had at least when they were younger. The girls went to church with their parents every weekend. Beth remembered even being in a children's club at the church when she was younger. But after her mom died, she stopped going to church so much, only on the important holidays. Her dad always asked her to go, but eventually she said no enough times that he stopped asking. She hadn't given a thought toward God in a long time.

She glanced at Johnny's Bible one more time before she had gone back to organizing her things, including the items she had gone shopping for with Ellie, like face wash and shampoo. A part of her wanted to pick it up and read it. She wasn't sure why. Her mom had found so much peace in the Bible, but Beth was afraid all she would find was condemnation. She knew she wasn't a good person. There was nothing for her there. She had once prayed with her mother to let Jesus into her heart as a child, and then had done so many times since, but saying the words had gotten her nowhere thus far. So she went back to her organizing without giving it much more thought.

It was refreshing for Beth to have her own space to retreat to without the pressure of trying to please anyone and acting along to a twisted game. It was such a luxury, and she felt completely undeserving of having it. And she knew it wouldn't last. She knew that something would happen down the line that would make the Harris's want her out of their house, but for now she was going to rejoice that she had a place of her own.

Of course, the Harris's were extremely kind and continually made it clear that Beth was welcome. She had yet to make any other meal but breakfast in her little apartment, even if she was solemn and uncomfortable around their dining table. They just kept inviting her, and she was surprised at how much she enjoyed being part of a family, simply listening to them talk even if she didn't join in herself, but it scared her as well. By the end of the week she had found herself getting more and more vocal, which was more natural for her—she was bubbly and outgoing at heart. She felt wanted, genuinely wanted, for the first time in years. She had a new family that let her into their lives and decided to bestow unconditional kindness upon her. They didn't care about Beth's twisted past—they didn't even ask her about it. They wanted her anyway. It made her fear for the day when they would be gone from her life. They wouldn't want her forever. No one wanted her forever. And what scared her the most was that she suddenly wanted them, too. She had been with them for a week, and already she felt completely changed inside.

Beth was pouring herself a glass of orange juice when she heard a soft knock on the door of her apartment.

"It's open!" she yelled.

A moment later, Ellie appeared in the doorway.

"We should probably head out soon. You almost ready?" she asked with a wide smile.

"I've just got to grab my jacket and I'm good to go," Beth replied, putting her half-filled glass of juice back in the small refrigerator.

Beth followed Ellie through the mudroom to the main part of the house and waited for Ellie to grab the car keys.

"You really don't have to do this for me, you know," Beth said as Ellie reached for the door.

Ellie paused with her eyebrows raised.

"What did I tell you last night?" she asked.

Beth smirked. "Not to keep apologizing and to stop complaining that you're doing too much."

"Exactly," Ellie stated. "So no more of that."

Beth smiled. "Okay."

The two of them walked to the car. It was a brisk fall day, and the tops of the mountains were covered with clouds, where Beth knew fresh powder was falling. It was amazing to her how much she liked being in this small ski town, even though she had only been there a week. It felt comfortable to her, probably because it was so much like where she had grown up in Colorado. The familiarity of it made her heart ache. She hadn't realized how much she missed the mountains. She had been trying so hard to be away from home to realize how much she missed it.

It was a short drive to the doctor's office. Ellie insisted on Beth's first night at their house after Beth moved into the garage apartment that they set up a doctor's appointment as soon as they could after Beth revealed to her that she hadn't been checked by a doctor since finding out that she was pregnant, except when Johnny took her to the hospital. Ellie told her that they had to make an appointment for her as soon as possible to do a thorough exam and to make sure that everything was going as it should, and that the baby was healthy. Ellie called the very next morning and set up an appointment for Beth.

They sat in the waiting room for less than ten minutes when Beth was called to come back to an exam room. It was the shortest wait she ever had at a doctor's office.

Beth stood up and grabbed her purse, and then turned to glance at Ellie. Without anything needing to be said, Ellie stood up and grabbed Beth's hand, and the two of them headed back into the room together.

The past week had been a struggle for Beth. She had started working in the flower shop, learning how to arrange bouquets and leaving the customer service part to Ellie, and Crystal when she was there. Part of Beth wanted to avoid interacting with other people as much as possible, which was different for her in many ways because she once had been so outgoing. But she loved the atmosphere of the small shop. It also gave her an opportunity to be get to know Ellie a lot better. She still felt guilty that this family was taking her in, but she couldn't help but open up to Ellie a bit. It was impossible not to like her. So she had explained some of her story to Ellie, much like she had to Johnny— never the whole thing. Beth couldn't trust anyone with her darkest secrets. She was afraid to trust at all, but she was trying. And just like Johnny, Ellie listened and it didn't change her opinion of Beth at all. It was amazing for her to have someone care about her knowing what she had come from and what she had done to her own family. Ellie reminded Beth so much of her own mother. It made her long for her mom in a way that she hadn't for years—and brought back the same pang of guilt that was always there when she thought of her mom for too long.

Beth put on the gown that the nurse handed her, and then sat down on the exam table, unsure of what to expect.

"You'll be fine," Ellie said with a comforting smile.

A few minutes later there was a knock at the door, and then the doctor entered. She glanced down at the folder in her hand before speaking.

"Hi Elizabeth, I'm Doctor Abernathy," she said, sticking her hand out. She was younger than Beth would have expected. She was picturing an old man with gray hair that was starting to bald. For some reason, Beth was immediately put at ease after glancing at Doctor Abernathy.

"Nice to meet you," Beth responded, taking her hand.

She started asking Beth tons of questions, ranging all over the place from the guessed date of conception to how much Beth was eating on a daily basis. After that she covered Beth's legs with a sheet and pulled the gown up over her stomach. She put cold gel on her abdomen, causing Beth to flinch, and then proceeded with a sonogram.

The machine hummed, and then there was a ticking sound coming from the screen.

"You hear that? That's the baby's heartbeat," Doctor Abernathy explained with a smile, as if the miracle of new life never got old to her.

Beth's mouth opened in a small "O" as she listened to the sound of the baby's heartbeat. It made the baby inside of her more real than ever before, more than the small flutters of movement she had been feeling for a couple weeks now. And it was her baby inside Beth, and it was depending on her to bring it into the world. She felt a sudden attachment to it that she had never felt before.

"And if you look on the screen, you can see the heart beating," Doctor Abernathy pointed out.

Beth turned her head to the screen and saw not only the heart beating, she saw the little baby growing in her stomach. Doctor Abernathy continued pointing out hands and feet, and then the baby's head and little button nose. She was utterly amazed, thinking that there actually was a life growing inside of her. It wasn't just an idea anymore, she could see her baby on the screen. She didn't notice that there were tears streaming down her face.

"Would you like to know the sex of your baby?" Doctor Abernathy asked.

"You can tell me the sex of the baby?" Beth replied, astounded. Going from being in denial about it, to actually seeing the baby on the screen and hearing its heartbeat, to now knowing its identity was extremely overwhelming.

"If you would like to know, yes."

"It's not too soon?"

Doctor Abernathy glanced at the screen. "You're a little bit farther along than you guessed. You're about twenty-one weeks."

Beth counted in her head. "Five months? But I'm hardly even showing!"

Doctor Abernathy nodded. "Pregnancy is different for every woman. First of all, this is your first pregnancy, so that plays a role in determining when you start to show, plus the fact that you're only twenty-two. You also have a slender body, and from the information you've been giving me, you've been extremely active and eating fairly well, perhaps a little less than you should be. All of those things can contribute to when a woman starts showing."

"Wow," Beth said. "So in four months I'm going to have a baby?" She was amazed that her pregnancy was already halfway over.

The doctor smiled. "In four months you're going to have a baby."

Beth took that in for a few minutes. She hadn't been preparing at all for a baby. But it was coming.

"So would you like to know the sex of your baby?" Doctor Abernathy asked again.

Beth glanced at Ellie, who had tears in her eyes as she looked at the screen. When she felt Beth's gaze she turned to her.

"It's up to you," she stated, taking Beth's hand and giving it a squeeze.

Beth turned back to the doctor. "Yea, sure. I want to know the sex of the baby."

"You sure?"

Beth nodded.

The doctor switched the image on the screen.

"Congratulations Miss Monahan, it appears that you'll be having yourself a little baby girl."

"It's a girl?" Beth asked.

"It's a girl," the doctor confirmed.

Beth turned her head back to the screen, tears pouring down her face. Beth was really going to have a baby. The child within her wasn't an "it" anymore, it was a little baby girl. Her daughter.

"It's a girl," Beth said again.

The doctor left the room after recommending vitamins that Beth should be taking. She told Beth that she would have some pictures of her daughter printed, and could pick them up at the desk when she signed out and scheduled her next appointment.

Ellie left the room as well, so Beth could get dressed. She put her clothes back on, and then stood in front of the full-length mirror on the back of the door, looking at her stomach. She cradled the tiny bulge as if feeling it and really noticing it for the first time.

"You're really in there, aren't you?" she said to the baby she knew was there.

In that moment, everything seemed crystal clear to Beth. It no longer mattered what she had been through in the past two years. It no longer mattered how this child was conceived. She would do right by the baby within her. Her life wasn't just about herself anymore. She had a daughter to prepare the way for. It was a scary reality to know that she would hold a baby in her arms in just four months; that she would be responsible for someone else's life and happiness. But as she stood there looking in the mirror, she was surprised with herself for wanting that responsibility. The baby she carried inside of her offered her the hope of a life that she didn't have before. This baby would give her a chance to have a new beginning. She needed a new beginning.

When Beth left the exam room, she left a changed person. She left as a mother who had just grown to love the child within her. And she was determined to become the best mother she could be for her baby—however scary that idea was. It was hard to picture herself as a mother, but she was going to do it. She was ready to keep going for this little baby growing inside of her.

Ellie and Beth left the office having scheduled Beth's next appointment. Beth carried the pictures of her daughter in her hands, afraid to let them out of her sight. She wasn't prepared at all to have a baby, and she was terrified out of her skin, not only for the labor part, but for the baby that would be placed in her arms afterward for her to raise on her own. But she was going to do it. She was going to have a baby. And she was excited. Totally frightened, but thrilled.

"I was thinking we could make some stops before we head back home," Ellie stated.

"Sure, whatever you need," Beth agreed. She figured that they would just stop at the grocery store to pick up a few items, so she was surprised when Ellie pulled up in front of a salon.

"What are we doing here?" Beth asked.

"I figured, since we were going to be out already, that now would be as good a time as any to do something about your hair."

Beth stared at Ellie for a moment and then burst out laughing—a laugh that came from somewhere deep down in her stomach that brought tears to her eyes. It felt good.

"It's really horrible, isn't it?" she said through her laughter. Her hair was totally uneven, and she had worn it up everyday just so that she didn't have to deal with it. But it was time to do something about it, for sure.

Ellie dropped Beth off and told her that she had an errand to run, so Beth went into the salon alone. The woman who cut her hair looked at Beth like she was crazy when she inspected her hair.

"I tried to cut it," Beth explained before the woman asked too many questions.

The woman smiled good-naturedly. "Do yourself a favor and just come to me next time."

Beth smirked. "I promise."

The woman washed Beth's hair and then went to work cutting it. She evened it out and added a lot of layers. By the time she was done, it rested about an inch below Beth's shoulders, which was a striking difference from the length it used to be. It made her look so much older. It made her look like a woman who could attempt to care for a newborn in four months time.

"Wow, I love it!" Beth declared, glancing in the mirror. Suddenly she felt like she resembled her mother more closely than she ever had before, but it wasn't just the change of hair. It was something in her face, something from down deep.

When she went to the register to pay, Ellie was back. And she realized that Ellie had already paid for Beth to get her hair done.

"Really, you shouldn't..." She was cut off by Ellie raising her hand to stop her from what she was going to say. Beth was amazed by the generosity of this family. She knew she would have to repay them someday, for everything. She didn't know how she was going to do it, especially with a baby on the way that she had to prepare for as well. But she was determined to try.

When they got to the car, Ellie handed her a little gift bag.

Beth took it, feeling guilty. "What is this?" she asked.

"Just something I got you to celebrate. Open it."

Inside the bag was a small card that said congratulations on it, and Ellie wrote a sweet little message about how glad she was that Beth had come into their lives. Also inside the gift bag was a cute little package of three purple onesies, all of which had different designs on them—perfect for a baby girl.

"The first of many that I'm sure you'll receive. I picked purple because I have a feeling you'll get overloaded with pink."

"Thanks," Beth said, wanting to cry all over again. How was it possible that any single person could be so wonderfully kind? Beth hadn't been around people like Ellie in a long time. "You really didn't have to, but thanks."

Ellie gave her the same knowing look that told her to stop apologizing. Beth rolled her eyes and laughed, leaning over to give Ellie a hug.

"Your hair looks fantastic by the way," Ellie said into Beth's ear.

"Thanks!"

Ellie treated Beth to lunch after the hair appointment. Beth pursed her lips when the check came and Ellie reached for it and gave Beth a look as if daring her to say anything about it. After their lunch date they went shopping. Beth got the vitamins that the doctor recommended, as well as a pair of running shoes that fit, and some slippers and a pair of flats. At the insistence of Ellie, she also bought some maternity clothes even though she was still fitting into the clothes she already had. But Beth knew that it was only a matter of time before she couldn't get into them anymore. She already could no longer zip her jeans all the way. Ellie still insisted on paying, but Beth really tried to fight her this time.

"Beth honey," she said as she handed her credit card to the cashier, "today I'm treating you. So stop fighting me on it and just consider yourself one of the family."

Beth breathed deeply and pressed her hand to her small bulge. In a week's time she had been saved from her own personal hell and had found a new home and a new job. She had grown to love the child within her. And she was part of a family again. It had been such a whirlwind of a week that she almost needed to catch her breath.

Chapter Nine

When Christmastime came around a month later, Beth wished she never complained about the fact that she wasn't showing much. Now every morning when she got dressed, she was very aware of her ever-widening stomach. She loved the baby girl within her, but she didn't love watching her stomach expand. And she had three more months of watching it grow until she had to deal with losing all the weight that she was sure she was gaining. Ellie kept telling her that she was tiny. Beth went running every morning. Doctor Abernathy had told her that it was okay since Beth had always been a runner. She just warned her not to overextend herself. But even with running and trying to stick to a healthy diet, although eating more than she ever had in her life, she still felt huge. And she knew she wasn't going to get smaller anytime soon.

"Stop staring at yourself in the mirror!" Crystal yelled, walking into the bedroom of Beth's apartment. Lately, she had been keeping the door of the garage apartment completely open, as if it was just an extra room in the house. The door leading into the kitchen was always wide open unless Beth wished it closed. She didn't want to shut herself away anymore. She had always been a people person anyway.

"I can't help it!" Beth complained.

"Seriously, for a pregnant woman, I still think you're kind of skinny."

"Do you not see this stomach?" Beth asked, pointing at her belly.

"Yea, but you're not getting, like, *huge*. From behind no one can even tell that you're pregnant."

Beth raised her eyebrows in disbelief and stepped away from the mirror.

"Whatever you say."

Beth followed Crystal through the mudroom to the main house. Now that Beth was a month and half into her new living situation, she was getting much more used to it. She no longer complained about the Harris's doing too much for her, even though she didn't stop believing it. But being with this kind-hearted family was teaching her a lot. It was teaching her that she really could trust the people around her, and it had been a long while since there had been anyone she could rely on. Not everyone was out to steal her money or just try to get with her. Some people actually cared about her. She truly felt like she was a part of this family. Crystal was like her little sister, and Mark and Ellie were like second parents. And then, of course, there was Johnny, who was still kind of a mystery to her in terms of what she felt for him. She definitely didn't view him as a brother, but she wasn't sure what that meant, and she didn't particularly want to explore that thought enough to find out.

Two weeks after living in her new apartment, Beth learned that the previous tenant was Johnny himself, which explained the few things left behind that had his mark on them. He moved out a few days before bringing Beth to his parents' home. What was even more earth-shattering was for her to learn that he moved out in anticipation of bringing her there. Apparently he was planning on pulling her out of her deadbeat life no matter what. It had merely been a miracle that he was there when Tyler decided to take out his aggression on her. Crystal told her that Johnny had gone back to San Francisco for her. Beth confronted him about it, and he confirmed the story unashamedly. She still had no idea what he saw in her to want to help her, or to simply sit on a street corner waiting for her to get out of work. And she still hadn't asked. But Johnny had saved her, and she couldn't help but love him for it. She'd never understand why, either, but she would be forever grateful.

Christmas put Beth in a cheerful mood. She hadn't celebrated Christmas since she had runaway from her family two years before. Of course, she had attended some grand Christmas parties when she had been away in Europe, but it wasn't the same as being with family. She had so much fun decorating the Christmas tree that the whole family had gone out and picked together. She loved the fresh scent of pine as it filled the open family room. She had loved helping Crystal and Ellie make endless amounts of cutout cookies and decorating them with homemade frosting. They gave a lot of them away, but there was a tin on top of the refrigerator that they dipped into a little everyday, and another tucked away in the pantry saved for Christmas. Beth showed Crystal how to make caramels like her mom had taught her, and together they wrapped them all in wax paper. Crystal had taken a ton to school and passed them out to her friends. The holidays were feeling joyous again. She had missed celebrating Christmas. She loved being with family—this felt like her family now. It was a happy season.

Beth was growing to love everything about Lake Tahoe. It reminded her so much of home that it literally hurt sometimes, but in a good way. It felt familiar to her, especially seeing the beautiful town blanketed in snow. It would be a white Christmas.

"What can I do to help?" Beth asked, coming through from her apartment into the kitchen. It was the morning of Christmas Eve, and she knew that Ellie was busy getting everything ready for the big dinner tomorrow. Mark's parents were coming over for Christmas dinner, as was his brother's family. Ellie wanted to get as much ready beforehand so that she wouldn't have as much to do when the guests arrived the next day.

"If you don't mind slicing the apples, you can help me get them ready for the pies."

"Sure," Beth answered, going to work as Ellie had asked. She had gotten used to her station in the kitchen helping out. Beth loved to cook.

They spent the morning baking three separate pies, as well as getting the potatoes ready for the next day, and making sure everything was in order. Ellie sent Johnny out to make sure they had enough drinks for everyone for the small dinner party. Beth was a little nervous for the family gathering, but she had met everyone before. She had met Mark's parents a few times. They had come over for dinner twice since she had been living there, and then the family went over to their house on occasion as well. She had only met Mark's brother's family once when she went with Ellie to drop something off for the family. She wasn't sure how much they knew about her past. But they had accepted her with the same love that the Harris's had. She kind of hoped that they didn't know about her past, that they could just get to know her now. But she knew that some explanation had to have been provided for why Beth had just appeared in all of their lives. It was clear that she wasn't just a tenant renting out the garage apartment. She was a part of their lives.

Christmas Eve was a quiet night with the family that Beth was coming to adore. Each one of them had found a special place in her heart. Mark was so kind and goodhearted. He cared for his family and loved them no matter what, even when it came to disciplining his daughter, which Beth had witnessed on a few occasions. Ellie was the most tenderhearted person that Beth had ever met, with the exception of her own mother. Ellie was the closest thing that she'd had to a mom in a long time. Crystal was the little sister that Beth never had, the little sister that Beth wished she had been, and they got along so extremely well that it was mind-blowing to Beth. It was nothing like the relationship that she had shared with her own sister over the years. Maybe it was because she and Crystal weren't actually blood related. But even so, Crystal and Johnny got along extremely well, too.

Beth thought it extremely cute how overprotective he could be at times. Crystal pretended to be annoyed with him, but Beth could tell that she actually appreciated it deep down. They were a complete and whole family, and loving them was making Beth a better person. But the closer she got to them, the more terrified she became. Loving people hadn't turned out well for her in the past. Everyone she loved had deserted her, had used her and taken things from deep inside of her that she would never get back. She trusted the Harris's, sure, but she wasn't sure she completely trusted herself yet.

Christmas morning donned crisp and white, just like a dream. Beth loved it. She was the first to wake up, the baby inside of her moving around so much that Beth became restless. Beth brushed her teeth and washed her face, but didn't bother getting ready for the day as of yet. She had gone to church with the Harris's the afternoon before. She had been accompanying them to church every Sunday, something she hadn't done in years. They had a small family dinner before all sitting before the television, a fire burning in the fireplace, and watched a Christmas movie. She knew that there was no rush to get ready for the day.

Beth made her bed and then walked to the main area of the house, turning the lights to the Christmas tree on. There were many beautifully wrapped presents under the tree. She remembered Christmases as a little girl, waking up before dawn, so excited to open her presents. She would run to the landing overlooking the great room and peer down at all the presents and the enormous tree below her. Her mother always made a grand Christmas brunch, and they all stayed cozy in their pajamas until they got ready for dinner. The family always came to Monahan Ranch for Christmas. If Beth thought brunch was grand, it was nothing to what her mom prepared for Christmas dinner. Elizabeth Monahan seemed good at everything she did, at least to Beth. She was the perfect wife and mother, and one of the most genuinely kind people that ever existed, so much like Ellie. Her mom always wore a gorgeous dress and moved liked royalty as she served her family. She was always serving her family. Beth's mom was the most selfless person that Beth had ever known.

How in the world did she end up with a daughter like me?

Beth turned away from the Christmas tree, trying to bury thoughts of happy Christmases down inside. She was far away from her childhood. She would never have those days back.

Walking into the kitchen, Beth glanced at the clock. It was only seven in the morning. She decided to put on a kettle of water to make a cup of herbal tea. While she was waiting for the water to boil, she stared out the window of the kitchen, which looked out over the deck and the backyard. It was snowing lightly, yet she could see blue sky ahead. It was the perfect Christmas day.

The kettle started to whistle, and Beth pulled it from the burner before it made too much noise. She didn't want to wake the sleeping family upstairs. Johnny had spent the night in his old room upstairs as well.

While sipping her tea, Beth thought of what she could do to help make this morning more special for the family. They had done so much for her in the month and a half that she had been with them. They gave unconditionally and showed her love she didn't deserve. Thanking them never felt like enough. She knew that they didn't have any plans until the family came over later, so Beth decided to take a cue from her mother and prepare breakfast for the family, or brunch depending on when they decided to wake up.

"What should we make?" Beth called out quietly, her hand rubbing her swollen abdomen. She had started talking to her baby after her first appointment with Doctor Abernathy. Ever since then the little girl inside of her had become so powerfully real. The pictures that the doctor had printed out for her were taped on the wall next to her bed. Beth loved the baby inside of her. She was terrified of being a mother, but she was determined to try.

She hadn't cooked for the family since her first morning at the house, when she had made omelets. She dug through the cabinets, scouring through all the shelves until she came up with all the ingredients she needed for her mother's homemade cinnamon rolls. She hadn't made them in years, but she had watched her mom make them so many times that she was sure she could do the recipe by memory. She missed sitting in the kitchen watching her mother cook.

Once she got the cinnamon rolls in the oven, she started cutting up fruit to make a fruit salad, as well as putting on a pot of coffee for the family. While the coffee brewed, she prepared icing to pour over the cinnamon rolls. She glanced into the oven to see how they were doing, and declared them to be done. Beth pulled them out and placed them on top of the stove. When she turned around to reach for the icing, she noticed Johnny coming down the stairs, running his hands through his messy hair.

"Morning," he said, stopping short when he saw her in the kitchen—like he had been expecting someone else, once again. He inhaled deeply. "Hmmmm, that smells wonderful."

Beth smiled. "I'm glad."

"Merry Christmas by the way."

"Merry Christmas."

The rest of the family came down shortly after Johnny had. Crystal came running down, saying that she was roused by the scent of cinnamon. Ellie came and wrapped her arm around Beth in the kitchen, where she was dripping the rest of the frosting over the warm rolls.

"What a treat!" she exclaimed. "Thank you, Beth."

They all sat down around the dining table after Mark started another roaring fire, bringing a wonderful ambiance to this perfect Christmas morning.

After enjoying the warm, homemade cinnamon rolls, Crystal moved everyone to the family room in view of all the gifts under the tree. She looked at them with a gleam in her eye.

Beth had worked hard to try to come up with gifts for the family. Nothing ever felt like enough. She didn't have a lot of money to spend. Thankfully, she had saved up some from all of her tips back from San Francisco that Tyler hadn't snatched from her, but even so, she needed that to pay for all the expenses that this baby would bring. But she had to do something for the family. Crystal was easy enough. She spent a lot of time going through Beth's wardrobe—or the little of it she had managed to bring from Tyler's. A lot of it didn't even fit her anymore. She didn't mind sharing with Crystal at all. They were close to the same size, and Crystal kept telling Beth that she had the best taste in clothes. So, Beth went and picked out a cute outfit for her, sure that Crystal would enjoy it.

For Ellie she had found a cute tea set. She had been strolling through some of the little shops in town and went into an old antique store while out on a walk. She hadn't been doing as much running since it started snowing, afraid she might fall and slip. But she found the shop on her new walking route and went in one day, hoping to find the perfect gift. None of the cups matched at all, but somehow they all coordinated well with one another, as well as the teapot. Beth hoped she would like it. She got the set for dirt cheap, but she thought it was beautiful.

Mark and Johnny had been more difficult. Beth had asked Johnny what his dad might like, and Johnny told her not to worry about getting gifts for the family, but of course she wasn't going to listen to him. She knew that Mark liked books, so the only thing she could think to get him was a gift card to the bookstore in town. It was an impersonal gift, but the best she could come up with. Johnny's gift, on the other hand, was partly a joke.

"A lift ticket?" he said with dread, turning to her with a look of terror on his face. "You've got to be kidding me."

Beth smirked at him. "You have to give it a shot," she told him. "Trust me. Skiing is so much fun."

She had looked online and had found an ad for discount lift tickets if she bought them in advance. She was determined to get Johnny on a pair of skis.

"No way," he said, putting the card with the voucher for the ticket down on the coffee table, pushing it away.

"You can't grow up in Lake Tahoe and never try skiing," she chided. She had talked to Mark, Ellie, and Crystal. All of them had at least tried skiing. Crystal actually quite enjoyed snowboarding and went with her friends frequently.

He gave her a calculated smile. "You can't even take me," he stated, glancing down at her stomach. "Didn't your doctor recommend not putting the life of your unborn child at undue risk?"

Beth rolled her eyes. "First of all, I never think of skiing as putting my life at risk—it's just pure fun. And second of all, the baby is due in March, so if everything goes according to plan, there should be some of the ski season left." She smirked at him. "And I've seen women skiing while pregnant, anyway," she added, not sure what her point was. She wouldn't do it, as tempting as it could be. It surprised even Beth to realize how overprotective she was of the child within her.

Johnny looked at her with foreboding and everyone laughed.

"You have some presents to open as well," Crystal told Beth.

Beth was overwhelmed as the family all turned to her and gave her gifts. They shouldn't have. They had already given her a home and paid for more than should ever be allowed. They just kept giving, giving, giving. She wanted them to stop. She would never be able to repay them. But they brought gift after gift.

After all the gift giving was over, Ellie made everyone clean up the wrapping paper, which had somehow got cast around the entire family room, and everyone organized their things and carried them to their rooms. Beth brought what she could into her apartment, but some of the stuff she couldn't lift, like the crib that Mark and Ellie had bought her.

"You seemed overwhelmed in there," Johnny said, coming through into her apartment behind her. She was standing over the gifts she had thrown on the couch, looking at them all. She received so many nice things, mostly all for the baby. She couldn't believe it all. She received tons of baby clothes, a lot of it in pink. When she bought outfits of her own, she'd have to stay away from the pink. She also received a changing table, a stylish looking diaper bag, and some blankets and plush toys. Johnny had also given her a little kid Bible, which didn't really surprise Beth. Although it wasn't like the baby would understand any of it until she was older. Her baby already had so much stuff and she wasn't even born yet.

Beth gave him a tentative smile. "I feel really unworthy of all that your family is doing for me. I don't know how I'm ever going to repay you for it all."

Johnny gave her a look that had become really familiar to her over the past month, a look that told her to stop feeling sorry for herself. She couldn't help it, though. She didn't deserve anything that she was getting. Sure, she had been in a horrible place and she was beyond grateful that Johnny had somehow cared enough to help her out of her own pit—but that's exactly what it was, her own pit. She had dug her own grave. She had put herself there. It had been her fault, and she had been dealing with the consequences. And now she was surrounded by people who were continually showing her a love that she felt completely unworthy of receiving.

Johnny smiled at her, a warm, genuine smile that melted her heart a little every time she saw it. It wasn't the boyish grin she received whenever he was teasing her—it was a smile of compassion, a smile of love.

"Can I tell you something?" he asked her.

"Sure," she said.

"We're all unworthy."

Her brow furrowed.

"Unworthy of what?"

His eyes narrowed on her slightly before he answered. "Everything."

Chapter Ten

Beth stood in the kitchen, glancing out into the open family room and dining area. Ellie had prepared a splendid dinner for the family and their guests. At dinner, Beth had sat between Crystal and her cousin Rachel, who was a couple years younger than her. She had listened to their high school banter about various people they both knew. High school seemed like such a long time ago to Beth. She had been amazed listening to them talk—Crystal and Rachel were good girls. They were just good. They listened to their parents and were amazingly kind. They were serious about their schoolwork and wouldn't do anything to jeopardize their futures. Being popular seemed like no big deal to them. They weren't swayed by the crowd. And they were both striving to live a life pleasing to God, like it was their top priority. Beth had been the complete opposite in high school. She probably was still the opposite.

She enjoyed being around the table with all of the Harris family. Mark's parents were so adorably cute, and Beth was amazed watching them—a husband and wife still so much in love with one another after so many years of marriage. Mark had read out the Christmas story before they sat down to dinner, and Beth watched as his parents sat close to one another on the loveseat, holding hands. She tried not to wish the same thing for herself when she was older. She figured it must be a wonderful thing to see all of the family together, the fruit of their love down through two generations.

Mark's brother, Dan, also came, with his wife Joanna and their three kids, Ben, Luke, and of course, Rachel. The two boys were younger, and spent more time playing with some of their new toys rather than socializing. Everyone was so warm and friendly. It sent a yearning straight down deep into Beth's heart that she couldn't explain. Even now, as she watched them from the kitchen after helping Crystal with the dishes, a part of her wanted to cry. She felt like she was a part of this family. She knew they all considered her to be, even the ones she didn't know so well. But watching them all interact, laughing with each other and sharing one another's company, made her miss her family in a way that she'd never experienced before. Years and years of Christmas memories flitted through her mind as she watched the generations of Harris's in one room. This is what she had given up when she left home.

Beth tore her gaze from the family around her and glanced out on the deck. Taking a look behind her shoulder, she managed to slip out before anyone noticed that she was gone. A moment alone to clear her head seemed like a good idea to her.

Holding her arms across her chest, Beth looked up into the dark sky, seeing her breath rise into the night air. It was absolutely gorgeous outside. The ground was covered in snow, and the sky was crystal clear. The stars were shining like a brilliant protective canopy over all the earth. She was able to pick out lots of constellations that her mother had pointed out to her as a child. In the summer they used to lie out in her mom's garden at night and look up at the stars, the scent of flowers wafting over them. Beth cherished those moments with her mom. Some of her happiest memories were of she and her mom outside in the garden late at night in the summer—usually after Amy had gone to bed so Beth got her mom all to herself. Her mom used to tell her stories of her childhood and what it had been like to grow up on a farm in Iowa. She also told Beth over and over again the story of how she had met Beth's father and had just known that she wanted to spend the rest of her life with him. Beth wished that she had gotten to spend a lifetime with him. Her life was cut too short.

Beth turned when she heard the sliding glass door open behind her. Johnny walked up to her and placed his jacket around her shoulders without questioning what she was doing outside in the cold. He glanced up to the sky, following where her gaze had been.

"Beautiful night," he said.

"Yea," she agreed.

"The stars make me feel insignificant," Johnny stated.

Beth looked at him in surprise, sliding her arms through his jacket, appreciative of its warmth. He was always surprising her with his words—like earlier when he had said that everyone was unworthy. He hadn't explained past that. He and his dad decided to spend the afternoon in Beth's apartment putting the crib together while Beth helped Ellie prepare dinner. But Johnny was constantly catching her by surprise. She couldn't put him in a box.

"Is that a good thing or a bad thing?" she wondered.

He smiled at her. "Good." He didn't explain more than that.

"Well, the stars always make me think of my mom," she said casually, and he looked at her in surprise. "What?" she asked him.

"I've never heard you mention your mother," he said.

She bit her bottom lip. "I don't talk about her much."

"Why not?"

She felt tears surfacing. It surprised her. Maybe it was because she hadn't been able to stop thinking of her own family all day. She truly missed them. With all her heart, which was equally startling and painful.

"It hurts to think about her too much," she admitted. She knew that she could talk to Johnny. She had thrown so much at him already and he hadn't run yet. He was the first man in a long time that she had been able to trust.

He nodded. He wasn't going to push her to talk if she didn't want to. She knew that. But she wanted him to know. She felt like she needed to unload, that it would help him understand her better, why she was the way she was. In some ways she hoped that telling him more about her would push him away some more. As much as she trusted him, she was afraid of getting too close to him. She knew he loved her. She just didn't know how much. It scared her. She also had no idea what she felt in return, which was even scarier.

"She died when I was thirteen," Beth said, looking back up into the sky. She wondered if her mom could see her. She had no idea what happened once people died. Sure, she believed with all her heart that her mom was in Heaven, but she had no idea if her mom could see her. Beth hoped she couldn't. Her mom would be shaking her head in dismay. All the good principles her mother had tried to instill in Beth as a little girl, she had thrown out the window the first chance she got.

"I'm sorry," Johnny said.

Beth gave him a sad smile in response. "It's not your fault." She looked back up into the sky. "If anything its mine," she said, barely above a whisper.

A tear escaped down her face and she could feel Johnny's gaze on her. After a moment she turned to look at him. He was studying her.

"Are you okay?" he asked her.

She pressed her lips together and looked away, tears streaming down her face. No, she was not okay. Why did he keep asking? She had changed a lot in the month and a half she had spent with his family, but she didn't know if she would ever truly be okay again.

"I killed her," she said, looking at him again with a slight shrug of her shoulders.

"What do you mean?" he asked, brows furrowed.

She closed her eyes, almost visualizing the scene. Over the years the picture of her mom had faded in her mind, but suddenly, as she relived the time leading up to her death, she could see her with perfect clarity.

"I made her take me out. She didn't want to go," Beth said, glancing at Johnny. She knew she wasn't making sense, but she kept going anyway. "It was a Sunday, after church—November. It was pouring rain outside, and my mom didn't want to go anywhere. She was supposed to have lunch with someone, but she didn't want to be out on the roads so she cancelled." Beth looked away from Johnny's intense gaze. She wasn't even truly looking at him anymore—she was seeing the scene inside her head.

"We had a few days off from school, and I was supposed to go to a friend's house—she had moved that summer, a town about 40 miles away from where we lived. I hadn't seen her since she moved, but Mom said that she didn't want to go out on the roads. I pleaded and pleaded, and finally she gave in."

Beth hated herself for it. She would never forgive herself for making her mom take her. She would do anything to take it back, to trade places with her. But her mom finally relented. They got in the car and headed out of town in the heavy rain, driving out onto the highway. Beth didn't remember much. She felt it when the car started to skid, she remembered hearing her mom scream, but everything that came after the crash had buried the memories of the crash itself. She had been told that the car had flipped over the barrier in the road, that her mom had died on impact.

"The only thing I remember was waking up in the hospital very early the next morning. I had a huge concussion, not to mention a huge gaping wound on my head." She instinctively reached up to touch her hair. She hadn't examined the scar in her scalp in a long time, but she knew it was there. "Other than that, there wasn't much damage done—just some bruises and cuts. The doctors said that I needed to take it easy and recuperate, and that I would be completely fine." She made a sneering face, a grimace. "I even had a doctor's note that said I wasn't allowed homework for two weeks because he was afraid of me straining my eyes and hurting my head."

Beth looked back into Johnny's face, coming back to the present.

"I'm sorry," he said again. "For your loss, I mean. I can't even imagine."

Beth grimaced. Her dad had been in the room when she had awoken. He was asleep with his head resting on her hospital bed, his big hands holding hers. He felt her stir and woke up, and then told her that her mom was gone—forever.

"It wasn't your fault, though," Johnny stated.

She closed her eyes and sighed. "Yes, it was."

"You couldn't control what happened, Beth. You couldn't control the weather, or the car. It wasn't your fault."

She looked up to him. "I made her go. I made her get in the car. If I hadn't, it wouldn't have happened."

"You didn't make the accident happen."

Beth sighed loudly. Of course, she knew that. The car had lost complete control and she couldn't have helped that. But she was the reason they were in the car to begin with.

"I still made her go," she said again. "My own selfishness made her get into the car that day. And my own selfishness has been ruining my family's life ever since."

Beth hated herself. She truly did. Sometimes she wished that she could just curl up into a ball and die. Death didn't come that easy. Sometimes she wished she could switch places with her mother. She had ruined everything. She had made her mother get in the car that day. She was the reason her sister hated her. She had been the cause of so much sorrow to her father. And she had ruined her own life. She had brought it all on herself. And there was nothing she could do about that. It would have been much better if her mom was the one who had survived the crash.

"Have you really not talked with your family at all since you left?" Johnny asked her.

Beth shook her head. "They wouldn't want to hear from me. They're probably glad to be rid of me."

"I doubt that, Beth."

She looked at him with surprise. "You don't get it," she told him. "What you have with your family in there," she said, gesturing to the house, "that's what I had, and I ruined it. I can never get that back again. I was crazy for ever giving it up."

She didn't know what had happened to make her turn out the way she was. She told Johnny how after her mom died, she stopped going to church with her dad and sister. Beth started hanging out with a different crowd at school. She dated a much older guy when she was only fifteen, losing all of her childhood innocence much too early. Then she started dating the captain of the basketball team, hanging out with him and his friends, drinking on the weekends and staying out late, sometimes not even coming home. When she'd gone away for college, she had been super excited to get away from home. Although, her freshman year she spent way too much time partying and not enough time on her schoolwork, which her grades reflected—except for her art classes. Somehow she had always managed to do exceptionally well in her art classes.

At first, college had seemed so glamorous and wonderful to Beth, which she thought was because she was away from home, away from her father and her sister and the endless cycle of life running the ski resort, but after a while she still felt like she wasn't going anywhere. It was part of what propelled her to run from home, to walk into her father's office and demand that he give her what she felt was her due. She thought the farther she got from home, the easier it would be to find herself and her own identity apart from her family. How wrong she had been.

Beth looked up into the sky again and laughed, a mocking laugh. "I disowned my family, Johnny." She looked back into the house. "I had that and I didn't want it. I had that and I don't even think I realized it. What kind of person does that make me?"

"We all have our own faults and failures, Beth. We all make mistakes. We all have regrets."

She just shook her head. Johnny was a good person. He'd never done what she had done, never would have even thought of it.

"I ruined my family, Johnny. I went into my father's office one day and told him that I didn't want him anymore. I brought the most unbelievable shame on him—walking out of his life. And I'm sure he had to answer for it. My dad's a pretty public figure, especially in Colorado, and his little girl just walked out on him one day," she said with biting sarcasm. She was silent for a moment. He didn't say anything. She figured she had finally silenced him. "I'm the most selfish person ever!" she yelled to herself.

"No you're not," Johnny said right away.

"Are you kidding me?" she asked. "Did you not hear a word I just said?" She could tell he was about to respond but she just kept going. "And here I am trying to make something of myself, but nope—I'm still so selfish. I'm just taking things from your family that I know I'll never be able to repay. But I can't go anywhere because I have nowhere to go!"

"Beth!" Johnny said, looking at her almost angrily. "Really, after all this time, this is still how you see us? We're not asking anything from you!"

The tears came back strong again. "But that's the scariest part, don't you get that? Everyone expects something from me and I keep disappointing them."

Johnny shook his head in sadness. "You really don't see yourself clearly at all. Stop having a pity party over all the mistakes you've made in your life, and just keep going on from here. I'm sick of listening to you beat yourself up."

She didn't know what to say to that, and somehow the words stung just a little bit.

"Well what do you want me to say?" Johnny asked angrily, when she didn't reply. "Do you want me to try and make you feel better and lie and say that you never messed up? That you did what you thought was right? Cause I can't do that!"

"I'm not asking you to," she replied quietly. "Believe me, I know how horribly I've messed up."

"I know, it's all you ever talk about—how badly you think you've screwed up everyone's lives, including your own. So if you can recognize the mistakes that you've made, how come you can't recognize how much you've overcome?"

She gave a sarcastic laugh. "I haven't overcome anything. I've just been put in a different situation."

Johnny glared at her. "You are a completely different person than the girl I met walking out of a strip club last summer—completely different."

"No I'm not."

"Are you kidding me? Beth, you were so hard when I first met you, so coiled up inside of yourself. But since coming here, you've learned how to open up—you're finally letting other people carry your burdens with you, and it's changing you. No—what you really need to learn is how to stop condemning yourself."

She wasn't quite sure what to say to that. She didn't know why it was so hard for her to admit that she had changed a lot, that maybe her life was turning around. It was just so hard to believe. But she knew he was right. The Harris's were the first people that Beth had truly been able to trust and depend on in a long time. But they were the good ones—not her.

"And look at everything you're doing for your baby. You're reading baby books, you're almost obsessive about everything you eat. You're saving all of your money so that you can take care of her. You're becoming a mother."

Beth bit her bottom lip. "Because I have to."

"No, because you want to," he said in a gentle voice.

She looked up into his face. She wanted this baby inside of her—wanted this little girl so badly. Her baby had become her reason for going on. But it hadn't been that way at first, and a part of Beth couldn't forgive herself for that.

"Do you remember when I first got here and your sister asked me if I was going to have an abortion?" Beth asked.

Johnny nodded his head in response.

"I told her no, but I almost did. I literally was on the table about to have the procedure. When I first found out I was pregnant, I thought I had to get rid of the baby. I wasn't in a place where I could take care of a child, and I certainly didn't want one," she paused, thinking back to that time. It seemed like a lifetime away. "But I couldn't go through with it. I don't know why. Maybe it would have been the right thing to do, I don't know. I have no idea how to offer this baby a good life," she stated, shaking her head. "But instead of getting an abortion, I used my pregnancy as my excuse to get away from Tyler, to leave my horrible life in San Francisco behind." Beth put her hand on her stomach. "I used my baby as my reason to leave. I certainly didn't want her—not at first. But I used her to get me out."

"Yes!" Johnny said, almost happily. "Don't you see? You left for your baby."

She scoffed. "No, I used her so I would have a reason to leave. I didn't want her—I was seconds away from ending it. I used her so that I would have a reason to get out, Johnny—my own selfish reasons."

He glared at her. "Do you really think you left Tyler because you were being selfish? Seriously? That guy probably would have kicked you out on the streets eventually."

She knew he was right. Beth knew Tyler. He would have been furious to learn that she was carrying his child. He probably would have forced her to get an abortion.

"Don't you get it, though? I used my baby."

"For a better life!" Johnny yelled. "Don't you think there's something in that? Don't you think there's a reason why you couldn't go through with the abortion? You talk about how you're scared to become a mother, scared to have someone need you, but don't you see? You need her, too."

Beth was stunned by his words, so stunned she didn't know what to say in response, once again. Somehow, he kept silencing her. She let his words mull around in her head. Could it truly be possible that somehow beneath her desperation, beneath the horribleness of her life that she had brought on herself, that what she viewed as selfishness was really her fight, both for her and her baby, to get out? To be free from the darkness that was her life?

Beth practically hugged her stomach, so grateful for the baby within her. Her baby was everything, maybe the only way back into the life that Beth had fled from.

Later that night after the extended family had gone home and Beth was curled up in bed in her apartment, she reached for the Bible that was still on the nightstand. She hadn't given it back to Johnny. She knew she really should, but she had been curious. She kept chiding herself for keeping it, but he also hadn't asked for it. Her very first night as she lay in bed, trying to fall asleep, she had reached for it and started reading. And she had been reading a little bit of it each day ever since, just reading it straight through. Most of the stories were very familiar, things she had learned as a child. She didn't know what was compelling her to read the Bible everyday, but she was getting used to it. She also read all of the notes that Johnny had placed in the margins. She was learning so much simply from his own study of the Bible.

Although Christmas Day was truly almost at a close, Beth opened up to the book of Ezekiel, where she had left off. She had already heard the Christmas story in church the day before, as well as when Mark read it before dinner, and didn't feel a need to open to it again. Plus, she wasn't sure exactly what it had to do with her, so she continued reading in the book of Ezekiel.

Beth read for quite a while, finally pausing on the story of Ezekiel and the valley of dry bones, where God called Ezekiel to prophesy, and life was brought back into these bones strewn about a valley floor. Their dry and broken pieces were put back together again, given life. It made her think. Dead and dry bones were obviously beyond repair, but God commanded them to be put back together again. He commanded breath and life back into them.

She read the passage twice before closing the Bible and putting it on the nightstand, turning the light off. She glanced at the clock and realized that it was well after midnight. She tried to get comfortable, but her mind was still racing, thinking on everything Johnny had said to her, and everything she had just read.

Johnny kept trying to make her realize that she was changing, that she was becoming a new person; that the things that she had done in the past didn't define who she was now. She could make something better of herself, and Johnny was convinced that she was already doing so. He kept telling her that she wasn't a hopeless case. And tonight she had read a story about God bringing new life into dead and dry bones. She wasn't sure what it all had to do with her.

In the quiet night, Beth whispered aloud, "Does that mean You can breathe life into my broken areas?"

It was the first time since her mom had died that she remembered calling out to God.

Chapter Eleven

After making sure that her father wasn't inside, Amy crept into his bedroom and walked up to her mother's vanity. The room hadn't changed much at all since her mother had died, even though it had been over nine years. A part of her loved how it was just the same as when she was a little girl watching her mother get ready day after day, but part of it tore at her heart. She glanced wistfully to the door, as if expecting that her mom would walk through it, but Amy knew that she never would. But still, even after all these years, there was still a sort of unreality to her mom being gone at times. Sometimes it felt like she was in the next room. Although, no amount of wishing so would make it true.

Amy sat down in front of the vanity, opening her mom's old jewelry box. Her dad had told her that she was welcome to anything in it, even encouraged her to take it, but she hadn't wanted to move it from the place her mom had kept it. But it was Christmas, and Amy was trying to keep up the tradition that her mother had started. She grabbed her mother's pearl earrings—her mother had loved pearls—and put them in her own ears, then closed the lid on the box. She was wearing a new dress she had gotten for the day. Her mom had always worn ivory or white on Christmas, so Amy had searched until she found the perfect dress. She had looked in some of her mom's old things, but none of them fit her. Amy was built differently than her mom had been—slightly taller and a little more broad-shouldered. With a grimace she realized that all the beautiful clothes still left of her mother's would probably fit Beth perfectly. She prayed that she'd never have to find out. Amy was sure that her sister would never come back. Beth had left them all behind, and Amy was glad to be rid of her.

She didn't dawdle in her parents' bedroom. She had a lot to prepare to make sure everything was ready for Christmas at Monahan Ranch. Her father's entire family would be there, as well as Aunt Mary and her husband, Don. Her father had also invited some of the employees that worked at the ski lodge, especially since many of them were away from their families for the holidays to work. He had a great relationship with many of his employees, and strived to always have some sort of friendly relationship with everyone who worked closely with him at the ski resort. Amy was trying to follow her father's lead when it came to how he handled business. She wasn't sure how many of them would come over to Christmas brunch and dinner at the house, but she had prepared for many. She absolutely loved Christmas.

Amy, already dressed for the day, went downstairs before the guests were scheduled to arrive to make sure that everything was in place and ready. Only the family would come for brunch, though people were invited from far and wide for dinner. But she wanted to make sure that everything was ready just the same.

It had been an extremely busy month for Amy. She was trying to spend as much time as she could planning her wedding, but it was hard with all of her other responsibilities. Mostly, she spent her time working with her father, learning how he did everything and trying to take over some of the jobs he had previously done. She had truly turned into his second-in-command and was excited for the day when she would be in charge of it all—although it was a bit daunting. She was glad that her father would be around to help her out and advise her, even when she was in charge one day. And then, of course, there was David who backed her up in pretty much everything she did. He was an employee of her dad's as well. And on top of all of that, she had Christmas to prepare for, and she would expect no less than the grandness of Elizabeth Monahan. She wanted to do everything just right. Her wedding plans could come later. After all, she wasn't getting married for another year.

It had nearly broken her heart, but she realized she couldn't pull off a wedding in time for summer. Winter was much too busy of a time to plan a wedding, and she didn't want to compromise on it being the day of her dreams because of work. So she and David had both agreed to wait until it was more convenient. Of course, Amy had continued to dwell on the fact that her dream of a garden wedding wouldn't happen, but had come up with a perfect idea instead. They would be married on New Year's Eve—her parents' anniversary. Once the idea had come to her, she had started to love it even more than being surrounded by her mother's flowers. That way she could plan the whole wedding in the summer and the fall, so by the time ski season started the next year, everything would be ready. And her father had already said that it was completely fine for her and David to take off on their honeymoon even in the midst of the busiest time of the year. Amy was in love with the idea of following in her parents' footsteps—her mother in particular. Amy would even be the same age her mom was when she got married. She would make sure that her mother's touch was at her wedding, as well as Christmas Day at Monahan Ranch.

Walking into the grand kitchen, she smiled at all the food laid out. Paulina, their cook from time to time, had been working hard all week to get everything ready for the big Christmas event. She left plenty of instructions for Amy on heating up the food and timing everything, which she was grateful for. Amy enjoyed cooking, to an extent. She was learning a lot, but didn't think of herself as that great of a cook. She didn't have the time to devote to it that she wished she did. There were way too many other pressing needs upon her. But she had to. Paulina wasn't there everyday to meet their needs, nor were the other staff that worked at the house.

Her father, although he could afford it, didn't want his house full of people paid to meet his needs. He could do it himself. There were people there from time to time, but mostly he liked having the house to himself. Amy agreed with him. She probably would agree a little more if it meant that she wasn't left helping him run the business as well as the home. Sometimes she couldn't catch her breath. When Beth was around, she helped out a lot around the house. Amy didn't realize quite how much she did until she wasn't there anymore. Amy hadn't learned to cook, at least not well, until after Beth left. In fact, she hardly did anything at home until Beth had left. It made her so angry with her sister. She didn't have time to herself anymore, instead she had to pick up Beth's slack.

"Merry Christmas, honey," her dad said, coming into the kitchen. He gave her a hug and kissed her cheek. "You look radiant."

"Why thank you," she said with a smile.

"Got everything ready for the big day?" he asked. She had been filling him in about the big dinner prepared for this evening all week. Sometimes she caught something in his eye that made her wonder if he wished it was just a small affair for Christmas, rather than a big dinner. Sometimes, she felt the same way. But she wanted to honor her mother's memory, and her mother had loved Christmas. Plus, she knew her dad would enjoy having all the family over, although they were all over often enough as it was. There always seemed to be someone walking around the house everyday, over for some reason or another, or even spending the night in one of the many guestrooms.

"I just have to set everything out." Amy glanced at the clock. The family would start arriving around eleven, so she had an hour to get everything together.

After putting an apron on, not wanting to get anything on her dress, Amy baked the rolls in the oven—Paulina had helped her prepare her mom's delicious cinnamon rolls ahead of time so all she had to do was pop them in the oven and pour frosting over them. She mixed together the ingredients for waffles, making sure the waffle iron was on. Her younger cousins loved making waffles. She had tons of toppings for them as well. Everything was pretty much set—she just had to put it all out. There were eggs and sausages and bacon, tons of fresh fruit as well as freshly squeezed juice. Her mother would be proud, and Amy was satisfied.

Right before eleven, David came over to help her put everything in place. All of the food was in the kitchen, more of a buffet style, but they could all sit down together at the big dining room table.

Amy was determined not to stop moving until her family arrived, and even then she was sure she wouldn't stop going, going, going all day. But David pulled her away from stacking plates and turned her toward him.

"I have to make sure those are out and ready for when everyone gets here," she stated, looking at him like he was crazy for stopping her.

"Can't I just have you to myself for one second before the craziness starts?"

She smiled up at him. She adored David. He was so kind and supportive. He knew that she was a busy person, that she had a lot of demands on her life, and he was there standing beside her through it all. She had met him two years ago when he had started working in the finance department for her dad. She started interacting with him right away, working with him as he got settled into his position. As a new employee, her dad had invited him over to dinner a few times, his family as well, in order to get to know him a little better. She saw him everyday, and eventually they just started spending all of their time together. She couldn't remember an exact moment when their acquaintance became a personal relationship. It all had just flowed so naturally. She fell in love with him quickly, surprising herself. She knew she always wanted to get married one day, she just didn't think it would happen this early on in her life. But she loved him, and she wanted to spend the rest of her life with him. Sometimes she worried that she was too busy to be the kind of wife that David deserved, but he continued to stick by her through her hectic life. He was a blessing to her.

"This time next year we'll be days away from getting married," he stated, giving her a warm smile.

She nodded. "I can't wait."

"Me either."

He held her close, and she was content there, his arms around her. David was the more romantic one of the two of them. Sure, she had dreamt about her wedding for years on end, especially as a little girl. But as she got older, she had gotten a lot more responsibility and didn't have as much time to daydream about falling in love. And when she did actually fall in love, it happened so suddenly that it took her by surprise. But David was her dream come true.

"Ahem," someone cleared their throat. Amy backed away from David. Her dad was standing in the entrance to the kitchen, smiling sheepishly. "Nice to see you, David."

"You too, Julian. Merry Christmas."

"Merry Christmas."

Amy knew her father loved David. There was a tiny part of her, though, that felt guilty marrying him. She didn't want to leave her father behind. She knew she wouldn't actually be leaving him behind. Obviously they'd be working together nearly everyday, but still. She was all he had left sometimes. He had worked hard to raise Amy and Beth on his own after their mom died, and he had done a wonderful job. In many ways, Amy felt like her dad was one of her best friends. She didn't want to leave him behind by himself. She loved her dad but she didn't know what to do about him when she married David. Of course, he was fully capable of taking care of himself, but she had just gotten so used to it over the years. She didn't want to hurt him by leaving him. He'd already been hurt too many times—first by grieving for his wife, and then when Beth left.

Stupid, selfish Beth, Amy thought.

Family started arriving at eleven, right on the dot. Amy loved being surrounded by her loved ones. David's family came as well, and she enjoyed the quality time she got to spend with them. She didn't know them as well as she wished she did. Sometimes she hated being so busy all the time, but they were wonderful people. She noticed her dad spending a lot of time chatting with David's parents. It was a little mind-blowing for her to realize that she was joining another family. What would happen when David's parents wanted them to spend Christmas at their home, and not at Monahan Ranch? She wasn't sure how she would handle that. Amy loved her traditions, especially those started by her mother.

"You did a great job," Aunt Mary said, coming up to Amy later that night, well after both brunch and the fabulous dinner had been served.

"What do you mean?" Amy asked her.

"You did Christmas just like your mother."

Amy smiled. "I wanted nothing less."

"I know," Mary answered. "You must have had your hands full getting all of this ready."

Amy nodded her head, releasing a deep breath. Part of her was extremely glad that it was all coming to an end. She had thoroughly enjoyed herself throughout the day, but it was hard being the hostess. Her mom must have had endless energy. Amy certainly did not.

"When do you have time to enjoy yourself?" Mary wondered.

"I do enjoy this," Amy answered.

"But do you ever have time for yourself," she asked, then glanced about the room, her eyes coming to a rest on David, "or for that handsome fiancé of yours?"

Amy glanced over at David. He was talking to her father and Uncle Don. Amy studied him for a moment, so happy that he was a part of her life. He would fit in really well with her family. In some ways it was like he had always been a part of her family.

"He is handsome, isn't he?" Amy said with a smile. David had light brown hair and brown eyes. He had just gotten a new pair of glasses the week before, and she was still adjusting to the change. They were quite different from his old pair—much more trendy.

"Have you two been working on the wedding at all?" Mary asked.

Amy's face scrunched up. "I know he really wants to get everything planned out, I've just been having a difficult time making time. Plus, we do have a lot of time to plan."

Mary raised her eyebrows, like she was going to reprimand Amy. Amy knew what she was going to say even before she opened her mouth.

"People first, then the business."

"I know," Amy said. It was her dad's tactic as well. He may never stop moving, he may have uncountable responsibilities resting on his shoulders, but he always made time for his family first. She needed to become more like him, she needed a better balance in her life.

"I'll come over tomorrow and sit down with you and David and help you get some plans underway."

"Are you sure?" Amy asked with surprise.

"Of course. You're my niece—I want this to be the most special day of your life, even if it is a whole year away from now. I would love to help out."

"I would love that," Amy told her.

"Unless, of course, you were planning on hiring a wedding planner or something. But in any way that you need me, I'm here."

Amy smiled warmly at her. Mary had always been a huge part of Amy's life, but even more so since her mom had died. Mary had stepped in and taken over that motherly role that Amy needed in her life. Of course, no one would ever replace her mother. No one could replace Elizabeth Monahan.

Mary smiled. "Let's plan this wedding!"

Chapter Twelve

Amy was so grateful to Aunt Mary and David. They were both so patient with her. The day after Christmas the three of them sat down and Mary talked them through everything they needed to get ready for their wedding, including many little details that Amy had never thought about. Amy didn't back down on the fact that she wanted to get married at the church in town that she had grown up in, even though it wasn't where her parents had gotten married, and then she wanted to have the reception at the Ranch in the big backyard, all on New Year's Eve. They could set up a marquee out back, which her father had done for various celebrations, and they could put heated lamps all around, making it warm and cozy even though they would be outside in the winter.

Amy thought it would be beautiful, she only wished that her mother's garden bloomed throughout the winter as well. She would had loved her mother's flowers wafting into the marquee, making the night even more enchanted, but there was nothing she could do about that. She would still technically be celebrating her wedding in her mother's haven.

The garden hadn't even been that well attended to over the past few years. Unfortunately, with Amy's time already overextended between so many different things, she didn't have time to take care of her mother's garden as well, which was probably a good thing as she felt she killed plants more than she made them flourish. It hadn't been as grand at all since before Beth left. That was another thing that Beth had taken care of before she walked out of everyone's lives. She had loved their mom's garden just as much as Amy had—and truthfully had much more of a green thumb.

Throughout the next week, Amy and David made lists of who they wanted to invite. When they had finalized their list after lots of discussion, it was handed over to Mary. A month after Christmas, so much had been planned it amazed Amy, especially since they had so much time left to make plans. She was sure that their guest list could change in the next year, but was happy to have a foundation. Mary had helped out so much. The invitations were picked out, even if they would be just sitting around for months, and Mary had a friend who would print them for Amy and David. They had picked out the caterers, and David's older brother played in an orchestra and agreed to get some of his band members to supply the music at the wedding. They would play when Amy walked down the aisle, as well as for her and David's first dance. They also hired a deejay for the reception. All in all, things were going great. Amy was pleased with how everything was progressing.

When February rolled around, Amy found her schedule lightening up just a little. Of course, the ski season would still continue for months, but she was starting to find a good balance between work and personal time, and she was so glad. She was enjoying having more time for herself, and she tried to spend as much time as she could with David. But it also meant more time for her friends, as well, for which she was glad.

Amy turned into the shopping center where she was meeting Shana, a longtime friend. They had been really close in high school and had stayed in touch when the girls went to different colleges. Shana had been the one friend that Amy had always been able to depend on through the years. They didn't get to spend as much time together as Amy would have liked, but every time they saw one another it was like no time had passed. She hadn't seen Shana since before the ski season started, and they hadn't talked much in that time either, but she was looking forward to seeing her friend.

Amy parked outside of the small café that she and Shana always met at. They served lots of great Panini's and homemade soups. It was the perfect day for a good, hearty soup.

Walking into the café, Amy looked around for Shana, but she didn't see her yet. Taking a seat at a table near the window, Amy started perusing the menu. She ordered a cup of tea while she waited. The waitress came back over and asked if Amy was ready to order when Shana walked into the restaurant.

"So sorry I'm late!" she said, smiling widely at Amy as she raised her sun-glasses up on her head. It was a beautiful sunny day outside, bright as the rays of the sun reflected off the snow. Shana's short black hair was pulled up into a messy ponytail, shadows under her eyes.

She sat down quickly and looked up at the waitress, ordering a drink before she walked away.

"So how are you?" Shana asked brightly.

"I'm doing well," Amy laughed at her exuberance. "How are you? It's been a while."

"I know, I know! Life's been kind of crazy, but before we talk about me, catch me up on your life. I want to hear all about David's proposal."

Amy complied right away. Shana had met David a few times, but they hadn't spent a ton of time with one another. Amy was hoping that would change.

With the wedding plans truly underway, although her wedding still ten months away, she was ready to start putting together her bridal party. She had been avoiding it, the voice of her mother in her head every time she thought about her maid of honor. All she could hear was "Beth, Beth, Beth," over and over, but Amy didn't want Beth to be her maid of honor. Even if she did, it wasn't like Beth was around anyway. No, she and Beth may share blood, but that was all. They didn't have a relationship with one another. Amy didn't want her sister anywhere near her wedding. She had been gone for over two years, anyway. Why did she still feel obligated for her sister to be there for her important day?

Not happening, Amy thought to herself. No, Beth would not be her maid of honor. She wouldn't be at Amy's wedding. And Amy was glad. But it meant that she had to think long and hard about who her maid of honor would be. She thought about all of her friends, and realized with a kind of sorrow that she wasn't as close to her friends as she used to be, not since she had taken on more responsibilities at the ski resort. But out of anyone, she knew that Shana would be the perfect maid of honor. She and Amy were so much alike, and she knew that Shana would be dedicated and attentive. She was the closest friend that Amy had.

Shana smiled with excitement as Amy told her how David had proposed. It had come as a surprise to Amy. It had been just a normal Friday at work. She was in her office and had spent the majority of the day on the phone with their advertisement representative, talking about updating the resort website. It had been a long and stressful week trying to get in touch with the representative.

They had played a bunch of phone tag, so she had ignored everything else that day when she finally got in touch with him, hanging up the phone with satisfaction when they talked through everything on her agenda.

During that time, her father's secretary had continually dropped papers on top of her desk to look over, but Amy had ignored them while she had the advertisement representative on the phone. When she finally got around to giving them a look over, she completely flipped out. It was an updated financial report to the one that she had processed the week before stating that the financial department calculated the tax report incorrectly that they were preparing for the end of the year. This meant a major setback, and no weekend for her. She had already stayed extremely late for the day and knew now that no end would be in sight for quite some time.

Amy stormed out of her office and down the hall to the financial department, annoyed because she had been so ready to start her weekend, but now would have to stay late and try to fix the mistake. But when she walked into the financial office, it had been completely made over. Sure, the desks and cubicles were still there, and everyone was gone, but set up in the middle of the room was a small table with candles lit on top, a bouquet of a beautiful mix of flowers in a vase. She stopped short, amazed at the office. Classical music was playing quietly around the room, and David stepped out from behind one of the cubicles, smiling at her adoringly. She was clutching the financial report in her hand when he walked over to her.

"I had to think of something to get you away from your desk," he said, taking it from her. "I've been having Carla going in there for hours trying to get your attention."

Amy glanced at the report in her hands and then back to his face, not sure what to make of it. She glanced at the table, and then back at him.

"I ordered dinner, by the way," he said, taking in her shocked expression. "Chinese—your favorite. I even got the gourmet kind you like."

She and David had spent many long nights in the office in the past and had ordered food to keep them going as they poured over various financial reports. It was all kind of fitting. But this night was entirely different.

The food was delivered right to the office, and Amy finally realized that David had played a trick on her and was able to relax—only after she made him prove that the tax report was calculated correctly. She was still shocked by this gesture, not sure what to make of it until he got down on one knee with a ring box in his hand.

"Amy, I love you with all my heart. Will you marry me?"

She covered her mouth with surprise. "Yes!" she yelled, an excited squeal. "Yes!"

David stood up and pulled her into a hug.

"I would love to marry you," Amy said, her head buried in his shoulder.

They sat there in the office, talking and laughing, dreaming aloud about their future together. It had been such a wonderful evening. David placed a ring on her finger that he told her Mary had helped him pick out. She had been extremely excited to go home and see her father, even though she had already called him right after saying yes to David.

"That's adorable!" Shana stated, bringing Amy back to the present. "Super sweet, but casual. Just like you guys."

"It took me a while to realize that he was kidding about the financial report, though. I made him drag up the real one on his computer and show me."

Shana laughed. "Yea, that sounds like you."

The waitress came back over and they ordered their food. Amy was interested in what Shana had been up to in the last few months since they had seen one another. The last she had heard from Shana, she had been teaching second grade at the elementary school in the next town over, and really enjoying herself.

"How's teaching going?" Amy asked.

Shana pressed her lips together and looked down at her hands, like she didn't want to say.

"Is everything okay?" Amy wondered.

Shana looked back up at her. "I'm not really working at the elementary school anymore. I'm actually not working in general right now. I'm sort of going over my options, trying to figure out what to do next."

Amy sat back in her seat, perplexed. Teaching had been all that Shana had talked about doing growing up. She remembered listening to all her stories when she did her student teaching. She wondered what in the world would have suddenly taken her away from that, make her not want to do it anymore.

"What happened?"

"Honestly, I don't know if I want to tell you," Shana responded, and Amy was surprised, and hurt.

"Okay," she said slowly, trying not to show that Shana's words had stung.

Shana bit her lip and glanced out the window, like she was searching for words. "I think I'm just a little afraid that you'll judge me."

Amy's brow furrowed. "Why would I judge you? I would never judge you!"

Shana turned back to her. "Look, I made a mistake, okay? I did something really stupid that I can't take back," she sighed heavily. "I was such an idiot!"

"What'd you do?" Amy asked.

"Do you promise not to judge me?"

"Why do you think I would judge you?"

"I don't know, I guess I'm just afraid that it will change how you think about me."

Amy shook her head. "That could never happen," she tried to assure her. "I'm sure it wasn't that bad," she added. She knew Shana really well. They'd known each other for years. If Shana made a mistake, Amy knew that it couldn't be that bad.

"Okay," Shana said. "I started dating this guy a few months back."

"Yea, Jared, right?" Amy asked. She remembered Shana talking about him the last time they had hung out.

Shana nodded. "Okay, so here's the thing. Jared's kind of had a rough life. His mom has just always kind of been too caught up in her own life to care about him and his dad has been a drug user for years."

"Wow," Amy said, leaning back in her chair and crossing her arms.

"Yea," Shana said. "Jared's been trying to do some sort of intervention for years, but nothing's worked," she paused as the waitress came over with Amy's soup and Shana's sandwich. Amy thanked the waitress, but Shana went right on talking as soon as she left.

"About a month ago, Jared had to go to his parents' house for something or other—I can't remember what it was. I went with him but waited in the car. Anyway, he saw a full canister of prescription pain killers for his dad and he took it."

"He took it?" Amy asked, feeling a sense of dread inside her. She had the feeling that something good wasn't going to come from where this story was headed.

"Yea, I mean, he wanted to get the pills away from his dad," Shana said, like it was a logical decision.

"So what happened next?" Amy wanted to know.

"Well, he showed them to me when he came back out. I felt so bad for him. I know he thought his father was doing a lot better lately, but apparently his dad was just putting on a good show."

"That's horrible," Amy stated.

"Yea, I know," she sighed. "Jared wasn't sure what to do with them. Somehow they ended up in my purse, which was where the trouble started. When I went to work that Monday, I accidentally dropped my bag—I forgot that they were in there. Well, my boss saw them and picked them up and saw that they weren't for me and it was just bad."

Shana explained to Amy how she ended up getting suspended for being in possession of prescription drugs that didn't belong to her or anyone in her family, and bringing them onto school property, which was obviously a no drug zone.

"That's horrible, Shana! Did you even get a chance to explain why you had them?"

"Yea," she said, "And Jared came in and backed up my entire story. But it doesn't matter—I still brought prescription drugs that didn't belong to me to work. Oh man, if one of the kids had somehow gotten into those accidentally…" Shana shuddered at the thought. "The suspension had more to do with Jared, anyway. He kind of used to sell his dad's pills during college, and got caught and had to be bailed out of jail. So the fact that he was involved at all didn't exactly bode well for me in front of the administration. They thought I may be involved with what he used to do, so when it came to a vote with the school board that was kind of all they focused on."

Amy tried to keep her jaw from dropping in surprise. Her best friend was dating a drug dealer? Her levelheaded best friend was suspended from her dream job and didn't even seem to care?

"So you're just not working now?" Amy asked to try to keep the conversation going. She felt sick to her stomach. Surely there had to be something Shana could do to defend herself.

"They'll take me back for the next school year, but I don't know what I want to do."

It was a horrible thing for her friend to have gone through, especially when it wasn't her fault, but still, she could have done something better to prevent it from happening in the first place. But her fears only escalated when Shana told her that she had moved in with Jared, and that he didn't believe in God, which went against everything Shana used to want in a man and how she wanted to live her own life. Amy was afraid Shana was digging her own pit to fall into. Obviously she wasn't thinking clearly.

"Be careful," Amy warned, wishing she could simply pull Shana from the clutches of this new lifestyle she was embracing. An image of her sister came into her mind.

Shana gave her a look of disbelief. "What do you mean?"

"Obviously this guy has been through a lot, and he's not a believer. And he sells drugs."

"He's still a good person," Shana said, defending him. "And he only dealt in college—he really needed the money. He's not doing that anymore. And it's not like he was ever taking the drugs."

Amy pressed her lips together and nodded. "I'm sure he is a good guy," Amy acquiesced. "Just don't compromise who you are for him."

Shana shook her head, as if that were impossible, but obviously it already had happened. She was living with the guy, after all. And she told Amy that she had been too busy to go to church for the last month or so. Amy was wondering what kept her so busy now that she didn't have a job and all. No, she could tell simply by the way that Shana talked about him that Jared had already had a profound impact on her dear friend, and Amy didn't like it. She wished that she could do something about it. Part of her wanted to call the authorities and have them do a thorough check on this Jared guy to make sure he wasn't wrapped up in drugs like he claimed not to be anymore, although she knew that was a bit drastic.

They finished their lunch, Amy feeling more unsettled than ever when she finally got in her car and drove away. Shana asked her if Amy was available anytime in the next week to get together again, and Amy told her that she'd have to check her schedule and get back to her. Honestly, Amy wasn't sure if she wanted to have lunch with Shana again, not now that she wasn't the same person anymore, not now that she was compromising her morals and everything she had strived for in her life to live with a guy who clearly had a lot of his own issues to work through and who was changing her dear friend.

When she got home she realized that she had completely forgotten about asking Shana to be her maid of honor. She felt profound relief at that thought.

Chapter Thirteen

After returning from lunch with Shana, Amy was extremely frustrated. She felt uncomfortable about where her friend's life was headed. She and Shana had been so close when they were teenagers, and Amy had believed that everything about her character had been completely above reproach, but apparently she had been horribly wrong. The friend that she used to attend Bible studies with in high school and various youth group events, the friend that Amy had always looked up to for her relationship with God, was now living with a guy who clearly had a lot of issues of his own, and was suspended from her job. What had happened?

Amy had always admired her parents' dedication to God as a child. They had taken she and Beth to church with them every Sunday and they went to various kids' clubs from time to time. She had watched her mother read her Bible nearly everyday. Sometimes her parents would even study it together. And she had continued to attend church throughout high school and even college. She still went there with her father every week. Amy liked the people she met there—people a lot like her, who were goal-oriented and striving to do good, people unlike her sister and the person that Shana would quickly become if she continued down this road she was on. Amy feared she would get mixed up with drugs if she didn't get out of the situation she was in now.

To make herself feel better, Amy decided to finally think about her wedding dress. Her dad was gone at the office for the entire day, and she had the large house to herself, which suited her perfectly. She had already talked to him about wearing her mom's wedding dress, and he told her that it was ready and waiting for her.

She headed straight upstairs to her parents' room, going right for the back of the large closet where she knew the dress was hanging. Her mom had shown it to her countless times as Amy was growing up. She never got tired of seeing it. It was so lovely.

Grabbing the dress from the closet, she laid it on the big bed, unzipping the garment protector. She smiled widely when it was opened, wishing that her mom were here to share this moment with her. She wanted to make her mom proud on her wedding day. Amy had told her a long time ago that she fully intended on wearing her mom's wedding gown. She wished her mom would be there to see it. Amy was doing everything she could to re-create everything her mom had ever told her of her own wedding.

Amy held up the dress and walked to the big full-length mirror in the large closet. It was absolutely gorgeous—sophisticated and elegant just like her mother had been. The dress wasn't white, rather it was ivory, just like her mom's Christmas dresses. It swayed to the floor, the bodice decorated with small pearls. It had a sweetheart neckline, and small sleeves that rested slightly off the shoulders. She absolutely loved it.

Amy took her clothes off and stepped into the dress, pulling it up and holding it to her chest, trying to figure how she was going to close it. She was able to pull some of the hooks closed, but the dress wasn't fitting her comfortably. She took a step back from the mirror to get a full look at herself. She wasn't completely pleased with what she saw. The dress was gorgeous, of course. She just wasn't content with how she looked in it. She didn't even want to think it, but as beautiful as the dress was, it wasn't quite her style.

Amy was three inches taller than her mom had been, but she thought the dress would have been long enough that it wouldn't have mattered because the material simply flowed elegantly to the floor, but she was wrong. It looked too short, like there should be more to the dress. And it was tight in places where it shouldn't be, and not tight enough in other places where it needed to be. She felt like she was going to cry.

Amy pressed her lips together, seething with anger. Would nothing go right? First of all, her mom wasn't going to be there for her special day, and now she wouldn't even get to wear her dress, have a part of her there. Sure, she could take the dress to a dressmaker and have them alter and change it so that it fit Amy perfectly, but she would never dream of making a change to her mother's dress. She wanted to preserve it just as it was. Plus, she wasn't quite sure that the style even complimented her. Secondly, she had gone to lunch expecting to enjoy a great time with one of her closest friends and even ask her to be her maid of honor at her wedding, but apparently Shana was falling in with the wrong crowd and wasn't the strong Christian and moral person she had thought she knew. She felt like everything was falling apart.

Without thinking much, Amy stepped out of the dress and kicked it into the wall, tears streaming down her face. It had been her dream beyond all dreams to wear her mother's dress on her wedding day. Now she wouldn't even get that. And with a heavy sigh that made her even more angry, she realized that the dress would probably fit her sister perfectly—and she would look great in it. Beth was the spitting image of their mother, although she couldn't be more opposite from the woman who had raised them. She hoped beyond hope that Beth would never get near that dress.

Amy quickly got dressed again, and then bent down to pick up her mom's dress, feeling remorse for kicking it into the wall. She may not get to wear it on her wedding day, but she didn't want to harm it. She would just have to look for its mirror image in a size that would fit her perfectly so that it at least resembled her mom's even if she wasn't sure she even liked it for herself. But still, she had wanted to wear the exact dress that her mom had worn—had practically even promised her mom she would.

Furious, Amy hung the dress back up and placed it in the same spot back in the closet. She marched out of the room when she was done, slamming the door to her own bedroom as she entered. She laid down on her bed, grabbing a pillow and clutching it to her, angry tears still falling down her face. She was surprised when she heard a knock on her door.

"Amy?" a voice called through, but she didn't answer. A moment later the door opened a crack and David stuck his head through. She wondered what he was doing over in the middle of the day, but didn't care to ask. When he noticed her curled up on her bed and crying, he came into the room.

"What's the matter?" he asked right away, sitting down on the edge of the bed, putting his hand on her foot.

"Nothing's going right!" she yelled.

"What do you mean?"

Amy sat up. "My mom's wedding dress doesn't fit me. The one person I actually wanted to be my maid of honor is about to go off the deep end. My stupid sister is ruining everything!" she yelled, throwing her hands down on the bed.

David looked at her with surprise. "What has any of that got to do with your sister?"

Amy glared at him. "She's been gone two and a half years and still she manages to ruin everything!"

"What do you mean?" David asked again, his brows furrowed. He had never met Beth—had literally missed meeting her by about a month or so, when he had started working at the resort. She was so glad that he was the one thing she hadn't been able to taint, but even still, she was messing up her wedding. "Has she come home? Have you heard from her?"

Amy laughed sarcastically. "Beth will never come home." It was something Amy was positive about. Her sister would never show her face here again. She may appear strong to everyone around her, but Beth was a coward. Amy was sure that she was out there somewhere making a mess of her life, but Beth would never come back, even if she did get herself into a mess of trouble. She had too much pride to come running back home to Daddy.

"So what could she have done that's bothering you so much?" he asked, trying to understand.

Amy took a deep breath, looking down at her hands. "If she could have just turned out right, everything would be okay. But no, Beth had to have everything her way."

"What are you talking about?" David persisted.

Amy knew she wasn't making sense. None of this made sense. But she couldn't help but see how all of this had to do with Beth. If she had just grown up into the woman their mom was raising her to be, there would have been no problem. If their mom hadn't died when Amy was fifteen, she was sure that Beth would have probably been a much different person. First of all, she would still be home, Amy was sure. And she would have been her maid of honor at her wedding, just like she was supposed to be. But no, Beth messed everything up when she ran away from home two and a half years ago. She messed everything up the day that she forced their mom to take her to a friend's house. And Amy hated her for it. But Beth just never listened. Amy would never forget that day.

It had been raining out, pouring. There was a winter storm warning placed over the entire county for the day. It was mid-November, which weather-wise could be an unsteady time. Sometimes fall lasted clear on into November. Sometimes winter came early. But a winter storm warning that time of year meant be careful, especially when it was pouring outside and close to freezing and you lived in the mountains. There was the danger of black ice on the roads. Even though they were all experienced with the weather patterns—it being one of several storm warnings per year—there was no reason to go out on the roads if it wasn't absolutely necessary.

They had gone to church that morning, the whole family, but they had all been relieved to be back home. Dad had to go over to the stables because they were short on staff due to the storm and he wanted to make sure that the horses were all boarded up and safe from the elements. It was just Mom, Amy, and Beth.

Amy was sitting in the kitchen, getting a head start on her homework that was due in a few days. The girls had two days off from school, a mid-November break. She was content sitting inside in a big comfy sweater and a pair of sweats, ready to hibernate as the storm came through, glad to be warm in her large home.

"Are you still going out to meet Aunt Mary?" Amy asked, her mom coming into the kitchen with the phone in her hand. She had changed out of her nice church outfit and into some comfortable home clothes, just like Amy.

"No, I told her we better reschedule," Mom answered. "It's raining cats and dogs out there and I don't want to get on the road." It could be especially scary coming down the mountain where they lived. It was a narrow road leading to and from Monahan Ranch. Amy had been in possession of her learner's permit for many months now, and still felt nervous as she drove up and down her driveway. The fear was starting to pass, but there was no way that she'd ever want to do it when the weather was as horrible as it currently was outside.

Amy smiled at her and went back to her homework while her mom put together a small salad for lunch, always eating healthy, and making a sandwich for Amy in the process. She was glad that her mom wasn't going out. Amy wanted to finish her homework quickly and then suggest that they curl up on the couch with a plush blanket and a roaring fire, and watch a movie. She was about to suggest it when suddenly thirteen-year-old Beth barged into the kitchen.

"Mom, are you going to take me to Julie's?" she asked.

Mom turned and glanced out the window. "You can barely see through this rain, Beth. We can't go out right now, honey," she said gently.

"Mom!" she pleaded. "I haven't seen Julie in months. You promised you'd take me after church!"

"I'm sorry, Beth," Mom said calmly, but Beth kept pushing.

"But she's expecting me," Beth told her. "We've been planning this ever since she moved. Please, Mom? Please! I really want to see Julie."

"Beth, I said no!" Mom said more firmly.

"Then when am I going to get a chance to see her?"

"You'll just have to reschedule," Mom stated.

"No!" Beth yelled. "I promised Julie I would come! You promised you'd take me! We already had to reschedule because of that stupid church picnic last month!"

"Beth!" Amy yelled. "Stop being so selfish. Mom said no."

Beth simply turned to her and sneered. Then she went right back to her pleading. Eventually Mom said she would take her, partly to get Beth to stop whining. Amy rolled her eyes when Mom said she would take her. Somehow Beth always ended up getting what she wanted. It drove Amy crazy.

Beth ran upstairs to get her stuff for the two nights she planned on spending at Julie's house. Julie's mom would bring her home on Tuesday. Amy was happy that she'd have the house without Beth around for two whole days.

"It looks like it's clearing up a little," Mom said before she left. Amy glanced out the window and saw the lighter sky ahead.

"Yea," she agreed.

Beth came back into the kitchen, her overnight bag ready, and they left.

Amy continued doing homework, finishing right before her dad came back in from the stables. He was soaked to the bone, having helped bring all the horses in out of the storm, but he told her everything was safe and boarded up. She was glad. She had gotten a horse the previous summer, and she didn't want Belle out in the cold rain. It made her shiver just thinking about it. She decided she would start that roaring fire for herself. Mom could join her when she got home.

Her dad went upstairs to take a shower and put on fresh clothes. The phone rang while he was up there, but Amy didn't answer it. Most of the calls were for her dad anyway, so she let it go to voicemail—they were mostly business calls. It rang again, and the second time her dad picked up. When he came back down, he was shaking and pale. He told her that there had been a car crash, that Mom and Beth were being rushed to the hospital. Amy gasped at his news, this dreadful pit starting to make its way into her stomach. They left right away, running to the car through the now light drizzle. They weren't too far behind Mom and Beth, even being slow and careful on the highway.

Amy remembered when her mom's car came into view. The road was blocked on the other side and there was a tow truck getting ready to pull it off the road. It was flipped upside down on the other side of the highway, the driver's side completely smashed in. Her heart started pounding wildly in her chest as they continued driving, feeling faint. She knew her dad had seen the car as well, but he tried hard not to react to it, which she assumed was for her sake. He had a mission before him, to get to his wife and daughter at the hospital.

When they finally made it to the hospital, the doctor who approached them in the waiting room gave the news that changed their lives forever. Mom was dead—she had died before a team was dispatched to the crash scene, but they hadn't mentioned so on the phone even though it had already been assessed that she hadn't made it. Amy sank back down into the chair in the emergency room. She didn't even hear the part when the doctor talked about Beth.

She didn't remember much after that. She knew her sister had been banged up pretty badly, but it seemed like she would be okay, although they couldn't make a full assessment until she woke up. She remembered Aunt Mary coming for Amy at the hospital and taking her back home. Dad stayed behind with Beth, phoning really early in the morning when Beth finally had awoken. Mary had been ready to take Amy over to the hospital first thing in the morning, but she had refused to go. She didn't want to see her sister at all. Mary was upset with her, she and Don both trying to force Amy to get in the car to go, but she refused. She never wanted to see her sister again.

Eventually, they convinced her to go, telling her that her dad needed her—that's what cracked her resolve. He couldn't leave Beth right now, not in the condition that she was in. But he needed Amy with him as well. So she went. She went to the hospital for her father and no one else.

Dad was waiting for them outside the hospital when they arrived, needing some fresh air. When Amy came walking up he ran to her and held her so close it almost hurt, but she clung to him with the same intensity. They cried together. She wasn't sure how long they stayed like that. They walked back in after a time—it had been freezing outside. The doctor came to her dad and said he wanted to discuss Beth's head scans with him. Aunt Mary and Uncle Don took Amy to see Beth. She was sleeping when they came in, a huge bandage on her head. Her arms were on top of the covers and Amy could see that she had a lot of small cuts on her arms from the shattered glass, a big IV in her hand. None of it made her feel any sympathy for her sister.

Aunt Mary and Uncle Don left her alone with Beth for a moment, thinking she might want a moment alone with her sister. Amy sat down in the chair next to her bed. After a little while, Beth began to stir, her eyes blinking profusely for a few moments like she was getting her bearings, and then coming to rest on Amy.

Amy opened her mouth to speak. "I hope you're pleased with yourself," she said with biting sarcasm, not afraid to let all the anger and malice escape in her tone. "You killed mom."

Chapter Fourteen

Beth hadn't reacted to what Amy said—or at least she didn't respond with words. She just started crying—silent tears, and Amy was glad.

"You blamed your sister for killing your mom?" David asked, bringing Amy back to the present. He gave her a calculating look, like he was seeing something in her that he had never noticed before.

"Yea," Amy said with a shrug. "I mean, if Beth hadn't persisted that day, then Mom never would have agreed."

David's eyebrows pulled together. "You don't really think that your sister killed your mother, do you?"

"Well, she didn't make the car spin out of control, no."

David nodded his head once, letting out a deep breath. "Did you ever tell her that again after the hospital?"

"What?"

"That Beth killed your mom?"

Amy thought. She was sure she had, in moments of anger. But what did it matter? She shrugged in response.

"And you guys were never close again after the accident?"

"Nope," Amy answered. "Although, we were never really that close to begin with."

David looked down at his hands and Amy leaned back on her bed. They were silent for a long time, both deep in thought, when David suddenly spoke.

"It wasn't your sister's fault, you know that right?"

She sat up in surprise. "The accident?"

"Yea."

She opened her mouth as if to respond, and then closed it again, not sure what to say. Was David actually trying to defend Beth, the sister that had been the cause of so much pain and frustration in Amy's life?

"Because it wasn't her fault," David said.

"I know," Amy stated reluctantly.

"Your mom didn't have to give in. It was her decision to take Beth."

Amy nodded her head in answer. Of course, she knew that David was right. It wasn't actually Beth's fault, but still. If it hadn't been for her sister, her mom would have still been alive. True, her mom was the one who decided to take Beth. She didn't have to say yes. But Beth had a hand in the equation, and Amy couldn't separate her from all the rest.

"I know," Amy finally relented, wanting to let David know that she didn't actually think that it was Beth's fault. Beth couldn't control what had happened.

David gave her a small smile. "Can I ask you something?"

"Of course," Amy replied right away.

"Why do you dislike your sister so much?"

She was surprised by the question. Why? Well, why not? How could someone like the person who has been the cause, or at least part of, so much pain, who has created such a mess?

Amy was about to unload on him when David stuck his hand out to stop her from speaking.

"Tell me honestly," he said. "I don't want to listen to you rant on and on about how your sister ruined your life. Think about it. Why do you really dislike Beth? What has she really done to you to make you so upset with her?"

Amy sighed, thinking about his question. There were so many different things. Although she hated to admit it to herself, she had been jealous of Beth when she was younger. Beth was the one who had the charming personality, who captivated everyone who came within twenty feet of her. Amy was always the more shy, reserved one. And, of course, from the moment she was born, Beth was a beauty. Amy was beautiful too, but in a different way. People were immediately taken in by Beth's sparkling blue eyes. And of course, Amy had to hear over and over again just how much Beth resembled their mother.

And then there was always the fact that Beth was the most selfish person that Amy knew. Sometimes she still couldn't believe what her sister had done to their

father. Walking into his office, demanding his money, and then fleeing. She completely turned her back on him—on her as well. And he had given her everything
over the years. He had loved her, had provided for her. Beth already had everything she could have ever needed, but no—her sister wanted out. She wanted out
of life at Monahan Ranch, at Holy Cross. She wanted to do everything on her
terms and expected to do everything on her terms. She acted without thought to
the consequences. As long as her own needs were met, she was satisfied. And she
had no idea, of course, what her leaving had done to their father.

First of all, she had completely shamed him. Their dad had always been a
well-known figure in the town, as well as the business world. And it was also a
well-known fact that the whole family was involved in running the ski resort.
But then Beth just left, and her father was plagued with questions about her
whereabouts. Amy even heard rumors from time to time about things that
had happened in their family to make Beth leave. None of them were true of
course, but she hated that they were said all the same. She hated that anyone
thought ill of her father, of her. Beth was the one to blame.

More than anything, though, she hated how much it hurt her father when
Beth left. Amy knew he didn't like to show it, at least when others were around.
And his life was so demanding that he was on the go all the time. But Amy
heard him at night that first week, crying in his room. They both knew that
it wasn't simply a phase—Beth was gone for good. She had been slightly surprised, though, at just how upset he was. Her dad had mourned Beth's depar-
ture as strongly as he had grieved for the passing of their mother, if not more.
And he was worried about her, as well. There was no telling what kind of
trouble Beth was getting into, and Amy was sure it was finding her wherever
she went. More likely, Beth was creating the trouble. But Amy knew that he
was worried still. He would never stop missing Beth. And she could tell when
he was thinking about her. A look always came over his face—a faraway look,
mingled with sadness. She didn't want him to hurt, and she was angry at Beth
for doing this to him, for continually doing this to him. Amy had been working
herself so hard since Beth left, partly to try to overshadow Beth's absence, but
she knew it wasn't working. Stupid, selfish Beth.

Why did Amy dislike her so much? How could she not?

She didn't have an answer for David, at least nothing that she could narrow down into a few words. She held her tongue. David had told her that he

didn't want to hear her rant on about Beth. He had heard a lot of that already throughout their relationship, and a part of her felt bad for that. He was probably sick to death of her complaining about Beth. She'd have to watch herself better in the future.

"I don't know," she finally stated, wanting to provide some sort of an answer.

David nodded. "Maybe you should think about it, about what really bothers you."

Amy's eyebrows furrowed. What good would it do? But she nodded her head anyway. Everything about Beth bothered Amy, but she knew that wasn't what David wanted to hear.

David squeezed her hand. "On to other things—your mom's wedding dress doesn't fit you?"

Amy's face crumpled. Why'd he have to remind her?

"You can always get it altered, can't you?"

"Yea," Amy said. "But I don't want to touch her dress. I'll just have to find something different."

"I'm sure you'll find the perfect dress—perfect for you and not because you feel like you have to wear it."

Amy gave him a strange look. "What do you mean because I feel like I have to wear it? I wanted to wear my mom's wedding dress."

"Okay," he said, not pressing it, but she could tell that he had something on his mind that he wasn't saying.

"What do you mean?" she asked him again.

He sighed. "Nothing, really. Just be careful that you don't keep doing things because you feel obligated. Nobody likes it when someone's just acting on empty obedience."

She had no idea what he meant by that, and didn't ask.

Amy told him everything about Shana, and he listened without interrupting. When she finally finished, all he said was, "Wow—we should keep her in our prayers."

"Well, yea," Amy agreed. "I guess there's nothing else to do."

"Well she's still your friend," David pointed out.

"I know." She was just a friend that Amy didn't mind having some distance from for a little while.

They remained silent for a time, Amy thinking over the day. She really could only shake her head at it all.

"Let's get out of here," David said after a while, standing up and pulling Amy up as well.

"And do what?" Amy wanted to know.

David smiled at her. "Something fun."

"What do you have in mind?" she asked.

"Well there *is* a ski resort in your backyard."

Amy laughed. "I hadn't noticed," she teased.

"I say we go sledding."

"Sledding?" she was surprised. They didn't normally do things like that. The tubing park was a few miles from Amy's house, part of the resort. She hadn't been there in years. "Really?"

"Really."

The two of them got dressed up in winter gear. It was getting dark out, but the tubing park was lit at night. By the time they were in the car and pulling up to the park, she was excited, her sense of adventure starting to seep through. She had been doing so much business over the past three years that she had forgotten how to have spontaneous fun. And it wasn't until her first run down the hill on a tube right behind David that she realized how much she had missed the resort part of being at a resort. She missed having fun. She was so glad she had someone like David in her life to remind her how do it, or even how to slow down and smile. He was such a blessing to her—her perfect counterpart in so many ways.

Sure, she was happy doing what she was doing. She really was interested in the ins and outs of running the ski resort, but she hadn't necessarily anticipated just how much it would consume her life when she had started working side by side with her father. And with Beth gone, she had tried really hard to keep things at home going at the same pace. Amy had taken on so much since Beth had left, but as she felt the cold winter air on her face and heard the excited laughter of those around her at the tubing park, she couldn't remember why she had felt the need to take on so much. Was it simply to overcompensate for Beth's absence? Or because she felt she had to? She just didn't want work to compromise having a life, especially now that she planned on spending that life with David by her side.

So many times he had stayed with her in the office at night when she had tried to get more work done, never complaining. He had just wanted to be with her. Had she ever done that in return? She couldn't think of ever stopping what she was doing just to be with him, and she felt horrible for it. And she knew her father had never asked her to make work her life, she had just done it because she felt she had to. She didn't want to do that anymore.

Amy looked over at David as they were preparing to head back up the lift to the top of the hill.

"This is fun," she said with a big smile. She needed him in her life. She needed his partnership. He was making her a better person, and she loved him for it.

He looked at her, a twinkle in his eyes. "We should do more of this."

"I agree," she replied. "I definitely agree."

Chapter Fifteen

In the month that followed Amy and David's trip to the tube park, she had made a point of spending a lot more time doing things for herself. She made herself leave her work desk by five o'clock no matter what, deciding that whatever was left for her at the end of the day wasn't pressing enough and could wait for the morning. She was still committed to helping her dad run the business, but if she really wanted to do it like him, she had to be more like him. He always put family and people first, and Amy had to do the same thing. She wanted to do the same thing.

If it were possible, Amy was even more in love with David than she had been when she said that she would be his wife. He was always there for her, no matter what. He was always giving of himself, and she wanted to be the same in return. She planned a whole adventure day away for the two of them. She even took a day off work, and made him take one off, too. Instead of spending the day running the business side of the lovely ski resort where they worked, they enjoyed it instead. Amy and David went skiing for the entire day, and it had been so much fun. Amy had been skiing since she was a little girl, but hadn't done it in a while.

As a kid, her parents had taken she and Beth on many ski trips to different mountains—some in Colorado, some in other states, and they even went skiing in Austria once when they took a big trip to Europe for Christmas one year. It had been the only year that Christmas wasn't at Monahan Ranch, although a lot of the family had come to Austria as well. They had rented a big cabin, and it had been pretty much the same. But throughout high school, she hadn't skied quite as much. And once she started working for her father, she had even less time. Of course, she took a run here and there, but she hadn't spent the whole day on the mountain in a long time. It was a good reminder of what all her hard work went toward.

She had packed a picnic for her and David to enjoy for lunch. She brought the basket up on the gondola with them—sandwiches, fruit, and hot chocolate. Simple, but great. And it was so amazing to just be on top of the mountain and sit with David in the snow, overlooking the town below. She loved her home. Amy never wanted to leave Colorado. She never wanted to leave Holy Cross. She loved her home and her mountain, and had missed it so much, even though it had always been there all along. She enjoyed going down the trails with David.

He was a snowboarder, and hadn't been at practice as long as Amy had, so they stuck to some of the easier trails, which suited her just fine. She enjoyed skiing, but the harder trails had always scared her. She had saved those for her father and Beth as a kid. She just liked to go steady and peacefully down the mountain. And since her date with David, she had skied every weekend since. She didn't want the ski season to end, but she knew it would draw to a close eventually. But then she had a summer of a lighter workload to look forward to, with plenty of time to spend with David having fun. And then she would also get to see her mother's garden bloom, which was always such a joy. Amy was truly content for the first time in a long while.

———

"Thanks for coming with me today," Amy said to Aunt Mary. Mary had picked Amy up at the house early in the morning. They wanted to get an early start. Mary was taking Amy to Denver to look for her wedding dress. She had made peace with the fact that she wouldn't be wearing her mother's dress. She had talked to Mary about it, and Mary had been all for Amy taking the dress to be altered, or even taking pieces of it and making it into her own, but Amy didn't dare touch it. She wanted to preserve it just as her mother had left it, so Mary offered to take Amy shopping for her perfect dress.

"Sweetheart, I'm honored that you'd want me with you to do this."

Amy smiled at her as they neared the city—the skyline in the distance, and the beautiful Rocky Mountains behind them. The two of them were spending the night at a hotel in the city, enjoying the rare chance to get away for a night. Her father had really encouraged it, telling her she could use some time away from the resort, as much as she had fallen in love with it again.

They checked into their hotel before they made their way to the dress shop. Mary apparently knew exactly where she wanted to take Amy. She had made an appointment for Amy to meet with one of the consultants at the shop, who hopefully would help her find the perfect dress. Amy wasn't so sure what she wanted anymore. She had studied her mom's dress many times over the past month, and although she loved it, it had been the perfect dress for her mother. Maybe it wasn't the perfect dress for her. The idea of wearing a dress unlike her mom's was surprising to Amy, especially since she had talked of little else when it came to her wedding for so many years. But it was kind of exciting to pick out her own dress, to do what she wanted.

Walking into the dress shop, Amy was overwhelmed by the amount of dresses that she saw hanging up. She had no idea how she was supposed to pick one.

Someone walked right over to them as soon as they came in and showed Mary and Amy to a large dressing room. Amy was surprised when the owner of the shop walked in and gave Mary a warm hug. Apparently they had gone to college together. Amy was quickly introduced to Lisa, who seemed very excited for Amy. When the consultant who had scheduled the appointment walked in, Lisa told the woman that she would personally see to finding Amy the perfect dress. Amy was honored.

"So, do you have anything in mind?" Lisa asked her. "A particular style you wanted to try?"

Amy took a deep breath. "Honestly, I'm open to trying a lot of different things. Originally I wanted to wear my mom's dress, but I want to try something different."

Lisa had Amy explain her mom's dress to her to which Amy showed her a picture, and then asked her a few more questions about what Amy envisioned herself to look like on her wedding day, and then went off to find her the perfect dress. While they were waiting, they were served tea.

"I can't believe you know the owner," Amy stated, adding a little sugar to her tea.

Mary smiled. "Lisa and I go way back. We even shared an apartment our junior year of school. Granted, there were also four other girls living with us."

"Wow," Amy replied. She couldn't imagine what it must have been like to share an apartment with that many girls. She'd have to ask Mary about it sometime.

Lisa came back after a little while with four different dresses for Amy to start with. The first one was strapless and had a lot of beading. She liked the beading because it reminded her of the pearls on her mom's dress, but she didn't want to wear a strapless dress. It just didn't suit her. The second dress she tried had thick straps and a V-neck. It was pretty, but it just wasn't the right one. But when Amy stepped into the third dress, she was smitten. It was a beautiful A-line gown, with small straps that were nearly off the shoulders, kind of like her mom's dress. She loved the beaded bodice as well as the full skirt. She thought she had wanted a simpler dress with a skirt that just flowed straight to the floor, but she liked the bigger shape of this one. It made her feel like a princess.

"I absolutely love it," Amy said with tears in her eyes.

Lisa smiled at her and nodded.

"It's beautiful," Mary agreed.

"I think this is the one."

"Are you sure you don't want to try on anymore?" Mary asked. "This is only your third dress."

Amy looked at herself in the big mirrors. "No, this is the one. I can feel it."

Mary seemed like she was about to suggest that Amy try on a few more, but she glanced at Amy's radiant face and decided to think better of it.

"When it's the right one, they know," Lisa stated.

Mary and Amy locked gazes, both of them with tears in their eyes.

"You look gorgeous," Mary stated. "You look like your mother."

Amy turned around from where she was glancing at Mary in the mirror and stood facing her instead. "Really?"

"It's your smile," Mary told her. "You have the same smile."

If possible, Amy grinned wider. It was the first time Amy could remember anyone saying anything about her looking like her mother. Her heart swelled.

"You're going to be a beautiful bride," Mary said.

"Thanks."

Amy kept the dress on for a little while as Mary and Lisa talked and caught up on each other's lives for a bit. She looked at it from every angle in the big mirrors in the dressing room. She was sad when she had to take it off. All her measurements had been taken for the alterations that would have to be made, but Amy had found her wedding dress. Lisa was much too generous and gave them a great deal on the dress. Not wanting to say goodbye to her college friend just yet, Mary invited Lisa to join them for lunch the next day before she and Amy headed out.

They had spent hours in the dress shop, but both of them had a lot of energy when they left. Instead of heading back to the hotel for a rest, they kept going, enjoying their day away in Denver, filling the rest of the afternoon with shopping. They deposited their bags in their room before going out to dinner.

Amy was having so much fun with Mary. She loved her aunt so much and was so grateful that she had always been there for her over the years. Amy's mom and Mary had always been really close, even when they were young. They were so different from Amy and Beth. When her mom had met Amy's dad, she moved out to Colorado to be with him, leaving the farm where she was raised in Iowa. Mary followed shortly after they were married, going to school out in Colorado and then staying after she graduated, and after she married Uncle Don, who was also from Iowa. The two sisters hadn't wanted to be far from each other. It had been really hard on everyone when Amy's mom died, of course. For a while, Amy thought that Don and Mary might return to Iowa, but they stayed, for which she was so grateful. They never had kids of their own, but they had always treated Amy and Beth like their own.

"Aunt Mary, I have something I want to ask you," Amy said as they were sharing a slice of cheesecake for dessert. She had been thinking about this for a while now, and decided that the time was right.

"Ask away," Mary said with a smile, going for another bite of cheesecake.

"Would you be my maid of honor?"

Mary put her fork down, surprised. "Your maid of honor?"

"Or matron of honor, or whatever the technical term is?"

"You want me?" Mary asked, clear from her expression that she never guessed Amy would ask this of her.

"Of course. I love you, Aunt Mary. You've always been there for me. There's no one else I'd rather have than you," she stated honestly. She didn't know why the idea hadn't occurred to her from the beginning. Beth obviously wasn't going to be anywhere near her wedding, and even if she was, Amy didn't want her to be her maid of honor. And she hadn't spoken much to Shana since they had lunch. Yes, they had been good friends when they were younger, but they had grown apart over the years. Mary was the perfect person.

Mary pressed her lips together and looked deep in thought. From the set of her face, Amy guessed where her thoughts had flown.

"You're thinking of Beth, aren't you?"

She nodded her head slowly.

Amy crossed her arms. "Beth's not going to be at the wedding," she stated, shrugging.

"What if she shows up?" Mary asked.

Amy rolled her eyes. "She won't. You know she won't." But for a moment she saw the same look that came into her father's eyes from time to time. It had been nearly three years since Beth had left home, but they still hoped. They still held out hope that one day she would come home. In some ways it made Amy mad, wishing they could just get over it. But mostly it just made her sad to see how sad they were, and how hopeless their hope was.

"You may be right," Mary said after a moment.

"Please, Aunt Mary, will you be my maid of honor?" Amy asked again.

Mary smiled at her. "I would love to, honey, if you're sure."

"Of course I'm sure!"

"Then yes."

Amy clasped her hands together and grinned. She was happy that everything was starting to work out. After all that she had been through over the years, the pieces of her life were finally falling into place. Her mom wasn't going to be there for her special day, and she also wouldn't get to wear her mom's dress, but she had found the perfect dress for her. And Aunt Mary was going to be her maid of honor. David was the greatest blessing of all. She loved him so much and couldn't wait to be married to him. She had overcome a lot of hardship in her life—the passing of her mom when she was a teenager, her sister leaving home and abandoning what was left of their family, the business, taking care of her father. And now everything was turning out right. She was happy.

Chapter Sixteen

"So how do you feel?" Johnny asked Beth as they strolled through the still snowy streets of Lake Tahoe. It was near the end of March, a week away from Beth's due date. "I mean, about everything."

Beth laughed. "It still blows my mind that pretty soon someone's going to place a baby in my arms." She was nervous, extremely nervous, but excited as well.

"I think you're going to be a great mom," he told her.

She smiled. "Thanks." She was trying to convince herself of the same thing, but the reality of having a baby was terrifying. Lately, she hadn't been able to think past the labor part. That certainly wasn't going to be fun.

The week before, Ellie had held a baby shower for Beth. It had been a surprise, so of course Beth had been completely overwhelmed at first, but she had enjoyed herself. Mark's entire family was there, as well as a lot of the people from the church that the Harris's attended that Beth was starting to get to know since she went with them week after week. They were actively involved in their church, so sometimes she found herself there for various weeknight activities as well. It hadn't been extraordinarily big, which Beth appreciated. Some of the older women had cooked, and Ellie had decorated the house with pink, girly balloons. Beth was getting entirely sick of the color pink, and the baby hadn't even been born yet. She had gone clothes shopping on her own and picked out a few outfits, none of which would fit the baby for a few months anyway, but they had no trace of pink in them whatsoever.

Once again, Beth received so much stuff that she felt completely unworthy of receiving, but she was grateful as well. After her talk with Johnny at Christmas, after dwelling on the fact that she was broken yet finally deciding to believe that she could be put back together again, she had opened up a lot more. She learned how to open up her heart to those around her and really let others in. The Harris's were truly like her own family, and she was so grateful to have them. She knew that they would always be a part of her life, no matter what happened. She loved them too much for them to not ever be there. She wouldn't make the mistake again of leaving those she loved behind. Beth was a changed woman. She still had a lot to work on, and a lot of new things she was about to embrace, but she knew she had already come so far. She was beginning to love her life in Lake Tahoe. She loved the ski town—it felt so much like home that it almost hurt. She loved working in the flower shop and being surrounded by flowers, and had learned so much. Someday she wanted to have a huge garden, just like her mother's.

"Did you find room for all your new stuff?" Johnny asked her.

Beth laughed. "It's like a baby store has exploded in the house." She was no longer able to simply confine it to her garage apartment.

He smiled.

The two of them were walking through some of the shops that were right at the base of some of the ski slopes. Beth was yearning to get on a pair of skis, but that didn't seem likely to happen in the near future, although she did still hold out hope of taking Johnny skiing. Ski season lasted until about mid-April, even into early May depending on the weather, and it had been an especially cold winter. Hopefully everything with the delivery would go well and Beth would have some recuperation time, enough to catch the ski season right as it came to a close.

It was cold outside. The two of them were bundled up in jackets and scarves. Beth was sipping the hot chocolate that Johnny had bought for her in a coffee shop they passed as they headed toward the church. Beth was still very dedicated to getting as much exercise as she possibly could. She felt huge, and she wanted to lose her pregnancy weight as quickly as she could after the baby was born. She figured being in as best shape as she could throughout the pregnancy had to benefit that somehow. Although, there was always room for hot chocolate. Certain things couldn't be compromised. However, she had finally learned to love her growing stomach. She had fallen in love with her baby a long time ago, but eventually she learned to love watching how her body grew to accommodate her little girl.

Easter was coming in the very beginning of April, and Johnny had helped to create a flyer to be sent out to all the homes in the area to invite people to come to his church for Easter Sunday. He had some more printed, and was leading Beth in that direction so that he could drop them off at the church.

"Have you thought of a name yet?" Johnny asked her. She was getting that question a lot these days. Honestly, she hadn't thought of it too much until recently, and still she had no ideas. She wanted the baby's name to mean something, but she wasn't sure what. Beth was named for her mother, but she wasn't so sure she wanted to continue on that trend.

"No idea," she laughed. "I'll let you know when I do. I don't know if I'll even be able to pick a name before she's born. It might help to see her first."

Johnny smiled. "What, you think you're going to look at her face and the perfect name is just going to come to you?"

She swatted his arm. "It could happen!"

Everyone was excited about the baby coming, especially Mark and Ellie. It was like they were about to be grandparents. It was amazing to Beth. She knew that this child was already extremely loved.

After stopping at the church, she and Johnny headed home. He helped her try to organize some of the baby things. She finally figured out how she wanted to arrange everything so she could almost partition off a spot for the baby. The crib, changing table, and a small dresser she had to get to fit all the baby clothes were where the couch and lounge chair used to be. She had found some cute curtains that matched the style of the apartment at the same antique store that she had bought Ellie's tea set for Christmas, which could be pulled closed if she wanted them to be over the baby's area, but mostly they had helped to just partition off the room.

The small dining table was now out in the shed in the backyard, and the couch was where the table used to rest. She rarely used the dining table anyway since she spent the majority of her time in the house, but even when she did sit in her apartment it was more comfortable to sit on the couch and eat than at the table. Plus, she never really ate in there anyway. Most of the time she was with the rest of the family. She only ate in her apartment when no one was home and she was too bothered to take the few steps through the mudroom into the kitchen. Although, she really only kept juice and some granola bars and fruit in her apartment—and fruit only because she grabbed it from the basket in the kitchen on her way through to her apartment.

At the baby shower she received loads more clothes and blankets, as well as a stroller and a baby carrier. The only gift that she received that was more for herself than for the baby were some canvas boards, as well as an easel and paints—from Johnny. He told her that he wanted to see her paint. She always talked about how much she missed painting when she was working in the flower shop because the one thing she loved to paint were flowers. It was a truly touching gift, very thoughtful. She couldn't wait to paint again. She told herself that the first thing she painted would be a gift for the Harris's, family she never asked for, but a family who had given her more than she could ever ask for and who loved her unconditionally.

She put the paint materials outside in the space between the entrance to the apartment and the washer and dryer. The mudroom was becoming her own storage area. She wasn't so sure how Mark and Ellie felt about that, but they hadn't said anything yet. Beth was more and more amazed at how much stuff one little tiny human needed.

Walking back into the apartment after putting the painting materials outside, she paused in the doorway. Johnny was thumbing through the Bible that had been left out on the couch—his Bible. His back was to her, so she couldn't see his face. After a minute he put it back down where he had found it and went back to folding blankets and putting them away in the drawers under the changing table. He didn't say anything about finding his Bible in her room, and she didn't bring it up.

———

Two weeks later, Beth was sitting uncomfortably in church next to the Harris's. It was Easter Sunday, and although she was thoroughly enjoying listening to the wonderful songs of praise surrounding her, she just couldn't sit still. She couldn't get comfortable—and hadn't been for a while. It was the second of April, four days past her due date, and still no baby. She had gone to see the doctor two days ago, and she had said that it still could be another few days. Beth was ready for this baby to come out. Too much longer and they would have to induce.

She glanced over at Johnny, who was standing and singing with his palms up, his eyes closed tightly and a small smile on his face. He was singing with all his heart. Everyone was standing around her and singing their hearts out. She was the only one sitting, only because she had stood throughout the first few songs and her feet started to hurt. She couldn't see the words that were flashed onto the screen in the front anymore, not with everyone standing around her. Instead of singing along, she listened to the voices of everyone harmonizing together as they sang for joy on this resurrection day. She had sung the first few songs, and could feel this yearning in her heart, this yearning to understand the joy of those around her. She felt like she was inches away from grasping this peace and joy that was clearly evident in everyone else, but she didn't know how to reach for it.

She listened as the pastor talked all about this joyous day, the resurrection of Jesus, and how He is still alive today and that all who call on His name will also be resurrected from the dead as well. Beth was soaking up his words. She had continued reading Johnny's Bible straight through. She had read all four Gospel accounts a month or so ago, and had read all about the resurrection of Jesus. Since then she had been reading all the New Testament letters and they were all filled with this hope, hope in the resurrection of the risen Christ. It was a hope she yearned for, yet didn't completely understand. She had read over and over again that Christ died so that she may live, so how did she grasp that hope that was so often talked about?

After the church service the family all relaxed back at the house. Ellie cooked a wonderful dinner, and they had fun just being in each other's company. Beth, Crystal, and Ellie went for a walk after dinner at Beth's insistence. Everyone told her to just lie down and relax, but Beth wanted to stretch her legs. She hoped that the exercise would make the baby come—Doctor Abernathy had even suggested it. She was so ready to have this baby. She had truly loved being pregnant, at least once she made peace with the fact that she was going to have a baby. She had loved watching her stomach grow, of feeling the baby move and kick inside her. But she was ready for the little girl inside of her to get out. Beth wanted to meet her!

Although she had forced Crystal and Ellie to go walking with her, she had been happy to get home at the end of their stroll. She put her pajamas on—a pair of sweat pants and the t-shirt of Johnny's that she had found waded up in the back of a drawer when she had moved in. It was one of the only things that felt comfortable for her to wear, even though it had started feeling tight a few weeks ago. She watched a movie with the rest of the family, going to bed like the rest of them when it was over, although she wasn't tired.

That night, Beth lay awake yet again, not able to relax. She was thinking about resurrection, trying to remember everything the pastor had said as he talked about new life.

She reached over and turned on the light next to her bed, reaching for Johnny's Bible. She was getting so near to the end.

Beth started reading the book of Titus and came to a halt in chapter three. Johnny had underlined verses 3-7, as well as bracketed them off. Usually when he did that, there was a note in the margin, but this time there was just one word next to the verses, "Beth."

"What in the world?" she called out into her quiet room.

She tried her best to prop herself up some more. Ellie had brought in some extra pillows to try to help Beth be more comfortable, and she used them now to get into a full, upright sitting position.

Beth stared at the text in startled surprise. She didn't know what to make of it. She flipped through Johnny's Bible, glancing at all the underlined verses throughout the entire thing. She had read almost the entire Bible, and had read everything he had written in it as well. He hadn't ever written anyone's name next to any of the verses. There were lots of notes, some on what the passage said, some reminders, and even some prayers. But no names, except for hers.

Flipping back to Titus, she stared at it again. It was a short book, and although he had underlined other parts of it, her name was the only note he had next to any of the verses. As far as she knew, he didn't know any other Beth's. What in the world had compelled him to write her name, to think of her, as he read his Bible?

Holding the book up closer to her face, Beth read the verses that he had underlined. She closed her eyes and tried to let them sink in, but opened them again quickly, wanting to read them over again.

Whispering into the silence of the night, Beth read. " 'At one time we too were foolish, disobedient, deceived and enslaved by all kinds of passions and pleasures.' " Yes, that part certainly seemed to apply to her. She had been all of those things, foolish, disobedient, deceived, and enslaved. She had deceived others as well as herself, had enslaved others as well as herself.

She kept reading aloud. " 'We lived in malice and envy, being hated and hating one another. But when the kindness and love of God our Savior appeared, he saved us, not because of righteous things we had done, but because of his mercy. He saved us through the washing of rebirth and renewal by the Holy Spirit, whom he poured out on us generously through Jesus Christ our Savior, so that, having been justified by his grace, we might become heirs having the hope of eternal life.' "

Beth read it a few more times out loud and then sank back into her pillows, a sense of relief like she couldn't explain washing over her. Somehow, those words explained everything she had been through, everything she had been and everything about who she wanted to become. She read those verses with a sense of relief, with a sense of hope.

Once again, Beth spoke out into the quiet night, but this time she spoke to God.

"I've been all of those things, God—You know more than anyone the horrible thoughts in my heart, the horrible things I've done. I've hurt so many people, have hated those who've only loved me, despising what they've had and wishing for more," she paused, wiping the tears that sprang to her eyes.

"You were there through it all, weren't You, God? You were loving me despite it all. You're the One who offered me a way out. You're the only One who can fix all the broken pieces within me. That's what I pray, God. Please, I ask You with all my heart to fix those broken pieces. Make me into the person that is described in these verses."

She was in disbelief of the words on the pages before her—in disbelief because they completely filled the yearning that had been in her heart for so long. Suddenly she understood that all of the good things that had come into her life over the past months had nothing to do with her—it was because of God's mercy. She had continually strived and failed to pick herself up, but she couldn't hold herself together. She was never meant to. Only God could hold her together. He was her hope. And in the darkest moments of her life, He was the only One who remained, covering her with His love. She could see that now.

"God, I pray for all of these things in these verses. I pray for the washing of rebirth and renewal by the Holy Spirit in my life. I pray that You would take all the broken areas of my life and make a new creation out of all of it. It was You who lifted me from the grave that I dug for myself, wasn't it? It was You all along offering me a way out, a chance at a new life. God, I want a new life, with all my heart I want a new life."

Beth was crying tears of joy. Suddenly, she completely understood the resurrection story—understood it because that's what she had been through in a way, her own kind of resurrection. God had taken her from the broken pit she had been in and taught her how to love and trust those around her, surrounding her with people that had been showing God's love to her through their very actions and words all along. He had brought her from death into a new life. And she felt new. She felt whole in a way that she couldn't ever remember feeling. And mostly she felt this hope, this hope beyond words that completely filled her heart.

Chapter Seventeen

Beth had finally fallen asleep the night before with a huge smile plastered on her face. She longed to tell everyone what she had read the night before, what she had gone through in her heart, but it had been late at night and she knew everyone was asleep. She had thought about calling Johnny, though. More than anyone, she wanted to tell him about the revelation she had made while reading the verses that he had somehow bracketed off just for her. She knew he would have come over from his apartment if she just asked, but she decided it could wait until morning.

When Beth awoke, she was surprised that she had slept in so late. It was after ten in the morning when she finally got up from bed. She normally was getting no more than three or four hours of sleep at night, being so uncomfortable. She was pleasantly surprised and felt refreshed. Not bothering to change out of her sweats, she walked through the mudroom to see if anyone was around. Mark was gone at work, and so was Ellie. Ellie left a note telling her to call if she needed anything. Beth knew she would be there in a heartbeat when she got the call that the baby was finally on the way, and she knew everyone was pretty much waiting for that call. Beth went upstairs to see if Crystal was awake. She had the week off for a school break and Beth figured she'd be sleeping in, but when she got upstairs she saw that Crystal's bed was made. She called out but was met with silence. Apparently, Beth had the house to herself.

Going back downstairs, she was a little sad that she couldn't share everything that she had gone through the night before, but nothing could dampen her mood. There was a euphoria in her every swollen step that she couldn't quell, and never wanted to.

Beth grabbed an apple from the bowl on the kitchen counter, and then went back through to her apartment to grab the Bible on her nightstand. She wanted to keep reading. She climbed back into her bed, ready to keep going.

From the main house she heard the front door open, and a moment later a voice call out, "Beth?" It was Johnny.

She got out of bed more quickly than she had thought possible, which surprised her since she was moving a lot slower these days, and yelled, "In here." She started walking toward the mudroom to greet him, apple in one hand, Bible in the other, when she froze. She looked down, feeling the trickle of liquid go down her legs. When she looked back up, Johnny was standing in the doorway with a shocked expression on his face.

"I think my water just broke," she said in disbelief. Sure, she had been ready for the baby to come all week, but now that it was actually happening she wasn't even sure what to do.

"Yea," Johnny said in response.

They stared at each other for a long moment, both clearly unsure of how to react, and then, as if on cue, both started moving at the same time. Johnny told her he was going to call his parents, and Beth went into the bathroom to change her pants. When she came back out, he was standing in the doorway again.

"Do you have a bag to take to the hospital or anything?"

"Huh?" she asked.

"You know, clothes and stuff? They do it in the movies!"

She laughed, a little hysteria behind it. This was really happening. "I didn't really think about it."

She and Johnny each grabbed a few things, neither of them noticing what they grabbed. Beth also grabbed a pillow from the bed, feeling pressure in her stomach that made her want to curl over, but Johnny reached for her and held her up. He led her through the house and straight to his car.

"My dad was in a meeting—I left a message for him," Johnny explained. "And Mom picked up, but she had to make some deliveries this morning while Crystal stayed in the shop. She said she just has to finish the ones she has left, then the two of them will come over. So I guess I'm taking you to the hospital," he explained, helping her into the seat. She was still wearing his t-shirt, not even feeling the cold air around her. "I called your doctor and she said she'd meet us there."

"Okay," she said, going along with anything that got her to the hospital.

Johnny ran to his side of the car while Beth squeezed the pillow across her chest. She lifted her hand and realized that she was still clutching Johnny's Bible. She must have picked it up again before they left.

"Do you feel okay? Are you in pain?" he asked in a slight panic as he backed the car out of the driveway.

She laughed. "I'm fine, Johnny. The contractions haven't really started much." Although as she said it, a pain seized her stomach. She pressed her lips together until it passed. It didn't last long, but she knew right then that labor would certainly not be fun. She had read enough about it beforehand to know that, but feeling it was a completely different thing. She had been experiencing a few contractions here and there for the past few days, but she could tell that this was different.

"Did you not have work today?" she asked him.

"I did," he said, "but I knew that you were alone in the house and I just wanted to check on you."

"Thanks," she said with a smile. "I actually really wanted to talk to you."

"Yea?"

She was about to explain why when he took a turn sharply and then stomped on the brakes to avoid a dog that had run out into the road.

"Whoa!" she cried out.

"Sorry," he said.

"It's not like the baby's going to come out right now. We have plenty of time—don't rush."

She took a few deep breaths. She didn't like the feeling of the car turning sharply. Not only was it uncomfortable because she was just completely uncomfortable to begin with, but it reminded her of another time when she was in a car and she felt that car losing control. She never wanted to repeat that situation. Beth had been careless about many things in her life, but the one thing that she took very seriously was driving.

Beth opted for silence as Johnny drove her to the hospital. He stood hovering close to her as they checked her in and filled out some forms. A nurse directed them to a room and helped Beth to a bed after she changed into a gown. She told her that Doctor Abernathy would be in to check her soon. She grimaced as they poked her with the IV, and set her up to the machines. There was a really awkward moment when the nurse left and she addressed Johnny and Beth as Mr. and Mrs. Monahan after a glance at some paperwork. Heat flooded Beth's cheeks when it was said, and she avoided eye contact with Johnny for a few minutes.

"So," Johnny said, trying to bypass the awkwardness, "are you ready to have a baby?"

Beth's face crumpled up in pain for a moment before she responded. "The actual having part—not so much. But I'm ready for what comes after." She was, she really truly was. She was young, and she was still figuring out her life. But Beth was ready to be a mother.

"I have something to tell you," Beth said, a smile on her face despite the fact that she was clearly not comfortable.

"Go for it," Johnny said, returning her smile. He walked over toward the window to reach for a chair, but Beth scooted over in her bed and patted at the narrow spot next to her. She wanted to be close to him, and she wanted to thank him from the bottom of her heart.

Johnny looked uncertain for a moment, an unreadable expression on his face, and then sat down next to her. She put her hand on his arm, and he wrapped it in his own.

"I wanted to thank you."

He looked confused. "For what?"

She grabbed his Bible from under the covers, which she had taken into bed with her, and placed it on her lap. He looked at it with surprise.

"For this," she responded. "Actually, maybe I should apologize first. I know it's yours and I probably should have given it to you a long time ago, when I first found it. But I'm really glad I kept it. So I'm sorry, but not that sorry."

He nodded, giving her a calculating look, partly amused. She was sure he was wondering where she was going with this.

"I've read it pretty much straight through," she told him, and she could tell that really took him by surprise. "And then I found this."

With her free hand, not wanting to let go of his, she opened to the passage in Titus.

He pressed his lips together, his cheeks slightly red, as if he were embarrassed.

"Why'd you put my name in here?" she asked him.

He looked to her. "It made me think of you," he replied slowly. "It was after the first night you agreed to have coffee with me and I was reading it, and I just felt this overwhelming need to pray for you right then, as I read those verses, so I did. And then every time I prayed for you since then those verses just kept coming back to me."

She felt like she was going to cry. She was touched. "You've been praying for me?"

His face melted into a smile. "Of course I've been praying for you," he stated in a husky voice, his hand giving hers a gentle squeeze.

She stared into his face for a long moment. "What made you keep coming after me?" she asked.

He took a deep breath, as if trying to search for the right words to say. "Honestly, I don't know," he said quietly. "I could just sense something about you. I just knew you needed me—or needed someone. That day when we met in the flower shop, I don't know. I just had this feeling about you, and then I saw you again later that night. Your brokenness was written all over your face, and I just wanted to help, to somehow be there for you."

She did start crying this time and buried her head in his shoulder. She squeezed his hand as another contraction rippled through her stomach and relaxed again when it was through.

She looked up at him when she regained control of herself. "I'm so glad it was you," she stated, "that it was you who reached out. You're the best person I know, Johnny Harris."

He smiled at her, his handsome face close. When she had first met him, she compared him to all the other guys she had known, all those she had been friends with and dated, and she knew that Johnny was different from all of them. He was a truly decent man, and she meant what she said. He was the best person she knew.

They smiled at each other, and it looked like Johnny was about to say something when a knock at the door produced Doctor Abernathy, who said she was coming in to check Beth. She gave Beth an apologetic look, like she had just interrupted something. Beth wasn't sure if she had just interrupted something.

Johnny left the room while Doctor Abernathy did the exam. Beth was so glad that she was the one who would be delivering her baby. She had felt so comfortable in Doctor Abernathy's hands after all of her appointments in the past months. She trusted her completely.

Doctor Abernathy asked Beth questions about her water breaking and how she was feeling. Her contractions were about 5-6 minutes apart, and after an exam, Beth learned that she was just over 3 centimeters dilated—she still had a ways to go.

After the exam, Johnny came back in, asking how everything went, coming over to sit down next to her on the bed again.

Beth opened the Bible back to Titus, which had been moved during the exam, and told him everything she had been thinking and feeling over the past months, how she had started calling out to God after reading about Ezekiel and the valley of the dry bones, of how she felt in the Easter service the day before, and what had happened to her heart last night when she had read those verses. He was nearly crying when she finished the story.

"I'm so happy for you," he told her.

She smiled, an excited smile, despite the fact that she was in a lot of pain. Labor was getting more uncomfortable by the second, but she didn't care. She was so happy that she could tell Johnny everything that was on her heart. He understood her, for some reason. He had seen her in her deepest brokenness, and instead of turning away, it only made him want to pull her out—it drew him closer.

He continued to sit beside her, not bothered at all whenever she squeezed his hand in pain. She was comforted by his side.

There was another knock at the door. Beth was expecting Doctor Abernathy again, but was surprised when Ellie and Crystal were the ones who came through. They had huge excited smiles on their faces, which turned to surprise at seeing Johnny sitting next to her in bed, on top of her covers, holding her hand.

Chapter Eighteen

Johnny sat up quickly and got off the bed, standing next to Beth instead, although he didn't let go of her hand.

"How're you feeling, honey?" Ellie asked, coming up to the bed and stroking Beth's hair. Beth gave her a strained smile.

"I've felt better," she said honestly. Ellie grinned.

Johnny left to go under the pretense of getting an Italian ice cup for Beth while Crystal tried to entertain Beth with a story about a customer that morning. Doctor Abernathy came back in to check Beth again, and Crystal left the room, but Beth asked Ellie to stay. She could tell by the look on Ellie's face that it truly warmed her heart to have Beth ask her to stay.

She was progressing moderately, and Beth could feel it, too. Her body was in so much pain—it was utterly exhausting.

Mark came on his lunch break and throughout the afternoon, he, Johnny, Ellie, and Crystal all took turns trying to keep her spirits up as contraction after contraction seized her body. She tried to focus on what they were all saying, appreciating their company. She wished beyond belief that her mother could be there with her through the whole thing, but she was so grateful for Ellie. In so many ways, Ellie was fulfilling the role of the mother that Beth had lost, and Beth loved her for it. Elizabeth Monahan was irreplaceable, but that didn't mean that there wasn't room for other people like her in Beth's life.

Throughout the day, Beth explained to the entire family what she had told Johnny, about how she had read the passage in his Bible, which they all took a turn to look at and read, and how it had truly changed her life. She could tell that they were all simply delighted at the news. She couldn't keep the excitement over it within her and was so happy to share it with them. They were her family, after all.

Johnny didn't like to leave her side—Beth could tell. He only did it when Doctor Abernathy came to check on her, or the few times that Ellie made him leave to get something, or just so she could talk to Beth alone.

After what felt like the longest day of Beth's life, Doctor Abernathy finally proclaimed that it was time to have Beth start pushing. The baby was coming.

Ellie stayed with Beth, refusing to leave her side unless Beth asked her to, but there was no way that Beth was going to do this without her.

It was a long and exhausting delivery. Ellie held Beth's hand throughout the whole thing. But it was the most rewarding pain of Beth's life, especially when a tiny baby was placed into Beth's arms and she heard a wail of protest as this infant met the world for the first time.

Tears were streaming down Beth's face as she looked down at the little baby the doctor had just placed in her arms—she couldn't get them to stop. Her eyes didn't leave the baby even as the nurses took her to clean her off and weigh her.

"Congratulations," Doctor Abernathy said, "you have a beautiful, healthy baby girl, six pounds, two ounces."

Beth looked up at Ellie, who was crying just as much as Beth was. She kissed Beth on the forehead.

"You did beautifully," she told her, taking Beth's hand and giving it a squeeze.

Eventually a little baby swaddled in warm blankets was placed once again into Beth's anxious arms. She looked down at the precious face of her baby, instantly in love. She was perfect—absolutely perfect. Beth's breath caught as the baby let out a little yawn and opened her eyes. She blinked a few times before her eyes steadied on Beth's face. Beth's heart swelled. She had been through so much over the past two and a half years, had made so many mistakes. Of course she had regrets, but she wouldn't ever take them back now. All the pain, all the mess, was worth it for the little baby in her arms. She couldn't believe that after everything she had been through, after all the hurt she had caused others, that she received this little blessing despite it all. Now she knew what Johnny meant about everyone being unworthy.

"She's absolutely precious," Ellie crooned from above her.

"Yes she is," Beth agreed, not taking her eyes off of her daughter.

"What are you going to call her?" the doctor asked, cleaning up around her.

Beth looked up at the doctor and then back down at the baby. She hadn't had a name picked out beforehand. She had thought through tons of them, but nothing had felt like it was the right name. She hadn't expected to have the perfect name simply come to her after seeing the baby's face—she and Johnny had once even joked about it. But suddenly, she had the perfect name. It just came to her. She told Doctor Abernathy and then looked at Ellie to see what she thought. If anything, she had more tears in her eyes.

After a time Beth was able to clean herself up a bit, but she hated to take her eyes off her little girl for long. The nurses brought her to a different room with fresh bedding, and Beth once again cradled her daughter, feeling refreshed after a shower.

"How would you feel about me bringing some visitors in?" Ellie asked. She still hadn't left Beth's side, aside from when Beth took the quickest shower she could manage. "I know there are some people in the waiting room who would be very anxious to see you—both of you."

Beth smiled. "Please, bring them in."

Ellie left the room. Beth could hear everyone coming back before she saw them. She heard Crystal's excited squeal in the hallway, and suddenly the door burst open and there she was. Crystal ran right up to the bed.

"Oh my goodness! She's adorable!" she yelled.

Beth looked at her and smiled.

Mark, Ellie, and Johnny came into the room, all of them coming up close to the bed.

"She really is beautiful," Mark said, a catch in his throat. Beth looked at Ellie and saw her radiant smile.

When Beth looked at Johnny, her heart seemed to melt. He glanced from the baby to Beth, tears swimming in his eyes. The smile she was getting used to—the one she only saw when he was looking at her, crossed his face. He didn't say anything. He didn't have to.

"What'd you name her?" Crystal asked. "Crystal, right?"

Beth smiled wide, not taking her eyes from Johnny's as she answered. "Eden," she said. "Eden Elizabeth."

"Paradise," Johnny whispered.

Beth nodded her head. It was the perfect name. Eden was the blessing that came out of Beth's disastrous past, one that she didn't deserve. She had read in Johnny's Bible of God's love for His people. From the very first page she read of how He created the world, of how He created man in His image. They messed up, but even so, He offered them a solution, a way back into a relationship with Him. She read all about the nation of Israel, at times frustrated with their unfaithfulness although able to relate to it at the same time, but God always proved Himself faithful and always stood by His people, preparing a way out of death and destruction. He was always there waiting for His people to turn back to Him, always watching over them and protecting them. And then He sent His Son to offer a way back into relationship with Himself, a way to know the Almighty God personally.

She had made her life a miserable wreck. She had fallen down into the pit that she had created, but He pulled her out of it. He brought her back from death and brought light to her darkness, offering her a way back to life. He had taken all of her broken pieces and put them back together again into a completely new creation. None of it had anything to do with her. She was in a relationship with God despite herself. But He loved her enough to bring her into His loving arms, sustaining her when she was lost. He offered her a way back to life, and He gave her a beautiful little baby as an expression of His wonderful love, of His beauty.

"That's such a pretty name!" Crystal exclaimed. Beth was glad she agreed. It was so absolutely perfect. "Eden! Aw, I just love it!"

"Do you want to hold her?" Beth asked. She didn't even need to ask, she could see the yearning on Crystal's face.

She handed Eden over to Crystal and watched as this wonderful girl, who had truly become a sister to her, crooned over the baby.

"Does Elizabeth have a meaning?" Crystal wondered. "Or did you just pick it because it sounds good?"

"It was my mom's name," Beth told her. "And mine, too. It means 'consecrated to God.'" Beth glanced up at Ellie. "And it's your name as well, isn't it?"

Ellie's hand was resting over her heart, tears streaming down her face. "Yes, it is. Although I've been going by Ellie for as long as I can remember."

Beth smiled. "Well, it's for my mom and for you," she told her. Ellie wrapped her arms around Beth.

"Wow," Crystal said. "You've got quite the name, little one," she said to Eden, slowly swaying the baby in her arms.

"How do you feel?" Mark asked.

"Exhausted," Beth answered right away. It was beyond late, going on two in the morning. They had stayed with her the entire day, even waited patiently while she got cleaned up, and she was sure they were ready for a good night's sleep.

"I'm sure. We won't stay too long. You need your rest."

But they did stay for a while. Beth really didn't want them to leave. They didn't leave her side until everyone had a chance to hold Eden. And Ellie remained after the others left, ready to spend the night with Beth at the hospital. Beth was so grateful to have her there.

The nurse came in and talked Beth through the mechanics of breastfeeding. She had given a lot of thought to it beforehand, not sure if she wanted to go through with it or not, but she decided to give it a try. Eden didn't catch on at first, but the nurse brought her in again throughout the night, and eventually she caught on. It was the strangest, most beautiful feeling that Beth had ever felt—strange because it wasn't strange, but completely natural. It was crazy how instantaneous her love for this little baby came. In a matter of moments, little Eden completely changed Beth's life.

She was able to sleep after Eden was fed and changed, and handed to the nurse. The nurse took her to the nursery so that Beth could rest. She didn't like seeing the baby wheeled out of the room in a little bed, but she knew it wouldn't be long until she got to hold her again. She was a mother now. This was the beginning of the rest of her life.

———

Caring for a baby was the most glorious, most humbling experience that Beth had ever been through. She was released from the hospital a day after Eden was born, her tiny little daughter entrusted completely into Beth's care.

Beth had learned so much in the first week.

First of all, she was extremely grateful that the Harris's were around. They were completely enamored with Eden, just as Beth was. She was always in someone's arms, loved by everyone around her. Although Beth cherished all the moments she got to spend with Eden alone. It was extremely tiring being roused from sleep night after night to a wailing baby, but a part of her loved it. She loved the moments she spent with her baby feeding, the bond she felt to her. Eden relied on her completely and needed her for everything. It was the most humbling experience of Beth's life to have someone else need her so implicitly and who instinctively trusted her completely. And she had to be everything for Eden. She loved it.

After two weeks, a routine was starting to develop more easily of when Eden was sleeping and eating, making things a little easier on Beth. She felt exhausted most of the time, but she didn't care.

After three weeks Beth was starting to feel more rested, overall, and feeling much more confident in her abilities to take care of Eden. Ellie had taken off work the rest of the week after the baby had been brought home and stayed with Beth, but everyone went back to their lives after that. Her first week alone was nerve wracking. She wanted to make sure she was doing everything right. But then she came to a point when she didn't worry so much about doing everything right. She was simply enjoying her baby, and enjoying being a mother.

Ellie still popped in every day around lunch time, and her schedule was a little more flexible since one of the older women from church was helping out at the store until Beth was able to come back, so she was still around from time to time, but Beth was doing fine on her own.

"Beth?" Johnny's voice called out, coming into the house.

"Over here!" she yelled. She was folding laundry. It amazed her how many clothes a little baby could go through, especially one so tiny. But Beth was determined to stay on top of everything as best she could.

Johnny came through the open mudroom and smiled at her when he walked into the door of the apartment.

"How're you doing?" he asked.

"Good," she said. "Just trying to be productive."

"You want some help with that?"

He didn't wait for her answer, but took the laundry basket from her hands and started folding everything in it. She took the folded pieces from him and put them away.

"Is the little princess sleeping?" Johnny asked.

"Yes, and please don't wake her!" Beth pleaded. Crystal had come in from school the other day and had woken Eden up, and it had taken such a long time to get her to go back to sleep. She wanted to keep Eden to a schedule as much as possible, and so far she seemed to be cooperating. Beth didn't want to mess it up.

"Don't worry," Johnny said. "I wouldn't dream of it." Although, he couldn't stop himself from going behind the curtain closed around the crib and sneaking a peek at Eden, leaning down to kiss her forehead. "I've never seen a prettier baby," he told her.

Beth smiled. "She's gorgeous, I know. I can't deny it."

Eden was born with a full head of dark hair, just like Beth's. Her eyes were blue and bright. She appeared to have Beth's nose as well. Beth wished she could see a picture of herself as a baby. She wanted to compare the two. She had a feeling Eden had much more of Beth in her than Tyler, for which Beth was really grateful. She hadn't even given much thought to Tyler at all. He wasn't apart of who Eden was at all. Sure, he may have provided half the DNA, but that was the extent. And that's the only thing that Beth would ever thank Tyler for.

"What are you doing over here on a Wednesday afternoon?" she asked him. They headed through the mudroom to the kitchen to make some lunch, Beth switching on the baby monitor on the kitchen counter.

"It's my lunch break—I have to head back to the office soon, but I came across something on my desk at work that I had forgotten about." He walked over to his jacket and picked an envelope up with his name written on it in Beth's handwriting. She smiled wide.

"Woohoo!" she shouted, then clamped her hand over her mouth, glancing toward the door leading to her apartment. Although she realized she was being unnecessarily quiet as Eden slept through pretty much anything anyway.

Johnny grimaced. "I figured I couldn't let it go to waste."

"You're going to let me take you skiing?" she asked, her eyes bright with excitement.

"If you promise not to kill me."

She rolled her eyes. "Why are you so terrified?

He gave her an exasperated look. "Have you seen those mountains?" he asked, gesturing through the wall as if they were really at the base.

"You mean the beautiful Sierra Mountains that you can't miss the second you look out the door? Yea, they're gorgeous. They remind me of home," she said cheerfully.

"They're huge."

"They look awesome to me. Where's your sense of adventure?"

Johnny smirked. "I'll go with you, okay? If you're up for it. But you might have to supply the adventure part."

"Deal," she said, holding out her hand, glad that winter seemed to be persisting throughout April. He took it and gave her a firm shake. "When do you want to go?"

"I can't this weekend, but maybe the next as long as the snow holds out?" he asked. "So a week and a half."

"I'm there," she stated, right away. Her body was yearning to hit the slopes just at the mention of it. She could feel it. She had no idea of how much she should be exerting herself after just having a baby, but she felt fine. It had been a full three weeks already and she was still walking everyday. After dinner she took a long walk, and had even started jogging again. Ellie was always more than happy to have a moment alone with Eden. Being active made Beth feel good inside. The thought of skiing made her feel euphoric.

She smiled widely at Johnny, dreaming about fresh powder beneath her skis. It had been much too long.

She walked over to him and jokingly roughed up his hair. "We're going to go skiing!" she yelled, and he laughed at her.

He narrowed his eyes on her. "I hope you can teach well. You better not take me up that chair lift and just set me off on top of the mountain and expect me to figure out my way down."

She smirked at him. "It could be a good learning tactic," she stated.

He gave her a look of dread.

"Relax, I'll start you on the bunny hill. It will be fun."

"Right," he replied. "Fun."

Chapter Nineteen

True to his word, a week and a half later, Johnny came over to the house early in the morning to pick Beth up for their skiing adventure. Crystal and Ellie were thrilled at the chance to have Eden to themselves for the entire day, and there wasn't anyone else that she could fully trust her with and not worry, although she still felt nervous being away from her for so long. Beth couldn't believe how much Eden had changed in the past five weeks. She couldn't believe that Eden was already over a month old.

She had to borrow some of Crystal's winter clothes, not having any of her own. But she was so excited she hadn't been able to sit still for the past few days. She only got more bouncy as Johnny parked the car near the slopes, her qualms about leaving Eden for an entire day completely gone.

They got everything they needed—lift tickets, and rental skis. They were good skis for rentals, although Beth missed hers at home. She had loved her skis. They had fit her so perfectly. But she didn't care what was under her feet at the moment. She just wanted them to make contact with the snow, and she would be happy.

While Johnny put his ski boots on, Beth studied the trail map. They had been informed as they were picking up their rentals that due to the lateness of the season and the weather starting to warm up, that some the trails were now closed, but not enough to stop them from making a day of it. She thoroughly hoped that he enjoyed skiing.

She had skied this mountain as a child, but it had been years. It was refreshing to try a mountain she was unfamiliar with. She knew Holy Cross like the back of her hand. A part of that made her love it all the more. She knew all the ins and outs, and had even explored, making trails of her own where she could. She had been elated when her dad had new trails added during the summer she turned twelve. But it was always fun to try something new.

"You ready?" she asked with a big smile.

He swallowed hard. "You promise not to kill me?"

She rolled her eyes. "I'll do everything in my power to keep you alive."

He nodded. "Okay then. Guess I can't ask for much more than that."

Johnny had a hard time picking up his skis and poles at first, holding them correctly so that they stuck together. It was second nature to Beth. She led him to the bunny hill—the small and easy slope set aside for beginners just like Johnny. He looked nervous as he stepped into his skis after watching her do the same thing. There were lots of younger kids in ski school milling about.

"You're going to go easy on me, right?" he asked.

"Sure," she replied, a mischievous dazzle in her eyes. She fully intended to get him to go down at least one real slope by the end of the day. It was her own personal goal.

He caught her eye. "I mean it."

"Johnny, I was teaching four and five year olds how to ski when I was only in high school. I got my first pair of skis when I was one and could barely walk. Don't worry."

She tried not to laugh at Johnny as his nervousness clearly showed. But he was being a good sport. She knew that he was doing this for her, but she really wanted him to enjoy it. If he grew to enjoy skiing, it could be something that they do together in the future.

He made it to the top of the bunny hill without any mishaps, and she snapped into ski instructor mode. Even after all this time, she was learned and rehearsed in how she conducted learning sessions, although she was able to have a little more fun with Johnny than she did with the kids she taught—at least she could tease him more.

Johnny did really well his first time down the slope. He only got better as the day wore on. He had fallen a few times, mostly when he made himself nervous or someone got too close to him, but he always got right back up. He was so endearingly terrified that Beth couldn't help but smile. Overall, it seemed like he was having fun.

She taught him everything she taught her students in multiple lessons in just the first few hours. She taught him how to bend his legs right, how to make a pie-shape with his skis to slow down. She showed him how his poles were used to aid him in skiing—not as a balance support as he had originally tried to use them. She didn't even let him use them his first few runs down the hill. Beth even showed him how to parallel his skis so he could see what it was like when he got a little more experienced, although it was kind of hard to show on the tame bunny hill, especially as the snow became more mushy on this mild day. But he was doing great. He had a lot of natural talent.

Beth didn't care that she'd only been going up and down the bunny hill. She was having so much fun simply having her feet in a pair of skis. She watched as Johnny went down the hill again. She stayed at the top this time, encouraging him from behind.

"Excuse me, are you an instructor?" a man asked, approaching her on skis, leaving a small ski school of young kids behind with the two other instructors with him. He was wearing the same light jacket that many of the other instructors wore who worked on the mountain.

"Uh, I used to be," she said, surprised. "I'm just trying to help a friend out."

"But you've done it professionally?" he wondered.

Beth's eyes narrowed. "Yes."

He smiled. "I've been watching you instruct your friend for the past hour that we've been out here. You're really good at it."

"Thanks," she replied, not sure if she should feel embarrassed or flattered.

"I'm Todd Carter," he stated, holding out his gloved hand for Beth to shake. He laughed and took his glove off then offered her his hand again. She shook it, not even wearing gloves on this mild day. "I'm one of the managers of the ski school here."

Beth's eyes widened in surprise. "Really?" She hadn't expected that response. It was always interesting to talk to other ski instructors, compare experience. She was good at talking snow.

"Did you work around here?" he asked her.

"Colorado," she answered.

"How long did you teach?" he wondered.

"All throughout high school, and then when I was home on school breaks."

His eyebrows raised in surprise.

"You taught ski school when you were only in high school?"

"Well, I was always with another instructor, but yea. Mostly kids."

"Wow," he stated, impressed. "Which mountain?"

Beth exhaled slowly. "Holy Cross."

He smiled. "I've skied there many times myself—great place."

She grinned widely. "I'd have to agree."

"You grow up there?"

"Yea—practically had the slopes right in my backyard." She literally did have the slopes right in her backyard.

"Awesome," he stated, as if it was his dream. She nodded in agreement. "I think that's one of the only family operated ski resorts left, am I right?"

Beth pressed her lips together and tried not to smile. "That's what I've heard—yea." She hoped that her cheeks weren't bright red. They felt like they were.

Beth looked down the slope to see where Johnny was. He was heading back up the hill, and she could tell his gaze was fixed on her as she talked to this man.

"Are you visiting Tahoe?" Todd asked.

"I live here," Beth answered, looking back at him.

Todd smiled, as if that was exactly what he was hoping for her to say. She drew back from him a little, wondering why. Why had this guy come over to her? She had a lot of experience with guys seeking her out in the past, and none of them had turned out well. What did this Todd guy want?

"I know this may be a little forward, but would you be interested in teaching ski school here?"

Beth balked. "What?" That was the last thing she had expected him to say.

He laughed nervously. "I'm sure you have a job and everything. I know you said you used to teach, but we're expanding our staff at the moment, preparing for next season and everything, and we could always use more people—especially people with lots of experience, like you."

"Are you offering me a job?" Beth asked in shock.

"You'd have to interview and everything, but I can say from watching you that you're pretty much already in, if you want it."

"Are you kidding?" she asked. Johnny was slowly making his way over to the two of them. When he reached them, he glanced back and forth between Beth and Todd in confusion.

"Not at all. I know the ski season's basically over, but we're always planning ahead for next year."

Beth smiled widely. "I don't know what to say." Skiing everyday, and being paid to do it? It was like her dream come true again. Who knew the one thing she had blamed her father for making her do would be the one thing she had wished she had been doing all along? And now it was being offered to her once again.

"Tell me you'll think about it and give me a call."

He reached into the pocket of his pullover jacket and pulled out a card.

"Thanks," she said, taking it. She'd definitely think it over.

He nodded and glanced at Johnny. "You've got yourself a great teacher."

"Yea," Johnny agreed, confused.

Todd glanced at Beth again. "I didn't catch your name."

"Beth," she supplied right away.

"Nice to meet you, Beth."

"Nice to meet you, too."

She watched as Todd headed back toward the ski school, picking up with the other instructors right away. After a moment, she turned back to Johnny.

"What was that about?" he asked darkly, like he was hurt.

"That guy is one of the heads of the ski school here. I think he just offered me a job."

Johnny's expression changed upon learning what he told her. "Are you serious?"

"Yea," she stated, still amazed.

"What do you think?" he asked with a smile.

"Well, it would be starting next season."

"Yea," he replied, his smile widening.

"But I do love skiing—and teaching."

"Yea," he said yet again.

"And I have Eden to think about."

"I'm sure you could work it out somehow."

"What do you look so excited about?" Beth asked him.

Johnny gave her the smile, the smile that was only meant for her. "It means you'll be staying in Tahoe."

She glanced at him in surprise and without thinking, replied, "I never want to leave Tahoe."

Their gazes continued to lock for a moment, as if they were silently communicating to one another. Johnny kept smiling at her, and it was making her heart race. He was the one who turned away first, and she realized that she had been holding her breath. What had just happened? What had just passed between them?

"So what do you say?" Johnny asked, turning to look at her again, this time his teasing, boyish grin in place, with one side of his mouth pulled up slightly further than the other. "You going to make me get on one of those chair lift things?"

A different kind of shock flitted across her face. "Are you serious?"

"I think I can do it."

She put her poles up in the air and shouted excitedly. "Woohoo!"

They took the chair lift up half the mountain, to a set of easy slopes. They were more advanced than what Johnny had been doing down on the teaching hill, but nothing he couldn't handle, she was sure. The only moment of uncertainty for him was when she lifted the bar and they got off the chair lift. She told him not to think and just go for it. So much of skiing was instinctive.

Johnny did great, going down the bigger slopes. She stayed alongside him, encouraging him all the way. They took many, many runs, laughing and enjoying each other's company. She had switched out of her instructor role and was having so much fun skiing with her dear, dear friend.

They were about to take the chair lift back to the top when Johnny turned to her.

"I want to see what you can do," he stated, as they moved forward in the line and sat down, headed back up.

"What do you mean?"

"You're the ski expert—show me what you're made of."

"As much as I'd love to, I'm supposed to be taking it easy. I did just have a baby, in case you didn't notice."

"Oh believe me, I noticed."

She wasn't quite sure what he meant by that.

"One run. Do it for me."

"For you? How would that be for you?"

He smiled. "You did this whole day for me—do one run for yourself."

It took a few more minutes to talk her into it, but she agreed. He was able to ski down to the bottom of the mountain. She went with him, surprised that he chose an intermediate trail to take him to the bottom. He was slow on the bigger hills. She would ski down them and then wait at the bottom for him. But he made it down beautifully.

Johnny told her he would be waiting for her at the bottom of the trail. She chose a black diamond that would bring her out at the end of the same trail they just came down, so he could stay put.

Beth left him behind and got on the chair lift, feeling like maybe she shouldn't be exerting herself so much. Ellie had warned her to be careful, but also assured her that as long as she was careful, she would be fine. It took a while for a body to get back to normal after having a baby, but Beth was feeling better everyday. She had talked to Doctor Abernathy as well, and she seemed to think that Beth would be fine if she took it easy—it had been five weeks. And Beth was a bit of a daredevil when she wanted to be, anyway. And really, what was she to do? Her feet were in a pair of skis for the first time in far too long. It was a risk she was willing to take.

Getting off the chair lift, she skied to the top of the slope and looked down, feeling the yearning to just go for it in the pit of her stomach, so she did. Her thoughts fled from her head as she allowed her body to lead her, acting of its own accord as she moved with the skis—it was a motion her body would never forget. It was completely exhilarating—it felt like freedom.

She reached the bottom of the hill much too shortly, tears in her eyes, but it had been the run of a lifetime. She did feel free, free from her head to her toes. But it had nothing to do with skiing, although that did make her feel great. The freedom came from inside her, came from living a new life that had been washed clean by the blood of Christ.

Beth was a new creation, ready for whatever lay ahead. She just didn't know what that was yet.

Chapter Twenty

"Why is this so hard?" Beth said to herself, aloud.

"What's so hard?" Johnny asked from behind her. She turned, not realizing he had come into the shop. He was standing near the entrance, pushing the stroller back and forth, where Eden slept. They had been walking around, enjoying the gorgeous sun even though its warmth was fading as the season changed, when Beth had come upon a tiny little art shop that she had never noticed before. She couldn't help herself, she had to go in. And there was such a great selection of paints and oils.

"I'm trying to pick some colors. I want to paint the leaves as they change in your mom's backyard," she told him, thinking of the large trees that towered near the back of their property line. She was debating between the perfect yellow, but she knew that she could always change the color to fit her needs. But there were so many different shades, it blew her away.

Picking a yellow, she brought it to the counter and paid for the paint. Johnny had stepped out of the store ahead of her while she had a silent debate between the pros and cons of each shade. It wasn't exactly a debate that he was interested in.

"Did you get what you wanted?" he asked her when she came back out. She held up her little tube of paint and showed him, and he feigned interest in her find.

Beth had loved watching spring come upon Lake Tahoe. She had been a little sad to see winter go. It was her favorite season. But there was such a renewal to the land with the coming of spring. Everything seemed greener and brighter to her than it ever had before. And the flowers had come up, adding a different kind of cheeriness to this town that she loved. The world was full of rebirth, and it matched Beth's spirit. Her heart had undergone a kind of rebirth as well. She had seen God's handiwork all over the changing of the seasons. And spring had quickly turned to summer. May had flown by, as did the other summer months. Now October was upon them, the last days of summer fading weeks ago. It had been the greatest summer of Beth's life.

Beth and Johnny kept walking as he pushed the stroller, not quite on the main drag anymore, which was no longer filled with summer tourists. There was so much to do in Lake Tahoe in all seasons, kind of like Colorado. She missed her home so much sometimes. She missed summer there as well, all the hiking she used to do, or horseback riding, or even simply going for long walks. But she could do all of that in Lake Tahoe as well. The town was filled with tons of visitors coming to enjoy the mountains in the summer and the splendor of the lake. A friend of Johnny's had a boat, and she had gone out with him and his friends a few times and had gone into the frigid water. It had been gloriously refreshing.

"Did you ever call that ski instructor guy?" Johnny asked her.

Beth glanced at him as they kept walking. "Yea," she stated, surprised that he had brought it up, especially since she had just called the other day. She had finally decided after a lot of debate to give Todd a call about the position of a ski instructor for the next season. He had remembered her from the day she and Johnny had spent skiing and asked her to come in and interview for the job toward the end of the month. Everyone had to interview. So as fall was making its arrival, winter looming ahead, she was planning on interviewing for a position as a ski instructor. She only agreed to interview with him after having a long discussion with him on the phone about daycare, explaining her situation with Eden. She told him that she was only interested in working part-time because she wanted to remain working at the flower shop as well. Eden came with her to work everyday, brightening up the place even more. Eden had brightened up Beth's life.

Beth absolutely loved being a mom. She loved caring for her precious daughter. She was still amazed at how much her life had changed in just a matter of months. She was a completely different person. God had truly lifted her from the pit she had dug and brought her to a new place, a place she could have never imagined. He took her from the bottom of the well and placed her on top of the mountain. She couldn't stop praising her wonderful, merciful Savior. And her time of darkness had produced the most beautiful blessing Beth could ever imagine, Eden.

Beth delighted in everything that Eden did. She couldn't believe how fast she was growing. She had nearly cried the first time that Eden smiled at Beth when she had entered the room, smiling because she recognized her mother. Now she smiled at her all the time. She had rejoiced as Eden rolled herself over, and as she learned to hold herself up. She loved her baby, and she was such a happy little girl as well. She loved listening to the sound of Eden's laugh, or the sound of her feeding, or even her deep breathing as she slept. At six months, she was truly starting to show her own personality, and Beth loved it, embracing each change and growth. Eden had changed everything.

"I'm sure you'll get the job," Johnny said.

"I hope so." Beth loved the idea of teaching skiing again. It was almost ironic that she was practically being handed the job that she had resented having to do when she was younger. There was just one thing that stood in the way of her being thrilled over the possibility of this job—it wasn't at Mount of the Holy Cross. It wasn't her mountain.

Beth and Johnny walked back toward town. She loved the feel of the sun on her face and the breeze off the lake, blowing her hair off her shoulders, chilling her slightly. Her wavy hair had grown a lot since she had sheered it off when she had arrived in November. It was now many inches past her shoulders, growing quickly.

The two of them stopped for soft served ice cream in town, eating it as they continued on their way back to the house, although it wasn't quite warm enough for ice cream. Johnny was over all the time. Sometimes it seemed like he spent more time at the house then he did at his own place.

No one was home when they reached the house. As soon as they came in, Eden started to stir, giving a little cry of hunger. Beth took her from the stroller and brought her into to the apartment to feed her. After feeding her and changing her, Beth headed back out onto the back deck where Johnny was sitting on the wooden rocker loveseat. Beth set out a blanket in the soft sun for Eden to sit on and put some toys in front of her and then joined Johnny shaded by a big maple tree.

A bird started nibbling away at the bird feeder on the side of the deck, drawing Eden's attention. She started laughing joyfully at the sight of the bird, and as others chirped above it. Beth smiled at her delight.

"She's beautiful," Johnny said, looking at Eden.

"I know," Beth replied.

Everyone loved Eden. Mark and Ellie were like grandparents to her. Crystal loved whenever Beth asked her to watch the baby. And Johnny loved her most of all, with the exception of Beth, of course. He loved holding Eden as she fell asleep at night. He volunteered to change diapers. He loved going for walks with her and Beth. He loved playing with her and taking care of her. It was impossible not to love Eden.

Johnny got up off the chair and walked over to Eden, who waved her arms excitedly as he approached. Eden knew Johnny well. He picked her up and brought her over to where he and Beth had been sitting. Eden sat on his lap, chewing on a toy.

Yes, Beth knew that Johnny loved Eden. She also knew that Johnny loved her. But what scared her the most was realizing how much she loved Johnny. She had been trying to define what she felt for him for months. He was the one person who had sought her out in her time of darkness. God had brought him into her life when she had needed someone most. He had taken her from the horrible situation she was in and brought her to his home, giving her the family of her dreams. And she had learned to love and to trust again. She had turned her life around. And he had been there through all of that, encouraging her and supporting her, praying for her. He had left his Bible behind, which ended up changing her life.

He confessed to her that he realized within the first week that he had forgotten it, but when he went into the apartment to take it he noticed the marker in it where she was reading and decided to leave it for her. He said he had a spare and had been doing just fine with it ever since.

Johnny had underlined verses that he had prayed specifically for her over and over, verses that had bridged the gap that had been getting narrower and narrower over the months between her and God. He had been there for her when she went into labor. He had been over to the house nearly everyday since Eden was born, except for the few times he had to go to San Francisco on business. And he adored Eden.

Beth suspected that she had started falling in love with him from early on. The fact that she had trusted him with her story, with her pain, showed her how much she truly did care about him. But seeing him with Eden only made her love him more. It terrified her. She had already received so much more than she could ever deserve. She knew she didn't deserve for Johnny to love her. Yes, she had changed a lot over the months, especially since Eden was born, but she still felt that Johnny deserved someone better than her, someone who didn't have a past like hers, or a child by another man. All of that didn't mean that she didn't love him, however.

Beth was in love with Johnny. She loved his entire family. She loved the town she was living in, but sometimes she had the feeling that it couldn't last, like it was too good to be true. She knew it couldn't last forever.

———

"Elizabeth Monahan?" called a tall broad-shouldered man, stepping into the front room of the small alpine office building. It was Todd Carter, the guy she had met on the ski slope with Johnny. He had been in full ski attire that day so she didn't really remember what he looked like.

"Hi, Todd," she stated, meeting his offered hand. "Just call me Beth."

"Right, Beth. If you'll just follow me back to my desk, we can talk more comfortably," he stated.

Beth walked behind him past rows of cubicles, stopping at the doors to a small office. It all felt so familiar, it made her heart race. He closed the door behind her once she stepped in.

It was the last week of October, and ski season was rapidly approaching—could begin in a matter of days if a storm came through. She yearned for this job in a way that hurt.

"Take a seat," he offered, gesturing toward a set of chairs placed in front of his desk. She did as he said, glancing nervously around the office. She felt the stirring of something in her heart and she didn't know what it was.

"So, Beth," Todd began. "I've glanced over your application. I'm impressed with the amount of experience you've had for someone so young. I know you said that you were teaching in high school, but this is seriously impressive."

Beth smiled, hoping that her amount of experience would work in her favor, and also that it would help him overlook the fact that she didn't actually put any references down from Holy Cross.

"Most twenty-three year olds who come to us haven't taught at all before."

"I guess that's what happens when you grow up in the mountains," Beth stated. "I've been skiing all my life."

"In Colorado," Todd supplied for her, glancing down at her application.

"Yes, in Colorado."

He looked down at her application again like he was unsure of something. "Monahan. Monahan. Why does that name sound familiar to me?" Todd asked himself, and she pressed her lips tightly together, her jaw clenched.

She could tell when the moment of comprehension crossed his face. He glanced down at her application, as if to double check the location of her past experience as a ski instructor, not to mention her name, before he looked at her in amazement.

"Are you related to Julian Monahan?"

Beth swallowed hard, feeling a lump in her throat, her heart giving a little pinch at the sound of her father's name.

"I'm his daughter," she stated quietly, her heart beating faster.

By the look on Todd's face, she could tell that he wasn't expecting her to be the daughter of the owner of Holy Cross Ski Resort, maybe just a distant relative—after all, her aunts and uncles and even her cousins were also in the business. He was looking at her like she was a celebrity or something. She should have known this would happen. Her father's name was well known to those heavily involved in the world of snow and mountains.

"And you want to work here," Todd asked her, amazed, "when you already have your own mountain?"

Beth was about to say yes when something in her throat caught. She couldn't get the word to come out, the one simple word, yes. This is what she wanted, wasn't it? To be able to teach skiing?

With a stunning force the realization hit her. Yes, that is what she wanted to do, but she didn't want to do it here. Beth dreamed of working on the slopes again, of living in a quaint little mountain town to raise her daughter in. True, she was already in one, but not the one she saw in her head.

Beth closed her eyes for a moment, pressing her hand to her throat and feeling her pulse racing. With her eyes closed she could see the outline of Mount of the Holy Cross like she had just been looking at it. It shocked her.

Beth stood up in alarm, and Todd gave her a puzzled look.

"Everything all right?" he asked.

She didn't know what to say, but suddenly she knew that taking this job, which she was sure would be offered to her, wasn't the right thing to do. It would be the easy way out, but she was never meant to travel the easy road, only the straight and narrow.

With a certainty that nearly knocked her off her feet Beth realized what she had to do.

"I...I mean..." She wasn't sure what to say. "I have to go," she stated and turned, pushing the door open ahead of her and practically running out of the office. She ran to Ellie's car and slammed the door shut, leaning her head back into the seat rest.

"You want me to go home, don't You?" she called out. She didn't even need to ask the question. She knew the answer before she asked it. God was calling her home.

Tears sprang to Beth's eyes, tears that came with knowing what would await her if she did go home. She had destroyed everything when she left. She had kicked her father out of her life, as good as proclaimed him dead to her. How could she go back now? After over three years had passed?

But, how could she not? Beth had never felt more certain of anything in her entire life. God wanted her to go home, to go home and apologize. She knew that it might not be accepted, but she had to offer it just the same. She knew that her father might never forgive her, that her sister certainly wouldn't—she certainly didn't deserve it, but she had to try. Beth had to go home and tell her father that she was sorry.

Pulling out of the parking lot, terrified yet resolved with what God was calling her to do, she realized with a deep pain from within her that going home would take her away from Johnny. But she thought that would be a good thing. She would never hope to have him.

Chapter Twenty-One

I t was a short drive back to the house, but by the time she arrived, everything was settled in her heart. Despite her fears, despite what awaited her, she knew that this was what she had to do. And it tore at her heart to think about what lay ahead, but she knew it was the right thing.

"Hey!" Crystal called out when she entered the house. She was sitting on the ground leaning up against the couch with Eden leaning against her chest, a TV program on quietly in the background. Crystal was holding a little book, which Eden was trying to put into her mouth. "Are you okay?" she asked, taking in Beth's face. "You look a little out of it. Did the interview not go so well?"

Beth came over and took a seat on one of the armchairs. Eden looked up and noticed her, smiling wildly, dropping the book that was becoming soggy with her drool and extending her hands, the signal for Beth to come get her. Beth got up and picked her up, sitting down again. Eden nuzzled her head near Beth's chest.

"Hey, I just fed you some cereal little girl!" Crystal called out. "You can't still be hungry!"

Beth pulled the blanket off the back of the chair and threw it over herself and started feeding Eden. Usually she went into her own apartment to feed her, feeling self-conscious, but she knew that Crystal was the only one home, having just gotten out of school. Mark and Ellie were both at work, and Johnny was in San Francisco.

"What's going on?" Crystal asked.

"I have to go home," Beth stated.

Shock flitted across Crystal's face. "Home, home? Like Colorado home?"

Beth nodded.

Crystal's eyes got huge. "Are you serious?"

Beth let out a heavy, pent up sigh. "Yea."

She peeked down at Eden, who instead of being hungry, had started to doze in Beth's arms. Beth pulled her shirt back down, throwing the blanket off of herself, glad to have it off. It was warm in the house.

"Why?" Crystal asked her.

Beth explained what had happened in the interview. When she was done, she was surprised by Crystal's response.

"That's awesome!" she yelled, standing up.

"Awesome?" Beth questioned with surprise.

Crystal sat down on the couch. "I think it's really admirable what you're doing—going home and apologizing. That takes a lot of courage, Beth."

Beth smiled weakly. "I just know that I have to do it."

"You're following God's call. That's an awesome thing to see."

Beth merely nodded in response, looking down at Eden's peaceful face. She wondered what her father's reaction would be to her having a child—that is, if he would even agree to see her at all.

"When are you going to go?"

"As soon as possible," Beth answered, afraid that if she didn't she would lose her nerve.

Crystal nodded her head. "Wow."

"Yea," Beth said with another heavy sigh. "Wow."

Beth had wanted to leave nearly the second she had understood that she really was supposed to go home all along, afraid if she didn't she would never be able to make herself go through with it. She had practically started packing right away. When Mark and Ellie got home that night from work, Beth once again explained that she had to go. They seemed just as thrilled as Crystal was that she was going home to try to offer her apologies. She was tempted to leave the very next day, but she didn't. She had to wait until Johnny got home from San Francisco. She couldn't leave without saying goodbye.

"I can't believe you're seven months old today," Beth said to Eden as she lifted her from her crib. It was the third of November. She couldn't believe how quickly the time had passed. She had nearly been in Lake Tahoe for a year.

Beth brought Eden into bed with her, enjoying the quiet as Eden woke up in her arms, wondering if she would eat this early. It was still dark, but she wanted to get away as soon as possible. It was a long drive to Colorado.

After changing Eden and dressing her for the day, Beth made sure the bed was made and all was tidied up. She had already gotten dressed before she pulled Eden from her crib. She put the baby in her car seat, where Eden fell happily back to sleep, clearly not hungry enough yet to stay awake. Beth was throwing her off her routine.

Beth walked through to the kitchen. Ellie was making coffee and Mark sat with the newspaper at the table, which must have just been delivered. Crystal was lying on the couch pretty much asleep, and Johnny was leaning against the front door with his arms crossed, like he wasn't going to let her out.

He had returned home in the afternoon the day before and had come right over to the house. She had waited four days to explain to him why she had to go home, and he listened as she told him what was on her heart. But he was the only one who saw through her, and they both knew it. Beth made it sound like it was going to be a quick trip to say she was sorry, and that's all that Ellie, Mark, and Crystal thought it was. And maybe that's all it really was going to be. Beth had no idea what was ahead of her. But she was determined to try, to stick it out and try as hard and as long as it took to make it clear that she was truly sorry for what she had done to her family, and to prove that she wasn't that person anymore. Johnny knew that she was saying goodbye for a while. He knew her too well. She was sure he knew how much she felt that she had to do this, but that there was also a tiny part of her that was running from him at the same time.

He went and got her bags from her apartment, bringing them out and placing them in his car. He offered to let her borrow it to drive home. Mark and Ellie agreed that it was a good idea. In the time being Johnny could just borrow one of their own cars, until Beth came back. Beth had already thought ahead. She planned on placing his car on the back of a truck that would deliver it to his doorstep.

It was a quiet morning. Everyone was still sleepy—they probably would go back to bed after Beth left, anyway. It was just after 6:00 in the morning by the time Beth had a light breakfast and was ready to go. It was extremely early. The sun was barely beginning to rise. But Beth was wide-awake.

Everyone walked her out. Johnny placed Eden into the car, her seat all rigged up in the backseat, after everyone had a chance to place a kiss on her forehead. She was still passed out completely, which was good. Beth hoped she would sleep for a while. She usually woke up around seven thirty in the morning, anyway.

After saying their goodbyes to the baby, everyone turned to Beth and gave her warm hugs and told her they'd be praying for her, wishing her well on her journey. Johnny was the last person to say goodbye to her. He had gone back into the house for something while Beth said her goodbyes to the rest of the family, thanking them for everything over the last year without making it too obvious that this could be goodbye for a while. But not forever—never forever. They were her family now as well, and Eden's. But she still had to try with the family she already had, that she had turned her back on. They were her family, too.

"You forgot this," Johnny said, holding out his leather bound Bible to her.

"It's yours," she answered.

Johnny placed it in her arms. "No, it's yours. It became yours the first moment you picked it up and started reading it."

Beth felt tears spring to her eyes, but she couldn't cry, not now. If she did, she might not stop. It was tearing her up to leave Lake Tahoe, to leave her new family behind. Especially Johnny. But she kept telling herself that there was a part of her that was leaving for him, as well, and she knew he knew that.

Beth took the Bible, knowing that he wouldn't take no for an answer. Plus, she liked the idea of having something of his with her. That, and the t-shirt of his that she had taken as well.

"Thank you," she said, placing it on the front seat of the car.

They stared at one another for a moment, both having so much to say, but neither saying anything. Before she did something she'd regret, like tell him she loved him, Beth quickly stood on her toes and planted a quick kiss on his cheek, then walked swiftly to the driver's seat and climbed in. She glanced back at Eden, who was still sleeping, and then back out at the family gathered in front of the house.

"Bye!" Beth yelled out. "Please pray for me! I love you all!" There, she said she loved him without saying she loved him. With that, Beth reversed out of the driveway and set off. Mark had let her borrow his portable GPS navigational system, which was programmed for her pit stop for the night just outside of Salt Lake City. He had also programmed it for home. Her home. Mount of the Holy Cross.

"We're going home, Eden," she told her sleeping child. It was a long drive, nine hours or so for today. She knew it was ambitious of her to do it in two days, especially with a seven-month-old baby, but she was going to go for it as best she could. She'd stop if she had to, and she was sure there would be many stops to feed and change Eden, and just make sure she was all right. Yet Beth knew that there would be nothing stopping her from going home now, nothing but the tremor of fear within her that she was trying to suppress.

Beth got a good three hours into the drive before she made a stop to change Eden and feed her, as well as stretch her legs. She continued on like that throughout the day, stopping for lunch along the road. She praised God that she had such a happy, content baby. Eden gave no complaints to spending the day in the car. Beth played music softly, singing along occasionally, and praying every time she felt the stir of fear in her heart.

Beth just kept driving, talking to Eden when she was awake. Eden had always enjoyed riding in the car. Beth knew that it would probably be harder as she got older to travel with her in the car for so long. It was the perfect age for her to be doing this. Beth had anticipated it being much worse, especially since she was throwing Eden off her schedule. Eden was perfectly content chewing on the few toys that Beth had pulled out for her, or simply looking around. But she slept a lot of the way, lulled to sleep with the motion of the car. Beth knew it meant that it was probably going to mean a long night in the hotel, but she would deal with that later.

As Beth ventured east out of Salt Lake City, the mountains started to appear more closely together. She stopped for the night at the hotel Mark had arranged for her, having traveled nearly eleven hours with the stops she had to make. She checked in and carried as little into the room as she could, having to hold onto Eden as well. Eden seemed suspicious of her new surroundings, but she ate dinner peacefully and enjoyed playing in the bathtub. Beth was exhausted but didn't get that much sleep that night, as Eden stayed up until after midnight, having slept most of the day. She got a late start the next morning, but she was ready. Ready for what came next. Ready to go home. And she had never felt so terrified in her entire life, or so certain of what she had to do.

Beth packed everything back up and got Eden comfortable in the car again, and then she left. She kept going east, driving toward the mountains that continued to grow as she drove. It felt like a reprieve to her aching heart, seeing the Rocky Mountains come closer and closer. She hadn't seen them since she left home. She never realized how much she missed them, missed the familiarity of home. She let out a cry of relief when she crossed the border into Colorado, the number of butterflies instantly increasing in her stomach.

She stopped at the first rest stop once across the border to stretch her legs. She hadn't eaten since lunch, but her appetite was fleeing the closer she got to home. Eden, however, was pleased to enjoy an early dinner. It was cold in the mountains, especially since the sun had already set. Beth put a sweater and a jacket on Eden and sat her on a bench and drank in the scent of the mountains. They both needed some fresh mountain air. She could hear the noise of I-70 around her, but she didn't care. A big part of her was home already. It was the last part of the trip that would be the hardest.

Beth put Eden back into the car and pulled back out onto the highway. She was going to get there tonight, in a matter of hours. She couldn't believe it. She knew two days had been ambitious with Eden, but they were doing it. She wasn't even tired, even after all the driving she had already done. She had to go to the end. She knew that.

Beth drove into the darkness, enjoying the beauty around her. It wasn't completely dark. The tops of the mountains were covered in snow, even the area around the road at times when she was higher up. She was careful in the dark, fully aware that the weather and the roads this time of year could pose a perilous threat. But she knew inside her heart that she would reach home with no glitches.

Eden fell asleep soon after Beth had started out on the journey from their last pit stop, and awoke in the last twenty miles from Holy Cross.

"We're almost home, Eden," Beth said. "I hope you grow up loving the mountains as much as me."

When Beth saw it, tears started pouring out of her eyes. Her mountain. She could recognize it anywhere, even in the dark. She'd even seen it from a plane before. She was home.

Pulling into the town of Holy Cross was so surreal. A part of her felt like she had never left. At the same time she could see that a lot of changes had been made, a lot of new places opened up. It was going on seven o'clock when she entered town.

She pulled into the parking lot of the big grocery store shopping center to stand up, glancing up at her mountain, at all the familiar trails that she had skied down countless times. And high up in the hills were the blazing lights of Monahan Ranch.

Beth got back in the car when her eyes grazed over her home. The big cabin-style house looked out over town, and Beth could see the lights shining through the windows.

"There it is," she said to Eden, who just looked at her and smiled. It was all she needed to keep going forward.

It took all the strength within Beth to put the car back in drive and follow the familiar roads leading up into the hills. She was crawling by the time she came to the gates of Monahan Ranch, parking the car. She knew all she had to do was press the button and she could ask someone to open the gates, no longer knowing the key code herself, but Beth stopped. She turned the car off and opened the front door, staring at the last part of the drive, and the part of the house that was visible through the trees and the gate—which wasn't much. But she had made it. She was home. She only had to get past the gate. She didn't know how she was going to do it. She was terrified to walk over and press the button and deal with the consequences of every bad choice she had ever made.

Beth thought about getting a hotel room for the night in town. It had been a long day, and she had to get Eden out of the car. Maybe it would be a good idea to come back in the morning, in the light of day. It was dark, and it was cold outside, much colder than Lake Tahoe had been.

As Beth warred with her options, clutching the open door of the car, the gates opened before her. She stood there with shock on her face, figuring that someone must be pulling out. She would have to back up to let a car out. But she didn't hear a car approaching. Instead, she heard feet pounding into gravel, like they were running. Her heart started thudding loudly when around the corner of the drive her father came right toward her.

"Beth!" he called out when she was in view.

She pressed her lips together, feeling a sob deep within her trying to force its way out.

"Beth," he said more gently as he stood in front of his daughter, tears falling freely down his face. He smiled warmly at her and then pulled her into him, hugging her fiercely. "Beth," he said again as he held his daughter. Her name sounded like a sigh of relief.

Chapter Twenty-Two

Beth fell apart in her father's arms. She started sobbing, tears that she had held in for years. She cried for the pain that she had caused him. She cried for all that she had done in the past three years, all of the messes she had created. She cried for all the blessings she had received that she felt unworthy to possess.

Mostly she cried because she had forgotten how much she had missed her father, and she was heartbroken about what she had done to him.

"You're home," he said, stroking her hair.

Beth looked up at him, brushing tears from her face, not that it mattered. They weren't stopping. Her father gave her a tender smile. He looked just as she had remembered, but with a little more gray to his hair, a few more lines in his face. There was peace in his eyes, love pouring from them—a look she knew had always been there. It left her speechless.

"I've been waiting for you to come home," he told her.

"I can't...I'm not..." she choked on her words. She could barely see her father through the waterfall pouring from her eyes. "I'm sorry," she finally stated. "I'm so, so incredibly sorry."

He pulled her close again, his hand resting on the back of her head. She felt so warm and protected in her father's arms.

"I was horrible," she said against his chest, crying the words out. "What I did to you—it was horrible."

Her dad put his strong arms on her shoulders, putting a little bit of distance between them so he could see her face clearly.

"I messed everything up," she said. "I sinned against you. I sinned against God." Her transgressions were so huge she felt like they could swallow her whole. But she knew, she knew in her heart that God had forgiven her. And now He had sent her to make things right with her father.

Dad smiled tenderly at her, his hand cupping her cheek. "You came home."

Beth simply shook her head. "I'm not worthy of being here. I'm not worthy of being your daughter." Maybe she never had been. Maybe that was the point.

In the back of her head, she heard Johnny's voice telling her that no one was worthy. How right he was. No one was worthy of the blessings they received. Everyone did wrong. Everyone deserved punishment. But God offers everyone a way out of that because He loves His creation and made man in His own image. He offers them life and then blesses them on top of it.

"Elizabeth, I have been waiting for you to come home for three years."

She was shocked, although in some ways she knew she shouldn't be. Beth hadn't expected forgiveness to come easily, but she should have known that her father loved her just that much. She was angry at herself. She had never tried to see him clearly. He had already forgiven her a long time ago. He had probably forgiven her the moment she walked out of his office, the moment she had cut him out of her life. And he had been hoping that she would come back ever since.

"I've been praying for you to come home for three years," he added.

"I'm so sorry," she stated, over and over again. "I'm so, so sorry."

She knew he had forgiven her, but she didn't know if she could ever fully forgive herself for what she had done. Beth had known that she had disgraced him the moment she had walked out the door after demanding that he give her what she felt was her due, but she hadn't cared enough about how he felt at the time to go back. It had taken time to get her to the point of being able to realize her wrongs, but now she could see that this reconciliation had been a long time coming. Even so, it hadn't fully hit her until Eden was born, until Beth experienced the awesome wonder of connecting with a child, of falling in love with her baby in an instant. The bond that Beth felt with Eden was what she had taken from her father. It wasn't until she had felt that love for herself that she truly realized what she had taken away.

"My dear child," her father said, holding onto his baby girl once again, "welcome home."

Beth pulled away and looked up at him, shaking her head. "I've disgraced you! I left! How can you just welcome me home?" She knew she was yelling, but it was at herself, not her father. And she knew that he could see that.

Surprise flitted across his face, surprise that she should even ask the question.

"Love," was his simple answer.

Beth smiled through her tears, smiled as the weight on her chest seemed to lift as she realized that he really had forgiven her. He had never stopped loving her. He had never stopped waiting for her to come home. And she knew she was home. God had been working on healing her heart for a very long time, and now the real journey of healing was just beginning. And it would be beautiful.

He put his arm around her shoulder like he was going to lead her forward.

"Come on, Beth. Come inside."

He took a few steps forward, but stopped when Beth's feet stayed planted where they were. He turned to glance at her.

"I don't deserve ever being let into that house again. I don't deserve your forgiveness."

Dad merely smiled at her. "It's time to come home now."

Beth grinned, the cold breeze from the mountains drying the tears on her face. She couldn't help it. Happiness was swelling in her heart. She had been preparing to camp outside Monahan Ranch until her father would even agree to talk to her. But instead, he came to her. She hadn't been able to make the last steps back home, so he had come to her. He came to her with his arms wide open, having forgiven her a long time ago, and merely waiting for her to ask for it. He had been waiting for her to come home. It was a beautiful picture of love that sounded familiar to Beth, a love that paralleled everything that she had read in Johnny's Bible—her Bible. God's love letter to the world.

"Really?" she called out.

"Really," he stated firmly.

Beth nodded, taking a deep breath.

"I missed you," she said, barely above a whisper.

He grabbed her hands. "I missed you, too, Elizabeth." He took a good look at her. "You've grown up a lot, into a fine young woman."

She continued to gaze into his face. She knew that he didn't mean years, although she knew that she had probably changed a lot in the three years that she had been gone. But Beth knew he was talking about her heart, about how much she had grown. She had faced a lot of difficult things and had Someone fighting for her the entire time. And she had learned to let that One in to fight her battles for her. It had changed everything.

"You're beautiful," he stated, shaking his head at her. "You look just like your mother." His voice caught as he looked into her face. Beth couldn't believe what she had done, that she had caused this man pain. He had never been anything but the best father in the world, loving her unconditionally. She didn't deserve it, but she felt so blessed at having it. She was home, and she felt it in her heart. She felt true freedom, freedom that only comes with forgiveness.

"Let's go inside," he said again, his arm extended toward the house.

Beth took a deep breath and looked back at the car.

"Don't worry about your stuff," he said, as if that was what she was concerned about. "I'll have it taken care of."

Beth looked back at him, her heart beating a nervous tune. She was truly astounded by her father's continual love and forgiveness. She was amazed that she was being offered back into the home she had fled from. But she had no idea what he would say to the fact that his twenty-three year old baby girl had a baby girl of her own.

"Um…before we go in," Beth began, turning from him and walking to the back seat of the car. "I have someone you need to meet."

She caught his puzzled expression before she opened the door and reached in to unbuckle Eden from her seat, who happily grasped for Beth and freedom from the car, even if it was into the cold night. She smiled at Beth as Beth pulled her out of the seat. Eden had been a perfect angel all day. Beth was grateful that she had been such an easy traveler, although she had slept a lot of the day. Beth hoped she wasn't awake most of the night yet again.

Beth wrapped a blanket tightly around Eden as she turned back to look at her dad. Her breath caught as she took in the expression on his face. He was crying openly, unashamed, as sheer delight came over him as he looked at the baby in Beth's arms.

"I'm a grandfather?" he asked, walking toward the two of them. Eden glanced at him as he came close, ducking her head closer to Beth, and he smiled widely at her, and then looked up at Beth. The expression on his face made her want to weep, but she did her best to maintain control.

"This is Eden," she said, looking down at her daughter who was studying her grandfather as she held tightly to her mother. "Eden Elizabeth Monahan."

"Eden Elizabeth," he repeated, glancing down at her again. "Welcome home Eden Elizabeth." He put his arm around Beth's shoulder. "Welcome home, the both of you," he stated as he began walking them forward toward the house.

Beth felt a multitude of different things walking into the house that she had grown up in. Everything was nearly the same, just a few upgrades here and there. In some ways, she felt like she had never left. Pictures of her growing up were still where they had always been. She had never been forgotten in her time away, although she was sure that some would have wished she had been forgotten completely, her sister in particular. She didn't ask where Amy was; she couldn't form the words. But her father told her that Amy was gone for the day to the stables. Beth was nervous for her return.

Dad led her to the big open living room, with large windows on each side of the house overlooking the lights of the town below, and her mother's beautiful garden in the back, which at this time of year was just shrubs. Beth couldn't even see them now. It was too dark outside.

She sat down on the comfortable leather sofa, her father running to the kitchen to bring back something warm for her to drink. She could hear him rummaging in the kitchen. She didn't want him bending over backwards to get something for her, but he appeared in the living room a few minutes later with a whole tray of things for her to eat.

"Thanks," she said when he sat down, reaching for the big mug of tea he had poured for her, noting with a pang in her heart that it was in her favorite mug. It felt so soothing after the long day of driving. She had expected to be utterly exhausted after a ten-hour day in the car, but she had a second wind now.

"You're more than welcome," he responded, a smile never leaving his face.

They started talking, talking like there hadn't been a strain of three missing years in their relationship. As Beth held her darling daughter in her arms, who was curiously looking about yet content to sit with Beth, she talked about her life. She didn't give him all the details. There was a lot that didn't need to be said. But she told him that she had gone to Europe and then ended up in San Francisco, getting herself into a bit of a rough situation. She told him about Johnny and how he had befriended her for seemingly no reason. She told him about the Harris's and how they had been there to pick her up from her broken place and walk alongside her. She told him about reading Johnny's Bible, of the verses she had found. She told him about Eden, about what her name meant to Beth, about what Eden meant to Beth. She told him how much she loved being a mother. And she told him about interviewing for the ski position, about how she had fled from the office with the realization that it was time to come home.

When she was finished, there were tears in both their eyes. But Beth felt free. She knew her dad had forgiven her. She felt like the last of the chains that had been binding her had finally been released. Telling him what she had been through had been freeing for her as well. It was the first time she had ever talked to her father like this, and she certainly hoped it wouldn't be the last.

"Can I ask you something?" Dad asked when she was done with her tale.

"Of course, anything," Beth said, her feet extended on the ottoman, Eden sucking her finger.

"May I please hold my granddaughter?"

Beth smiled. "Absolutely." She shifted her weight and placed Eden into his arms, her grin only growing as she watched how her dad smiled down at her, as he began talking to her. Eden already had him wrapped around her finger. It certainly hadn't taken long. She loved seeing her dad holding her daughter, even if Eden was a little skeptical at first. It only took Dad making a few funny faces for Eden to produce a smile and feel comfortable.

"She looks just like you, you know," Dad said.

"You think so?" Beth asked. She couldn't deny that a lot of Beth's features had seemed to transfer to Eden.

"Definitely. How old is she?"

"Seven months, as of yesterday."

Beth continued to smile as her dad held Eden, listening to her nonsense talk and reaching for safe things for her to grasp. She was completely surprised when the doorbell rang. It was just after eight o'clock at night, but it was very dark out.

"Who could that be?" Beth asked. It was late for visitors.

"Why don't you go and answer the door and find out?"

Beth's eyes narrowed slightly. "You know who it is, don't you?"

He feigned innocence. "I have no idea what you're talking about," he stated. "I'm just admiring my granddaughter over here."

Beth rolled her eyes and got up with a sigh. Her heart picked up its pace as she walked toward the door, hearing a small cry of resistance now that Beth was out of Eden's sight. Her dad's forgiveness had given her so much freedom, but she knew that she hadn't just walked out on him when she left home. There were many others that she still needed to make her peace with.

Beth opened the big wooden door slowly, bracing herself for whatever awaited her. A huge smile spread across her face as she took in the shocked faces of the two people on the doorstep, a smile she couldn't contain inside her despite the knot of fear in the pit of her stomach. She wasn't expecting to be accepted by everyone.

"Beth?" Aunt Mary called out in disbelief, her hand pressed against her heart. A second later she had her arms around Beth, and was holding on as if she never wanted to let go.

It was another tearful reunion, and another one that completely surprised Beth. Uncle Don and Aunt Mary couldn't have been happier to see her, to have Beth come home. Aunt Mary held onto her for a long time as the two of them simply cried together, their tears conveying a multitude of things that didn't have to be said aloud. Then they came into the house and joined her dad, delighting in little Eden and both requesting chances to hold the baby, the three of them fighting over her. It stressed Eden out a little, being lovingly smothered by three strangers. Beth took her again and Eden settled contentedly in Beth's arms, giving her charming smile to the adults in the room now that she felt protected again.

Beth was surprised when more people continued to come. Her dad confessed that he had called the entire family while he left her in the living room when he went to get her something to eat. He had been so thrilled to have her back that he couldn't help but share the good news with everyone.

More of her aunts and uncles appeared from her dad's side of the family, as well as some workers from the ski resort—some that Beth knew, some that she didn't. Her family was happy to see her, none as happy as her father and Aunt Mary, however. She hadn't been as close to her father's family as she was with Mary. But it was a happy occasion. She was happy to see her family, and they seemed happy to see her, however shocked and confused they were at her reappearance, especially with a baby. Thankfully, they didn't ask too much, like they were wary of what she would say. Her father simply told everyone that Beth was home and that was a cause for celebration.

Beth was surprised how this party continued to go on even though it was late at night. She was amazed that so many people came over, although Monahan Ranch always had a reputation for throwing great parties. At ten o'clock someone fired up the grill in the backyard to make burgers like they planned to enjoy themselves all night.

Beth stayed inside as the party continued. It was fun being surrounded by the people that she loved, even though she hadn't ever shown it well in the past. She loved them just the same. But the party could continue on without her. It was more of a celebration for her father than anything else. She wanted an excuse to leave, as touched as she was by this display of love from so many.

Eden let out a little cry of frustration, which was just what she needed. Beth could use a moment alone, just to collect her thoughts for a moment. Beth took her from Mary's arms and carried her upstairs. She'd have to go out to the car eventually to get her things. Her father had driven it up to the front of the house for her. Eden would need to be changed after she had some milk, and Beth needed to put her in a pair of pajamas and get her to bed. After the stress of so many people, Beth knew Eden would sleep.

Her dad told her to go upstairs to her room, that it was ready and waiting for her. She ascended the stairs slowly, once again overcome with gratitude at how her father had welcomed her back with open arms. She couldn't believe she was home.

Beth walked to her closed bedroom door, standing in the doorway for a moment after she opened it, peering inside. It was dark, but the light of the moon was shining through the windows, illuminating the large space. She reached for the light and switched it on. The room was just as she had left it, although just a little bit tidier. For one thing, her bed was made, which never had been Beth's favorite thing to do in the past. Everything was in its place, but she was sure she hadn't left it quite that way. She loved it.

"I'm really home, Eden. We're both home."

Beth walked over and sat on her bed and began to feed Eden, enjoying a moment of tranquility with her daughter, the special closeness she always felt when Eden was feeding. Eden's eyes began to flutter a few moments later as she drank happily, sleep coming over her once again. Beth was sure she would sleep through the night now. She had felt bad about messing up her normal routine for the past two days, but after being admired by so many people down below, her little girl was utterly exhausted.

A knock on the door sounded, and a moment later Aunt Mary peeked her head through. "Mind if I come in?" she asked.

"Of course not," Beth said, turning a little bit for modesty's sake as Eden continued to drink lazily.

"I just wanted to see how you're doing," Mary said. "I'm sure you're a little overwhelmed."

Beth smiled at her. She felt exhausted more than anything else. Beth could use a good night's sleep. But instead, they talked for a bit, Beth opening up more to Mary than she had to her father. She knew that Mary could take it better than her father could. Beth loved Mary so much and had missed her tremendously over the years. She had been such a special person in Beth's life. She couldn't help but hate herself for leaving.

Eden had long since fallen asleep cradled in Beth's arms when Beth could hardly keep herself awake any longer. She handed Eden to Mary and went back downstairs, asking her to watch her for a few moments of which Mary was all too happy to oblige. She had to get Eden's bag out of the car so she could change her and dress her for bed and put her down. And her portable crib was also in the car, which Beth planned to set up next to her bed if she could find the strength to do so tonight.

She walked outside the front door into the cold night, walking straight toward Johnny's car. There were a few people out front sitting in the small courtyard off to the side of the house under the outdoor heaters, but no one bothered her as she ducked her head into the trunk and rummaged for the things she needed, placing things on the ground that she wanted to bring in as she decided what was important to take up now, and what could wait. She was so tired, so emotionally drained, that all she wanted to do was sleep.

Beth closed the trunk and reached for the things she had placed on the driveway at her feet. She turned to go back into the house when she stopped dead in her tracks.

Amy was home.

Chapter Twenty-Three

Amy had been having a great day. It was Friday, the end of the work week, but hers had ended early. She was loving this time of the year. The end of summer had meant that she had to get ready for the coming winter ski season, although the summer and fall had kept her occupied as well. The resort was still as busy as ever. Just because the summer and fall meant no skiing, it didn't mean that all the fun ended in this resort town and work was able to stop. No, there was still so much to do at the resort even without snow.

However even though the snow was beginning to fall, and it was getting cold enough to make it, she was still finding that balance in her life of doing her own things and having fun. She had been indulging in one of those things this very afternoon. She had gone over to the stables after having a quiet lunch with David in town. Her father had encouraged her to take the day away, especially since the wedding was getting closer and closer. He had taken the day off as well to enjoy a quiet day at home, which was surprising now that November was upon them. It was so refreshing for her to realize that she could actually have a life outside of work.

David hadn't come with her to the stables, although she had pleaded with him to spend the day with her. He did have to go back to work after lunch, however. Not everyone could take time off as the busy season approached. But once she pulled up to the familiar spot, she was content to be there by herself. She spent part of the afternoon helping the workers wash some of the horses, brushing them out when they were through. After a while she couldn't help herself, and she saddled up Belle and took her out into the mountains. Lots of tourists came and did horseback riding tours through the trails in the woods. She followed as a tour set out around dinnertime, but met up with some of the regular horse trainers out exercising some of the horses, and they took off further up the mountain, stopping to rest the horses on the top of one of the ski trails, admiring the town below in the autumn evening. She had forgotten how fun some of the workers could be when she could be their friend and didn't have to be their boss.

They didn't start coming down until the sun began descending, not wanting to be caught up in the mountains in the dark. It wasn't safe, especially when in the woods. Amy wasn't particularly comfortable up on the mountain at night—at least not when covered by the dense trees. The sounds made her nervous, as did the thought of all the animals that she could meet up with. Plus the fact that it was cold.

Their riding party got to the stables as the last rays of the sun disappeared. They put the horses in the stables for the night, making sure they had ample food and water, especially after their adventure, and Amy spontaneously decided to join them for dinner in town. She had a lot of fun getting more acquainted with those she worked with. They didn't leave the restaurant until they started closing up for the night.

Amy blasted the heat in her car as she drove up the long mountain road. It was a beautiful clear night, the moon shining brightly. She told herself that she'd have to go out onto her balcony when she got home and look up at the stars, however freezing it may be. Her dad was probably in bed already, anyway.

When Amy pulled off the road to the drive leading to the house, she could see that there were cars parked along the road. She reached for the opener to the gate, realizing that it was wide open as she got closer. There were even more cars parked in front of the house. The house was ablaze with light, and there were some people talking outside in the small courtyard. What in the world was going on?

Amy was unable to bring her car around toward the front, where she always parked. She stopped the car where she was able to find a spot to pull over out of the way. She got out and could hear laughter coming from the house.

"Hey, Amy!" someone shouted from the courtyard, waving to her as she walked closer to the house. She recognized him as Wesley, one of the full-time ski instructors. What was he doing at the house this time of night, and outside in the cold, no less?

"Hey!" she called back across the drive. "What's going on here?" she wondered, feeling a little silly for asking. After all, she did live here. She felt like she should know what was going on.

Wesley laughed. "Your dad's throwing a party."

"Why?"

"Don't you know?" he called out. "Your sister's home, safe and sound."

Amy stopped walking, shocked. Did she just imagine Wesley saying that Beth was home?

Before she had a chance to verify what he said, the front door of the house opened, and Beth herself came walking out. Amy took a deep breath, biting hard into her lip. Her sister walked to a car right in front of the house, opening the trunk and pulling some things out, setting them at her feet. Amy couldn't believe what she was seeing. Her sister was a mere thirty feet away from her. Amy had thought she would never see her again. And what was more, Beth was pulling things from a car—bags, like she intended to stay awhile.

A few minutes later, Beth closed the lid of the trunk and picked up the things at her feet. When she turned to go back to the house, she noticed Amy standing there and stopped walking, staring at Amy.

Beth couldn't be back. She just couldn't. This wasn't her home anymore. She had left them. She had forsaken them all for her own life. How could she be back?

Amy pressed her lips together, trying to keep the angry tears from pouring out of her eyes. Neither of them moved as their eyes stayed locked on one another. Amy didn't know what to do. She didn't know what to say. Beth was the one who broke the silence.

"Hey, Ames," she called out, calling Amy by Beth's own personal nickname for her as a kid.

Amy shook her head in angry frustration. She couldn't believe this was happening. Beth couldn't come home. She just couldn't. Amy didn't want her to come home. Beth had already ruined everything once. Amy couldn't let her do it again.

"What are you doing here?" she asked quietly.

She heard Beth's loud exhale of breath. "I came home," she said with a slight shrug.

Amy closed her eyes shut tightly, the hot, angry tears finally coming. This was a nightmare.

"Are you coming inside?" Beth called out quietly, and Amy opened her eyes and glared at her. Beth continued to gaze at her for a moment more before she gave a slow nod and turned and walked back into the house.

"This can't be happening," Amy whispered into the quiet night. "Please God, no. This can't be happening."

Amy stood there, rooted in place when the front door opened again, her father coming out this time. He walked right to her, his arms open to her, but she didn't enter his embrace. Instead, she crossed her arms and looked away, angry beyond words.

Her father put his arm around her. "Let's talk," he said. She didn't fight him as he pulled her forward with him. They walked over to the courtyard where Wesley and his friends had been chatting, her father asking them if they minded going someplace else. He led her to a seat under one of the heaters, sitting down across from her. As soon as she was seated, her anger boiled over.

"How could Beth be back?" she yelled. "How could you let her come home?"

Her father gave her a sad sort of smile.

"She left!" Amy called out, standing up in her anger. She started pacing in the small courtyard. "She left us all behind. She messed everything up. How can she just come home?"

She was yelling, venting all her anger. No, it wasn't fair for her to come home—not after everything she had done. It wasn't fair at all. And what had her father done? He let her in and decided to throw a party.

"How could you let her come home?" she asked again, stopping this time. "It's not fair," she told him, glancing at his face.

She couldn't read his expression, but she could tell that he was trying to read her face.

"Why do you think that?" he asked.

"Why do I think that?" she repeated. "Because it's the truth!" she yelled. "She doesn't deserve to come back here, not after what she did to you! She doesn't deserve *anything*."

Amy started pacing again. She couldn't get control of herself. She was so angry. Her mom had once reprimanded Amy for saying that she hated Beth. Amy never used the word again to describe what she felt toward her sister, toward anyone. Her mom told her to never say that she hated someone. She wouldn't say it now, but she was feeling it in her heart. She had never disliked anyone so strongly as she did her own sister. How could she come back?

"Beth has messed everything up, and God knows what she's been up to these past three years! Have you given any thought to that? She's probably been making a huge mess of herself, probably ruining other's lives in the process."

Amy stopped again when the anger burst over. "These past three years, I've been doing *everything*. *I'm* the one who's been there for you. *I've* been the one helping out the business. *I've* always done what you've told me. *I've* never done what Beth has. I never would. And what do I get for it? *Nothing!*" She shook her head, her heart pounding fiercely. "Yet you welcome your *other* daughter home with open arms," she said more quietly. "You're celebrating."

She was quiet now, trying to contemplate how this could all be happening, trying to understand. She had no answers, no explanation.

Her father stood up and walked over to her, putting his arms on her shoulders, the same sad smile on his face.

"Yes," he said, nodding his head for emphasis. "Yes, I'm celebrating. Of course I'm celebrating. Your sister has been gone for three years. She completely lost herself, but she's back. She's alive again. How can I not celebrate?"

Amy glared at him and was about to interrupt when he silenced her.

"But you already know that all of this," he said, looking over her shoulder at the house, so much more than simply the house in his eyes, "is yours. Everything is yours. It has been yours for a long time. All that I have is yours. You've always been with me. But your sister was lost to us—to herself, and now she's found. She's home."

Amy was stunned. She didn't know what to say. His words silenced her. She still didn't get it, how he could let her come home again. She didn't understand. He was too forgiving, too loving.

"So, Beth's really home?" Amy finally asked after searching for a response that would please her father, coming up with nothing.

"Yes," he stated.

"For how long?" she wanted to know, rolling her eyes and looking away. Her father paused, not answering until she turned to look at him.

"They can stay as long as they want," he said. "I hope they're home for good."

Amy's eyebrows raised as she took in his words. "They?" she called out. "Beth didn't come alone?"

His eyes narrowed on her slightly before he answered. "They, as in Beth and Eden, your gorgeous little niece."

Amy shook her head, taking in his words. "Beth has a baby?" she asked. She couldn't help herself, she started laughing—a cold, mocking laugh. Of course, Beth would get herself into so much trouble. Beth would get herself knocked up by some guy. She was so irresponsible. Amy was surprised that she went through with having a baby in the first place. She felt bad for the kid, having Beth for a mother.

"And where's the father?" Amy asked after a moment, a sneer on her face. Although, once she caught the look in her father's eyes, the pain on his face, she calmed down. It was like what she was saying about Beth was wounding him personally.

"Beth said he's not a part of their lives."

Amy nodded and looked away. She didn't want to upset her father anymore, which clearly her words were doing, however much she felt that Beth deserved it.

"Amy, you have a choice to make," her dad said, drawing her attention back to him.

"What do you mean?" she asked, confused.

"I'm going back into the house," he said, gesturing behind him. "I'm going back in there to celebrate the fact that your sister has come home." She nodded along as he talked. "But you have to decide what you're going to do."

"About what?"

He gave her a piercing look, like he could see deep down within her. "You need to decide whether you're going to come into the house or not. I hope you do."

She was puzzled by his words. He stood with her for a moment more, watching her, before he turned and walked back into the house, leaving her in the courtyard. She sat down on one of the wrought iron chairs that decorated the space, trying to understand what he had just asked her. Was she going to come into the house or not? It was where she lived, after all. Where else was she going to go? She wouldn't go somewhere else simply because her wayward sister was home. No, that would please Beth, and Amy didn't want to give her that satisfaction. But she knew that her father's words had a much deeper meaning, she just didn't know what. If he wanted to know if she could just forget the past and forgive Beth, that answer was no. Beth didn't deserve her forgiveness. And she certainly wasn't giving it.

Amy sat outside for a while, not bothered with the fact that it was cold, the breeze cutting through her jacket even as she sat under the heat lamp. She wished she had her heavier winter coat on. She was flabbergasted that her father had let Beth come home, but more than that, that he was celebrating her homecoming.

Amy was startled when all of a sudden Aunt Mary sat down next to her. She hadn't noticed her approach.

"I've been wondering where you were," Mary said. "Your father mentioned that you were home."

Amy turned to her and sighed heavily. "I'm just trying to understand all of this. He just let her come home."

Mary nodded, not saying anything. Amy loved her for it. She didn't come outside to pick up where her father had left off. She was simply just being there for Amy, like she had always been there for Amy.

Mary reached over and grabbed Amy's hand. "It's getting pretty late," she told her. "It's after midnight."

Amy just shook her head. "I just can't go in yet. I can't. I don't want to see her."

Mary didn't say anything, not for a while at least. She just sat there quietly with Amy while Amy's brain went a mile a minute. She was exhausted from thinking.

Eventually Mary stood up. "Come on," she said. "Come inside."

Amy looked up at her, not sure what to do.

"Beth went to bed well over an hour ago. You don't have to see her tonight."

Amy took a deep breath and stood up. She walked behind Mary and into the house. Her father was still awake. She could see him outside in the backyard talking with people. The outdoor fireplace was lit, and that's where everyone seemed to be congregating. Amy didn't have the strength to go outside, to celebrate. She couldn't celebrate Beth's homecoming.

Amy said goodnight to Mary and walked upstairs to her room, pausing in the hallway outside her door. Beth's bedroom was right across the hall from Amy's, looking out over the backyard. She couldn't help herself. Quietly, Amy opened the door to her sister's bedroom, peering in. She could see the outline of Beth under the covers of her bed, the moon shining through the tall windows and doors that led out onto a balcony. She also saw a small portable crib right next to Beth's bed. She was too far away to see her sister's face, or her sister's baby. But it was really true. Beth was home, and she had brought a baby with her.

Amy shook her head in disbelief, closing the door quietly behind her. She was spent. She was absolutely spent. All she wanted was to go to bed and forget about this horrible mess.

Chapter Twenty-Four

Beth rolled over in bed, reaching for the nightstand on her right for the clock that rested there. She reached and reached, but only hit empty space. Opening her eyes slowly, against the light, Beth got her bearings. And then she realized that she wasn't in her garage apartment at the Harris's. She was home, in her bedroom, in Colorado. She was home.

Sitting up quickly in bed, everything from the night before came back to her: her arrival in Colorado, and her arrival home.

Beth hopped out of bed, glancing at the big clock over the fireplace in her room. It was only seven in the morning. She couldn't believe that she hadn't slept longer, especially after the long drive the day before, and everything that followed it. She had collapsed into her bed the night before after gently changing Eden into her pajamas, trying not to wake her. She had expected to sleep a lot longer, but she had slept soundly. She felt well rested.

Walking over to the portable crib, Beth leaned over it and looked at Eden's contented face as she slept. She hadn't woken at all through the night, and Beth was glad. She hoped that she would sleep a little longer. Eden had started sleeping through the night around eight weeks, although there was the occasional night when she would cry out in the early hours of the morning. But usually she slept soundly, just as soundly as Beth.

Leaving Eden sleeping, Beth crept to the big French doors that opened up to a balcony that overlooked the back of her father's property. She could see some of her favorite ski slopes close by. When she was twelve years old, she had attempted to find a way through the woods off the trail closest to her house that would deliver her right into her backyard. She had to carefully make her way past many trees, but she had managed to make it pretty close. She had skied off the beaten path before. Of course, the property was completely fenced in coming off the mountain, so she ended up having to walk through the woods with her skis to her front door. Since then she had stuck to taking the trail to the end. It wasn't far from home, no matter where she came out at the end. The closest ski lift was pretty much right on the other side of the property line, through the trees. She could see it as it trailed up the mountain from her balcony. She loved the view, but mostly she loved that her room overlooked her mother's garden.

She looked out over it in the morning light. It was frosted over, but Beth was sure it had bloomed beautifully throughout the summer. Beth used to take care of it after her mom had died. She had loved spending hours out in the garden. It made her feel close to her mom. She wondered who had taken care of it these past three years. Staring at it now, however, sent a pang through her heart. Strangely, it wasn't for her mother. As she gazed at the garden from the height of her second story bedroom, she thought of Ellie. She had been gone a little over forty-eight hours, and she already missed them so much.

Beth knew that they would be waiting for her to return to Lake Tahoe. A part of her wanted to, but she knew she wouldn't. No, she was home, home to stay, at least for now. The unbelievable had happened. Her father had already forgiven her a long time ago. She would not leave and turn around now. She had prepared herself to stay as long as needed to make things right with him but her father had graciously invited her in right away. She was ready to show him how much he meant to her.

Taking a deep breath, Beth walked back into her room, closing the doors behind her. She strolled around her room, looking at all the little trinkets she had placed on various shelves over the years, of pictures of old friends from high school and college, some of whom never wanted to talk to her again. She stood in front of the fireplace in her room for a while, examining a picture of her mother and her at a mother-daughter luncheon they had attended through the church her parents had taken her to shortly before her mom had died. She really was the spitting image of her mom.

Beth walked over to her large walk-in closet, examining the clothes she had left behind when she had left home. A lot of them she would never be caught dead in nowadays. A lot of them probably didn't fit anymore. Her body was pretty much back to normal after having Eden. Beth had been determined to be in shape throughout her entire pregnancy, and then tried to get into a strict workout routine after Eden was born. At first it had started off as long walks and light jogs, and then six weeks after Eden was born Beth started running again. She loved it. She loved the awesome feeling when her endorphins kicked in, giving her energy to keep going. She loved the ache in her muscles after a good run. And it helped her lose the weight she had gained during her pregnancy, which Doctor Abernathy had informed her had been a bit lower than average to begin with. It helped that Beth was twenty-three. She had always had a lot of energy.

Beth walked into the bathroom off her bedroom. It was a Jack and Jill bathroom, connected to the smaller room next door, which had been a playroom for Amy and Beth when they were younger. Opening the door on the other side of the bathroom, she saw that it still had a lot of toys in it, although some of them were more for decoration than anything else, like the wooden rocking horse the girls' grandfather had made when their dad was born. That rocking horse used to terrify Beth as a child, and had to be covered with a bed sheet until she was about six years old before she would comfortably play in the room. She glanced at it now with a smirk. There were some stuffed toys sitting on top of a shelf, as well as the old, large toy box.

Back in the bathroom, Beth explored under the sink, surprised to see some of her old makeup and beauty products still there. They had probably dried up or gone bad a while ago. She would have to run into town for a few things. She had some bath products in her suitcase, but not much. And either way, her bag was still in the car. She had been too focused on getting Eden's things the night before that she hadn't thought of herself.

Hearing Eden stirring, Beth left the bathroom and walked back into her large bedroom. It was still so surreal in so many ways to be back here, but she loved it at the same time. She was happy. She was really and truly happy. But she knew she still had a lot more to make up for. Everyone wanted to know why she left, and why she had come back. And she knew that a lot of people wouldn't be ready to forgive her—her sister most of all. But putting that behind her for the time being, Beth went to take care of Eden.

"Good morning, Miss Eden!" Beth cooed over the top of the crib. Eden smiled up at her mother and kicked her feet. Beth reached for her and kissed her head. "You slept so soundly last night," she declared. "Mommy got to sleep all night. Thanks for that."

Beth walked over to the large windows where there was a loveseat and a coffee table. She put her feet up and settled in, holding Eden as the sleepiness fully left her eyes. Afterward, she dug through Eden's things and dressed her for the day in a cute, fall outfit, with pumpkin colored pants and a leaf print top, putting a headband on her as well. Beth loved shopping for baby clothes. Eden dressed so much better than Beth these days, although looking nice had always been one of Beth's things. She still did own a lot of very fashionable and expensive clothing that she had brought back from Europe.

"What should we do now?" Beth asked Eden, picking her up from the bed where she had laid her down to change her, knowing that the first thing she needed to do was get Eden some food. It was not quite eight o'clock yet, and everything seemed silent in the house, although it was so large that the silence didn't necessarily mean anything. Someone could be on the other side of the house rocking out on a drum set, and she probably wouldn't notice.

With Eden on her hip, Beth opened the door to her bedroom, surprised to see the rest of her belongings outside her door. Someone must have brought them up late at night, saving her the trouble. She was touched.

Amy's room was right across the hall, the door closed. Beth was sure that it was probably locked as well. She could see how shocked Amy had been at seeing Beth again—shocked and angry. Dealing with her would be a long, slow process, but Beth was determined to set everything right, as much as she could. She knew Amy would be the hardest part.

Walking down the stairs to the main floor, Beth explored the house, giving Eden a little tour, more because Beth was happy to see the home that she had grown up in. She walked through the large living room where she had talked with her dad the night before. She walked through the more comfortable entertainment room with the large TV screen and sound system. Off to the side was the game room, with a few old arcade games, as well as a pool table and shuffleboard table. She walked through the library, something her father took great pride in. He loved books, much like Johnny's dad. She also walked into his study after making sure no one was in there. The last time she had been in that room she had cut her dad out of her life. She could almost see herself standing there as she had been three years ago, demanding a right that had never really been hers. She didn't stay in there long. She walked Eden through the sunroom that overlooked the garden and gave the feeling of being outside. She walked through the huge dining room, with a table that could fit twenty people, and finished by coming into the kitchen.

With one hand supporting Eden, Beth opened the large double-door fridge, surveying the contents. There was a ton of food, but she didn't want to dig through it now. Instead of seeing what was in the mix of containers and meandering through the shelves, she opted for a piece of fruit. There was a big basket of fruit on the kitchen island, and Beth pulled a pear from it, rinsing it under the faucet and biting into it, trying to figure out what to give Eden. She knew she probably had a few jars of baby food, but she didn't know where they were at the moment. And she normally gave Eden baby cereal for breakfast, as well as milk. As she stood against the counter eating her pear and gently swaying Eden back and forth on her hip, her father walked in, greeting her with a smile as bright as day.

"Good morning, Beth," he said, walking right over to her and planting a kiss on her forehead. Then he looked down at Eden. "And good morning to you, little Eden," he stated, repeating the gesture and kissing her forehead as well. "How'd you sleep?" he asked Beth.

"Like a little baby," she answered with a smile. "I don't think I moved the entire night."

"I'm surprised you're up so early. I was hoping you'd sleep in so I could have a big breakfast waiting for you when you got up. Although I guess I shouldn't be surprised. You were always a morning person."

Beth was truly touched. Her dad was always giving so much of himself. How could she have ever left him? How could she have ever wanted to leave this place that meant so much to her? Although it dawned on her as she sat down in the breakfast nook, talking with her dad, trying to see if Eden would eat some pear, that maybe she had needed to leave in order to realize what she had. She never would've appreciated all the blessings she had in her life, never would have recognized them, if she hadn't been without them. Beth had so much to make up for, she knew that. She would do anything to set things right—with everyone, including her sister.

After a while, Beth was hungry for a bigger breakfast, and could tell by Eden's crankiness that she was, too. Instead of having her dad cook for her, she handed Eden to him and decided to cook for him instead. He had tried to fight her off until she placed Eden into his arms, then he was completely smitten by his granddaughter as she ate pieces of dry cereal off the table in front of her, or at least sucked on them to the best of her ability. She wasn't quite into finger foods yet. Beth was sure that her dad would spoil her rotten.

Going to the refrigerator, Beth pulled out the ingredients to make omelets, almost laughing to herself once she got them cooking. It was what she had made for the Harris's that first morning in their house as a small gesture of appreciation for what they had done for her, almost exactly a year ago. And now she was doing the same for her father. She never could have imagined this day a year ago.

She placed a steaming omelet in front of her dad, cooking one for herself afterward. She brought it over to the table when she was done, sitting down with him again. She couldn't help but smile broadly as she watched him with Eden. He was so good with her, and she seemed content enough to sit on her grandfather's lap.

"What have you got planned for the day?" her father asked her, taking a bite of his omelet, his attention continually drifting back and forth from Beth to Eden.

"I don't know," Beth said. She didn't really have any plans at all, other than trying her hardest to make up for what she had done to her family. "I suppose I'll have to make a run into town for a few things, stock up the bathroom again and get some things for Eden."

Her father nodded. "Sounds like a great idea."

Beth grinned and glanced out the window for a moment, looking out on the small courtyard out front, remembering the look on Amy's face from the night before.

"Amy's mad that I'm here," Beth said, her gaze still focused on the world outside. The frost had lifted, but Beth knew that real snow would be on the way shortly. It already covered the upper part of the mountain, and she knew that meant they were making snow on the slopes. She loved it.

Her dad didn't respond right away. Beth turned and looked at him, compassion shining from his eyes. Of course, what Beth had done had been horrible, and she knew she had hurt her sister. But the feud between her and Amy went back way further than from when Beth had left. They had been at odds with each other for most of their lives.

"I'm praying that she'll come around in time," her dad finally said. Beth nodded. She'd take a cue from him and do the same. Her dad's forgiveness was proof that it had nothing to do with Beth anyway, it was all God. And He could do anything.

Beth didn't ask anything more about Amy. She had gone right to bed once she had come in the night before, but she guessed that Amy hadn't just walked into the house and pretended that everything was all right. Beth knew that Amy was the one person in the world who disliked her most. She could feel it radiating off of Amy the night before when they had stood face-to-face after all this time.

"If you want to go into town, I don't mind taking care of this little one," her dad said, smiling down at Eden, who was gripping his finger and trying to munch on it.

Beth grinned. "You don't have to take care of her."

"I want to," he told her. "You could use a little break," he said. "I know it wasn't easy for you to come back here, Beth."

She bit her lip, nodding. No, it hadn't been easy. The thought of coming home after all that she had done, after all the time that she had been away, had been terrifying. But she had been given strength to conquer this greatest fear by her God who had always been watching over her and protecting her, even when she was too stubborn to notice.

"I could use a little time to get to know my granddaughter, anyway," he said, like they would spend the morning in serious conversation about each other's lives. Beth laughed.

"If you really want to," she answered. In some ways, she didn't want to leave Eden behind. She had almost become a security blanket to Beth. Eden was the gift that God had given her that had been the reason Beth had changed her life around. She never felt burdened by motherhood. She never left Eden behind. Of course, she would get her shopping done much faster without having her along. However, Eden was also going through a stage right now of crying whenever Beth left her—even with the Harris's. Johnny was the only exception. Eden was perfectly comfortable with him. But Eden didn't know her grandfather, and even though Beth wanted them to bond, she was nervous that she would be leaving a cranky baby behind. Although she was sure that Eden would warm up in time. She would have to with the amount of doting her father was already bestowing on his granddaughter.

"Take the morning for yourself," her dad said. "I'm sure you could use some time to think," he stated, giving her a knowing look. Yes, she did need to think about what was next. She needed to figure out how she was going to deal with everything she had left behind in Lake Tahoe, especially the family that she loved. She didn't want to leave them behind. She didn't want to leave anyone behind ever again.

"Okay," she said. "If you're sure you don't mind."

"Not at all."

Beth stood up, taking the dishes to the sink.

"I'll do those," her dad said. "You cooked breakfast. Let me clean up."

She thought about arguing with him, but knew it would do no good. She took Eden from him as he washed the dishes, sitting back down in the breakfast nook, chatting contentedly with her father. As her dad was drying the plates, Amy walked into the kitchen, stopping quickly when she saw Beth sitting there, her eyes narrowing slightly. Without a word, she turned and left. A few seconds later, Beth heard the front door slam. She could see from the window in the kitchen that Amy was getting into her car. She pulled out of the driveway and through the gates, gone in seconds.

Making up with Amy would not be easy.

Chapter Twenty-Five

Amy was furious as she drove quickly down the driveway, much too fast for the windy road, away from her house and closer to town. Beth was everywhere all of sudden. Amy couldn't escape her. She had gone into her room the night before, hoping to fall right to sleep, only to be kept awake for hours unnerved by the fact that her sister was in the next room. She still couldn't believe that Beth had come back after all this time. Amy was sure that she wanted something. Beth didn't come home for no reason. She probably wanted more money and would play nice to their father until he was wrapped around her finger again, and then would devastate him again by leaving. Amy was sure of it. And her sister had the perfect bait this time—a baby.

Once she had finally drifted off to sleep, she was bothered by a series of dreams, all of them including Beth. She couldn't even escape her in her sleep. She had been hoping that when she woke up this morning that she would be able to have some peace and quiet before dealing with the inevitable meeting with her sister again, but she had run into Beth right away as she walked into the kitchen to make her morning coffee. Yes, Beth was everywhere, and Amy hated it.

She drove straight to David's apartment, needing to unload on someone. She had been so angry the night before after her talk with her dad that she hadn't even thought to give him a call. He had probably been sleeping anyway by the time Amy had finally fought with her pride and gone into the house.

Amy parked the car in the guest parking area, walking to his building. She walked up the stairs to the second floor of the condominium complex, knocking urgently on his door. He seemed surprised to see her when he opened the door.

"Hey," he said, greeting her with a smile as he pulled a sweater on. He was still in his pajamas, looking like he just woke up. It was Saturday, after all. She knew he liked to sleep in on his days off.

She barged into the condo and flopped down on his couch.

"Everything all right?" he asked, walking over to her. He left her there for a moment and walked into his bedroom, coming back out with his glasses on. "What's the matter?" he wondered, taking in her expression.

"You'll never guess what I came home to last night," she said with evident sarcasm.

His eyebrows pulled together. "What?"

"A party—a celebration, rather."

"For what?" David asked, waiting for her to explain the whole story. She could tell that he was still mostly asleep.

"Oh, you'll never believe it," she stated. "My father was having a celebration, celebrating the fact that my selfish, wayward sister has finally come home."

David simply blinked at her for a second, as if her words were sinking in. "Beth's home?" he finally asked.

"Oh yes!" Amy declared, unable to keep the sarcasm from her tone. "My beloved little sister has finally come home."

She could see the surprise on David's face. She told him about her small encounter with Beth in the driveway last night, and then vented about her discussion with her father, finishing with how she had rushed over to his condo this morning after seeing her sister and father talking in the kitchen.

"Oh, and I haven't told you the best part yet," Amy added. "Beth has a baby."

David didn't react to that piece of news like she thought he would. In fact, he didn't react at all.

"Did you hear me? Beth has a baby."

"I heard you," he said quietly, taking a seat on the couch.

"She's the most irresponsible girl alive," Amy stated, sitting back into the couch and resting her arms over the back as if she could breathe again now that she had told her tale.

Neither of them spoke for a little while. Amy was just glad to not be at the house where her sister was probably moving all of her stuff in and making herself right at home. After a time, David spoke.

"So, you and Beth haven't talked at all?" he asked her.

Amy gave him a confused look. "Why would we talk?"

"Well, you are sisters," he answered her.

"Did you hear anything I just said?" she asked him. "I've told you all about Beth. I don't want anything to do with her."

David sighed, looking troubled. "You know, she's probably changed a lot in three years. I'm sure having a baby has really changed her."

Amy glared at him. "Are you defending Beth?" She couldn't believe her ears.

"No," he said. "I'm just saying, I'm sure she's changed a lot. I'm sure she came home for a reason."

"Yea, to demand more money or break another piece of my father's heart."

David looked at her reproachfully. "You don't know that."

"Well, you don't know that she won't," Amy countered. She couldn't believe this. She couldn't believe that they were actually arguing about Beth. That's what Beth did, ruined everything everywhere she went. There was no way that Amy was going to let Beth ruin anything with David.

"Maybe you should give her a chance," David said. "I'm sure it wasn't easy for her to come home after all this time."

Amy bit her tongue, wanting really hard to lash out at him, but not allowing herself. She couldn't fight back. She couldn't fight about Beth with David. She needed him to be on her side.

When Amy didn't say anything, he seemed to take it that his words had given her something to think about.

"Are you going to invite her to the wedding?" David asked.

Amy balked. "Are you kidding me?"

She could tell by David's expression that he most assuredly was not.

"She is your sister," he stated.

"No, a sister doesn't do what she did to our family. She's not my sister."

David shook his head and looked away. "You know, you probably didn't make life easy on Beth either. You can't blame her for everything."

"I can't believe you!" Amy yelled, standing up. So much for not fighting about Beth. "How can you even say that?"

David stood up, looking straight into her eyes. "I've been thinking a lot about what you told me a while back about when your mom died."

"What about it?" Amy asked, folding her arms.

"Well, I'm sure it messes with a thirteen-year-old girl when her sister blames her for killing their mom."

Amy couldn't help it. She kicked the coffee table with her foot, reacting without thinking. David stepped back and looked at her, startled. She closed her eyes, realizing that she was getting carried away, feeling horrible in an instant, especially when the table toppled to the side as the one leg gave way. She had more force than she realized.

"I'm sorry," she said right away. "I don't know what came over me."

David took a few deep breaths, not saying anything.

Amy felt horrible, absolutely horrible. She had never reacted like that. What had come over her? David was only trying to help, and she knew that. He had never been anything but the kindest, most loving person to her. And this is how she thanked him, by breaking his furniture when they were arguing.

"I'm sorry," she said again, tears springing to her eyes. David nodded his head, clearly not at all concerned about the table, and came over and pulled her close, letting her cry against his chest. "I'm sorry. I just don't know what to do."

He held for a few minutes. When they pulled apart, she wiped her nose and dried her tears.

"I'm sorry that Beth makes me crazy," she stated.

David gave her a small smile. "Just promise me that you'll give her a chance. I know I've never met her, but I'm sure it took a lot of courage for her to come back like she did."

Amy nodded. She didn't want to forgive Beth. She didn't feel like Beth deserved it. But for David's sake, she would try not to make Beth an issue.

"And remind me when we're shopping next to get more indestructible furniture."

Amy laughed despite her tears. She couldn't help it.

"Sorry," she said once again.

"It's a coffee table. I'll get over it."

Amy took a deep breath, trying to calm down.

"Why don't we go over to your house?" David suggested, surprising Amy.

"Really?" she asked, clearly showing that she didn't like that idea.

"From everything you've said, Beth doesn't appear to be going anywhere for a while. You might as well try to make peace with that as best you can."

Amy nodded. She knew he was right. She would go home. She would face Beth and prove that Beth couldn't tear her down. Beth's presence couldn't bother her. She still didn't want to go back. She never wanted to have to deal with her sister. It comforted her slightly to know that she was getting married in two months and would be out of the house after that, although she hated the thought that Beth would be left to take her place.

Amy and David had purchased a house a mere mile and a half from her father's house, which suited Amy greatly. She had felt guilty about moving out, away from him, with no one to care for him. She didn't want him alone in that great big house. But their house was just a road over from the drive that led to Monahan Ranch. It was a nice mountain home, of course not as grand as the home she had grown up in. Nothing could ever compare to Monahan Ranch, but she was excited to live there just the same. She was thrilled to have a home for her and David. She was excited to marry him, however poorly she had shown herself to him today. She was grateful for his constant love, even if there were a few kicked-in coffee tables here and there.

David and Amy walked out to her car. She gave him the keys and he drove to her house. She took the short drive to try to compose herself. She wouldn't let Beth see how much her reappearance was affecting her. She would pretend that Beth had no impact on her whatsoever.

David pulled the car right up to the house, taking her hand as they walked through the door. Amy heard voices coming from the sunroom and headed that way with David. No more hiding. But when she walked in she was met with only her father and Aunt Mary—Aunt Mary with a baby at her feet chewing on a large toy.

"Good morning," her dad said to her as she came in, greeting her with a smile.

"Morning," Amy returned. He greeted David behind her as Amy glanced at Mary, who gave her an encouraging smile.

"I heard you had yourself a bit of a celebration last night," David said, as if it was no big deal at all.

"We did," her dad said, smile still in place. "Beth's home."

"I've heard," David said, sitting down in a suede armchair.

"She went out to run a few errands," Mary stated for Amy's benefit, Amy could tell. Amy took a calming breath. At least she had a little more time to get used to the fact that Beth was really, truly home.

Amy stood in the doorway of the sunroom for a few minutes, trying to find her composure. She could do this. She knew she could. She had been through so much in her life already. She could deal with the fact that Beth was back.

"Is that the baby?" Amy finally asked, feeling slightly foolish. Who else's could it be? For a fleeting second she wondered if Beth was really running errands, or if she simply had left her baby and run for it again so she wouldn't have the responsibility of raising a child. It was a possibility.

"Yes," her dad said, standing up and taking the baby from Aunt Mary's feet and walking over to Amy.

Amy glanced down at the baby in his arms, a surprise swell of emotion coming over her. She was dressed in the cutest outfit—burnt orange pants and a top covered in leaves. She had a matching orange colored cloth headband on her head with a flower on it. It was adorable. She was adorable. Amy couldn't deny it. She had Beth's dark hair and striking blue eyes. She was absolutely beautiful.

"What's her name again?" Amy asked quietly, not taking her eyes from the baby, who seemed to be studying her with the same curiosity. Tears came to her eyes again, tears that she couldn't explain. Why did glancing at her sister's baby make her want to cry?

"Eden," her dad answered. "Eden Elizabeth."

Amy's head snapped up. "Elizabeth?"

Her dad nodded. "Elizabeth."

So Beth had named the baby for their mom, for herself. Amy warred within herself, silently resenting the fact that Beth made a claim to the name even though it was her name as well, but also moved at the same time. This baby had been named for a great person—that is, as long as Beth didn't have herself in mind when she had picked it. Beth didn't deserve to be named for their mother.

"Do you want to hold her?" Dad asked.

Amy sighed. She didn't want to want it, but she couldn't help it. No one could resist a little baby, especially one as beautiful as Eden.

"Sure," she said, biting the inside of her cheek as her dad passed the baby into her hands. Eden continued to gaze at her, seemingly trying to decide what she thought of Amy. Amy took her and sat down in a chair by David, her eyes not leaving Eden's face, who was now looking at the toys on the ground out of her reach.

"Hi, baby," she said. Eden looked up at her again. "I love your little outfit," Amy told her, her voice warm for the first time in a day. Eden smiled at her, and Amy thought that she would cry again. This baby was just too cute. Amy didn't want to fall in love with her.

"She looks just like Beth when she was a baby," Mary stated.

"Yea, we were looking at pictures this morning," her dad added. "We found this one from when Beth was seven months old. Take a look."

Her dad handed the photo out to Amy and she took it, glancing from the photo to Eden.

"My goodness," she said, shocked. Beth and Eden at seven months old looked exactly the same, like Eden was a little clone of Beth from that time. She could be looking at the same baby.

"Let me see," David said, looking over.

"It's crazy, isn't it?" Mary asked. It was like this baby had the DNA from only one parent in her. Amy knew that she would grow up looking just like Beth, just like their mother.

They sat for a while, just talking happily. Amy knew that she and her dad had had a strained conversation the night before, but none of that showed now. She could see that he was happy. He was happy that Beth was back, and she could also tell that he was happy Amy was home as well. Amy could also see how delighted he was in little Eden.

When Eden let out a cry, Amy wasn't sure what to do.

"She's probably hungry," her dad said right away. "Beth said she usually gets some milk around this time before going down for a nap."

He stood up and went and left the room and came back a few minutes later with a bottle. He handed it to Amy.

"You want me to feed her?" she asked with surprise.

He nodded. "Unless you don't want to."

Amy glanced at the bottle in his hands and then at Eden. She was content to keep holding the baby, as long as Eden didn't mind. Amy reached for the bottle and held it up, surprised when Eden snatched it from her hand and held it up herself, drinking happily, making cute happy hums as she drank. Amy couldn't help but smile. She had to help Eden a little, propping the bottle up so that the milk flowed through.

Her dad left the room to answer the house phone, and Mary followed behind him, leaving Amy and David alone in the room with Eden.

"How're you doing?" David asked her with a smile.

Amy sighed heavily. "I'm so sorry for earlier," she said again.

"Don't worry about it," he said, and she could tell that he meant it. "You're going to be okay, you know. You're going to make it through this."

Amy nodded her head. She couldn't believe that she had ended up with this great guy. "You always believe in me."

His smile widened. "You're worth believing in."

Amy melted at his words, looking down at Eden. Her eyes were slowly closing as she continued to drink, fighting sleep.

"She's adorable," David said, glancing at Eden.

"She is," Amy agreed, smiling at the baby—her niece.

Eden let out a contented sigh when she finished her bottle, her eyes closing in sleep.

"Well, she seems happy," Amy remarked, gently rubbing Eden's chin with the back of her finger. Eden smiled in her sleep. She looked up at David and grinned, but he was looking past Amy. She turned around and saw her sister standing in the doorway, her hand over her heart as she let out a slight smile at Eden. Beth glanced up at Amy, their eyes locking on one another.

Chapter Twenty-Six

Beth's heart was moved as she looked at her older sister holding Eden. She had been praying about dealing with Amy all morning, and part of the afternoon, as she had been out doing some shopping and getting some things she needed. On her way back she took a small detour and drove to the main entrance to the ski resort, climbing a short way up one of the slopes and taking a seat on the frozen ground of one of the as yet unopened trails, looking out over the town below. She had missed this place so much and was beyond excited to be back. But she knew she wouldn't be able to feel completely at home until she could come to some sort of resolution with her sister, which she knew wouldn't come easy. But as Beth prayed, she knew that she had to keep trying. She wasn't about to give up on her sister. Beth had to at least apologize when she was given the chance.

"You must be Beth," a man said, standing up and walking over to her, holding out his hand. "I'm David."

"Nice to meet you," she answered, giving him a small smile.

"I'm your sister's fiancé."

Beth's eyes widened. No one had informed her since returning that Amy was getting married.

"Congratulations," Beth said, looking from David to Amy, a real smile spreading over her face now.

"Did you get in yesterday?" he asked, making small talk with her, trying to help clear the evident tension in the air between her and Amy.

"Uh, yea," Beth answered. "Drove all day."

"Oh yea?" David asked. Beth couldn't tell if he was feigning interest to keep the conversation going or not. "Where from?"

"Lake Tahoe. Well, yesterday, from Salt Lake City."

"Wow!" David said. "Tahoe! Nice place."

"Yea, I like it," Beth answered.

"Good skiing, I hear," David stated, keeping the conversation going.

Beth laughed. "Yea. Awesome skiing."

"Beth was working as a florist," her dad said, coming in behind her and putting his arm around her shoulder. "She's always loved flowers." She caught the look of curious surprise on Amy's face. Beth was sure she was expecting to hear worse, and Beth could tell her far worse. She knew that Amy probably wanted to hear how much Beth had messed up her life. She knew she had, but she hoped that what Amy could see was how much she had turned her life around. She hoped that Amy would be able to see that God had found her and brought her out of nothing into a brand new life.

"Great," David said.

Awkward silence filled the room.

"Eden's adorable," David blurted out.

Beth smiled at him. "Thanks," she answered. She looked over at Amy.

"She's sleeping," Amy informed her quietly. "I don't know if you want to put her down somewhere or something."

Beth nodded. "I can take her if you want."

Amy shrugged. "If you want to."

Beth pressed her lips together, trying not to smile too widely. She wouldn't take Eden from Amy if Amy wanted to keep holding her. Maybe Eden could help bridge the gap in their relationship. It was impossible not to love her darling daughter, or at least Beth thought so. She had watched as everyone got wrapped around Eden's finger. Even customers in the flower shop would always become distracted from making an order or picking out various bouquets to smile at the happy baby.

"I have something to show you," Dad said to Beth.

"What?" she asked.

"It's a surprise," he told her.

"A surprise?" Beth frowned slightly. She didn't want him to go out of his way doing anything for her. He had already given her so much. She wasn't going to ask him for anything, except for a job. She had been thinking this morning of what she was going to do for work now that she was staying in Holy Cross. She thought about asking her father for the very job she had run from, not sure if he would even allow it. But after the thought of teaching skiing had flitted across her mind after Lake Tahoe, she couldn't get it to leave. And she was back at her mountain.

Beth followed him out of the sunroom, noticing that David and Amy followed as well, at David's encouragement. She followed her dad upstairs. He stopped in front of the closed door to Amy and Beth's old playroom.

Her dad knocked on the door. "You ready for us?" he called out.

"Ready!" Aunt Mary's voice answered through the closed door.

Her dad reached for the handle and opened the door for Beth. Her jaw dropped, her hand coming up to her lips to cover her open mouth. Tears sprang to her eyes as she looked around the room, which had been completely transformed from when she had walked through it earlier that morning. There was a crib in the room, pushed up against the wall, with big white fabric letters on the wall over it that spelled out Eden's name. There was also a changing table and a dresser. The toy chest was still in there, and Beth was sure that it was filled to the brim with toys. Stuffed animals filled the shelves. There was a comfy looking rocking chair with a footstool that rocked with it. It was the most beautiful little nursery that Beth had ever seen. Everything was decorated in various cream colors, looking light and bright. It was gorgeous.

Beth looked to her dad, tears falling down her face.

"I don't know what to say."

"You don't have to say anything," he said with a warm smile.

She bit her lip, feeling horrible that he had done this for her. She just didn't deserve it.

"How in the world did you do all of this in the time that I was gone?" Beth asked.

"Well, I talked to Mary about it last night," her dad answered.

"And you know me," Mary began, "my mind went wild with decorating possibilities."

Beth smiled at her.

"Your dad talked a bunch of the guys into coming over this morning and putting furniture together at the party last night. Don helped me with the shopping. There really wasn't a ton to do other than put everything in place. It's not like we painted or anything."

Beth couldn't speak. She didn't know what to say. She was moved beyond words. It was a beautiful gift and a perfect space for Eden as she grew. And Beth loved the fact that she could walk through the bathroom right into the room.

"I looked online last night after you went to bed at baby furniture and picked this stuff out—even reserved a bunch of it and pulled up in the back of the store and they loaded it up in the truck. I really only had to go looking for the fabrics this morning."

Beth shook her head in disbelief.

"This is amazing," she said.

She walked around the room, touching the surface of the beautiful ivory dresser, reaching out to feel the padding in the crib. Her eyes finally focused on Amy in the doorway, who was looking around the room, shocked, still holding Eden.

Her dad followed Beth's gaze and he walked over to Amy, taking the baby from her. She handed Eden over freely then turned and left, David following her.

"Should we see if she likes her new crib?" Dad asked. He placed her carefully inside the crib, pulling a thin blanket over her. Beth smiled at her. She was also sure that Eden would wake with a shriek, finding herself in an unfamiliar place.

"We also hooked up a baby monitor system," Mary informed her, pointing to where the monitor rested on a shelf next to the crib. "There's a receiver in your bedroom, as well as downstairs in the living room with an actual screen so you can see her in here, although all the monitors are obviously portable so you can take them all over the house."

Beth simply nodded, taking everything in. She couldn't believe this. Those that she had walked out on, those that she had hurt and dismayed, had taken her right back in without asking any questions. And they just kept giving, giving, giving. She wished she had something to offer in return.

"This is beautiful," Beth said. "Thank you."

She hugged Aunt Mary, and then turned to hug her father. It didn't feel like a good enough thanks, but she hoped that they could see on her face how moved she was by this gesture. They wanted her home as much as she wanted to be home.

Amy and David left while Beth had been perusing the nursery. Beth was sure Amy wanted to spend as little time around her as possible, which made her sad. Beth was realizing that she had even missed her sister while she was gone. They had fought all their lives, and Beth knew that Amy had never really enjoyed her, but Beth had missed her older sister. Whether or not it was mutual, Beth had always loved her, had always looked up to her. She was her older sister, after all. Of course, she had disliked her much of the time as well, but she wanted to make up for that now, if Amy would let her.

Beth spent the afternoon talking with her dad and Aunt Mary, enjoying their company so much. Beth was filled in on three and a half years worth of news, and tried to tell them as much about her life that she had skimmed over the day before—at least the parts that were worth telling.

When Uncle Don came over to join them for dinner, he brought another surprise that Beth had been completely unprepared for. He brought her a brand new car, which her dad had picked out for her.

"You've got to be kidding me," Beth said, standing in the driveway looking at the white SUV. She would feel a lot better if people would stop giving her things.

"I thought you'd need a car," her dad said, putting his arm around her as she stood in shocked surprise, not sure how to react. The nursery had been so much already. Her being let home at all was more than she had expected. But a new car?

"Got it all cleaned up and ready for you," Uncle Don said, walking over and handing her the keys. "Your dad had me go out for it this morning and take care of it all."

She just shook her head, staring at the car.

"You always said you wanted a white car when you were younger," her dad said with a smile. "Didn't you want a car the color of snow?"

Beth laughed humorlessly and turned to her father. He had already given her a white car once when she was sixteen. She ran away from home in it and then later sold it because she needed the cash. "I can't accept this," she said. She just couldn't.

He smiled at her. "Of course you can. I won't take no for an answer."

Beth didn't know what to say. Her dad started spouting off facts about the make of the car, things that she knew nothing about and didn't quite understand. He told her that he had searched for an SUV that had great safety ratings, especially since Beth would be driving around with Eden quite a bit. Also an SUV that could handle the twisty mountain roads, especially in the winter.

While her dad talked to Uncle Don about how everything had gone at the dealership, unaware of how shocked Beth was, she glanced from the new car to Johnny's old one, feeling a small pang in her heart for him. She had been gone three days, and she missed him so much. She missed the whole family. She had to work on getting his car back to him. And then somehow figure out a way to see them all.

When they went back into the house, they came back into the living room. Beth spread out a blanket on the floor and sat Eden on it, who had woken up from her nap much earlier in her new nursery, upset just as Beth had predicted until she came in the room and got her. She picked up some toys, shaking them so that they rattled, watching as Eden grabbed for them and stuck them right in her mouth. She looked to Aunt Mary and smiled.

"Do you mind watching her for a second?" Beth asked.

"Not at all," Mary answered.

Beth asked her dad if she could talk to him alone. He directed her toward his study, taking a seat at his desk. She swallowed hard. This was all too familiar. But this time as she stood before her father, instead of demanding his money and telling him how much she hated her life, she spoke from her heart and told him that she didn't deserve all that he was giving her. And then, almost laughing at the irony three and a half years later, she humbly asked for a job at the ski resort—the very job that she had run from. With wonder, she realized that this was a redeemed moment.

"A job," her father said in shock. "You want a job?"

Beth looked at him strangely. "Well, I need to do something to provide for Eden."

She could tell by the look on her dad's face that she never had to worry about having enough to provide for Eden. It made her uncomfortable. That's not what she came home for. She had never even been sure that she would even live at Monahan Ranch, even if all the repairing of relationships had gone well.

Of course, that had already surpassed her wildest dreams, and she knew that she was home to stay for a while.

"Yea, I mean I can start showing you how things are done around here," he answered her like it was no big deal at all.

"Actually, I want to teach skiing again, if that would be possible. I'm sure you already have instructors lined up for this season and everything, but if you ever need an extra hand…"

Her dad looked at her, humorously surprised. "You want your old job back?"

Beth pressed her lips together, not sure whether it would be more appropriate to laugh or cry. "I know, crazy right?"

Her dad laughed a deep hearty laugh at the irony of it all, causing Beth to smile.

"Can't say I expected that one," her dad said, tears in his eyes by the time he quieted down. "But of course, if you want to teach, that'd be no problem at all."

Beth smiled widely. "Thank you." She wanted to cry. Her father had already given back everything to her that she had ungratefully thrown in his face when she left, that and so much more.

Later that night after a quiet dinner with her dad, Uncle Don, and Aunt Mary, Beth fired up her old computer, blanching as the computer wallpaper screen came on. It was a picture of her and some friends from school completely wasted and dancing in a bar. She merely shook her head at herself, changing the picture really quickly to a preset wallpaper of some flowers. She hadn't spoken to any of those friends in well over a year and a half.

Beth signed into an application to make calls over the Internet, hoping she'd be able to catch Crystal. She had promised the Harris's that she would check in as soon as possible.

Crystal was online, and Beth clicked on the button to start a call.

"Beth!" Crystal's voice protruded out of the speakers of the computer. "I've been on all day hoping I'd hear from you."

Beth smiled as the video portion of the chat kicked in, allowing her to see Crystal's face. Beth could tell that she was sitting in the family room, the kitchen behind her on the screen.

"It's so good to hear your voice!" Beth answered honestly. She held Eden up on her lap, picking up her hand and waving at the camera in Beth's computer.

"Eden!" Crystal squealed yet again. "Goodness, I miss you guys."

"We miss you, too."

Before Beth began to tell her tale about everything that had happened in the past day, Crystal started yelling, searching for her parents. A few moments later Ellie and Mark appeared in the picture behind Crystal, Eden clapping in delight at hearing their voices, although confused by the fact that they weren't with her. They offered her warm greetings. And then Beth spilled her story, starting with how she felt when the Rocky Mountains appeared before her to the moment she pulled up to the gate at her house. She told them everything about her dad coming out to meet her and walking her the last few yards toward home, like she had never left. She told them about the spontaneous celebration he had, about seeing more of her family, including Amy and how that hasn't started off well. She told them about the beautiful nursery and the car, and how undeserving she felt about it all. They listened with rapt attention to everything she had to say. When she was done, Ellie took the computer and said that she wanted to talk to Beth alone.

Beth watched as Ellie carried the computer through the house, finally resting it on her and Mark's bed. She smiled warmly at Beth when she sat down.

"You're not coming home, are you?" Ellie asked.

Beth took a deep breath before she answered. "I am home," she said honestly.

Ellie nodded. "You are home."

They looked at each other in understanding for a moment. Beth knew that she was right where she needed to be right now, and Ellie knew that, too.

"We're going to miss you here," Ellie told her.

Beth smiled sadly. "I promise to visit as often as I can."

"We'll hold you to that," Ellie stated.

Beth glanced down at Eden who was playing by her feet. She had smiled when she heard the voices of Mark, Ellie, and Crystal yet had long since given up trying to find them, losing interest. Now she was gripping the legs of Beth's chair, trying to pull it toward her.

"How's Johnny?" Beth finally asked. She couldn't help but ask about him. They had said nothing about him, and Beth simply assumed that he wasn't there. He didn't live at home anymore, after all. She wondered if he would move back into the garage apartment now that Beth was gone, although she had a feeling that he liked his independence from his family that the apartment didn't allow. He was twenty-six, after all.

"He's fine," Ellie answered quickly. "He's over at his place right now. He's headed back down to San Francisco again next week on business."

Beth nodded. "Well, tell him I said hello."

"I will," Ellie assured her.

Beth took a deep breath. "I really miss you guys. It's so surreal being back here. I just feel so undeserving of it all."

"Can I ask you something?" Ellie wondered.

"Of course."

"Have you forgiven yourself for what you've done?" Ellie asked her. "For leaving home and everything that came after?"

Beth pressed her lips together, feeling a sudden rush of tears spring to her eyes.

"I know that you've asked God to forgive you, and now you've returned to your home and you've asked others to forgive you. But have you forgiven yourself?"

Beth didn't respond right away. She knew that God had forgiven her. She could feel it in her heart. Her Lord and Savior had pursued her in the midst of darkness and called her into life. He had been waiting for her to run into His arms all along. And her dad was the greatest representation of God's love by doing the exact same thing. But she still felt guilty, incredibly guilty.

"No," Beth answered honestly. "I haven't."

"Why not?" Ellie asked.

"I guess I feel like I don't deserve to be forgiven and everyone already has." Well, almost everyone. Amy was a different story. "I feel like I should be held accountable for all the wrong I've done. But instead I was welcomed home with open arms, and then my dad's been going crazy giving me things on top of it all," she said, thinking of the nursery and the car, let alone the very job she had once refused.

Ellie gave her an encouraging smile. Beth wished so much that they were talking face-to-face. She longed to throw her arms around Ellie in a hug.

"Beth, none of us deserve any of the blessings we receive."

Beth nodded. She did know that. She knew that everyone was unworthy. Her gracious and loving Savior loved her so much that He gave himself for her, taking all that she did deserve for the things she had done and putting them on Himself. And that's what Ellie reminded her as they continued to talk. She encouraged Beth to think of the cross every time she was condemning herself for mistakes she had made in the past. She told her to remember her Savior, who had died for her and taken her sin. She told Beth to bask in God's grace and thank Him for it by living for Him. He had forgiven her, and Ellie wanted her to fully taste that freedom by forgiving herself. Beth was in tears by the time Ellie had finished speaking.

"Thank you," was all that Beth was able to say when she was done. And she didn't just mean for now, but for Ellie's constant encouragement. She meant it for everything, for taking her in when she had needed someone most and making her part of their family.

That night after Beth rocked Eden to sleep in the rocking chair in the nursery, placing her in her crib, she walked back into her bedroom, keeping the bathroom doors that connected her to the nursery open at both ends so she could hear if Eden woke, even though she had the baby monitor on. She was used to Eden being near when she slept.

Beth opened the tall French doors to her balcony and stepped outside, wrapped in a sweater, glancing up at the stars above her, remembering summer nights when she was a kid with her mother. Thinking of her mom gave her a moment of inspiration, and Beth reached for the baby monitor near her bed and quietly crept downstairs, walking out through the back of the house straight for her mother's garden, the smell of pine from nearby trees rising to meet her as she came near. She hadn't walked through it yet since returning home, even though there wasn't much to see at the moment.

Beth walked purposely toward a patch of grass near the dried rosebushes, lying down on her back and peering up at the heavens with a blanket she had grabbed in the sunroom, wishing that her mother were next to her. Strangely, she felt like she was close by as Beth lay there in her garden. But God felt even closer. She could feel Him in the night breezes, in the gentle scent of the pine trees above her head, as she saw her breath in front of her face. And she could feel Him inside her. And there, in her mother's garden, she prayed once again for forgiveness, and the strength to forgive herself. She praised God for

His grace and the freedom He had given her, all the blessings that she didn't deserve but that He gave anyway. And she told Him that she didn't want to wallow in guilt and self-pity any longer, but that she wanted to live her life for Him to the fullest. As she lay there, she felt like she had truly reached out and accepted the wonderful gift that God offers everyone if they but ask. She was forgiven. She felt forgiven. She felt free.

Chapter Twenty-Seven

In the weeks that followed Beth's return to Colorado, Amy tried her hardest to spend as little time at home as possible. She just didn't want to be around her sister. She was fully immersed with work and wedding plans, although her wedding was pretty much all put together. Aunt Mary had been a great wedding planner. Amy couldn't have asked for more capable hands.

She was spending plenty of time with David, which suited her just fine, although now that ski season had hit, their time together was sometimes more in the office than outside of it. The two of them started to go shopping for furniture for their house in their spare time. David made her promise that he got to pick out the coffee table. She was excited to get married, and everything that followed. She was simply looking forward to having her own home, especially now that Beth was back. Her wedding was only three weeks away now, and she was so ready.

Of course, it was impossible for Amy to be gone from home all the time. She still slept there every night, and she wanted to spend time with her dad. When Beth was around, Amy simply acted like she didn't exist. Amy had been holding a grudge against Beth for a long time, and resented her even more for coming home. Now their father's attention was divided between the two of them. Her family was all curious about where Beth had been, but happy at the same time that she had returned, and happier even still with a new baby in the family. Amy was sick of her presence. She forgot how much people liked her sister. Even the people that Amy worked with were excited that Beth was back. She had always been the friendly, outgoing one. Beth had always been friendly with Amy's coworkers back before she left. People were asking her questions at work all the time about her sister, and Amy wished that they would simply leave her alone. How had everyone already forgotten that Beth had left them all?

She resented Beth most of all because it had caused a slight rift between her and David. They had gone to dinner over at Monahan Ranch at her father's invitation. Uncle Don and Aunt Mary were there as well. And David spent a considerable portion of the evening before and after the meal chatting with Beth and getting to know her—he always seemed to do that when they were around each other. Amy couldn't believe her ears later that night when David told her that he actually *liked* her sister. He kept encouraging her to try and talk to her, to realize how much Beth had changed. He just didn't realize that Beth would never change. He never knew what she was like before she left. Amy knew she was simply incapable of it. Beth was still the same egotistical and thoughtless girl inside, even if no one else could see it. She wanted nothing to do with her sister. She had been walking on eggshells around her for the past five weeks.

There was only one thing about Beth that Amy couldn't deny, and that was that Beth truly loved Eden, and she actually was a good mom. Beth doted on Eden, always there to meet her every need and encouraging Eden as she grew. She seemed happy to take care of her, never complaining when the baby cried or when she had to go change her. She did it all with a smile on her face. Amy wondered how long it would last. Someday Beth would get tired of taking care of a baby, and Amy worried about what she would do. Yes, Amy was sure of who her sister was, of who she had always been. She was sick of everyone coming over to visit her, of all the attention they were giving her. She was surprised by her father most of all.

Her dad was doing everything for Beth, bending over backward to take care of her. She had been shocked to see her old playroom turned into a nursery for Eden, although it was a beautiful room. Secretly, she loved it and was glad that there was a comfortable space for the baby. It amazed her that despite Beth, Amy only wanted the best for that little girl. Amy might be upset and angry that her sister was home, but she couldn't hide the fact that she loved her niece. Eden was such a delight simply to hold and smile at, or to sit on the ground and play with. Beth let her hold the baby a fair amount, when Eden would tolerate it—she had recently started crawling and didn't like to be held for long, and Amy was glad to be there for that milestone but she would never say it aloud. She was always over the few times that she knew Beth was out of the house and had left the baby with her dad or Aunt Mary. She loved feeding Eden and taking her for walks in the stroller, all bundled up against the cold. It was fun being an aunt.

Amy had been even more surprised when her dad gave Beth a car. He had also set up a portion of the sunroom to turn into a paint studio for her because it looked out over the garden and the mountain and there was a lot of great natural light. She didn't deserve any of it.

"Hi honey," her dad said when she walked into the house after a long morning at work. Her dad hadn't come into the office for the morning. He had been out visiting some of the employees that worked at the lodge. She felt weird about taking a half-day when she knew there was so much she could be doing.

"Hi, Dad," she answered, giving him a smile. "How was your morning?"

"It was great," he told her. "We picked out the new linens for the rooms and sent the order in."

"Great," she replied. They were updating the rooms in the big cabin-style ski resort.

Her dad led her into the kitchen, and together they worked side by side and made sandwiches, laughing as they piled different toppings on them, building them up.

"Where's Beth?" Amy asked, curious.

"Out in the garden with Eden," he answered. "I think she's trying to make sure that child grows to love the snow as much as she does."

She nodded. She liked to know Beth's whereabouts. She liked to be prepared for when she was about to run into her sister.

Amy enjoyed lunch with her father, her sister never coming in. When she was finished, she went upstairs to her room. She had to find the contact information for one of their new finance executives that had recently been hired to work under David. She remembered bringing it home in her purse, and had never brought it back to her office.

Digging through a mound of papers on her desk, she was frustrated when she couldn't find it. Maybe she had left the information in her car. She was about to go and check when she turned and saw Beth standing in the open doorway to Amy's room, her hand poised like she was about to knock on the doorjamb.

"Hey," Beth said with a slight smile when Amy turned around.

Amy was shocked to see her there, shocked that Beth had ventured the hallway between their two rooms. It had been no man's land for weeks.

"Hey," Amy replied, pressing her lips together. What in the world did Beth want?

"Can I talk to you for a second?"

"Uh…sure," Amy replied, not sure that she actually wanted to talk to Beth for a second. She had worked hard at avoiding her sister, but in the times that they were together, Beth hadn't seemed that eager to talk either. What could she want now?

Beth looked unsure of herself for a moment as she stood in the doorway. As if in answer to a question in her head, she nodded and then took a step forward.

"Where's Eden?" Amy asked, stalling whatever Beth wanted to say.

"She's in the nursery. I just put her down for a nap."

"Oh."

Beth took a deep breath. "Look, I know things haven't really been easy between us since I've been back," Beth began, "or ever. But I just wanted to say that I'm sorry."

Amy's mouth dropped slightly, her defenses rising. She crossed her arms and glared at her sister.

"You're sorry?" she asked like she didn't believe her.

"Yea," Beth answered.

"Sorry for what?" Amy wanted to know.

"For everything," Beth replied. "For hurting you. For leaving."

Amy's eyes narrowed. "You didn't hurt me." It was a lie, of course. Beth had hurt her, but Amy wanted her to think that her little sister could have no power over her whatsoever.

"Okay," Beth said, giving her a sad sort of smile. "I just wanted to tell you," she stated before turning to go.

Amy was infuriated. "What right do you have to come in here and apologize?"

Beth just turned and looked at her.

"After all this time, why did you have to come back? You're just going to hurt everyone a thousand times more when you leave again."

"I'm not going anywhere," Beth replied calmly.

"Oh, sure you're not," Amy said. "Like I'll believe that."

"I hope that someday you will."

Amy rolled her eyes. "Yea right," she said sarcastically. "How could you come back here and show your face again after everything you've done? After you took dad's money and practically wished him dead? Did you even realize that you were tearing him to pieces?"

Amy could see tears coming into Beth's eyes, but they didn't fall down her face.

"Honestly," Beth began, "no. Not at the time. I was too self-absorbed and selfish to care what I was doing to the people around me."

"You're right, you were," Amy said. "You've always been self-absorbed and selfish. And you haven't changed."

Beth's face remained impassive, making Amy even more angry. Amy hated to admit it, but Beth was stronger than her. She was taking everything Amy was spewing at her and not even flinching. Amy would be in tears if the roles were reversed. Although maybe it wasn't strength. Maybe Beth was just numb to feelings.

"Where have you been these last three and a half years?" Amy asked, continuing on before waiting for an answer. "Ruining your life I suppose. Is that why you came back? You needed money to do it all over again?"

"I came back to say I'm sorry. I came back to try to fix things," Beth answered quietly.

"You can never fix what you broke. You have no idea what you did when you left. And I've been having to cover for you all this time, picking up the slack that you were also too irresponsible to deal with. I've been the one taking care of dad, running the business."

Beth didn't say anything.

"And now everyone's so happy to have sweet, little, beautiful Beth back," Amy said in a mocking voice. "No one cares about all the hard work I've been doing now that the life of the party is home."

"I'm sure everyone really appreciates all the work you've done," Beth replied. "And I'm sure you're very good at it."

Amy glared at her. She didn't want her sister's fake sympathy. So in response she completely unloaded on Beth, telling her just how selfish and ungrateful Amy thought she was. She reminded Beth about all the horrible things she had done in the past, and how badly she had treated people who had only loved her and cared for her.

"Seriously, I don't know what you came back for," Amy said, finishing her outburst. "I know dad's happy that you're back, but we were all better off without you."

Beth nodded. She hadn't said anything as Amy had talked. She had simply stood there and listened, and took it all.

"I'm sorry," Beth simply said again. "For it all." With that, she turned and left.

Amy was outraged. She wanted Beth to fight back. She wanted to tear her sister down. She wanted to hear everything about where Beth had been these last three years and what she had been up to, to continue to show her how much she didn't deserve being back here. But Beth had said nothing—except sorry.

Wanting to get as far away from her sister as she could, Amy practically ran from her room, once again fleeing to David's side. She hurried into his office, slowing down when she got inside, trying to appear semi-composed as she passed everyone working.

"What happened now?" he asked when Amy stormed into his new office. He was finally out of a cubicle.

She walked right past him at his desk and went over to the window. "Beth came to me to apologize—can you believe that?" she asked, turning around to face him.

David smiled at her, like this was a good thing. "That's pretty great," he said. "I'm sure that wasn't easy for her."

Amy glared at him, remembering when she had kicked in his coffee table weeks ago for defending Beth right after she had returned. She still felt horrible about it, yet at the same time she felt the slight urge to break something. What was that about? She had never been that angry before.

"Well why don't you marry her in three weeks if she's become such a favorite to you?" Amy spat out at him.

"Amy, why can't you see that your sister is a different person than she was three years ago?"

Amy shook her head. "Beth will never change."

David stared at her for a moment before speaking. She could tell he was deciding whether or not he should say what was on his mind.

"What are you thinking?" Amy had to know.

"Honestly," he began, "I'm just wondering how long it will be before you realize that you're the one who has to change."

Amy had to fight the urge to scream.

Chapter Twenty-Eight

Amy was sure she was going to break something now. She wanted to throw things at the wall and hear them crash. But instead she stood rooted in spot, her anger simmering around inside of her.

"What do you mean I'm the one who has to change?" she asked through gritted teeth.

David wasn't afraid of her. He walked over and sat down on the small couch along the wall of his office, which had been left there by the previous occupant, reaching for a book on the side table. "Can I share something with you?" he asked.

She gave him a look that told him to go on. He opened the book and she was surprised to see that he had picked up a Bible—even more surprised that he had it with him in the office.

"I want to read to you from Titus," David told her, flipping through the pages until he found the right spot. "Chapter three."

Amy took a deep breath, forcing herself to sit down in the chair across from him. He didn't begin reading until she looked him in the eye.

" 'At one time we too were foolish, disobedient, deceived and enslaved by all kinds of passions and pleasures. We lived in malice and envy, being hated and hating one another.' " David glanced up at Amy, as if to see that she was paying attention and listening to his words. He looked down again and continued on. " 'But when the kindness and love of God our Savior appeared, he saved us, not because of righteous things we had done, but because of his mercy. He saved us through the washing of rebirth and renewal by the Holy

Spirit, whom he poured out on us generously through Jesus Christ our Savior, so that, having been justified by his grace, we might become heirs having the hope of eternal life.'" David glanced up again when he was finished.

"Is there something you wanted me to get out of that?" Amy asked him, still trying to fight him.

"Yes," he answered plainly. "A lot, actually."

"Okay, shoot. Enlighten me." She put her feet up on the coffee table. She was almost surprised by the amount of sarcasm evident in her voice. She didn't mean to take it out on David.

He handed her the Bible and told her what passage it was and had her read it out loud to him.

"What do you think it means?" he asked.

She looked down at the passage again, reading the first verse. "That some people are foolish and disobedient, only caring about their own pleasures and passions, and hating others. Sounds familiar," she stated. "Sounds like someone I know."

David sighed. "Not some people, Amy, everyone. Everyone has been foolish and disobedient. Everyone has been enslaved by different passions and pleasures. Everyone has put their own needs first and has resented others that got in the way of what they want. Don't you realize that?"

"Okay fine," she acquiesced.

"It's a call to obey, to be ready to do good work and to speak evil of no one. It's a call to be gentle and loving, to be humble. It's a call to be merciful to all men because we all have been subject to our fallen nature."

"Yea, yea, yea," Amy said. "We're all fallen, we're all sinners. I know all this," she told him, thinking of everything she had learned in church over the years.

"Yea, I know you know it," he said forcefully. "But are you living it?"

She took a deep breath. "What do you mean?"

"I don't know about you, but I what get from this passage is the realization of how good and gracious God is. I get that we've all done horrible things, we all were born with a fallen nature, and that it isn't our own righteousness that saves us," he stated, looking directly at Amy like he was trying to point something out to her. "This passage makes me feel so humble and grateful at how God has changed me, and that it was Him at work that changed my heart, not anything I had done."

"We're saved by faith, not by works," Amy stated, something she had heard countless times in Sunday school and youth group, in many different sermons.

"Right," David said. "You know what else this passage teaches me? That I should show kindness and compassion to those who are still in that lost place, to those who are ignorant of what God can do in their lives. And it teaches me to have faith that God can change them, and I know He can."

Amy was finally calming down as they sat across from one another. She wasn't angry with David, after all, she was mad at Beth.

"Are you living this?" David asked her.

"Yes," she answered right away.

"You're showing love and compassion to those who are lost, those who have made foolish mistakes, those who have been enslaved by their own passions and pleasures?"

She knew he meant Beth, and she knew the answer was no. She wasn't showing Beth compassion. She didn't feel that Beth deserved compassion.

"Amy, you've been so obedient these last three years, but what's it all been for?"

She stared at him, confused. She had been working so hard because she had to. Didn't he know that?

"What are you trying to tell me?" she asked.

"I'm trying to encourage you," David said. "I'm trying to show you that your own righteousness gets you nowhere and that it is God working through us that keeps us going. Obedience means nothing without God."

Amy nodded, taking a deep breath. She knew he was right, of course, but it was hard to hear. It was hard to hear because that's exactly who she was. She had been trying to make up for the person she thought Beth should be all these years, trying to prove herself useful and a good person, but it meant nothing if she wasn't doing it for God—and she knew she hadn't been otherwise she wouldn't feel so drained. Obedience meant nothing if it wasn't for the right reasons. She remembered what David had said once when they had been having another argument about Beth. He told her to be careful that she wasn't just working out of empty obedience, but that's exactly what she had been doing.

Amy started crying, not even sure where the tears were coming from.

"Empty obedience," she said out loud.

David nodded his head slowly. She looked away, trying to control her tears, but it was as if a flood had been released inside her. Everything she had been doing over the past three years, even longer, had been because she wanted to be the good girl. She wanted to be the one everyone looked at and smiled at and trusted. Amy had gone to youth group in high school simply because Beth didn't. She went to church every Sunday with her father out of habit, but when was the last time that her heart had really been in it? She had been simply going through the motions for so long. Somewhere along the line her heart had stopped reaching out toward God, had stopped serving Him, but she continued to pretend she did anyway because she liked how it made others see her.

"I have a question," David stated. "What made you want to work alongside your dad, to run the business?"

Amy looked at him, swallowing hard. Everything was being put out in the open. She was seeing herself clearly for the first time in a long while. She told him the honest answer.

"Because I knew that Beth didn't want anything to do with it."

David nodded, giving her a slight smile, which she knew was because she was honest with him.

Amy bit her lip, still not able to stop the tears. David had said that she was the one that needed changing, and then he read verses that showed that Amy needed to learn to have compassion and mercy for those who had been lost, just like her sister. But right now, Amy was the one who felt lost.

Suddenly, Amy's mind went back to the day before when she had sat in church with her dad and sister. Amy was holding Eden. Beth had handed her over with a smile when she went up to use the restroom before services started. Amy had watched her sister throughout the service, how she sang with all her heart during worship, peace and contentment on her face. And she had listened with rapt attention to the pastor as he talked about two other sisters from a very long time ago, Mary and Martha—Mary, who had sat at Jesus' feet while He talked, and Martha, who was busy trying to prove herself useful, resenting the fact that her sister wasn't helping her. Suddenly, Amy realized which sister she was from that story. She had read herself into the person of Mary, telling herself that of course she would sit and listen as Jesus talked if He came walking into her house. But she wouldn't. She would be the one doing all the work, trying to show that she was the obedient one. Beth was Mary. She was the one who realized what was most important—worship, not empty obedience. Her sister, once given over to rebellion, to foolishness and disobedience, who had been enslaved by all kinds of passions and pleasures, had been lifted from that place. Amy was the one who was there now. She was the one condemning her sister for the speck of dust in her eye, all the while completely not acknowledging the plank in her own. She hadn't been able to see the person that Beth had become, because Amy couldn't even see herself clearly. Somewhere over the course of three years, they had switched places.

"I'm the fool," she said aloud. "I'm the one who's hating others, who's trying to prove my own righteousness."

David didn't say anything, but she could see compassion shining through his eyes.

"You know when you asked me why I disliked Beth so much?" she asked. David nodded. "Yes."

With a sigh of relief—relief because finally she was seeing herself clearly, she told him why. "I've disliked her so much because it's always been easier to judge Beth than judge myself." Amy leaned forward, putting her head in her hands. "Oh my goodness," she stated.

All these years she had been condemning Beth because Amy didn't want to deal with herself. She didn't want to admit that she had areas in her life that were just as ugly. She didn't want to admit that she made mistakes. She watched Beth struggle with right and wrong and she did nothing to help her, nothing to be there for her—and practically encouraged her to keep struggling, widening the gap between them. Amy wanted to be the golden child. She wanted to be the one that everyone loved. So she did all the right things, but in the end, it all meant nothing.

Yes, Beth had made a lot of mistakes in her life, but how much of that was because of something Amy had said and done to make her think that she was a bad person, that she couldn't do right? Especially after their mom died and Amy pretty much alienated Beth, blaming her for their mom's death. How much of Beth's rebellion was due to Amy herself? Yet, Beth had somehow found the meaning of life for herself. She had overcome the messes that she had made in life. She was the one that was truly living now. Amy was the one who had fallen down more and more the higher she had tried to climb. David was right—Beth had changed. Amy was the one that needed to. Amy was the one that had wanted everyone to love her, but Beth was the one who had learned how to love.

Amy thought over the argument she had just had with Beth that had brought her running over to David's office—and how one-sided it had been. Amy had lashed out at her, blaming her for all the wrong she had ever done, and Beth had just stood there and taken it all. She didn't fight back. She stood strong and simply took everything Amy threw at her—and then she apologized. Beth was the one who said she was sorry.

It was painful for her to realize how horribly she had fallen, but freeing in a way as well. It was proof that her own righteousness was worth nothing. She needed God. She needed Him like she needed air. She could not go on from this point without Him.

As Amy sat there with David, she cried out to God for the first time in years, with all her heart. She prayed for forgiveness, for acting with empty obedience, for the hand she had played in influencing Beth, and for refusing to forgive her. She prayed that God would change and renew her heart and overwhelm it with His Spirit. And she thanked Him that her salvation had nothing to do with herself. She had become so proud over the years, but there was a certain freedom in realizing just how weak she was. She had never felt so humbled in her entire life.

"I've been pretty blind, haven't I?" she asked David after tearfully praying aloud.

David smiled at her. "I think your heart had been in the right place to begin with, you just lost yourself after a time."

She nodded. "Thanks for helping me try to find the way back."

David got up and came over to her, reaching for her hand and pulling her up. "As your soon-to-be husband, and the man that loves you, I can tell you that that's what I'm here for—anytime."

Amy smiled at him, kissing his adorable face.

After washing all the dried, salty tears from her face in the bathroom, Amy walked with David back out to her car, ready to go home. It was time to start showing Beth that Amy could be a different person as well.

"You should come by for dinner when you get off work," Amy told him.

He smiled. "I'll do that."

Amy drove home, surprised when she pulled in the driveway to see the old car that Beth had come back home in parked in front of the house once again. She thought that had disappeared right after Beth had gotten her new car.

Walking into the house, she followed the sound of voices into the living room.

"Amy!" her dad said. "Where'd you run off to?"

She gave him a slight smile, her cheeks red. "I was with David at the office." She had plenty of time to tell him everything that she had gone through, that she had realized, later when they were alone. After all, she didn't just owe Beth an apology. She had been emptily following her father for years, showing him no gratitude for all that he had done for her. Although she had stayed, she had done the same thing as Beth. She had still demanded what she thought she deserved, and then harshly condemned him when she didn't think she was going to get it. She thought of what her father had said to her the night Beth had come home and he had come outside to talk with her. Before going back into the house, he invited her in as well. She was truly ready to come inside now.

Amy looked over to the person her dad was talking to. The man smiled at her, and she smiled back.

"This is Johnny," her dad said, and then turned to him. "This is Beth's sister, Amy."

Johnny stood up and held his hand out to Amy. "Nice to meet you."

"You, too," she said, slightly confused. She looked over to her father. "Where's Beth?" she wanted to know.

"Out walking Eden," he answered. "She left a little over two hours ago now, but you know her. Beth could walk all day and not get tired."

Amy was surprised that Johnny nodded in agreement to her dad's comment, like he knew Beth just as well. She was slightly upset that Beth wasn't home—which was shocking enough in itself.

Amy sat down, listening as her dad and Johnny continued to talk. They were talking as if they were old friends, but Amy was sure her dad had never seen him before. She could tell from the conversation that Johnny knew Beth—after all, they both had arrived in the same car. She was curious about him and what had brought him to Colorado. The license plate on the car said California. He probably knew Beth more than Amy had ever tried to.

They talked for a good half hour, Amy joining in, before she glanced out the tall windows and saw Beth pushing the stroller up the drive, bundled up against the cold. Amy liked Johnny. He seemed like a really great, genuine guy, and he had a lot of funny stories about working in a flower shop with his parents.

Amy noticed through the tall window as her sister came to a dead halt as she saw the car parked in the driveway. It took her a moment before she started walking again.

Amy heard the door open and then close again. She waited for Beth to come into the living room. She came slowly, holding Eden on her hip, surprise written on her face—surprise that only intensified when she saw who was sitting in the living room.

"Johnny," she said like she didn't believe it.

Amy looked over and saw Johnny smiling widely at Beth. Suddenly Amy knew exactly why Johnny was here. She could see it on his face as he looked at her sister. He was in love with her.

Eden started clapping, obviously recognizing a familiar face. A familiar and loved face.

"What are you doing here?" Beth asked him.

Johnny stood up and walked toward her. Amy couldn't help but watch.

"I came here to tell you that I love you," he stated with confidence. Amy was surprised at how he just blurted it out. She couldn't help but smile. Beth looked shocked.

"I…you…you can't just…" Beth looked around the room, glancing at Dad and then Amy, searching for words, but coming up with nothing.

"And I'm staying for as long as it takes for you to admit that you love me, too," Johnny informed her.

Beth's eyes shot back to Johnny. She was almost glaring at him.

"You're staying?" she asked.

"Yea," he said with a playful grin. "Your dad even said I could stay here."

"No," Beth said, right away. "You can't stay here."

"Why not?" Johnny asked.

Amy watched her sister's face as she stared at Johnny. She clutched Eden closer to her, almost as if she could shield herself with her baby, although Eden was reaching her arms out for Johnny to take her.

Shaking her head, she gave her answer. "If you stay, I'm not sure I'll have to strength to tell you no."

Johnny gave her a cocky grin. "I'm counting on that."

Amy's mouth dropped at Johnny's words and she turned and glanced at her dad, who only had amusement written on his face. He winked at Amy, then looked back to Beth.

Johnny walked closer to Beth, taking Eden from her. "Well hello, little princess. I've missed you! You're so big!" He kissed her forehead and walked back over to the sofa where he had been sitting, smiling at Eden, who was seemingly trying to tell him a story in a language only she could understand.

Amy looked at Beth and saw nothing but sheer terror.

Chapter Twenty-Nine

Beth pressed her back into the wall, glaring at Johnny. She couldn't believe that he was here, that he had just told her that he loved her. She never imagined that Johnny could be so bold. He was normally the more quiet type. Although a voice in the back of her head told her that he had never been that way with her. This kindhearted, quiet man had been bold enough to keep coming after her when she had needed it most. He had been bold enough to jump in the middle of a fight between her and Tyler and literally rescue her from his clutches. And he had brought her to his parents' house, giving her a home. There was even a boldness to the way that he continually prayed for her when there was no other way to fight for her. When it came to Beth, Johnny was always bold, always stepping up. He was just always *there*.

"Don't look so terrified," Johnny said, glancing up at her. He then looked back down at Eden, talking to her and smiling at her in a way that pierced Beth's heart. She knew that Johnny loved Eden dearly. It made her love him even more. She knew that it had probably torn him up when she left Lake Tahoe simply because Eden was no longer there, let alone her.

Beth shook her head. "This can't be happening."

"Oh, it is," Johnny stated, not taking his eyes off of Eden. "You could make it easy and just admit that you love me." He looked up at her, a mocking grin on his face.

"What makes you think…" But she couldn't finish her sentence, and she saw a challenge in Johnny's eyes, as if he dared her to try and say that she *didn't* love him. And she couldn't do it. She couldn't lie and pretend that she didn't love him. She just didn't want to love him.

Beth narrowed her eyes on him and gave him a daring smile. There was no way that he could just stay here. As long as it took? What did that even mean?

With a newfound confidence, Beth walked over to where her father and sister were sitting with Johnny. She took a seat across from him and gave him a playful smirk.

"When are you going back to Tahoe?" she wondered.

"I have no definite plans at the moment," Johnny stated, relaxing into the couch with Eden in the crook of his arm, chewing on her fingers. "At least, none but getting you to admit that you love me."

"What about work?" she wanted to know.

"I've got work all worked out. Benefit of working in the family business."

Beth sighed. "You work for an advertising agency."

"Yes," Johnny said. "And the majority of the work I do is for the flower shop, in case you didn't realize that already. The rest I can mostly do from home. Or here."

"You can't just not work," Beth countered.

Johnny shrugged, as if none of this was a big deal. "I'll figure it all out. And I'm still working—just working at something else. Some things take more of a priority than my job."

She rolled her eyes. "What about your parents?"

"What about them?"

"You can't just leave them," Beth stated, and then looked down at her hands, feeling ashamed. That's exactly what she had done. With a sheen in her eyes, she turned toward her father, but he only had a radiant smile in place. She was confident in the fact that he was confident in her—he knew that the person that Beth was now would never leave her family behind. She turned back to Johnny, and with a conviction born of knowledge, she told him again, "You can't leave them."

He gave her a compassionate smile, knowing what that admission cost her. He had seen her transformation over the past year. He had seen her struggling to survive and then watched her adapt to a completely different situation. He had met the Beth that wanted to keep running, and had been there when she realized that only place she wanted to be was the place she had run from.

"I'm not leaving them," he stated. "I'm twenty-six years old, and I moved out ages ago now. I'd be a little concerned if they expected me to stay forever."

"That's not what I meant," Beth replied.

"I know." When she didn't say anything, Johnny added, "They fully support me being here one hundred percent. If anything, you're the one who can't leave them."

"I would never," she stated.

"I know you wouldn't," Johnny replied. "You love them. And you love me."

Beth rolled her eyes. "What makes you so sure of that?" she demanded.

A look came over Johnny that made her melt inside—it was her look. He was looking at her with complete adoration and love that she could feel it inside of her. Her heart started pounding faster, and she felt a flutter in her stomach.

"I'm sure," he responded.

Beth didn't know what to say. She couldn't believe that he was here, that he had come all the way here not to proclaim his love for Beth, which, of course, he definitely was doing, but he came here for her to proclaim her love for him. She didn't know how to do it. She didn't want to love him. She had learned that she had been given so many blessings that she could never deserve, but Johnny was just too good for her, so much above her. He deserved someone who could give him what she never could. He deserved someone who didn't have a past, and definitely who didn't have a child with another man. She could never be whole for him in the way that he deserved, in the way that he would be for her.

"Well," her dad stated in the silence that lapsed. "I have to run into town for a few things for dinner," he stated. "Why don't you come with me, Amy?"

Beth glanced at her dad, and then to her sister. She had hardly been aware of their presence at all in the midst of this, except when she slipped up and made a comment about leaving home. She blushed, realizing that they had overheard it all.

"Uh, sure," Amy said slowly, glancing at Beth. She gave Beth a hurried smile, which caught Beth by surprise especially in light of everything Amy had spewed at her earlier in the day. She was actually acknowledging Beth's presence for once. "Have fun," she stated, almost like she was repressing a laugh.

"Um, thanks," Beth replied, even more surprised that Amy had spoken to her as she got up and left the room, their dad close behind.

Dad turned around in the doorway. "Don and Mary are coming over for dinner, and David will probably be here as well," he told Beth, then glanced at Johnny. "And Johnny of course."

Beth caught Johnny's face as he gave her dad a knowing grin.

"Beth, show him to the guest room overlooking the garden. I think he'll enjoy it." With a wink at his youngest daughter, he left.

Slowly, Beth turned her attention back to Johnny, having absolutely no idea what she was supposed to do now. Even though she had been nearly unaware of their presence, in some ways her dad and Amy had acted as a buffer. Now Beth was on her own.

"The guest room is upstairs, first door on your left."

Johnny smirked. "Thanks."

"Yea."

"You going to show me around this place?"

"Why should I?" Beth asked, getting slightly annoyed out of nervousness.

Johnny stood up. "You're going to have to get used to me being around here, whether you like it or not. You could just make it easier on yourself and stop fighting me."

With that, he left the room and Beth caught him heading up the stairs through the doorway, Eden in the crook of his arm. She stared after him, in utter disbelief that this was actually happening. She got up quickly and went after him. She opened the door to the guestroom, but didn't see him inside.

"Johnny?" she called into the room, met with silence.

She walked out and opened the door across the hall, but he wasn't in there either. She tried another room and then came upon him—in her bedroom.

"What are you doing in here?" she asked, hands on her hips, angry now.

Johnny looked around with wonder written all over his face. "This room is the size of the whole bottom level of my parents' house."

Beth shrugged. It wasn't quite true, but the room was large just the same. He was slowly spinning around, taking everything in.

"How many bedrooms are in this place?" he asked, his eye catching on something. Beth followed his gaze to the picture frame resting on the ledge over the fireplace. It was a picture of him and his family with Beth holding Eden in the hospital when Eden was born.

"Uh…seven," she replied. "Eight bathrooms. Ten thousand square feet. Resting on two acres of land." She looked out through the large windows at the mountain and pointed. "And that."

Johnny's eyes widened. "You're rich."

She shook her head, her eyes narrowing on his. "My dad's rich."

She could tell that Johnny was watching her face closely but she wasn't sure what he was looking for. Eden let out a tiny wail, but Johnny's gaze didn't stray from her face.

"It means nothing to you though, does it?" he asked.

"What are you talking about?"

"This," he said, his free hand extending in a wave over her room.

"Not anymore."

He smiled at her. "I really hope you realize just how much you've changed."

She bit her bottom lip, feeling that flutter in her stomach again. He took a step closer to her.

"Why are you so scared?"

"I'm not scared," she replied right away, her pulse increasing with each step he took toward her.

"You're terrified."

Eden let out another wail.

"She's hungry," Beth said, glancing down at Eden.

Johnny held the baby out to her and Beth took her. Eden calmed down right away, knowing that Beth would see to her needs.

"Why are you so afraid to admit you love me?"

Beth pressed her lips together, feeling like she was going to cry. Johnny had always been able to see through her pretenses. He could see right down into her heart.

Johnny lifted his hand and cupped Beth's face. "You've finally fallen for the good guy and that scares you more than anything, doesn't it?" Johnny asked gently. "Because it's a huge unknown for you."

Eden started squirming, wanting to be fed right now. Beth adjusted her in her arms.

Johnny let go of her face. "Feed Eden. Take a few minutes to breathe. I'll see you later."

With that, Johnny left her alone in her room with Eden. She stood rooted in place staring at the doorway he had just departed from. She was completely unaware that she was trembling.

And she didn't know how long her resolve would hold out with him so near.

Chapter Thirty

"So, Johnny," Amy began, pressing her lips together and looking for conversation. "Do you ski?"

He smiled wide at that, like he found it almost comical. "I've only gone once, but I'm looking forward to getting better at it."

Beth glanced over at Johnny and scoffed. She was standing on the other side of the long island, as far away as she could possibly be from Johnny in the kitchen, cutting up an onion, helping to prepare dinner. Amy had no idea what she was making, but she knew enough about her sister's talents to know that whatever Beth made would be amazing.

"What?" he challenged her. "I liked it!" He turned to Amy and explained that Beth had taken him skiing in Tahoe in May, and how great a teacher she had been. Amy just smirked. She was sure that Johnny would ski again, and she knew why he would as well.

Her father had forced Amy out of the house earlier, practically thrusting Beth and Johnny together. They went into town and had a cup of coffee, sitting there until her dad thought they had waited an appropriate amount of time before heading back to the house—they hadn't actually picked up anything for dinner. Amy thought it hilarious that her dad was trying to work as a matchmaker. He mentioned in the car on the way to the coffee shop that although he didn't know Johnny at all, he had a feeling about him. He told Amy that he thought he had just met his other new son-in-law.

Amy didn't know quite what to make of it. She could plainly see how much Johnny loved Beth, and how much Beth was fighting her love for Johnny, but she didn't understand why. When Amy and her dad got back to the house, Beth was sitting in the entertainment room, the big-screen TV on, yet she clearly was not paying attention to it. She kept glancing toward the stairs every few minutes. She told them that Johnny was resting after his trip. Evidently he had driven through the night from Lake Tahoe to get to Holy Cross. Beth had started dinner before Johnny woke up, who came down to everyone congregating in the kitchen, including Aunt Mary and Uncle Don. Although Uncle Don and her dad left the girls alone after a little bit, enjoying sitting by the fire and watching a football game more than preparing dinner.

Although they had both kept wondering what was going on back at the house, Amy had taken the opportunity to open up to her dad while they were sitting together over coffee, the beautiful snow-covered Mount of the Holy Cross outlined by the setting sun in the distance. It had been hard to begin—there was a huge lump in her throat when she tried to speak. But she had to apologize. And she had to take him up on his invitation.

"Dad," Amy sputtered. He glanced from the mountain to her, a peaceful smile on his face. "I need to tell you something."

He raised his eyebrows, waiting for her to go on. She didn't know where to begin.

She bit her lip, tears coming into her eyes. "The night that Beth came home you asked me if I was ready," she began, swallowing hard and blinking quickly, trying to keep the tears in. "I am. I'm ready to come inside the house now."

The lines in his forehead smoothed out, a big smile coming over his face. He didn't need to say anything—she could see it all in his face. He had spent over three years waiting for Beth to come home, and just as long for Amy to come home as well.

"You don't know how happy I am to hear that," he stated, reaching for her hand across the table. He gave it a gentle squeeze.

She apologized to him. She told him how sorry she was for taking advantage of him, for not appreciating him enough, for being resentful toward her sister. She told him about Beth coming to talk to her earlier that morning, which felt like a lifetime away, and about everything that David had told her. She told him how freeing it was to let go and see herself clearly for the first time—faults and all. She felt like a new person.

"I love you Amy Grace," her dad said. "No matter what."

She nodded, squeezing his hand this time. "Thanks."

He gave her a look that told her that she never needed to thank him for loving her. But she felt so appreciative of her father. He had done everything for her over the years, and had given her everything that he had worked so hard for. He believed in her. He knew that she had what it took to work the ski resort. He knew that she had what it took simply to be herself, which she was learning was okay. She didn't have to be anyone else—she didn't even have to be her mother. All that anyone ever asked of her was to just be Amy, and that's exactly where she wanted to start now. Her father had already forgiven her for all her faults and failures a long time ago. She knew where she really needed to start.

"I need to fix things with Beth," Amy stated, wrapping her hands around her mug of tea, enjoying the warmth.

Her dad sighed heavily. She could guess what he was thinking. Amy and Beth had never been close before. There weren't warm memories of a once close relationship that she could go back to and try to build off of. Amy had to start from scratch, and she knew that she had to be the one to try with her sister. Amy had been trying to cast Beth out of her life since the day she was born. Beth was the one who had always reached out to her, even as kids. She had always sought to have a relationship with Amy, but Amy never wanted it. She pushed Beth so far away that eventually she gave up. It really saddened Amy to think of how well she had alienated her sister—the one person in her life that she should have always been looking out for. Even today, Beth had come to her to apologize, and Amy had pushed her away. In many ways Beth was much more mature than Amy. She wasn't afraid to reach out, even when it was hard. She wasn't afraid to confront her past mistakes and try to fix them. She didn't turn a blind eye to her actions, she had sought to make amends wherever possible. And Amy hadn't been letting her. Amy knew nothing about what had gone on in Beth's life in the time that she had been away, but she was sure that coming home after all that time and facing the things she had done had to have been one of the hardest things Beth had ever done—and the strongest. Beth came home of her own accord, Amy had to be prompted.

"I don't know even where to begin with Beth," Amy stated honestly, hoping that her dad would offer some insight.

"What do you want out of your sister?" her dad asked her, his eyes narrowing on her slightly.

Amy pressed her lips together, taking a deep breath before replying. "I just want her. I want to really know her. And I want to be a sister to her."

Her dad took a sip of his coffee, glancing out to the mountain again before addressing her. She could tell he was pleased to hear what she had to say, but proceeded with caution all the same.

"You're going to have to be patient with her," her dad replied. "You're going to have to earn her trust. Beth's been through a lot, and she's been betrayed by a lot of people." He paused before adding, "But she's always wanted to know you."

His words made her want to cry all the more. She knew her dad wasn't blind to the way that Amy had treated Beth over the years. But she also knew that she genuinely wanted to make amends of her own now. She was happy for his advice, willing to be patient where Beth was concerned. She had no idea what her sister had been through in the last three and a half years, and she knew her father wouldn't tell her. It would have to be Beth's choice. Beth would have to tell her because she wanted Amy to know, and because she trusted her enough to tell her. Amy left the coffee shop with her dad resolved to do anything it took to show Beth that she actually did care. And she knew she had one thing going for her. Even through all the years of their tumultuous relationship, the reason that Amy reacted so strongly to Beth wasn't out of competition or resentment, ultimately it was out of love. Deep down inside of her, she knew she loved Beth. Now it was time to show her.

"Do you need help with anything?" Amy asked Beth, who was wiping her eyes on her sleeves, having just thrown the onions she had chopped up into a big bowl.

Beth looked at her like she was surprised to hear Amy address her personally. Her answer was delayed.

"You can make the rolls if you want," Beth said with a shrug. "The dough's in the fridge."

Amy nodded and went to the fridge, grabbing the big metal bowl. She shaped the dough into little mounds like she had once seen Beth do before, placing them on a baking sheet.

"What can I do?" Mary asked, stepping right in and offering her assistance. Beth was about to answer her when a cry over the baby monitor caught her attention. She was about to wash her hands and head up the stairs when Johnny beat her to it.

Beth watched him go with a grimace on her face.

"So," Mary said, "explain."

Beth sighed and glanced at her. "There's nothing to explain," she stated firmly.

"Well he's clearly in love with you."

"I know," Beth groaned.

"And you clearly love him as well."

Beth looked at her sharply. "That's...so not the point."

Amy suppressed a grin. So Beth was admitting that she was in love with Johnny, just not to Johnny himself.

Before Mary could try to prod what exactly that point was, Johnny walked back into the kitchen with a sleepy Eden in his arms, who smiled upon seeing her mother, her pacifier falling out of her mouth.

"Mommy's busy right now Eden," Johnny said gently. Eden looked up at him and smiled, bouncing a little in his arms.

"The guys are in the other room if you want to join them," Beth said pointedly. "From the sound of their shouts, it seems like a good game." Aunt Mary smacked her arm.

Johnny gave Beth an amused smile. "You can kick me out of the kitchen if you want, but I'm still not going anywhere." With that he left, taking Eden with him.

"Be nice to that boy!" Aunt Mary reprimanded Beth.

Beth rolled her eyes and concentrated on what she was doing.

Once Beth declared that dinner was ready, Amy went into the living room to tell the guys to make their way to the dining room. David had arrived while she was helping with dinner. He gave her a big smile and pulled her aside before everyone sat down.

"How're you doing?" he asked her.

She gave him a radiant smile. "I feel like this has been the longest day of my life," Amy told him. "And that I'm a completely different person from when I woke up this morning."

He nodded. "In a good way, I hope."

"In a great way," she replied, wrapping her arms around his middle. He pulled her close and enveloped her in a hug. She couldn't wait to be married to this man. She realized that the tension that had been there between them since Beth had been home was only him trying to help her, to walk alongside her and carry her when she wasn't seeing clearly the road in front of her. He wanted nothing but to help and guide her. David brought out the best in her. She couldn't ask for more than that.

"I love you," he whispered into her ear.

She pulled away and gave him a quick kiss. "I love you, too."

They joined everyone at the table, Johnny sitting across from Beth, and David across from Amy. Despite the fact that Beth clearly wanted to pretend that Johnny wasn't there, they had an enjoyable dinner. Although Amy and Beth sat side by side and didn't speak directly to one another the entire meal, things just felt put together again. Amy felt light and free. She was happy in a way that she hadn't been in a really long time.

After they had finished both dinner and dessert, everyone lazily congregated back to the roaring fire in the living room. Amy hadn't noticed her dad leave, so was therefore surprised when he walked back in the room lugging two pairs of skis, both resting on his shoulder like he was ready to hit the slopes that instant. He took them down and rested them up against the wall, leaving the room for another moment and coming back in with two pairs of ski boots.

"I have a bit of an early Christmas present to deliver," he stated, addressing the room, putting the boots down next to the skis. "I was just so excited about it that I couldn't wait!"

He looked to Beth, who was sitting on the floor with her legs spread, Eden leaning up against her surrounded by her favorite toys.

"Since you'll be teaching again, I thought it only appropriate to get your old skis good and waxed so you'll be all set to go."

Beth looked at the skis her dad was holding, a slight crease between her eyebrows. Amy looked back at her dad.

"But they had rusted a bit over the years. So here, you'll be needing these."

He reached for one of the pairs of skis and handed them out toward Beth. They were brand new, top of the line. And Amy knew that her dad had them made to Beth's specifications, based off her old skis. They were shaped perfectly for her height, as well as her skill level.

Beth's mouth dropped, like she couldn't believe what she was seeing. Amy had to guess that she was a little overwhelmed after everything else their dad had already given her since she had returned. She had been there for the unveiling of the nursery, and had come home to see the new car as well. But it was the new pair of skis that made Beth cry.

Beth stood up and walked toward their dad, hugging him while clutching her brand new skis at the same time. She thanked him profusely and then began examining them. Amy knew that she had to be thrilled. She had been surprised when her dad mentioned that Beth wanted to teach again, but somehow it was fitting. They both loved this place so much. Skiing was a huge part of both of their lives.

Dad turned to Amy. "I got you a new pair as well. They were needing a bit of an update, too."

Amy was sure she was giving him the same shocked look that she had seen on Beth's face. She too went and hugged her father, reaching for her brand new skis, excited to try them out.

Amy glanced at her sister and caught her eye. Despite everything else, they both looked at one another and smiled. Every few years the two of them had both received new skis for Christmas.

"Oh and Beth," Dad started, "you better try those out and make sure you like them. You have your first client tomorrow morning. A private lesson."

"Tomorrow?" she asked, surprised.

"Yes, tomorrow." He turned to Johnny and winked. Beth clearly noticed, because she gave Johnny a thunderous look. And then, despite herself, she laughed.

Chapter Thirty-One

Beth awoke before the sun had even risen the next morning, completely exhilarated by the fact that today would be the first day that she got to ski her mountain in over three years. She had been feeling antsy as she had gone to bed the night before, her brand new skis propped up in the corner of her room right next to her bed. Excitement and adventure were coursing through her veins, memories of years and years on this mountain propelling her forward. She couldn't wait.

She had gone out early, leaving Eden with her sister of all people, who had willingly volunteered the night before. She had taken her skis, and her dad had driven her to the main entrance of the ski resort, parking right by the ticket counter in his designated spot. Beth was dressed in all her winter gear that had remained home in her absence, everything with the emblem of Mount of the Holy Cross printed on it. She was a walking advertisement, but she didn't care. This was a huge part of her homecoming, something she hadn't realized that she had missed so entirely much. She had gone skiing when she had been in Europe, and then the one time in Tahoe, but nothing compared to home.

Her dad didn't stay with her once she had gotten onto the gondola. Instead, he just sent her off. The resort was still a half hour from opening. The snow had been groomed, everything set for the coming day. And Beth would have the first run down the mountain.

She was alone in the gondola as it went to the lodge three-quarters of the way up the slopes. She grabbed her skis as it came in, hopping out and heading into the unblemished snow. With a smile on her face she put her new skis on and used her poles to help propel her forward to where a lift took her to the highest, steepest ski trails. Beth stopped right at the top of her favorite trail, looking out below her.

It was beautiful, of course. The sun was still coming up, casting a stunning golden glow to the still waking town of Holy Cross. She could see the whole town from where she was, including a portion of Monahan Ranch that wasn't tucked away in the trees. Snow was covering the branches of the trees, the lake in the distance was almost frozen all the way across. And Beth loved all of it.

She couldn't do anything but praise God for bringing her right back to this place before she headed down the mountain. And her prayer only continued through the swish of her skis, the movement of her body, as her uncontainable joy led her forward.

It wasn't the first time that Beth had been the first person of the day to head down the mountain—in fact it was a New Year's tradition in her family. They always went up all together and took the first run of the year on the first of January. But today it was extra special. Just Beth and God—and her humble, thankful heart.

By the time Beth reached the bottom, tears were in her eyes. She couldn't remember ever being so happy as she had been in the past year. And this beautiful run felt fitting to Beth's new start at a better life that came about when she had been taken to another little ski town. But this was home.

Others were starting to arrive when Beth got to the bottom of the mountain. Her dad was talking to the guys operating the gondola. She went right over to him, quickly stepping out of her skis, and greeted him with a big hug.

"Thank you," she told him.

They stayed like that for a while, until he ran back down to the car and grabbed his own skis, and the two of them took off up the mountain together. Beth and her dad skied together for well over an hour before she had to go meet Johnny and he had to go into the office. And she had loved every minute of it.

Beth walked over to the area where ski school always met, and Johnny was there waiting for her, holding his skis over his shoulder like he skied everyday. Apparently he had gotten everything he needed without any help from her.

"Good morning," he said when she came to a halt beside him.

"Hi!" she replied excitedly, unable to contain her happiness, forgetting that she was supposed to be upset by the fact that Johnny was there. But that was impossible. She was thrilled beyond belief that Johnny was with her.

He laughed at her exuberance. "I take it you've had a good morning so far on your new skis."

"The best," she answered. "You ready to ski some more?"

"It's been a few months," he reminded her.

She smiled wider. "It's not something you forget. Trust me."

With that, she took off toward the bunny hill, Johnny scrambling to get into his skis and follow behind her. She had him take a few runs on the bunny hill, reminding him of how to position his skis. He did great.

"You ready for something a little more advanced?" she asked when he met her at the bottom of the hill.

"How advanced are we talking?" he asked, looking up at the mountain. She followed his gaze.

"Not quite that far," she answered. "I'm not trying to kill you."

"Are you doubting my skills?" he asked her.

Beth gave him a sheepish smile. "Hey, if you want to go all the way to the top and ski some double black diamonds, you'll hear no complaints from me."

His nervousness came out at that, and Beth laughed.

"Come on," she said, and led him to a lift that took them up only a portion of the mountain to some of the easier trails. She knew that Johnny would be able to handle them.

They waited in line to catch the lift, Beth being greeted by many of the same workers that had been there when she'd left.

"So this is your mountain," Johnny said when the two of them were on the lift.

"This is my mountain," Beth stated. "And I love it."

"I can see that," Johnny said, looking at her inquisitively through his ski mask.

Beth tried not to look at him for too long. Of course she was beyond thrilled to see Johnny. She missed him, and all of his family. They were her family. But he terrified her.

They got off the lift and skied down some of the easier trails together for most of the morning. Johnny really picked skiing up quickly, which pleased Beth. But she wanted him to enjoy it for himself, and not for her.

After getting him to go down an intermediate trail, the two of them took the gondola higher up the mountain where there was a mountain lodge, which served cafeteria-style food, as well as a smaller log cabin, which was a sit-down restaurant. They left their skis outside the lodge in the designated area, and walked into the big room, warmth surrounding them as soon as they opened the doors. The one side of the lodge was floor-to-ceiling windows, looking out over the slopes and the town.

Beth and Johnny grabbed trays and plates, and worked their way through the buffet. Beth really hadn't had much to eat that morning when she left. She had been too excited to hit the slopes to sit down for breakfast. So she grabbed the last two pieces of French toast—they were getting ready to switch over the food for lunch—as well as some hot chocolate to warm up with. She was happy to eat now.

They paid for their food, everyone who worked in the lodge greeting Beth by name, before they walked over to a table right up against the windows.

"You're so popular," Johnny said jokingly.

"They all work for my dad," she corrected him.

He shrugged.

They started eating after Johnny said a quick blessing, Beth's eyes outside the window as skiers and snowboarders made their way down the mountain.

"This is quite a place," Johnny said, shaking his head.

"It's not that different from Tahoe," Beth stated.

"Yea, but your family doesn't own Lake Tahoe."

She bit her lip, her eyes narrowing on him.

"Sorry I'll stop talking about it," Johnny told her. "It's just kind of shocking to actually see it all in person."

Beth sighed. She couldn't hold her tongue for that much longer. She had been having fun with Johnny all morning, but her guard had been up the entire time.

"What are you doing here?" she asked him, wrapping her hands around her mug of hot chocolate to warm them.

"I already told you what I'm doing here."

"What does getting me to tell you that I love you prove?" she wanted to know.

He looked at her inquisitively. "Why does it have to prove anything? It's the truth."

"But what does it matter?" she asked, crossing her arms.

"Are you kidding?" He leaned closer to her. "It means everything."

"It's not going to change anything."

"Oh yes it will. You're just scared."

Beth looked out the window, tearing her eyes away from his face. It was just like their early morning visits to the diner over a year ago, when Johnny was trying to get Beth to see reason. Although in the last year absolutely everything had completely changed. Yet here they were once again, leveling with one another.

"You can't pretend that there's nothing going on between us, Beth," Johnny said, drawing her attention back to him.

"I wasn't."

"Then what's got you so bothered?"

"You know you can do so much better than me, right?"

He gave her a look like he couldn't believe she had just said that. She glanced away from him again.

"I don't want anyone but you."

"Johnny, you're a great guy. Probably the best guy I've ever met. And you've always been that way. I haven't."

"I know everything already, Beth. I know what you've been through."

"Exactly. I've made a lot of mistakes. I've done things you'd never even think about doing."

"Why are you bringing all of this up again? You let it go. You're not that person anymore."

"That doesn't mean that all those things didn't happen."

She felt tears coming into her eyes. Because no matter what she said, he would still love her, and she knew it. And she wanted that, too. He knew everything about her and all of the choices that she had made, and somehow he still had never condemned her or judged her for them. She knew he never would, not when he had seen her sorrow, her struggle for her life again. He didn't see the ugliness within her, he saw hope instead. In a way that shocked her, she realized that he saw what God did when He looked at her—her redemption.

"I could never be whole for you. You deserve someone who could give you everything."

"Don't you get it? You can give me everything I want."

"What is it that you want, then?"

"You, Beth. I want you. I want you no matter what. I want you despite the things you've done in the past. I want you for the person you've become because of all those things. I want you and no one else."

She just shook her head, trying not to cry. She didn't know what to say to that. She avoided his gaze.

"I want to marry you, Beth. I want to live here in Holy Cross, because I know this is where you need to be right now. I want to spend my life with you. And I want to adopt Eden."

That snapped her attention right back to him, surprise drying her tears.

"You want to what?"

He reached into his jacket pocket and drew out a stack of papers.

"I've had the documents made up," Johnny stated, placing them on the table.

Beth looked at them, unable to believe her eyes.

"Adoption papers?" she gasped.

"I contacted a lawyer the day you told me you were leaving Tahoe."

"And you felt the need to bring them skiing with you today?"

Johnny laughed. "I had a feeling you'd put all the cards out on the table somewhere over the course of the day."

Beth was flabbergasted. "You want to adopt Eden?" she asked, still unable to believe what was before her.

"Yes," Johnny stated. "And I want to marry you."

Beth had no idea what to say. She had no idea how to even react. She had loved Johnny for a long time, and he had loved her for even longer. But this was beyond anything that she had dared to dream for.

Johnny reached across the table and grabbed her hand. Beth didn't have the strength to yank it away.

"I love you," he said. "And I love Eden. I want us to be a family."

And Beth could see it. She could see the three of them together. Because somewhere over the last months she had started to think of Johnny as Eden's father. He had been there for everything. He was the one who had saved Beth from herself. He had been patient with her, giving her a place where she could open up. He had brought her to his home, and given her a new life. He had driven her to the hospital and had stayed by her side until it was time for Eden to be delivered. And he had been there ever since then. He was always there for Beth, and always there for Eden. In many ways they already were a family. But still, making it all official was a big step. And tying herself to Johnny forever terrified her. What if he was wrong? What if he didn't really want Beth after all? What if she messed up again?

"If it helps, your dad's all for it," he told her.

"What do you mean?"

"I asked him yesterday if I could marry you."

Her eyes narrowed. "He said you could marry me?"

"Yes."

"After just meeting you for the first time?" she asked loudly. She wasn't sure how to take that.

Johnny laughed. "Well perhaps he knows, as well as you and I know, that we're meant to be," he told her. "And speaking of your dad, we've got to go," Johnny said, standing up.

"What?"

"I told him we'd be back around noon. We're going to go cut down your Christmas tree."

Beth just stared at him, barely hearing what he was saying.

"Come on," he urged her, taking her tray with his and clearing their table. She followed him slowly outside. He already had his skis on and was moving toward an easier trail.

"Meet you at the bottom!" Johnny called, and took off.

Beth just stood there, staring after Johnny's retreating figure, like she couldn't believe what had just happened, her body trying to catch up to her brain.

She had to methodically think through putting her skis back on, but once she took off, excitement took over and she was able to let the thoughts flee from her mind.

Beth didn't follow Johnny down the easy trail, instead she took off on her own, down a black diamond, and although he had gotten a significant head start, she still beat him to the bottom.

Chapter Thirty-Two

Everyone loaded into her father's large SUV. David sat up front with Dad, Johnny in the middle section next to the car seat, and Beth in the backseat with Amy. They were all dressed up in their warm gear, ready to head out to pick out their Christmas tree. It was a Monahan family tradition to chop down their tree every year. They actually had multiple trees, but the biggest one went in the living room and was always elegantly decorated. It was the main feature for the season, so large that it could be seen from the town below if looked at from the right angle.

They also had Christmas trees in other rooms. There had always been an ultra-colorful one in the entertainment room, which had always been for Amy and Beth to decorate anyway they wanted to, which was always fun for them. They had made a lot of ornaments over the years, and just had special ones that had meaning to them. It was their tree. They had always had to pick it out together, which was one of the few things they didn't fight on. They both looked for the perfect tree, and seemed to agree on a good one together every year.

There were also smaller trees that went in Amy and Beth's rooms, as well as their parents' room. Elizabeth Monahan had loved Christmas more than any other holiday. Every room was decorated in some way.

Usually they began picking out trees the weekend after Thanksgiving, but with Beth's homecoming and Amy being absent from the house every chance she could get, they hadn't had a chance yet. Monahan Ranch was definitely behind on the decorations, but not for long. Beth couldn't wait to have everything decorated for Christmas. She was so excited to be home this year to celebrate with her family.

When they got to the Christmas tree farm, Beth was flooded with multitudes of memories. They came here every year, and it had always been their mother that had prodded Amy and Beth forward. Her exuberance for Christmas overflowed into the two of them. Their mom was the one delegating decorating duties to them both. And each year, once their trees were up in both Amy and Beth's rooms, she made it a special night for each of them. She would take Amy out for dinner and do some Christmas shopping, and then the two of them would come back and decorate Amy's tree, and then the next night she would do the same for Beth. She looked forward to that night with her mom every year. But this year she would be on her own.

With a thought that made her cringe, she realized that she could ask Johnny's help to decorate her tree.

Beth got out of the car behind Amy, turning around to help Johnny unbuckle Eden from the car seat. She felt bad for her little girl, who was wrapped up like an Eskimo in her winter clothes. She didn't want her to freeze, though. But Eden was being a good sport like always. She had been mad when Beth was zipping her up in all her attire, but she was fine now. Beth hoped she remained fine while they spent time picking out the perfect trees.

Johnny held Eden while Beth put her backpack carrier on. When she was ready, Johnny helped ease Eden into it, so that she was resting up against Beth's back. That way she would have her hands free while they trudged through the snow and looked at trees.

"What kind are we looking for?" David asked Dad.

They headed in the direction of the Douglas Firs, many other families out picking their Christmas trees.

"Does your family chop down their tree?" Dad asked Johnny, making conversation.

"We have," he replied. "Sometimes we just go to the lot and pick one out. But always real."

Dad laughed. "Beth once wanted one of those colored artificial ones. I think it was hot pink, right?" he asked her.

"It would have been amazing," she replied jokingly. Although really, it had potential, at least for fun.

"We should get a little baby tree for Eden," Dad said, taking off down a row of trees.

Beth glanced over to Johnny, who was right at her side now that Dad wasn't between them.

"We're starting new traditions," he said with her special smile.

She smirked. "Cutting down our own Christmas tree?"

"Well it is our second Christmas together, if you think about it."

"You're not staying for Christmas," she stated, matter of fact.

"Of course I am."

Beth stopped in her tracks. "I will not let you spend Christmas away from your family."

"I'm a big boy, Beth. I think they can handle it."

Beth looked at him harshly. "Don't miss out on opportunities of being with your family. I know what that's like."

He nodded, giving her a compassionate look while he put his hand on her shoulder, leading her and Eden forward.

"Don't worry, I've got it figured out," he told her. "And I am with my family."

Beth bit her lip. She wanted to cry. All she had to do was say yes to Johnny. She knew how easy it would be. All her dreams could come true if she could just say the words that he wanted to hear, that were already on the tip of her tongue. But she didn't.

Dad called David and Johnny over to look at a tree, David holding onto the saw. Beth stood back, and gazed at the large tree. She could tell by the way that Eden was leaning against her that she had fallen asleep against Beth's back.

"What do you think of this one?" Dad called to her. She walked up and joined everyone else around the huge tree, which must have been well over ten feet tall.

"It's huge," Beth stated.

"It's perfect!" Amy exclaimed.

"Then we'll take it," Dad replied.

Beth stood back while Dad bent down near the trunk, starting to cut. Johnny and David positioned themselves around the tree, ready to catch it when it fell. It didn't take long before Dad had cut through the whole thing. The two guys took it and headed back toward the entrance, where the bottom would be smoothed out and they would put it through the machine and wrap it to take home.

"What about you girls?" Dad asked, staying with them. "We need to pick your trees."

Amy and Dad took off, Beth kind of lagging behind, thinking over the morning. When she had met Johnny at the bottom of the hill, she went with him to take back his rental skis, and then the two of them had walked back to Monahan Ranch, Beth still in her ski boots. She showed him the shortcut back to the property, and then left him as soon as they got in the front door to change and find Eden, who was playing happily in Amy's room, Amy sprawled out on her stomach on the floor with her. Beth fed Eden lunch before the family had gone out to go Christmas tree shopping, and she had avoided speaking to Johnny as much as possible ever since. She still couldn't believe what he had said to her. Marry her? Adopt Eden? It blew her away.

And yet her heart yearned for those very things. She would love to spend her life with Johnny by her side, to make it all official, for the Harris's to really be her family. She wanted nothing more than for Eden to have a happy life with both a mom and a dad. And the only person she had pictured ever filling that role was Johnny. She wanted Johnny to be Eden's father. And she wanted to be Johnny's wife. She knew he wasn't like Marcello or Tyler or any of her old boyfriends. She knew he would never take advantage of her, would never hurt her purposefully. She knew that the two of them could be very happy together. But the words were so hard for her to say. Why was that?

"Beth! Come on!" Dad yelled.

They spent at least two hours looking at trees, but in the end they left with five big trees, and one tiny one that Dad insisted they cut down for Eden's room. Beth was glad they did. It was Eden's first Christmas. She wanted it to be special.

It took quite some effort to get everything loaded on top of the car, but Beth was excited to see the house come alive with Christmas cheer. Her dad had already worked hard on the outside, getting everything lit up and bright. He had been over at the resort as well, overseeing the usual outdoor decorations all over the place.

When they got back to Monahan Ranch, Beth was asked to prepare some hot cocoa while the guys brought the Christmas trees in and got everything set up. She placed Eden into the highchair in the kitchen, putting some dry cereal before her, while she warmed up the cocoa over the stove. She served it to everyone before heading back into the kitchen, working on another tradition. She got everything ready, but right before she started, she went out on a whim and found her sister, who was upstairs in her room watching David position her tree just right, Amy standing back to give it a look over.

"Hey, Amy," Beth said. She could see Amy's surprise at Beth addressing her. David glanced at her as well. "I'm making caramels, if you wanted to help."

Amy's eyebrows pinched together. She didn't say anything for a moment.

"Sure," she replied slowly.

Amy followed Beth back downstairs to the kitchen.

"Have you made any so far this year?" Amy asked her.

"Nope, not yet."

Amy nodded. "How many batches do you think we need to make?"

"Who all do we usually give them to?" Beth asked her. Amy and Beth both knew that the "we" she was referring to was their mother. Beth didn't even know how many caramels she used to make per year, but she had handed them out to seemingly everyone she met. Beth knew that there were always bowls of caramels in each of the different offices, and a small doggie bag was made for all of the employees. They never lasted long.

Amy thought for a moment, and then answered with a laugh. "Everyone."

Beth laughed too, and they smiled at one another for a moment.

"Maybe for now we can just double the recipe, and see where that gets us," Beth suggested. After all, their double boiler wouldn't hold more than that. She had no idea how her mom had made so many caramels every year. She must have been making them every day.

Beth told Amy how to do everything, basically overseeing everything she did. Amy had always wanted to be like their mom, doing everything the way she did. It seemed to take a lot of effort for her sometimes, but making caramels was something they had always seen their mom doing. And although Beth had memorized the recipe years ago, she knew that Amy wanted to be the one making them as well.

They spent the rest of the afternoon and evening working on the big tree in the living room. The guys worked together stringing lights on the tree, Johnny up on a ladder wrapping them around the top and getting them strung on the backside. The room was filled with the scent of Christmas, and Beth loved it.

Uncle Don and Aunt Mary came over and brought dinner, although no one really sat down for a real meal together. They just ate when they had a second. Everyone wanted to get the trees at least lit, before they could start decorating.

It was late before all the trees were strung with lights, including the three-foot pine in Eden's room. Beth was never asked to help, and she didn't offer, which was just fine with her. Instead she ended up back in the kitchen with Amy and Aunt Mary, the three of them working on cutting up the caramels that Beth had put outside to harden quickly, and then cutting up little pieces of wax paper to wrap the caramels in. They had a little production line going.

"I can't go this weekend," Aunt Mary said. "But we can go down next weekend. Would that work?"

Beth didn't know what she was talking about—she had left the room for a bit to put Eden down for the night.

"That would be great!" Amy said excitedly. "I can't wait!"

"I'm sorry I can't take you sooner. I know you must be anxious."

"That's okay," she replied. "I've got plenty to do around here to keep me busy."

"Do you want to come?" Aunt Mary directed toward Beth.

Beth had no idea what she was talking about, but she saw Amy's shocked glance at their aunt, which she quickly tried to hide.

"Come where?" Beth asked.

"Denver."

"What's in Denver?"

"Amy's wedding dress is ready, and just in time, too."

Beth nodded, glancing at her sister. She knew that Amy's coming wedding was a huge topic of conversation around Monahan Ranch, she just hadn't been a part of it, at all. As far as she knew she wasn't actually invited.

"We were going to make a night of it in the city," Mary continued. "A girl's night."

Beth took a deep breath, but before she could reply, Amy inserted her opinion.

"Yea, you should come."

Beth was so shocked by Amy's invite that she found herself saying yes.

Chapter Thirty-Three

"Maybe I should stay here," Beth said once again as they got everything packed in the car.

"Everything will be fine, Beth," Dad assured her, framed in the doorway with Eden on his hip.

Amy looked over at Beth, who was biting her bottom lip, looking at Eden. After a moment she let out an audible sigh.

"Fine," she replied, walking forward to kiss Eden's cheek one more time. Amy watched as she took one fleeting glance at Johnny before heading to the car, shaking her head.

"It's going to be fine," Aunt Mary stated, starting the car.

"I know," Beth answered quickly.

They headed out of the gate, down the long drive into town. Amy was sitting up front with Aunt Mary, excited for the weekend ahead. She hoped that it would give her and Beth the chance to open up a little more to one another, to at least try. Ever since her talk with David over two weeks ago, she had been trying to be friendlier around Beth. She was trying to keep in mind what her dad had told her, taking it slow to show Beth that she really could trust her. She caught Beth's looks of surprise every once in awhile when Amy offered to help her with something or when she simply asked how her day was or addressed her at all. She hoped Beth was noticing an improvement. She was slightly worried that Johnny being around all the time was a bit more distracting for Beth. Amy still didn't understand what was going on there.

"She's going to be fine," Aunt Mary stated again, looking at Beth in the rearview mirror. "She's got your dad and Johnny."

Beth scoffed. "I know she'll be fine," she stated assuredly. Amy had a feeling that was not what was consuming Beth's mind.

"What's going on with you?" Aunt Mary wanted to know. Amy was glad she asked.

"Nothing."

"Come on," Mary prodded.

Beth didn't say anything, just leaned her head up against the window as they continued to drive on toward Denver.

Amy couldn't wait to go back to Lisa's shop and see her beautiful wedding dress. Of course, she had picked it out months ago, but with the alterations that needed to be made, and the fact that she lived two hours away and had a demanding job, it had taken her a while to make it to the shop. She knew it was going to be beautiful. She couldn't believe that she was less than two weeks away from getting married. Christmas was coming up at the end of the coming week, and then her wedding was one week later. She simply couldn't wait, and neither could David.

Amy and David, in between making sure that everything was set for their big day, running around with last minute things to get done, had also been overseeing furnishing their house, on top of their full-time jobs. Amy couldn't believe that she was about to move out of Monahan Ranch for good. If she thought about it too much, it made her want to cry. Not that she couldn't wait to live with David, it was just hard to say goodbye to a chapter of her life. Things would be different from now on—a good different, but different nonetheless. Change was hard. Although she was only going to be about a mile and a half from her childhood home. She couldn't really complain about that.

Their house was a lovely home in a quiet neighborhood, each of the houses far enough away from one another to give the appearance that they weren't on top of each other. They would have a nice yard, although most of their yard was canvassed in by woods. It wasn't Monahan Ranch, but Amy wasn't complaining. It still had four bedrooms, three-and-a-half bathrooms. It was a fairly large house for their first home, but they both loved it. There was a part of her that had made her feel for a while that she should just move into David's condo while they figured things out. It's what some of her friends had done when they got married—they all had starter apartments, or townhouses and such. But Amy couldn't really compare herself to her friends. She had a slightly different upbringing than most people, what with the legacy of Mount of the Holy Cross. She could have gone a lot more crazy than the house that she and David had purchased. But they both loved the home, and they would be there for years and years to come. It was the home they would raise their family in. And Amy couldn't wait.

The closer and closer they got to their wedding, the more she and David had to work harder to keep physical boundaries in their relationship. They were waiting for one another, for their wedding night. They themselves would be a beautiful gift to the other. Amy couldn't help but think about what was coming a lot, and each time it filled her stomach with nervous butterflies, as well as a rush of excitement. She couldn't wait to be married to David, to be united in every way. She loved him so much.

But first, the wedding. And before that, the dress.

It was a fairly quiet ride to Denver. Mary had the radio on, turned to Christmas music. The Rockies were covered in snow, but thankfully it was a beautiful sunny day. They didn't have any weather to contend with.

They were staying in the same hotel that they did the last time. Mary had gotten them a suite this time so that they would have a little more room, and frankly it was a lot more fun. Mary had her own room, and Amy and Beth had a room with double beds to share. In a way it made Amy want to laugh. They had shared hotel rooms on family vacations and such in the past. But they were in incredibly different places now. Physical proximity didn't mean that they were close, although Amy yearned for that closeness that they had never shared before. She had never realized how much that had been lacking in her life over the years. Amy wanted her sister. She needed her sister. She was dying to actually know Beth.

"So, to the dress shop first?" Mary asked, popping her head into their room.

"Yea, please!" Amy declared excitedly.

The three of them filed out of their room, walking the short distance to the dress shop. Lisa once again gave them the warmest of welcomes when they came in. She wouldn't let any of her attendants help them, she wanted to do it herself.

While Mary and Beth sat outside the changing area, sipping cups of peppermint tea, Amy went into the dressing room with Lisa. Her dress was hanging inside, beckoning her to put it on. It looked just as beautiful as when she had tried it on the first time, and when she had come back in the summer after her first fitting. Pretty soon she would be walking down the aisle in it, declaring in front of her family and friends, and most importantly God, that she indeed loved David Carpenter and wanted nothing more than to be committed to him for the rest of her life.

Lisa helped her slip the dress on and lace up the back. Amy just stared at her reflection in the mirror, at the beautiful gown, and at herself. She couldn't contain her smile. Her long awaited day was almost here.

"You're beautiful," Lisa told her, helping to adjust the veil.

"Thanks," Amy said.

Lisa opened the door to the dressing room, waiting for Amy to step out and show her aunt and sister.

Amy stepped outside and onto the platform, in front of the large mirrors where she could see herself from every angle. And sitting directly opposite the mirrors were Mary and Beth. Amy turned to them, anxious for their reactions.

Aunt Mary stood up and came right to her, tears in her eyes, but smiling all the same.

"You look amazing!" she declared, walking around and checking out the dress. Amy laughed at her as Mary touched the end of her dress and her veil, like she was inspecting it.

"I'm so happy for you," Mary told her, hugging Amy, a tear falling onto her shoulder.

"Thanks," Amy told her.

Lisa told her everything they had done to the dress, going into detail about the alterations. It fit perfectly. Amy didn't want to take it off.

While Mary and Lisa continued to talk about the dress, Amy chanced a glance at her sister, who still hadn't said anything. Amy was completely unprepared for her reaction.

Beth was crying. She was looking at Amy and she was crying.

Beth cleared her throat when she realized that Amy was looking directly at her.

"You look like Mom," she said quietly. Amy's heart did a little flutter at her sister's words, the threat of tears building within her. She appreciated Beth saying so, but Amy was staring directly at the likeness of their mother.

It struck Amy as she looked at her sister just how similar they really were, mother and daughter. They both had an amazing confidence about them, despite different hardships they had been through in their lives. Beth had her same zeal for life, the same passion for those she loved, and the things she loved. Beth was the one who had an elegant presence around her, and she didn't even notice it. She was the life of the party, just like their mother. Beth was the one who had every recipe of their mom's memorized, the one who cared for her garden, who loved flowers just as much as their mom. She was creative and artsy. She was amazingly stubborn. And she loved fiercely.

Amy couldn't help but cry. She had wanted nothing more than to be just like her mother all her life, and she had tried to emulate her in every way that she could, trying to do things the same way she had done, even her own wedding. But Beth was just like their mom without even trying. And somehow that was suddenly okay.

"I wish she were here," Amy stated.

Beth nodded, fingering a long strand of pearls around her neck. "Me too. She would be so proud of you."

"She would be proud of both of us," Amy corrected.

Amy and Beth's eyes locked in a kind of shared understanding that only two sisters who had lost their mother could understand.

Amy reached her hand out toward Beth—perhaps for the first time in her life—who was still in her seat. She grasped it and squeezed it back. They only held on for a moment, but it meant everything.

"You look gorgeous, Ames," Beth said with a smile, brushing the tears from her face.

Amy and Beth were completely unaware that both Lisa and Mary had fallen silent, watching the two of them.

—⁓—

After a tearful, yet wonderful, time in the dress shop, the three girls walked through downtown Denver, bundled up against the cold, doing some last minute Christmas shopping. Amy had gotten most of her gifts already. She did most of her shopping online. She found it so much easier. She didn't have to go out in the crowds. Everything came right to her. Although she had to admit that shopping could be tons of fun if you had the right company.

Three hours, and many, many shopping bags later, the three of them headed out to a restaurant, needing fuel after the day they had. Amy was just happy to sit down.

"Is Johnny going to go back to Tahoe for Christmas?" Mary asked.

"Um…I don't think so," Beth replied, annoyance flashing in her eyes. Amy wasn't sure if it was because of the question, or Johnny.

"What did you get him for Christmas?"

"Nothing."

"Nothing? Beth! You have to get him something. What does he like? Is there anything he wants?"

Beth laughed humorlessly.

"What?" Mary wanted to know.

"I'm not sure I can give him what he wants."

"What does he want?" Mary asked. Amy leaned in closer, not wanting to miss anything.

Amy was about to give up on Beth answering when she finally spoke up.

"To marry me and adopt Eden."

"What?" Amy asked before she could control her reaction.

"Wow!" Mary replied. "That's huge."

"Just a bit," Beth said.

"That's great, honey."

The look on Beth's face said that it was anything but great.

Before more could be said, the waiter arrived with their dinner. Amy was famished, and couldn't wait to tuck into her smoked salmon. She was astounded by what Beth had just said. Marry Johnny? He wanted to adopt the baby? It was amazing. She knew that Johnny was crazy about Beth. It was written all over his face, in the way he spoke to her and acted around her. And he was definitely already a father to her beautiful niece.

Amy had gotten to know Johnny a bit in the last weeks. She knew all about his family and what he did. But he never said a word about his history with Beth, or anything that had to do with Eden's biological father. Of course Amy was curious. The only thing she did know was that Johnny and Beth had known one another a year and a half and that Beth had lived with his family. That was all. It was interesting getting to see Beth through Johnny's eyes. Amy was dying to know her own sister.

Mary kept glancing at Beth throughout dinner, who was refusing to say another word on the subject. The three of them shared a slice of chocolate cake before heading back to the hotel room.

Amy hopped in the shower while Beth called home to check on Eden and to say good night to her. She couldn't get what Beth had said at dinner out of her mind.

"Please bless her God," Amy called out, shampoo in her hair. "I'm pretty sure she and Johnny are meant to be, but she can't see it for some reason."

Amy kept praying as she finished her shower and put her pajamas on, mostly for her sister, and also that after all these years the two of them would be the sisters they always should have been.

She found Beth and Mary in the sitting room watching a Christmas movie. When it was over, they went right to bed, but Amy called David to check in with him. She was on the phone for a while, but she knew when she walked into the dark room where Beth was in bed that her sister wasn't asleep. She was lying on her back, her arm over her forehead, staring up at the ceiling.

And suddenly Amy understood perfectly why Beth was reluctant where Johnny was concerned. It wasn't because she didn't love him—anyone could see that Beth loved Johnny. It wasn't because she didn't want to marry him—Amy was sure that was exactly what Beth did want. But that wasn't the point.

"You don't think you deserve him, do you?" Amy asked, unable to help herself.

Beth looked over at her, a crease in her forehead. "No, I don't."

Amy's heart broke a little bit for her sister. Besides Beth leaving, Amy knew nothing about her sister's life during her absence. But whatever had happened, she knew that Beth couldn't let it go. She had made amends with everyone around her, but was continuing to punish herself.

Chapter Thirty-Four

They left Denver early, all three of them needing to get back to Holy Cross for different reasons. Amy had a lot of work to do before she could take off for the week after Christmas, then for her wedding and honeymoon. Aunt Mary and Uncle Don had various engagements all week before Christmas dinner at Monahan Ranch. And Beth wanted to kiss her little girl.

Beth hadn't slept well. She was glad for the night away, but she wished she had been in her own bed. It had been hard to leave Eden, but it was also good for her to have a little time for herself, as emotional as it had been. She had no idea that she would react so much to seeing Amy in a wedding dress. It had all just come crashing down on her how much she really missed her mom, and how much she had missed her sister all these years—and not just the years that Beth had been gone. But the two of them had shared a moment only they could understand. It was a beginning.

Beth hadn't meant to be so open about what was going on with Johnny, but in some ways she was glad that she had said something, not that she was looking for advice. It was just nice that someone else knew what was going on in her life. She missed Ellie, Mark, and Crystal more than she wanted to admit, especially now that she was back home with her family. But they were her family, too. She had shared everything with them—Johnny also. She didn't have that in the same way here. Although she could, if she could find it within herself to open up to Johnny. She knew he was waiting.

Honestly, Beth was surprised at Amy's perceptiveness. Yes, Beth didn't think that she really deserved to be with Johnny. He could do a lot better than her, she was sure of that. He could find someone who had shared his morals all of her life, who didn't have a kid with another man. But Beth also knew that it didn't matter that she felt undeserving. The truth was everyone was undeserving. Johnny had taught her that. Everyone was unworthy. But Johnny had chosen her. For some miraculous reason that Beth would never be able to understand, Johnny loved her. He wanted her—every part of her. And Eden, too. And she knew that he would say that he felt unworthy of her as well—a thought that completely mystified her.

No, it wasn't Beth's qualms about feeling undeserving of such a great man that was keeping her away from him now—however true those feelings may be. It was just that she had gotten so used to keeping up a big wall between her and Johnny over the past year. She had marked him as off limits from the very beginning, which hadn't stopped her from falling in love with him. But she was scared. She was scared of how much she wanted everything Johnny had said—getting married and raising Eden together. Raising a whole family together. She had never given that much of herself to anyone else.

Yet she knew how easy it would be, if she could just say yes. But it was hard. Beth had been fighting for so long. She had fought for independence against her family. She had fought for a way to fix the mess she made when she came back from Europe. She fought to get away from Tyler. She fought to start her life over. Her strength came from God, she knew that. But she was so used to fighting. Although she had already let her guard down with Johnny more than anyone. It would be so natural, so right. But it was just so hard.

"Are all the bridesmaids dresses ready?" Aunt Mary asked as they came off the interstate, almost to Holy Cross.

"Pretty much," Amy answered from the back seat, giving Beth the front for the drive home. Her wedding dress was in a zippered garment bag on the seat next to her, and it seemed like she didn't want to let it out of her sight.

Beth also had to learn to let her guard down with her own family, particularly her sister. Beth didn't know what was going on between them now, where they stood with one another, but she knew that things had changed. Amy was no longer looking at her with disgust, walking out of a room if Beth was in it. She was even addressing her, smiling at her, offering to help her. And this weekend was a little more.

Her eyes were beginning to close. She could use a nap. Her brain had been going a mile a minute for far too long now. She was too exhausted to put that wall back up between her and Johnny. She just didn't care anymore. Maybe she should just let it happen. It's what she truly wanted, anyway.

"Whose car is that?" Beth heard Amy ask a short time later.

Beth opened her eyes. They had just pulled in through the gates to Monahan Ranch. She was glad to be home.

And then she saw the car that Amy had pointed out.

"Oh my goodness!" Beth shrieked.

"What?" Amy and Aunt Mary both asked.

Beth bounded out of the car as soon as Aunt Mary came to a stop, running through the front door. She came to a halt when she walked into the living room, surveying the room quickly before she walked forward and threw her arms around Ellie, tears coming into her eyes.

She hugged her like she hadn't seen her in years.

Beth pulled away and looked around excitedly. Crystal was sitting on the floor playing with Eden. Mark and Johnny were sitting side by side across from Beth's dad, like they had been in intense conversation.

"What are you doing here?" Beth asked the room at large, but looked at Ellie.

"We've come for Christmas!" she declared, and, if possible, Beth's smile got wider. She was with her entire family now.

Beth glanced over at Johnny and gave him a mocking smile. "You're horrible," she told him. She was sure that he had done everything he could to bring his family here, reminding her of all that she would be saying yes to if she could just get herself to utter that very word.

"And that's why you love me, right?" He winked at her and she shook her head, unable to contain the huge smile on her face.

Mary and Amy walked into the room, Amy's wedding dress draped over her arm. Beth took over the introductions, her two families meeting one another. She couldn't have been more happy. Although one look at Johnny and she knew that wasn't true. Beth knew that Ellie and Mark would be thrilled beyond words for the two of them to get married. She was sure that they already saw Beth that way in their lives anyway. She knew they considered her to be their daughter. But she had a feeling that they had been waiting for the moment when they would be able to really declare that she was their son's wife, that Eden was their grandchild. And truthfully, they already were a family. Johnny loved her, and she loved him. Why not just say yes and make all of their dreams come true?

"I can't believe you're all here!" Beth declared, amazed at how her happiness continued to grow. Being accepted immediately into the family that she had left had been so overwhelming. And now being with the family of her heart was bringing her near to overflowing.

"I'm excited!" Crystal said. "We never go anywhere for Christmas, and this place is like staying at a five-star resort."

Mark nudged her with his foot.

"What?" she said, glancing at him.

Beth laughed. The five-star resort was down the road. This was her home. And now her whole family was here.

Beth looked at Ellie, who had tears in her eyes as she met Beth's gaze.

"I really missed you," Beth told her, a sheen in her eyes. Ellie held her for a long time. It felt so good to be in the arms of this woman, her other mother. In the same moment Beth was filled with amazing joy, and also profound sadness. She was so grateful to have Ellie in her life, but it made her miss her mother in such an overwhelming way.

"I'm always here, Beth," Ellie whispered into her ear.

Beth pulled away and smiled at her.

"Thanks for coming," she said, even though she hadn't exactly invited them. She was so thankful that her dad had thought to ask the Harris's to come.

It was one of the best afternoons of Beth's life. Everything felt put together. She was back home with her beloved family, feeling accepted by all of them, even Amy. There was a huge bridge to be built between the two of them, but Beth was sure that in time they would somehow meet in the middle. And she was thrilled to have Mark, Ellie, and Crystal there to celebrate the holidays. As happy as Beth had been in the last two months to be back home, she had really missed her other family. And now everyone was together, like one giant family. Her dad seemed happier than she could ever remember seeing him. Aunt Mary and Uncle Don were there. David came by after work to join them for dinner. Everyone was together. The only one missing was her mom.

And when Beth glanced down the dinner table at Amy, she knew that Amy was feeling the same way. They didn't see eye to eye on anything, but they understood one another's pain like no one else could.

Chapter Thirty-Five

It was late, yet Amy was restless. It had been a busy three days since she had come back from Denver with Beth and Aunt Mary. She had been at the office, cramming to get in as much work as she could before she felt like she could take a full two weeks off. She couldn't allow herself to think of all that would be awaiting her when she got back from her honeymoon—it was too overwhelming. But in a way she just didn't care right now. She was far too excited about celebrating Christmas, let alone her wedding and honeymoon. There was so much to look forward to. And she was ready. But one thing wasn't right.

Amy got out of bed and walked over to the window, looking out over the town below. Lights twinkled in the night, but Amy knew that everyone in this particular house was tucked away for the evening. Today had been her first day off, it being Christmas Eve. Amy and David, as well as her dad and Beth, and all the Harris's, had spent the entire day skiing and snowboarding. They ate dinner at the restaurant up the mountain, before coming back home and playing a board game next to the blazing fire. Everyone had gone to bed early, exhausted from a long, but extremely fun day. Yet Amy was wide-awake.

Turning away from the sleeping town below her, where she was sure many children were settled down in beds in anticipation of what the next morning would bring, Amy glanced at her closed bedroom door. Without hesitating, she opened the door and quietly walked across the hall into her sister's bedroom. Beth's door was open, and her bed was still made.

"Beth?" Amy called out. No answer.

She walked over to the French doors leading out onto her sister's balcony overlooking the garden. She saw Beth outside, sitting next to one of the lighted pine trees in the outdoor living room. It was partially covered, off the sunroom. She had a fire going in the outdoor fireplace.

Amy grabbed a jacket and headed down the stairs to join her sister. It was time to talk. It was time to get everything out in the open. It was time to apologize.

Beth looked over when she heard the door squeak open. She had a blanket wrapped around her, her sweats tucked into warm boots, holding a steaming mug. The TV was on in the corner.

"Hey," Amy said, walking toward her.

"Hey," Beth replied, clearly surprised to see her. "Did I wake you when I came down?"

"No, I couldn't sleep."

Beth nodded and gave her small smile. She held out a corner of her blanket for Amy to join her under.

Amy sat down next to her sister on the outdoor couch. They both stared at the TV for a while, old home movies of Christmases past playing. Amy guessed that she was about eight or so in the video playing, Beth six. They were opening their presents on Christmas morning, their mom sharing in their enthusiasm at everything they opened as their dad filmed the moment. It made Amy's heart ache.

While still glancing at the TV, Amy tried to compose her words. It was warm underneath the covered patio with the fire and the outdoor heaters on. The night was silent around them with just the fire crackling. The night was completely still, and so clear. There wasn't a cloud in the sky. Yet it wasn't that dark. The snow on the ground made the world around them glow.

"I couldn't sleep either," Beth said after a while, taking a sip of her drink.

Amy glanced over at her, not sure where to start, but unable to keep silent any longer.

"Beth," she began. Beth turned to her, tears in her eyes. Amy wished she knew what she was thinking. "Are you okay?"

Beth pressed her lips together and nodded, wiping a stray tear with the blanket around her shoulders.

"I miss mom," she whispered.

Amy took a deep breath and wrapped her arms around her sister, just like their mom would have done if she were there. It was the first time Amy could ever remember reaching out for Beth, aside from her small gesture when she had her wedding dress on. What had taken her so long? Why had she allowed herself to stand in the way of this for so long?

"I miss her, too," Amy stated, glancing at her mom's smiling face on the TV. Beth leaned her head on Amy's shoulder.

"She always loved Christmas," Beth said. "It was her favorite time of year."

"It was always beautiful."

"Yea."

They were silent for a while, both absorbed in memories of Christmases past, both listening to their mom's cheerful voice over the speakers. Not a day went by that Amy didn't think of her mom, but for some reason it was harder at Christmas.

"I miss you, too, Ames," Beth said into the stillness.

Amy bit her lip, tears springing to her eyes. She pulled away from Beth so that she could look into her sister's face.

"Beth," Amy started, hoping that she could hold herself together long enough to say what she needed to say. "I'm glad you came home."

"Really?"

Amy smiled at Beth. "Really. I wasn't at first, and I know you know that. I guess I never realized, despite everything else, just how much I missed you, too."

They were both crying now.

"I'm sorry I left," Beth said. "I'm sorry for everything. I know I never made your life easy and…"

"No, Beth," Amy stopped her, "I was the one who never made your life easy. I was never there for you—never. I pushed you away every chance that I could. I never tried to be there for you."

Beth wiped her eyes on her blanket. "All I ever wanted growing up was for you to let me in."

"And I pushed you away every chance that I got," Amy said again. She felt terrible about it, but also so relieved to be finally saying it out loud. She felt so healed by being able to look at herself clearly and admit the mistakes she had made.

"Well, it's not like I made it easy on you," Beth replied. "I was always thinking about myself above everyone else. And then I left," Beth said, her voice breaking with the pain of what she had done.

"You came back," Amy reminded her.

"Not before screwing up the lives of everyone I knew in the process."

"But you still came back," Amy said. She was amazed by her sister. She still had no idea what Beth had been up to in all the years that she had been gone, aside from what she had learned from the year that Beth had spent with the Harris's, but in a way it didn't matter. Amy knew that Beth's life hadn't been easy since she left. She knew her sister regretted leaving. And she knew what it had taken for her to come back and try to make amends. Beth reached out and admitted she was wrong. Amy only learned how terribly misguided she had become throughout the years, had only realized her part in Beth's perception of herself, when Beth had the strength to come home.

"They should have named you Elizabeth," Beth said.

Amy looked at her, everything seeming so crystal clear for the first time in her life.

"No, I think it was meant for you," Amy told her. It never would have fit her. It was never supposed to. And she was amazingly okay with that now.

Beth shook her head and glanced at the TV screen out of the corner of her eye. "She would be so ashamed of me if she could see me now."

"No she wouldn't. She would be proud of you, Beth. She would be proud of the person you have become. She would be proud of how you turned your life around, and how you have stepped up to raise Eden. She would have been so thrilled to be a grandmother. And she would have welcomed you back with open arms."

Beth didn't see it at all. She had run away from home years ago because she was running from her name. She was running from the expectation of who everyone thought she should be as the daughter of Julian and Elizabeth Monahan. And it had taken hitting rock bottom for Beth to truly find who she really is, and to be made new by the God who had been loving her all along. The irony was that Beth had grown completely into her name without even trying. And all the while Amy had been trying to prove herself, prove that she was just like her mother, and had lost herself in the process. And it had only been through seeing Beth clearly that Amy was starting to see herself.

"Beth, I'm sorry," Amy said. "I'm so, so unbelievably sorry. All these years, I've been blaming you for my own mistakes and my own failures. I've been blaming you for being who I thought I wanted to be. I've never let myself be there for you because I was way too proud. I haven't been a sister to you at all."

"Yea, well, neither have I."

"You've at least tried."

"If you can call it that."

"I do call it that," Amy said.

They both stared at the fire, which was starting to burn down to coals.

"David shared those verses with me from the book of Titus that you told him about. He told me all about how you read Johnny's Bible, and how it completely changed your life."

Beth smiled, a look of contentment flashing across her face. "Yea, it did."

"Those verses changed my life, too."

Beth looked back at Amy, and Amy started to tell her everything. She opened up to Beth about the past three years, of how she felt when Beth ran away, about how she had this compulsive need to overcompensate for Beth's absence by running herself into the ground. She told Beth all about the conversations she had with David about her, including the one about the day their mom died. She told Beth about David making her read those verses in Titus, trying to get her to truly hear them, and how they had opened her eyes for the first time in possibly her whole life to who she really was, and how they also allowed her to truly see the beautiful person Beth had become. And the tears continued to flow, washing them both clean. By the time Amy finished, they were both clinging to each other.

"I'm so sorry, Beth."

"I'm sorry, too, Amy."

They pulled away from one another, their hands still clasped.

"I want to be sisters, always. Really, truly, sisters," Amy told her.

"Me too," Beth agreed. "And I want to be friends."

They smiled at each other.

"And Beth?"

"Yea?"

"I love you."

Beth grinned at her. "I love you, too."

Amy looked down at her hands for a second.

"Can I ask you something?"

"You can ask me anything," Beth told her, and Amy knew she meant it. She was being invited into Beth's heart.

Amy took a deep breath and met Beth's warm gaze.

"Will you be my maid of honor?"

Beth clutched her chest, a new round of tears springing to her eyes.

"Really?" she asked.

"Really. I need you, Beth. It was always supposed to be you. And I want you there. We're sisters. There's a tie between us that nothing can break, as hard as we've tried."

Beth laughed. "I would be honored, Ames. I would love that."

It was the early hours of the morning on Christmas day, a day that had been a long time coming for Amy and Beth. As they held onto one another in sisterly love, they knew that it was the beginning of a beautiful relationship. And they felt the love of their mom surrounding them as they crossed the wide gap in their relationship and built a bridge together. They were sisters forever. And now they were friends.

"We should go inside," Amy said. The fire had died, and she could feel the chill of the winter breeze. "It's getting late."

The two girls walked back in the house together, their arms around one another. They climbed the stairs side by side, pausing in front of their bedroom doors.

"One last thing," Amy began.

Beth looked at her, waiting for her to go on.

"Johnny."

Beth rolled her eyes and then started to laugh.

"He loves you."

"Yea, he does," Beth agreed.

"And you love him," Amy said with a sparkle in her eyes.

"Yea, I do."

"So what's holding you back?"

Beth took a deep breath. "I honestly don't know anymore."

Amy smiled her satisfaction. Beth shook her head and looked away down the hall, a sheepish grin on her face.

"Goodnight, Beth."

"Yea, whatever."

Amy laughed and turned to go.

"Hey, Ames?"

"Yea?" Amy turned toward her again.

Beth gave her a playful smile.

"Want to sleepover?"

Amy laughed and shrugged her shoulders, walking into Beth's room.

"Sure!"

Chapter Thirty-Six

Beth quietly opened her bedroom door and peered down the hallway. Amy leaned over Beth's back and did the same thing.

"Everyone's still sleeping," Beth whispered.

"Well, we're always the first awake on Christmas morning anyway," Amy replied.

They were about to quietly creep out of Beth's room to go downstairs when Beth heard Eden starting to talk to herself. She glanced back at Amy.

"Okay, I'll get the baby, and you start making breakfast."

Amy rolled her eyes. "Beth, come on. I'll get the baby, and you start breakfast. Let's be real here."

Beth laughed at her. "Okay."

Making sure to be as quiet as possible since there were so many people spending the night, Beth tiptoed down the stairs and into the kitchen. She got out all the ingredients for her mom's cinnamon rolls. She got as far as rolling the dough to be curled into large rolls when she began to wonder what was taking Amy so long. Just as she put the first batch into the oven, Amy came strolling in with a smiling Eden in her arms.

"Sorry, I couldn't resist. I gave her a bath and then went through her entire wardrobe. This kid has a lot of clothes," Amy said, proudly showing off her niece dressed in the most adorable Christmas dress, a red headband in her hair.

"She looks like a little Christmas present," Beth said.

"She looks amazing."

"Of course she does," Beth agreed. "She's the cutest little girl in the whole entire world," she told Eden, who reached her arms out for her mother.

"Thanks for getting her ready."

"No problem," Amy stated, sticking her finger in the bowl of frosting. "So good!"

Beth smiled at her, bouncing Eden on her hip. She couldn't believe how last night had changed everything between she and her sister. They had talked absolutely everything out, and had both finally apologized for hurting one another over the years. Amy had spent the night in Beth's room, where they had stayed up nearly all night just talking about each other's lives. Beth told Amy everything that had happened to her since the day she had left Holy Cross—more than she had told anyone but Johnny and Ellie. It felt so good. And there was no condemnation from Amy whatsoever. Just compassion and love. In one night they had built the relationship that Beth had always wanted with her sister. And she knew that it was only the beginning.

They had finally fallen asleep around three in the morning, and only woke up so early because Amy's cell phone alarm went off when she usually got up for work. But Beth was wide-awake when she got up out of bed, and so was Amy, her internal clock not prepared for vacation time. So they decided to make breakfast for everyone. They were having their usual Christmas brunch, but with a much smaller crowd. This was the first year that there wasn't a huge dinner being given at Monahan Ranch. With Amy's wedding a week away, her dad had decided before Beth had come home and before the Harris's came, that Christmas would be a small affair. It was something that he had secretly wanted for years, anyway. So this year it would just be the immediate family, plus the Harris's and Uncle Don and Aunt Mary, who had spent the night as well. David's parents would join them later on. Beth thought it was perfect.

"What can I do to help?" Amy asked.

Together they worked in the kitchen to make another batch of cinnamon rolls, as well as some bacon and eggs, and some of Beth's famous hot chocolate. Amy cut up a bunch of fruit while Beth fed Eden breakfast.

"What's your secret?" Amy asked, taking a sip of warm chocolate, a great way to start the morning.

"I'll never tell," Beth smirked.

Amy rolled her eyes at her.

Beth laughed. "It's not much of a secret. I just started adding a pinch of salt and a little espresso. It makes a big difference."

"Salt?" Amy asked.

"Among other things," Beth stated, keeping some things to herself.

Amy narrowed her eyes. "I'll get it out of you somehow."

"I'd like to see you try!"

The two of them laughed.

"Smells good in here!" Aunt Mary said, coming into the kitchen in her cozy robe, looking between their smiling faces.

"We thought we'd get breakfast started," Amy said, throwing some apples into a big bowl.

Aunt Mary set the table as everyone else began to get up, the delicious scent of cinnamon, bacon, fresh coffee, and chocolate wafting upstairs. Amy and Beth sat across from one another next to their father at the head of the table, sharing in the joy of their newfound sisterly relationship. At one point their dad, as well as Uncle Don and Aunt Mary, stopped eating and stared at the two of them as they both laughed at something the other said.

"What?" Beth asked, looking around. She glanced at Amy, who was exchanging a smirk with David, who had joined them for brunch after already having breakfast with his own family.

"Nothing," Dad said with a huge smile.

After breakfast, everyone went into the large family room and sat around the Christmas tree, taking their time opening the multitude of gifts. Beth felt so loved by everyone. She loved having the Harris's there, and she also loved being home for Christmas. She wished that she had given more thought to gifts. She felt like she was receiving more than she was giving. But maybe it was just because for the first time Beth was truly giving of herself. She was giving her love.

After cleaning up all the wrapping paper and carrying gifts to everyone's various rooms, Eden's gifts outnumbering everyone else's combined, Beth finally started to get ready for the day. Dad and Uncle Don offered to clean up after breakfast, while Mary prepared the roast that would cook all day. Beth went upstairs to shower. While she was surveying her odd array of clothing left over from high school and her first years of college, there was a knock on her door.

"Yea?" Beth called, wanting to know who it was before she invited them in, being wrapped in a towel and all.

Aunt Mary let herself in. She was clutching Amy's arm, who had a dress in her other hand.

"Hey," Beth said, looking at the two of them.

"What's going on?" Aunt Mary wanted to know.

"What do you mean?" Beth asked.

"I caught Amy looking in your mom's old closet. She pulled out this ivory dress," she stated, pointing to the dress, "and mentioned that she was bringing it to you to wear for the day."

Beth glanced at the dress and then at her sister. "It's pretty," Beth told her.

"Yea, well, it made me suspicious," said Aunt Mary.

Beth gave her a teasing smile and glanced at Amy.

"You really should wear this," Amy said.

"I don't know." She felt strange about wearing one of her mom's old dresses. It was a gorgeous, elegant dress, and Beth could tell just by looking at it that it would fit her perfectly even though she had never worn anything of her mom's before. "Why don't you wear it?"

Amy laughed. "Mom's stuff doesn't fit me. And I already bought a new red dress to wear for today. I really think you should wear it," Amy said, holding the dress out to her.

Beth knew that Amy was offering her more than the dress. She was letting go of a huge battle within her own heart.

"Wear it," she said one more time.

"Okay," Beth agreed.

Aunt Mary walked between the two of them.

"Right. You two have never done anything nice for one another. Explain yourselves."

"Never is a long time," Beth said, grimacing.

"We had a long talk last night," Amy filled her in. She didn't go into extreme detail about everything Amy and Beth had talked about. It was between the two of them. But she didn't have to. Aunt Mary was wiping tears of joy from her eyes as soon as Amy mentioned that they had finally talked.

While Amy was filling Aunt Mary in, Beth had finished her makeup and slipped into the gorgeous ivory dress. When she faced her aunt and sister, they both stopped talking.

"Wow," Aunt Mary said.

Amy gave her a sad smile. "You really are her spitting image."

"You're beautiful."

"So are both of you."

The three of them hugged.

"Oh, Aunt Mary? I need to talk to you," Amy mentioned as she was about to walk out Beth's door to put her own dress on.

"You want Beth to be your maid of honor?" she surmised.

Amy glanced back at Beth, opening her mouth to say something, and found no words.

"It's what I had been praying for all along," Aunt Mary said. She turned to Beth. "I'll bring your bridesmaid dress over tomorrow. I had one made for you when we ordered the others just in case." With that, she turned and headed back down the stairs.

Amy was stunned, and so was Beth.

"That was easy," Amy said.

"Yea," Beth agreed.

Everyone took their time getting ready. It's not like they were actually going anywhere and had anywhere to be, but everyone wanted to look their best. Beth couldn't help but marvel that night after dinner how far she had come from Christmas the year before. Last year she was beginning to open up, invited into a new family, and truly realizing what she had run out on. And here she was, a year later, with both families surrounding her in love. She went from completely broken and pregnant with no options, and became a mother. She opened her heart to the Harris's, and in turn they taught her how to open her heart to her God. And she did. And life had been different ever since. She had been made completely new. Beth had never been so happy.

And yet, there was still one thing missing.

While everyone was transitioning from the dinner table to the family room before dessert and coffee would be brought out, Beth pulled Johnny aside.

"Can I talk to you?" she asked him.

"Sure," he replied.

They had been in the same house for weeks now, and had settled into a routine around one other. She spent a lot time with him, but there was usually someone else around. And when his family arrived, there were more people around to entertain and distance themselves from having alone time.

But now Beth needed Johnny all to herself.

She led him through the sunroom out into her mother's garden. She wanted to get away from everyone in the house so that they could have some privacy. What she had to say was for Johnny alone.

She led him to a bench near the place were her mother's roses bloomed, although instead of sitting down, she just turned and faced him, glancing back at the house for a second, where she could see through the large windows all of her family congregated around the Christmas tree in the living room.

"It's kind of ironic, don't you think?" she asked him. She could see her breath in front of her face.

"Huh?"

"Here we are again, Christmas day, outside in the backyard."

Johnny smiled at her. "Yea, but everything is different now."

She nodded. "Yes, it sure is."

"So what did you want to talk about?" Johnny asked with a smirk.

She sighed. "Well I was feeling kind of bad, because I didn't get you a Christmas present."

"I noticed," he said with mock hurt.

She narrowed her eyes on him. "Well you didn't get me anything either," she teased. Although his being here was more than enough. That, and the fact that he wanted to marry her and adopt her baby.

He crossed his arms. "You don't know that. Perhaps I just haven't given you your gift yet."

"You got me a present?" Beth asked.

"Let's not get off topic. You said you wanted to talk."

"Yes, I did say that."

"So talk."

Beth pressed her lips together, and glanced around the garden. She took a deep breath and let her gaze rest on Johnny's handsome face.

"I want to sign the papers," she whispered.

"You what?"

"Those adoption papers—I'm going to sign them."

A wide grin spread across Johnny's face.

"Although," Beth began, "technically we'll have to get new papers drawn up. I think I'm the one who has to file the papers. Plus I'm pretty sure they need to be signed by a witness after we sign them. And I haven't really looked into it all that much, but I also think that there is a hearing involved. So whatever lawyer gave you those papers didn't really know what they were talking about."

Johnny laughed. "Yea, I just printed them off the Internet."

Beth gawked at him. "Johnny!"

"What? The gesture was the same whether or not they were real!"

"I can't believe you!"

"What does it matter? Eden is my child, and now we're going to make it legal."

Beth gave him a wistful grin. "She really is your child."

Their gazes locked, and Johnny gave her the special smile that he reserved only for her. It took her breath away.

"Before we get carried away here," Johnny started, "I think I better give you my gift."

"Oh so you actually have a gift? You're not just bluffing, like with the adoption papers?"

He rolled his eyes at her, and reached into his pocket, although Beth couldn't tell if he actually pulled anything out.

"What'd you get me?" Beth asked excitedly.

"You really want to know?"

"Yes, I really want to know!"

"I got you this." With that, he held up a diamond ring in his hand.

Beth's mouth opened in shock. At the same moment Johnny went down on one knee before her.

"Beth, I love you. I've loved you practically since the day I met you, which I'm pretty sure you've known for a long time. I wanted to give this to you right after you had Eden, but I knew you needed time. But since we're about to raise a beautiful little girl together, I don't want to wait anymore. So, will you marry me?"

Beth looked down at Johnny's face, love and adoration pouring from her eyes.

"Before I say yes, and I'm going to say yes, there's something you need to know first."

"And what would that be?"

"That I love you, too."

"Yea, I know."

She scoffed at him. "Hey! That's the first time I've told you I love you!"

"And now you've said it twice. So, will you marry me?"

Beth smiled at him. "Yes, I'll marry you."

Johnny put the ring on her finger and then stood up before her, his dancing eyes never leaving her face. He pulled her close and brought his lips to hers. It was their first kiss. And it was electric.

It also didn't last long because everyone in the house started yelling and whistling. Beth looked past Johnny to see everyone in the sunroom watching the two of them and cheering at what they had just seen.

Beth started laughing. "I can't believe them!"

Johnny grabbed her hand and started walking toward their family. "I can. They're all happy for us."

Beth looked at Johnny. "I'm happy for us, too."

Chapter Thirty-Seven

Exactly one week later, Beth found herself once again outside in the large backyard of Monahan Ranch, near her mother's garden. She was dressed in a gorgeous midnight blue bridesmaid dress, under the giant marquee that had been set up for David and Amy's reception. Everything was decorated in beautiful winter colors, with white lights and glowing tea candles all over the place. It was an enchanted winter wonderland. It had been a beautiful ceremony, and Beth had been right at Amy's side as her sister said her vows. She felt so blessed by being able to share in this special day with Amy. She felt blessed by knowing that she was exactly where God wanted her to be.

"I just put Eden down," Johnny said, coming up behind her with two drinks in his hand. He gave one to her.

"Did she go right down?" Beth asked, tearing her eyes away from the happy couple on the dance floor. Amy truly looked radiant—a beauty that went far beneath the gorgeous dress she was wearing, and her perfectly styled hair and makeup. Her face was glowing, reflecting her contented heart. Reflecting her love—her love for her family, for Beth, for David, and for God most of all.

"I read her a book or two first, and then we rocked for a little bit. But she's fast asleep now. It's been a hectic day."

"It's been a great day," Beth corrected.

He smiled at her. "It has been a great day. And you look absolutely amazing, by the way."

"Why thank you," she replied with a big smile. "You look rather handsome yourself."

"Rather handsome is not the same as flat-out handsome. Do you want to change your answer?"

Beth shook her head at him. "You're so annoying."

"But you love me anyway. And now you're stuck with me."

"I wouldn't call it stuck," Beth told him.

Johnny gave her a warm smile and pulled her close.

"I think we should head out onto the dance floor, Mrs. Harris."

Beth placed her drink down on the closest table, and put her hand in Johnny's as he led her onto the crowded dance floor.

The day after Christmas, with the blessing of both of their families, Johnny and Beth had gotten married. It all happened so fast, but Beth was so happy about it. She felt bad about getting married right before her sister's big day, not wanting to steal any attention away from her sister, but Amy was thrilled for Beth and Johnny. With her sister standing next to her, and Johnny's dad standing beside him, the two of them had exchanged vows in her mom's garden in the late afternoon, after they had gotten a marriage license signed in the morning, and her dad had arranged for the pastor of his church to come over. Her dad had arranged it all. After Johnny had proposed on Christmas Day, her dad went right to work to make it happen right away.

Amy came to her once again with another ivory dress for Beth to wear—their mom's wedding dress. Beth couldn't believe it. She had always known growing up that Amy wanted their mom's dress for herself. But she surrendered it freely and offered it to Beth—a beautiful gesture given out of love. Aunt Mary did her hair, and Ellie and Crystal never left her side as she got ready. Johnny went into town and bought a suit. It was a simple affair—after the quick ceremony they all gathered together in the dining room and had a lovely dinner, but it was absolutely perfect. Beth didn't need a big wedding. She hadn't been dreaming about her special day since she was a little girl, like her sister had been. She just wanted to be married to Johnny. Because truthfully, she, Johnny, and Eden had already been a family for quite some time. And now it was all official.

Beth and Johnny spent two nights away in the nicest room at a hotel in another ski town a few hours away, before coming back to help Amy get all the last minute preparations ready for her wedding. After the New Year, Johnny would legally be Eden's father, although he had already been her dad since before she was even born. Going from engaged to married in less than twenty-four hours was certainly a rush, but it also was so natural. She and Johnny had reached this point in their relationship a while ago, even if Beth had been in denial about it at first. It may not have been the most conventional beginning, but they were right where they were supposed to be.

"So your dad offered me a job," Johnny said as he held her on the dance floor.

"No kidding," she laughed. "What kind of job?"

"He wants me to head the public relations department."

"Wow," Beth said, taking a step back so she could fully see Johnny's face. "That's big."

"Yea, that's really big," Johnny stated, pausing on the dance floor.

"Well, what do you think? It's kind of different than what you were doing before. And what about the flower shop?"

"Well, I'm definitely going to think about it, and pray about it, but to be honest it sounds absolutely amazing. I mean, that's what I went to school for. I just kind of fell into the advertising work because of the flower shop."

Beth gave him a smirk. "So, you're going to join the family business? The Monahan family legacy?"

"You did."

"Yea, well, it was born and bred in me. What's a girl to do?" she teased. They both knew it hadn't been that easy.

"Well, it's something to think about."

"Yes, it is."

"Especially since this is home now." The two of them started to slowly dance again.

Beth peered back up at him. "Are you sure you're okay with that?"

"My home is with you and our daughter. And this place is pretty much awesome."

Johnny pulled her close again, and they kept dancing. Again, it wasn't the most conventional way to start a marriage, but she and Johnny planned on continuing to live at Monahan Ranch. Her dad was the one who suggested that they renovate two of the rooms at the complete opposite end of the house from his room and make it into a large room of their own. For now they were both staying in Beth's room, but eventually they would probably turn it into Eden's room.

"Do you mind if I have this dance?" her dad said, cutting in between them.

"Absolutely," Johnny said, handing her over to her dad. She saw him pull his mom out onto the dance floor from where she had been talking with Aunt Mary.

Beth started moving around the dance floor with her dad.

"I'm proud of you honey," he said. "And your mom would be, too."

She smiled at him. "You really think so?"

"I know so."

"Thanks for letting me come back home. And for being the best dad in the world."

"You never have to thank me for being your dad. It's a privilege."

Beth rested her head on her dad's shoulder and hugged him tightly.

"I love you," she told him.

"I love you, too. And I'm so happy for you."

She nodded against his shoulder. "I'm happy, too."

After dancing with her dad, Beth also danced with her new father-in-law as well as Uncle Don. But as the night wore on, there was one person that Beth had to be sure that she had a turn around the dance floor with.

As a song came to an end, Beth approached her sister and asked David if she could steal Amy away for a song. David happily left them to go greet some friends. Beth grabbed Amy's arms and pulled her into a hug.

"I'm so happy for you, Ames!"

"I'm so happy for the both of us! I don't think I've ever been so happy before!"

They started swaying to the music, the photographer coming over to get a picture of them together.

"I'm really glad that you got to be here for this," Amy told her. "You're the best maid of honor a girl could ask for."

Beth smiled her appreciation.

"Actually, you're the best sister a girl could ask for."

"We'll, I'd have to say the same to you," Beth returned.

"Except for before," Amy laughed, and Beth joined her.

"Yea, except for that."

"Do you think mom's watching?" Amy asked her.

Beth nodded. "I'm sure she's watching and celebrating."

"With both of us," Amy added.

"With both of us."

"I wish she were here."

"Me too."

"But I'm so glad that I have you," Amy stated, gathering Beth in another hug.

"I'm so glad that I have you, too."

"We're sisters," Amy said. "Finally."

"And always will be."

Elizabeth Monahan had once told her two girls that there was a tie that bound them together no matter what life threw at them, and no matter what they did to try and destroy it. Amy and Beth were sisters, and their mom always knew that one day they would realize how much they needed one another, how much they loved each other. And she was right. God had used them both as an instrument of His healing in one another's lives. They were changed forever. And they had no doubt that their mom was watching.

Everyone came out from under the marquee and gathered to countdown the end of the year in their mom's garden despite the cold winter air, sparklers in their hands making the world around them glow. Fireworks went off over the resort once the hour approached, which could clearly be seen from the backyard of Monahan Ranch. Beth and Amy glanced at each other from across the garden. It would be a great new year.

A Parable of Two Lost Sons

There was a man who had two sons. The younger one said to his father, "Father, give me my share of the estate." So he divided his property between them.

Not long after that, the younger son got together all he had, set off for a distant country and there squandered his wealth in wild living. After he had spent everything, there was a severe famine in that whole country, and he began to be in need. So he went and hired himself out to a citizen of that country, who sent him to his fields to feed pigs. He longed to fill his stomach with the pods that the pigs were eating, but no one gave him anything.

When he came to his senses, he said, "How many of my father's hired men have food to spare, and here I am starving to death! I will set out and go back to my father and say to him: Father, I have sinned against heaven and against you. I am no longer worthy to be called your son; make me like one of your hired men." So he got up and went to his father.

But while he was still a long way off, his father saw him and was filled with compassion for him; he ran to his son, threw his arms around him and kissed him.

The son said to him, "Father, I have sinned against heaven and against you. I am no longer worthy to be called your son."

But the father said to his servants, "Quick! Bring the best robe and put it on him. Put a ring on his finger and sandals on his feet. Bring the fattened calf and kill it. Let's have a feast and celebrate. For this son of mine was dead and is alive again; he was lost and is found." So they began to celebrate.

Meanwhile, the older son was in the field. When he came near the house, he heard music and dancing. So he called one of the servants and asked him what was going on. "Your brother has come," he replied, "and your father has killed the fattened calf because he has him back safe and sound."

The older brother became angry and refused to go in. So his father went out and pleaded with him. But he answered his father, "Look! All these years I've been slaving for you and never disobeyed your orders. Yet you never gave me even a young goat so I could celebrate with my friends. But when this son of yours who has squandered your property with prostitutes comes home, you kill the fattened calf for him."

"My son," the father said, "you are always with me, and everything I have is yours. But we had to celebrate and be glad, because this brother of yours was dead and is alive again; he was lost and is found."

www.ingramcontent.com/pod-product-compliance
Lightning Source LLC
Chambersburg PA
CBHW070738180626
46818CB00007B/2905